Seven-Knot Summers

by

AF208021

Beth Hill

Horsdal & Schubart

Horsdal & Schubart Publishers Ltd.
Victoria, BC., Canada

Cover painting by Art Simons, Fulford Harbour, BC.

Unless otherwise credited, photographs and drawings appear courtesy of Beth and Ray Hill.

This book is set in Classical Garamond.

Printed and bound in Canada by Kromar Printing Ltd., Winnipeg.

Canadian Cataloguing in Publication Data

Hill, Beth, 1924-
    Seven knot summers
    Includes bibliographical references and index
    ISBN 0-920663-27-3

1. Hill, Beth, 1924- —Journeys—British Columbia—Pacific Coast. 2. Hill, Ray, 1927- —Journeys—British Columbia—Pacific Coast. 3. Pacific Coast (BC)—Description and travel. 4. Pacific Coast (BC)—History. I. Title.
FC3817.4.H54 1994   917.1104'4   C94-910205-9
F1087.H54 1994

Seven-Knot Summers

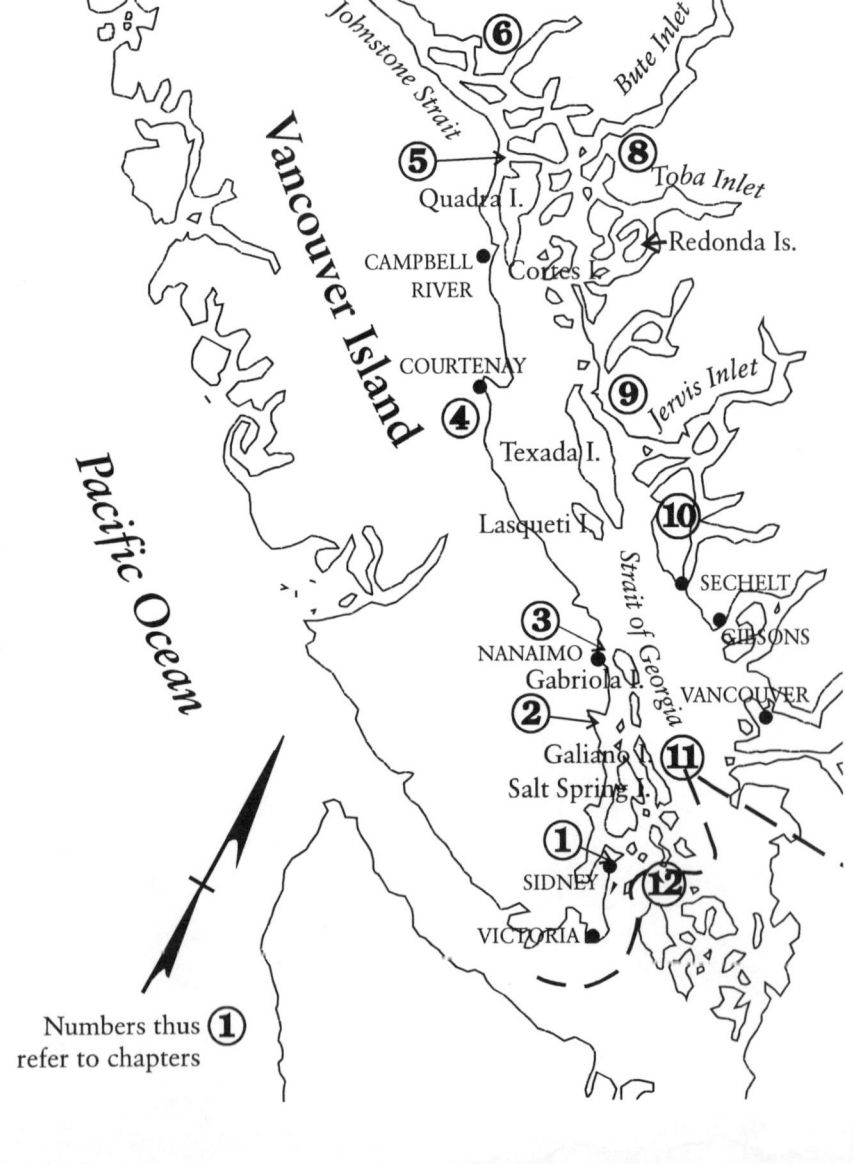

Numbers thus ① refer to chapters

B2 (3) 8.⁰⁰

Contents

INTRODUCTION

The End at the Beginning

There was never a moment when the end of the summer began, but one morning a few brown leaves lay on a path, like curled and crumpled hands. Unbidden, home thoughts intruded. The earth had swung round the sun and signalled the canning of tomatoes, the bottling of salmon, the chopping of firewood.

Ray and I had drifted through a summer at sea while I wrote about the places and people. There were some destinations, of course: notes scribbled on the charts, events and locations described in other people's books and articles. Sometimes old friends, or strangers, pointed us to sites and stories. In these assembled sea-pieces (see-pieces?) certain themes were persistent, like the summer's northwest wind, as I examined this inside coast (from Sidney to God's Pocket) through the lens of my life.

There is another dimension. It was unsubstantial at first, never clear to me, glimpsed briefly before it dissolved, ghost-like. It did not belong, perforce, to any one time or place or person, and yet it might manifest itself anywhere and anytime, a sparkle in the dewdrop cupped in a tiny leaf, a loon on the misty lagoon at Refuge Cove, the weathered grey of an old shed. I recognized the quality. I struggled to capture it in nets of words, but it escaped easily, like water through a seine net. I was usually left with the fish, which I valued, but I was not fishing for them. Joseph Conrad said that words were the great foes of reality.

Then, in *The Continuum Concept*, Jean Liedloff gave me some words to describe it. She wrote about a childhood moment in a forest when, as she hurried along a path, she saw in an open glade a single fir tree, sunlit. It was covered with bright, almost luminous green moss. The place had "such dense power that it stopped me in my tracks." Softly, as into an enchanted place, she entered and sat down with her cheek against the freshness of the moss. All anxiety fell away. Everything was as it ought to be...the tree, the earth beneath, herself. Seasons would circle around, the snow would fall, the spring would come, some plants would die, new ones would sprout: life was unspeakably RIGHT.

I felt I had discovered the missing center of things, the key to rightness itself, and must hold onto this knowledge which was so clear in that place.[1]

She promised herself that she would think about The Glade every night. She knew, even at age eight, that life would present "impenetrable tangles of rights and wrongs"[2] but if she could keep The Glade with her, perhaps she would not get lost.

Reading Liedloff, I recognized that I had been questing for that "missing center." Appropriately, I am at sea. Freud gave the label "oceanic feeling" to the infant's sense that it and the world flow together in a single, unbounded identity. The elusive dimension was this feeling of being intimately bonded to this world...not just the islands, tides and giant mountains, but the coastal people, both those I met and the ones whose ghosts faded as I tried to see them. Sometimes, as our prow cut into an uninhabited inlet, imagining myself the first person to enter, I would be overwhelmed by awe and loneliness. Sometimes just the rotting remnant of a log cabin stirred deep wells of compassion.

There's a certain Slant of light,
Winter Afternoon -
That oppresses like the Heft
Of Cathedral Tunes -

Heavenly Hurt, it gives us -
We can find no scar,
But internal difference,
Where the Meanings are.[3]

Kierkegaard remarked that life must be lived forwards but can only be understood backwards. There is only this moment as I sit at this computer and the *Liza Jane* rocks gently in the wake of some departed vessel. To know who I am, I try to read the pieces as if they had been written by someone else.

To measure their progress, sailors tied knots at about 50-foot intervals on a string called the log-line. Leaning over the rail while the ship slid through the sea, they let the string run out, counting the knots while sand slipped down from the upper chamber of an hour-glass. But a knot is also a ganglion, a meeting point of lines or nerves, sometimes something intricate, difficult to unravel or explain, a tangle. A knot can be a cluster of persons or things, associated in some way. The word comes from the old Teutonic *knutten* from which we also get the word "knit". The knots on a log-line have run through my fingers. Many strands have been assembled and entangled here.... I have knotted a book.

It is not our part to master all the tides of the world, but to do what is in us for the succor of these years where we are set.[4]

CHAPTER ONE

Northward out of Tsehum Harbour, Sidney

Like M. Wylie "Capi" Blanchet and Francis and Amy Barrow, we cast off our familiar life from Tsehum Harbour, near Sidney, feeling the way children do when schools close at the end of June: free as the wind...no telephone, no mail, no schedule, a thousand destinations...

Enchanted ports we, too, shall touch...
Nor other pilot need beside
A magic wisp of moon.[1]

Having no faith in the fickle moon, we set off with a compass, a Loran, a depth sounder, a carton of charts, the two Cummings gunkholing books, the John Chappell guide, *The Curve of Time*, *Upcoast Summers* and a ragged Morris and Heath Marine Atlas from 1952.

Thirty years ago Capi Blanchet's *The Curve of Time* was our first guidebook. "Only fools seek adventures,"[2] her son David remembered Capi saying, but adventures found her, nevertheless, in the way that outward events in a life usually reflect the inner state of mind. The Blanchets' Little House is no longer there, except in imagination, but as we departed we always saluted the Blanchet house that replaced it, at the tip of Curteis Point.

Little House is one of those fairy-tale places that exist forever in the mind. Edith Iglauer Daly described it as "an unusual house, a strangely mystical English cottage covered with ivy, with a big fireplace and billiard table on the first floor and four bedrooms up a

1

rickety flight of stairs."³ In summer, like the palace of the Sleeping Beauty, it was guarded by thorny roses. Unfortunately the house was on wretched foundations and full of dry rot, and by the time Capi tore it down in 1948, dining-room chairs were skidding across a listing floor, which must have challenged even the Blanchet sea legs. The Blanchets found Little House in 1922, deep in forest and "covered with the roses in bloom — on the paths — in the porch — over the house — up the roof...roses were everywhere."⁴ The *Caprice* was purchased the next year. Only four years later, in 1927, *Caprice* was discovered anchored off Knapp Island, where Geoffrey Blanchet had gone ashore to cook a meal. He was never found and is presumed to have suffered a heart attack while swimming.

Perhaps as a way of coping with this terrible event, the next summer Capi made the first of many summer odysseys whose highlights are collected in *The Curve of Time*. Daly described Capi as a woman of medium height, with a strong face framed in a halo of fine, upbrushed, blonde hair, dressed in shorts, khaki shirt, a Cowichan sweater and sneakers. Children and friends loved her, in spite of a somewhat domineering manner, and respected her competence. Her publisher and friend Gray Campbell found her to be a serious person with "a delicious, dry sense of humour" and "a delightful shyness."⁵ When her daughter Joan bought an old Indian dugout canoe for five dollars and crossed the Gulf of Georgia in five days, paddling at night to avoid traffic and heavy seas, Capi seemed angry. "Just because I'm a fool doesn't mean you children have to be!"⁶ she said, but one of the boys said she laughed herself to sleep that night.

We never met her. Three years before her death in 1961 at the age of 70, we first ventured to sea in a boat Ray had built in our city backyard. Her book changed our lives, for in 1965 we followed, in foolhardy ignorance, the track of the *Caprice*. Our experiences increased my respect for this remarkable woman who, in the year of her death, published this best of all books about our coast. No wonder we dip the flag to a certain bungalow at the end of Curteis Point, as we leave Tsehum Harbour in early summer, on that endless curve of time.

TSEHUM HARBOUR. AMY AND FRANCIS BARROW

Little House is gone but the Barrow house has survived, inside Tsehum Harbour, a massive, brown-shingled building rising boldly from Mill Point. Built as the Brackman-Ker mill, it was transformed into Francis and Amy Barrow's home after their marriage in 1906. A generation older than Capi Blanchet, the Barrows began their coastal cruising a quarter of a century before her; sometimes their meandering tracks crossed, but they do not seem to have been friends.

The Barrows' *Toketie* was at least 20 years older, and one foot longer, than Blanchet's *Caprice*. Unlike *Caprice*, which was accidentally burned soon after Capi sold it, the *Toketie* still plows the waters of Tsehum Harbour, elegantly restored and renamed *Merlin* by its present owner, the marine architect William Garden. One of the oldest yachts on the coast, *Toketie* was built for Francis Barrow in Vancouver in 1903 or 1904, and some of its travels have been described in *Upcoast Summers*. The Barrows went to sea from 1906 onwards, but the sea journals from which excerpts were chosen for *Upcoast Summers* chronicle the years between 1933 and 1941. The house, the *Merlin* and the journals (now in the Campbell River Museum) have remained to bear witness to their lives; as long as they are remembered, they are in a sense still with us.

> Yet meet we shall, and part, and meet again
> Where dead men meet, on lips of living men.[1]

So quickly does the British Columbian raincoast reclaim the little abandoned homesteads that it sometimes seems as if the lives of the pioneers were only a dream. During the 1930s, Amy and Francis and their two cocker spaniels visited coast people, and in the Barrow journals and photographs, they gave these friends an immortality not granted to many. More than 60 years later, we went in search of those ghosts and we visit them still.

From a float below the house, each year in June, the Barrows departed to cruise northward, happily joining the activities of their coastal friends. Along the channels Barrow made careful drawings or photographs of the pictographs and petroglyphs, and sent these records to both the National and Provincial Museums. Ray and I used Barrow's notes and drawings when we did our petroglyph research expeditions in 1973. As we age, we even seem to somewhat resemble Francis and Amy, for our *Liza Jane*, a 32-foot, wooden displacement boat built at Birdseye Cove in the late 1950s, is old-fashioned in the world of fibreglass palaces. But we are almost two generations younger than the Barrows; our coast is not their coast and our eyes belong to a different era. In contrast with their naive optimism, we live in an age of crumbling confidence.

We view the native people differently, neither romantically like Blanchet nor with Francis Barrow's prejudiced eye, but as partners with whom we share this province. We have the benefit of two generations of research to help us understand their past and our own. The stories we tell of the early, white-skinned, coastal pioneers evoke a time when there were still fish and forests apparently unlimited, but nowadays too many people squabble over too few fish and trees.

On the day we left Tsehum Harbour, clouds like whipped cream were piled on the horizon and some flat-bottomed clouds drifted above us, imitating islands. Out of the harbour, where the real islands floated in a glittering sea, sails sliced the sparkle like killer whales' fins. The flag fluttered at *Liza Jane*'s stern. We saluted the Barrows and the Blanchets and with hearts as light and bright as the day, we headed out for our own upcoast summer.

TSEHUM HARBOUR. SEATED HUMAN FIGURE BOWLS

The Barrow house stands at the end of a clam-shell beach. Several thousand years ago, when cedar dugout canoes lay there, a row of flat-roofed, cedar-plank houses stood on the bank above. Beneath those vanished houses, a 14-inch carved stone figure was found, on the Barrows' property, in the 1920s. It is one of about 75 such sculptures which fit (in date, distribution and style) into a group called the Seated Human Figure Bowls. If the long-dead people of the midden are to be more than cardboard "savages", we must probe the mystery of these sacred objects.

The figure bowls have been found in Salish territory: the Gulf of Georgia from Puget Sound to Courtenay and up the Fraser River to Kamloops. They were in existence between 2,500 and 1,500 years ago but some were still used (and may have been manufactured) until the arrival of white people. A sitting or kneeling human figure, whose upturned large head has huge eyes and mouth, holds a bowl in arms and legs which sometimes become a bird's wings. Some are embellished with snakes. On the front of the bowl there is an animal face.

Franz Boas in 1890 wrote that an Indian Agent at Yale saw a shaman lead a girl, at the conclusion of her puberty ceremonies, from seclusion to the centre of the village.

He carried a dish called tsuqta'n which is carved out of steatite, in one hand. The dish represents a woman giving

4

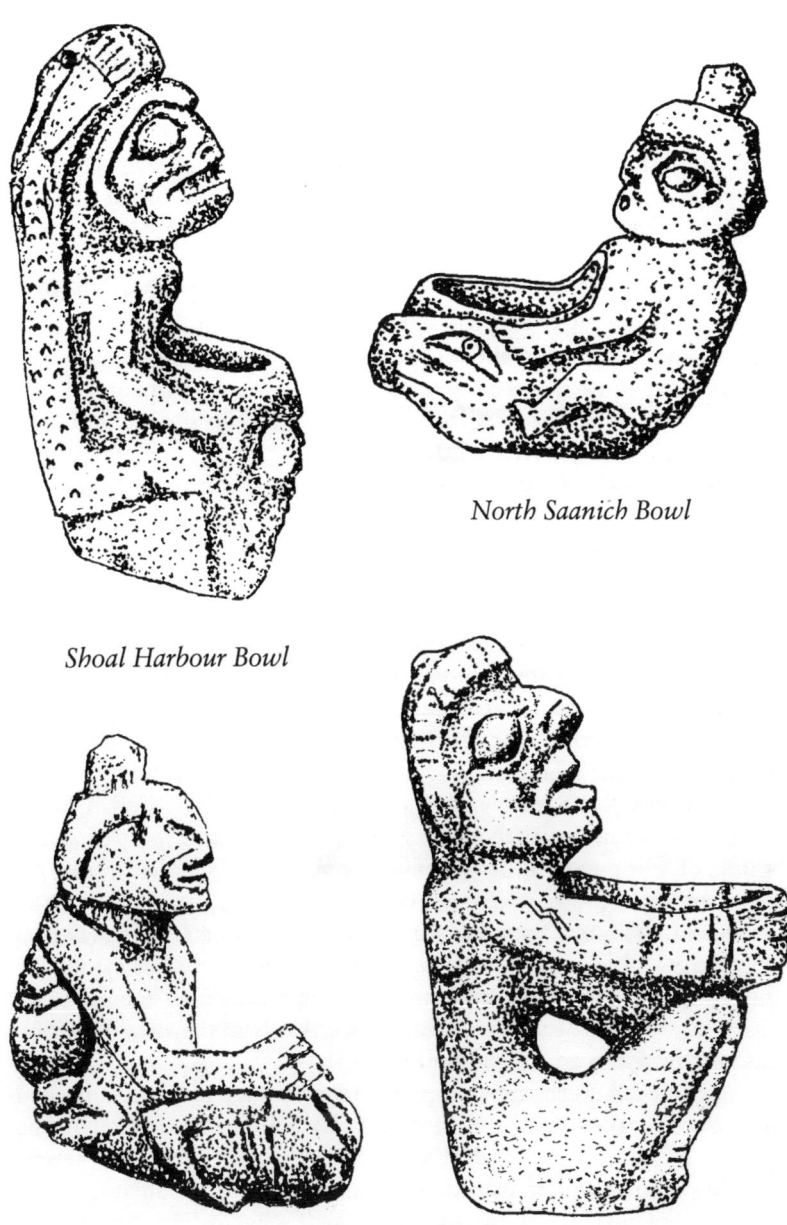

North Saanich Bowl

Shoal Harbour Bowl

Kuper Island Bowl

Cowichan Bay Bowl

Seated Human Figure Bowls.

birth to a child, along whose back a snake crawls. The child's back is hollowed out and serves as a receptacle for water. In the other hand the shaman carries certain herbs. When they returned to the village the herbs were put into the dish, and the girl sprinkled with the water contained in the dish, the shaman praying at the same time for her to have many children.[1]

The shaman (the priest), the bowl, the water of life — all these are familiar to us, but the difference between that baptismal ceremony and ours is subtle. These people, celebrating the onset of a woman's miraculous power to bring forth new humans, knew themselves to be animals like other animals, an intrinsic part of creation. The Christian god, separate from his creation, both perfect and male, occupies a place named Heaven from which other animals are excluded and to which the baptism is a passport. Perhaps the notion that humans are likewise "above" nature has led us to the foolish idea that we can "conquer" nature. The dichotomy Life/Death is the bedrock of consciousness, but we know little more of it than did the makers of the Seated Human Figure Bowls.

Most of the Seated Human Figure Bowls have upturned faces and "an expression of agonized ecstasy."[2] Many have prominent ribs, symbolizing the near-death knowledge from which the shaman's power emerged. The seated figure probably represented the shaman, and the snakes and birds her or his spirit power. The Indian Agent at Yale who witnessed the use of the bowl may have grasped something of the meaning of the object without being accurate in his interpretation. The attitude of the seated figures is humble, suppliant. This is a figure in prayer, aware of human dependence on fearsome and unknown powers. The snake is an ancient symbol of maleness and femaleness combined, and of rebirth; but the snake on the Fraser River Seated Human Figure Bowls is the deadly rattler, and the bird, the owl, is the bird of death.

The bowls were sometimes filled with water for far-seeing and for prophecy. At Yale, after a young boy had put river water in the Seated Human Figure Bowl, the shaman in trance predicted the size of the salmon run, the fish whose deaths gave life to humans. Some bowls were buried with their shaman owners and others were passed down through families. A man near Yale said his shaman uncle had three such bowls but hid them from visitors. "It must be because they would have made me sick," he remarked. "Some of his power was in those stones."[3] Anthropologist Homer Barnett wrote that Saanich shamans "sometimes gazed into a pan of water in which, with the aid of their spirits, they could see all the world reflected."[4] His further comment: "In Salish culture in general it is not uncommon for shamans and seers to use containers of water in which to see distant places and for shamans to use water in their curing procedures."[5]

These hints only scratch the surface of meaning. The medium is itself part of the message, for, in Wilson Duff's words, "Stone means eternal."[6] To live we must eat, so the Seated Human Figure Bowls make sense to me as begging bowls. Give us this day our daily bread. To live, we eat death. But the bowls, associated with the awesome power to give birth, may also beg for rebirth, for life after death. When we stop to contemplate these bowls, we feel our close kinship with the people of the middens. Our white yachts and designer jeans are the toys with which we distract ourselves from that intimacy with mortality which is wisdom.

Most of these sacred objects have disappeared into private collections or museums; it seems appropriate to restore some of them to history by reconnecting them, in this book, to the coast where their makers left them.

D'ARCY ISLAND

On the smooth grey surface of Sidney Channel the reflected clouds twisted and squirmed. D'Arcy Island lay ahead, flat and forbidding. With no sheltered anchorage on any side, with no white beaches, surrounded by reefs and rocks and kelp, blown by winds fetching from an invisible distance and swept by the rush of tides, D'Arcy was not welcoming. We approached with caution and by good fortune found immediately the three marine park mooring buoys on the north side; we then circumnavigated the island in the dinghy. Two great turkey buzzards rose lazily as we landed on the stony western beach.

We had the island to ourselves. One coast atlas stated that this island was "once the site of a leper colony, which served as an undisturbed storehouse for bootleg whiskey."[1] Designated a leper colony in 1890, at first it held only one wretched soul who later made the only known escape. He either fashioned a makeshift raft from logs on the beach, or was rescued by a friend with a boat; or he was drowned and his body carried away by the tide. In 1891 there were five lepers, all Chinese, housed in a building with six rooms, each opening off the porch that ran the length of the structure on the beach side. Every three months a supply vessel arrived to bring them food, clothes and opium but no medical aid, although a medical officer and sanitary inspector might venture ashore.

As we climbed from the beach into the trees we were walking in the footsteps of Dr. Hall and Dr. Nelson, who inspected in 1898. We found the cement foundation wall of the 1891 building where, in 1898, the lepers, "listlessness and indifference portrayed in their very attitudes", stood on the porch awaiting their visitors. Dr. Hall later wrote:

> The spokesman, a strong-framed man, betrays by the incessant twitching of the muscles of the face that the disease has attacked the nerve centres, accompanying which are the nameless pricking, burning and jerking features. Another has the tuberculated form. The upper lips are distorted, the eyes bleared, the ears enlarged and the limbs swollen. The most hideous form was that of one where the face had become a great mass of cruel half-healed sores.

The doctor, familiar with leprosy, advanced with a cheery greeting and asked the spokesman, "How many are there, John?"

"Sellen."

"Where is the eighth?" John pointed over his shoulder with a thumb from which the first joint was gone, then led the doctors behind the house, along a foot-path to a fenced garden.

> Splendid vegetables were here growing, including potatoes, lettuce, onions and cabbage. The station is maintained at a minimum outlay, though each man is allowed fifty pounds of rice per month and all the flour, pork, tobacco, tea, oatmeal, etc. which they can use, yet the annual expenditure does not exceed $1,000. They raise plenty of fowl for their own use, and at the time of our visit there were about one hundred and fifty chickens and thirty or forty ducks.

They pushed through the tangled luxuriance of shrubbery, and examined the little mound where the eighth was buried. When they came back to the beach, John saw one of the doctor's wives, who had accompanied the inspection trip. "'Oh, lady, lady,' he exclaimed...as he bowed repeatedly before her with Oriental grace."[2] In 1907, the surviving Chinese lepers were deported to a hospital in Canton, where they were not isolated and where members of their families may have found them. The buildings on D'Arcy Island were burned and two new ones constructed, for it was not until 1924 that the leper colony was moved to Bentinck Island. There are no lepers now, for sulpha drugs cure the hideous disease.

We sat on the foundation wall (about 30 feet by 20 feet and 15 inches high) to eat our sandwiches, a silent lunch, for the lepers haunted us. Northwards along the shore, we explored a substantial ruin, vine-covered, with trees growing through the walls. There was once a garden there, and a second building beside it, but only the cement steps remained. When Heather Corney and Doug Forbes kayaked to the island in 1992, Heather wandered through this ruin and into the garden and was suddenly overwhelmed by "an intense feeling of sorrow" as she stood on those steps. The misery ceased when she fled to the beach. Had she imagined the sorrow? She and Doug decided that she should walk again in that haunted garden. "At that same spot the feelings returned...I was now filled with a sense of complete despair and found myself standing over a pile of rocks, sobbing."[3] Only after her return from D'Arcy Island, did Heather learn that lepers had been incarcerated there.

We sat on the beach, our backs against a log, drinking the last of the coffee. The slow slap...slap...slap of soft waves broke the stillness, and the wind sighed in the alders. Philip Teece, writing *A Dream of Islands*, anchored between D'Arcy and Little D'Arcy one wet night, when the wistful rain fell gently on his cabin roof. In a total blackness peppered with raindrops, he thought he could hear sad voices. Perhaps it was only the leaves shivering as the rain tapped them, but the feelings of despair were undeniable.

ISLE-DE-LIS

It seemed a hoity-toity name for an ordinary islet. We preferred its first name, Rum Island, until we went there in April. Eastward from Tsehum Harbour the scattering of islands teased us, merging and shape-shifting. Forest, Domville, Brethour, Gooch, Comet and all their little islets can be confusing when you first venture among them. Ray and I have four degrees of eyesight: normal eyes which are good neither for squinting at sliding islands nor reading charts; sun-glassed eyes for admiring the mirage of islands in a glittering sea; eyeglassed eyes for reading charts and compass; and binocu-lared eyes for distinguishing distant marine markers from sailboat masts. We seemed to be constantly changing our eyes.

When we had found our way to the eastern end of Gooch Island, little Isle-de-Lis suddenly detached itself from its larger partner but remained tethered to it by a narrow neck of double beach. We were less than half a mile from the international boundary when we rounded the flashing light off Tom Point. The two marine park mooring buoys floated near the northern side of the isthmus and the sign above the dock announced "Isle-de-Lis Marine Park". But it was Rum Island in prohibition days and it was Rum Island when Mrs. Renee Nelson bought it in 1945. Mrs. Nelson, who lived in White Rock, had come to Canada from the United States when she was 12. It was still Rum Island when she refused to sell it to private owners, insisting that it should become a marine park. "I don't want it ever to be sold to Americans", she announced firmly.[1]

The reality behind her statement is worth examining. Springing up at the beginning of the Industrial Revolution, a period dominated by the Whig notions of individualism, the United States then welcomed millions of Europeans. For the children of these new Americans, the old connections with earth and seasons grew tenuous, displaced by the concept of individual freedom — as if the "freedom" of an individual were not constrained first by his and her brain-washing by parent, priest and pedagogue, secondly by the social nature of human life and lastly by the environment. Perhaps because we are a northern country, Canadians have more easily grasped the fact that human happiness is embedded in social relationships. In Canada, both public and private enterprise exist. Going upcoast again and thinking about both the prehistoric times and the changes I have witnessed, it seemed important to understand Renee Nelson; to value our distinctive world view, it must first be recognized.

Except that park outhouses have replaced Renee's cabins, the island is much the way she found it. It was not until we hiked around it that we discovered why the island had been renamed. On the north side, between the forest and the sea, where sandstone has been sculpted into stone waves, in moist soil pockets in broken rock ledges, we came upon dense patches of thousands of white Easter lilies, drooping petalled flowers four inches across. A hundred years ago *Erythronium oregonum* was as common as a dandelion, but now the first sanctuary has been established for it at the Thetis Lake

Nature Sanctuary. Here, on Isle-de-Lis, the island setting may preserve this endangered plant. Although it is now a public place, without the protection of "Private" signs, most of the visitors come when the rare lilies do not bloom.

At Tom Point on the eastern tip of the island, where a deep ravine sliced into the shore, we lost the path. Floundering in the underbrush, we came upon a small cave, the perfect place to cache contraband liquor. The Tom Point light which guides ships on Haro Strait could also have led the rum runners to the narrow beach where the ravine opened to the sea. How easy it would be, on cloudy nights, to slip in and out of this secret place.

On behalf of all cruising people, these pages acknowledge the generosity of Renee Nelson. Every year, when the April sun lures us out of Tsehum Harbour, we shall walk among the lilies and remember her.

PORTLAND ISLAND

My introduction to Portland Island was scary. This may even be a ghost story. In 1957, when the children were young, we four (and the dog) anchored in the little bay south of Chads Island, off the northern corner of Portland Island. Up a wide swath of meadow on Portland we could see an abandoned house. It was a hot, windless summer day, with no sound except the humming of bees. Through knee-deep grass, motionless in the heat, we followed a path up the slope towards the grey, weather-worn old house. As we neared the house, we paused. The silence seemed too quiet. Was the house, in fact, abandoned? We could not see curtains in the windows and no dogs ran barking to greet us, but we debated in whispers before proceeding. The path led us to the back of the house, where there were two windows beside the closed door. Our dog seemed nervous. Almost simultaneously we all put faces to the window glass, cupping our eyes to enable us to see the dark interior. Afterwards, we compared notes to confirm what we had all seen.

A woman sat in a rocking chair, rocking slowly and silently, staring at us with a dead, expressionless face. Back and forth, between her and our faces at the windows, paced two huge mastiffs, back and forth, neither dog looking at us. There was no sound. For a long moment we were glued to the window. Then we fled. We ran all the way back down the meadow, pushed off the dinghy, splashed into it, rowed to our boat, climbed in and hoisted the anchor. I can still call up the stab of cold fear as I looked at that woman. When we returned almost 35 years later, we found only a few foundation stones and the covered well. On the edge of the clearing, not far from the old pump, a visitor in 1958 had stumbled across a small stone tombstone with FLOSS cut into it, and not far away a wooden cross with the name KATTY.

This house must have been the one built by an American diplomat named Barker, who sold the island to the amazing Frank "One-Arm" Sutton. Sutton received the Military Cross for bravery at Gallipoli; when the Turks hurled grenades into the foxhole where he and his men crouched, Sutton heaved them back, but he wasn't quite quick enough with the one which cost him his arm.

He was an adventurer who, before World War I, became a sub-contractor in railroad construction in South America. After losing the arm at Gallipoli, he became a one-armed golf champion before departing to prospect for gold across Siberia. In a China wracked by civil war, Sutton served Manchurian War Lord Chang Tso-lin. In 1927 he arrived in British Columbia with millions to invest, his own and his Chinese war lord's money. He bought mansions, commercial property, mines, ranches, electric power sites, race horses, an airplane and Portland Island. For a few years he lived gloriously. He stocked the island with pheasants and built a race track and a barn to stable 40 horses.

Then came the great stock-market crash and his splendour shrivelled. Chang Tso-lin was blown to bits when a bomb exploded in his private railway carriage. In 1932 *The Colonist* reported that "Major-General Frank Sutton M.C., who was supposed to have been worth $14 million, has recently returned to Northern China."[1] His star continued to plummet. When the Japanese armies swarmed southward, Sutton was thrown into the Stanley Prison, a concentration camp. He died there in 1945.

In 1958, aging Premier Bennett the First gave the island to the lovely young Princess Margaret in a grandiose gesture, and then there was the long embarrassment of getting her to give it back without actually asking her for it. After she returned the deed in 1967, the island was designated a marine park. When we were there last, the sheltered bay at the south end was crowded with yachts. We knew where Sutton's barn once stood for we had ventured inside the rotting structure years before the Parks workers dismantled it. Too late for the plum crop, we watched children climbing the neglected, unpruned apple trees and pelting each other with wormy fruit. Probably the fruit trees were planted by the first settlers, the Hawaiians (Kanakas) or by John Norton, who farmed the island before One-Arm Sutton arrived. We followed other boat people across the island to the meadow with the old well, where we had seen the woman and her strange dogs. The yellowed meadow grass stood tall and silent in the heat, as I remembered it. The silence seemed oppressive.

FULFORD HARBOUR. SALT SPRING ISLAND. THE AKERMANS

Coming into Fulford Harbour before sunset, on our port side the massive southern third of Salt Spring Island darkened in the gloaming. At the west end of narrow Fulford Valley, the kindly guardian mountain, Mount Maxwell's Baynes Peak, lifted its rocky chin into the rosy sky. Behind the ferry slip, brilliantly illuminated, an eclectic collection of local craft crowded the government dock. We rafted against two trollers and slept uneasily. When the ferry came we all stirred and rolled, and at 5:30 A.M. the start-up roar of its four motors roused us.

In the morning we took the dinghy across the harbour to the overgrown log-dump. About 1970, this log-dump was built by bull-dozing together at low tide some of the boulders usually below the water, and when the marine growth dried and fell off one boulder, a deeply grooved petroglyph appeared. Bob Akerman, who was born here, told me that his Indian grandmother had said that the old shoreline below a vanished village crossed from the log-dump site to the present ferry dock; the mudflats threaded by outflowing branches of Fulford Creek were once dry land. Perhaps an extremely high tide, combined with a cyclone of a southeaster, washed the village away. The infinitely slow tilting of Vancouver Island (this eastern end going down and the Long Beach side rising) made the Fulford village vulnerable to such a catastrophe. The Fulford petroglyph boulder, now nestled in a close circle of cedar trees at Drummond Park at the head of the harbour, may have stood at the seaward end of a village, the daily rise of the tide washing the strange face. Perhaps it called the fish into traps and weirs built in the creek.

A hundred and fifty feet above this southwest side of the harbour there was a midden deposit which was gradually destroyed by the commercial removal of the deep gravel bed on which it rested. One day, the blade of a bulldozer working in the gravel pit nicked a stone figure which had fallen from the collapsing midden.

The operator's sharp eye noticed the stone — he stopped his machine and climbed down to pick up an unusual version of a Seated Human Figure Bowl. Not only does the figure have a lap bowl, but the elongated head has a small bowl in its top. The front of the lower bowl has been broken off, but the face of it was probably upside down and when the figure is upended, there is a third bowl in the broken base of the figure.

At the northwestern end of the harbour, the little Catholic church (now wrapped in pseudo-stone siding) was built between 1880 and 1885. Its windows, door and bell were brought in canoes from the Butter Church at Cowichan Bay to Burgoyne Bay and then moved by ox-drawn stone boat to Fulford Harbour. Martha Akerman, the first white woman in the valley, may have run out of her kitchen, her apron flapping, to watch them pass. Buried here are Michael and Mary Ann Gyves, Bob Akerman's other grandparents, and the Tahouneys and the Pallots, the Hawaiians. From the church we clambered down a steep path through the blackberry bushes to find a bowl made in the bedrock between the tide lines. The silken smooth surface of this bowl curved over the two ends of its oval shape.

When the old village was drowned, the new village was built where Drummond Park and the Fulford Inn are now found. When we were Salt Spring Islanders, white-bearded Mr. Drummond, who lived in the house at the corner of Isabella Point Road and the Fulford-Ganges Road, showed us a large collection of artifacts he had found in his vegetable garden. Mr. Drummond's collection may still be seen, a short distance up the Fulford-Ganges Road, in Bob Akerman's new log-cabin museum.

In the autumn of 1859, young Joseph Akerman came rowing down the harbour, hunting deer with friends, and stepped ashore on the beach below the midden. An English newcomer in Victoria, he was working in a market garden located where the Parliament Buildings now stand. He hoped one day to have a farm, and when he followed the trail along the Fulford Creek, he recognized the place of his dreams. He filed pre-emption papers for 160 acres. From spring until autumn he gardened to pay off the $160 cost and in the winter he felled the great trees to make the first fields and build a log cabin. In 1863, the "brideship" *Robert Lowe* brought Martha Clay and her two sisters to the new colony. Was Joseph standing amid the crowd on the dock, eager to see the young women? How did he manage to capture one of these precious "brides"? When she agreed to marry him, he brought Martha to this valley on their honeymoon. Their grandson, Bob Akerman, still lives not far from the old Akerman house; once called "Travellers' Rest", it was also the island's first hotel and store.

Walking in their steps, we went up the road to the museum, past the Anglican church, with its meticulously trimmed graveyard where words carved in granite note only the beginning and ending of pioneer lives, and maintain a stony silence concerning ecstasies and miseries; past the Fulford Community Hall where preparations for a giant rummage sale were underway. In 1992 Bob's museum was opened. We entered to the thump of drums, broadcast from a speaker in the porch. In the glass cases lay Mr. Drummond's artifacts, but Bob's collection included many items from farther afield: the stone head found on Galiano Island by Mrs. King, stones used in finishing deerhide, a shaman's soul catcher. There was the Tsweywey mask from the George family; because Bob's Grandmother Gyves belonged in that family, Bob is entitled to display it.

Tiny white paddles hung in rows on the deerhide jacket given to Molly Akerman's father, Frank Morrison. "When he danced they tinkled like a brook," Bob said. "It was like the sound of water dancing." Frank Morrison received it from the Cowichan people, who were grateful for the work he had done in writing down their songs for the magnificent native opera, *Tzinquaw*, produced in the 1950s. It is the CBC recording of *Tzinquaw* that is broadcast from the museum porch; as I admired the jacket, the round, clear, tenor voice of Abel Joe quivered around me. *Tzinquaw* is the story of the great seabird who killed Quannis, the killer whale who was preventing the Cowichan people from catching the salmon they needed to survive. What a magnificent production it was, and those who saw it talk about it still. And when it was over, Abel Joe crowned Frank Morrison with his own headband, naming Frank Chief "Tza-Qua-La", after "him who first came from heaven to descend upon Cowichan Valley." Today that headband, with a single feather, hangs above Frank Morrison's deerhide jacket.

Many of the Akerman family still live in the valley, their history bridging the meeting of two races who will, we hope, find a new harmony in the years to come. Bob Akerman is quietly proud of this continuity.

These artifacts, the trim churches, the midden remain; if we strain to listen, they can speak for the silenced folk who walked this road before us. Unaware of this landscape of ghosts, the impatient cars filed from the ferry and rolled past us, homeward bound.

CHAPTER TWO

Northward, Cowichan Bay to De Courcy Island

COWICHAN BAY. CHIEF TZOUHALEM

"There was thunder and the sky was like fire!" when Tzouhalem was born. The lightning flashed and they saw a wizened infant with a huge, ugly head. "See what the spirits have sent me! Throw it out on the shell piles!" shouted his horrified father.[1] But the grandmother intervened and the misshapen, unwanted child lived to be a ferocious war chief.

Besides the pain of carrying a grotesque head, the child suffered an invisible wound. When he was only three years old, great Haida canoes suddenly appeared in Cowichan Bay. His grandmother snatched him up and fled. Hidden in the trees, he watched as the Haidas tied the hair of the women to the thwarts of the canoes. He heard his infant brother crying and his mother screaming. Weeks later one woman escaped and returned to the village, telling how a Haida warrior had thrown the yelling baby into the sea and when Tzouhalem's mother would not stop shrieking, she too was tossed out of the canoe to drown in the swift tides of Sansum Narrows. His grandmother brought him up to be a vengeful warrior. Ridiculed by other children, he was also rejected by the young woman he loved, a third and fatal blow.

"My mother often used to talk about Tzouhalem because he was her relation," Mrs. Tz-Lal-Tzer told B. M. Cryer, "and she told me how he wore his hair long, but used to fasten it on top of his head with sticks, and in his hair — do you know what he had? A snake! There, twisted in his hair was a live snake! He would take the snake off his head and put it about his arms and neck, but nearly always it slept twisted in his hair."[2] Unwanted children may become feared and dangerous adults.

16

We came up Satellite Channel, heading for the shelter of Genoa Bay. Mount Tzouhalem rose, monstrous, above Cowichan Bay, the long arm of Separation Point stretching out to protect Genoa Bay. The marina was tucked close against the sheer mountain behind. The people at the store told us where to find the trail from Genoa Bay to the top of the mountain, 1,760 feet above, and that evening we followed the bright orange tape markers to a magnificent viewpoint over Tzouhalem's territory. Driven from his village, he lived in a cave on this mountain. From the heights where we walked, he watched the Cowichan River delta far below. And on this mountain his gods ordered him to go down and be the war leader of his people. He built a stockaded fort upon the promontory now called Green Point.

In 1844 he took his warriors to Fort Victoria, where Chief Factor Charles Ross had just died, leaving 26-year-old Roderick Finlayson, a clerk, in command. Tzouhalem moved into the Songhees village across the harbour from the fort and ordered several Hudson's Bay Company cattle shot for his feasting. He called in warriors from the neighbouring tribes to support an attack on the fort. Finlayson coolly armed all his men and set watches night and day, and although the Indians riddled the stockades and the roofs with musket balls, he would not allow his men to return the fire. Finlayson shouted to the Songhees chief, saying that he did not want to kill them and giving them a chance to withdraw and pay restitution. When this had no effect, he sent his native interpreter out, instructing him to pretend he had escaped the fort, and telling him to point out the lodge on which the fort's guns were trained, urging that it be evacuated. Then Finlayson ordered the nine-pounder carronade, loaded with grape-shot, to fire. BOOM! The lodge was reduced to splinters flying in the wind. The Songhees chief sued for peace and agreed to pay in furs for the slaughtered animals. Tzouhalem went home.

It was probably true that Tzouhalem had many wives, that he was brutal and that he had murdered men to take their women. The native people say he split women's feet so they could not run from the caves in which he imprisoned them. However, there is one story that shows another side of the chief. Hector Munro and his young wife had a little farm near Cadboro Bay. Shortly after their first child, a daughter, was born, Munro fell ill with pneumonia. With the baby in her arms, Mrs. Munro set off to get help. She met a distraught neighbour fleeing into the forest to escape Tzouhalem and a large band of Cowichans. Unwilling to leave her husband, Mrs. Munro returned to the cabin and bolted the doors and windows. The Cowichans arrived and easily broke down the door. The house was filled with shouting warriors. Suddenly they fell silent and Tzouhalem came in. He stooped over the bunk where Munro lay unconscious, and raised his axe. Mrs. Munro fell on her knees, pleading for her husband's life. Tzouhalem looked down at her and asked what she would give him. Mrs. Munro had heard of Indians adopting white children, so she held out her baby, the most precious thing she had. Tears streamed down her cheeks. Tzouhalem stood silent, looking at her. Then he motioned his warriors out of the house and left. When Mr. Munro recovered, he took his wife and daughter back to England.

In the end, Tzouhalem was betrayed by one of his half-brothers. Tzouhalem wanted a handsome woman named Tsaw-mea-lae, the wife of a Kuper Island Lamalchi man named Schelm-tum. He went to the Lamalchi village with some of his warriors, intending to kill Schelm-tum. However, one of his half brothers had removed the bullets from his gun. Tsaw-mea-lae stood half-hidden behind a large post inside her house, as Schelm-tum faced Tzouhalem, refusing to give her up. Tzouhalem levelled his gun at Schelm-tum and pulled the trigger. The gun did not fire. He backed up against the post to avoid being attacked from behind. But Tsaw-mea-lae quickly passed a stout stick around the post, in front of Tzouhalem's body. She held him there long enough for Schelm-tum to snatch up his axe and strike. Tzouhalem's decapitated body was sent back to Cowichan Bay. The native people say that for a week, Tzouhalem's head was kicked around like a football before it was brought back to Khnipsin village and mounted on a stake. When they wanted rain, the villagers turned his face toward the southwest wind.

In lurid prose, H. Davy wrote, "If you listen closely when dark clouds gather over Cowichan Bay and the wind howls through the tree tops, Indians claim you will hear the shrieks of the discarnate soul of Tzouhalem being tortured by the Cloud God. Beware of his shadow, they will also advise."[3] Dolby Turner, who lived on the site of Tzouhalem's house during the 1930s, saw that shadow on a number of occasions, and so did some of the visitors to her house. It took the shape of a "great black solid menacing thing."[4]

Dolby Turner has published an excellent book of Salish legends entitled *When The Rains Came*, told to her by native storytellers whose pictures and brief biographies accompany the tales. In one of the stories, she described the night she heard the ghost drums and chants on Separation Point. Dolby, her sister Edie and her daughter Carol were with friends camping overnight at Separation Point in order to be on the water, fishing lines out, in the first grey light of dawn. After a supper around a driftwood fire on the pebble beach near the end of the point, they scooped hollows to fit hips and shoulders, snuggled into sleeping bags and slept.

Dolby and her daughter and sister were awakened by the sound of drums. They were puzzled, because they knew the Indian people were all away hop picking in Washington state.

It was also the time of the harvest moon. There it was, hanging in a cloudless sky above the Saanich hills, a large, orange-red plate. The strange part was that none of the others with us could hear a thing — though everyone was wide awake by now — even though to the three of us the sound was as distinct and as real as though a dance was in progress just around the Point.[5]

Her native friend Danny Thomas told her that the people of Tzouhalem's village sometimes heard "things that happened a long, long time ago, just like it was happening now...some of us can hear the old people sing and the sound of drums...not many, but some do." He was quiet for a while and then he added, "Some night, when the big red moon comes up over there and puts out the light of the stars, you lie down on the earth near the water and you listen."[6]

MAPLE BAY. VANCOUVER ISLAND

We came in at sunset, when the masts of the tightly bunched sailboats at the yacht club looked like the teeth of an old comb. Maple Bay was the site of the last, bloodiest battle between the Salish tribes and the Kwakwaka'wakw people from the north. The Salish were the victors.

Chief David La Tasse heard the story from his father. In 1932, when N. deBertrand Lugrin interviewed him, he was very old and his hair was white, but when he spoke of that battle, "his age fell from him as though it were a garment, his eyes glistened and his thin voice became full and strong."[1] For many, many years, he said, the Yacultas had been coming down and killing men and taking the women to slavery. Every year they came, "for their war canoes are upon the sea as the salmon in the spawning season at the river mouth." Then the tribes of the south, the Cowichans, Malahats, Songhees, Saanich and "the men from Sooke, where the tall white waves come in from the ocean" decided they must join together to fight the Yacultas. When the Cowichan scouts came, warning that the Yacultas were paddling south, all the fighting men gathered together in Maple Bay, their canoes out of sight under the overhanging trees. They sent out into the bay a few canoes with warriors lying low in them and one or two men paddling slowly and feebly, like old men, as if no one was guarding the village.

"So quick and sharp like the seagulls swoop across the water, come two canoes, scouting. The men stand and look under their hands, and they laugh." The enemy scouts went back to tell the Yacultas that the Cowichans had fled before them. No need to paddle softly...

the noise of the Ukultahs' paddles against the sides of the canoes is like thunder and they shout and laugh and sweep like a cloud into Maple Bay. But see! Up in those canoes manned by old men, spring Cowichan fighters, a hundred to a canoe. And look! Out from the trees come more canoes full of warriors. Thumping of paddles, shouting of fighters, songs of the champions.

Chief David brought his hands together and interlocked his fingers. "Like that the boats meet. We use our great clubs made from the elk bone. Thump. Thump. Thump. Every thump a kill!" As Maple Bay turned red with blood, the Salish warriors sang their war song: "Ha ha a a yu tsenukwat sen qe qe qwa ha a a." ("Behold we are the great serpent people!")[2] With the establishment of British law and order, the fires of tribal war were extinguished and women were no longer taken as slaves. Perhaps the imposition of peace was secretly welcomed by the coastal people. Our anchor splashed into the bay, sunset-red. There were no screams, nor did I hear the great serpent people sing.

VESUVIUS. SALT SPRING ISLAND. THE GARNERS

Imagine the Garner kids dancing on a grey whale's back! Hoping to find the site of this crazy caper, we intended to match Joe Garner's

20

photograph with the rock cliff south of Vesuvius Bay. Tied to the Vesuvius Bay float, the *Liza Jane* bounded in the wind and ferry wash. With Joe's book (*Never Fly Over an Eagle's Nest*) in hand, we went in the dinghy around the point south of the ferry landing.

We found the spot easily: a slightly overhanging wall of sandstone, with 15 to 20 feet of softly eroded stone above the barnacle line, and one bit of sculptured overcurling gallery. Rough barnacles below served as a coarse rasp to file off the barnacles growing on the whales. At the waterline fat purple starfish clung to the rock and to each other. A rusty iron chain, once used to hold a float against the cliff, hung straight into the sea. Above this chain stood a great fir tree, around which the Garner children once tied their rope, to lower themselves onto the back of the grey whale rubbing itself against the cliff. There are other whale rubs known along the coast but only at Vesuvius were the whales assisted in this back-scratching by kids who liked to kick barnacles. Ethel, Tom and Joe took turns going down the rope, only one at a time while the other two watched to warn of any sudden movement from the whale, but the great beasts seemed pleased to have these small human animals easing their itch.

When I talked to Joe about it, he added the information that in the days when he was a child (he was born in 1909) the grey whales calved in the warm water at the outlet of Booth Canal and he remembered seeing blood in the water. There was always a midwife whale assisting, he said, and a lot of squeaking and squealing, and he saw the male whale swimming back and forth between Sansum Narrows and Vesuvius, every inch the pacing father.

The Garner children inherited the tenacious strength and independence of their pioneer family. Oland, a fierce eagle of a father, and Lona, a remarkable mother, escaped from the Ku Klux Klan in South Carolina and fled north until they found Salt Spring Island in 1904. Lona's first child, Ethel, was born in 1905 and her second, Tom, in 1907. Joe was born on an icy February morning in an eight-by-ten-foot log cabin on a Salt Spring hillside. When the children were old enough to remember things, Lona would show Joe her big milk jug, telling him that "for the first two months after you were born, I used to put you in that pitcher filled with nice warm water to keep you from freezing to death."[1] From this precarious beginning, Joe grew to be a husky, six-foot-two logger.

Lona was a hard-working, courageous woman, wise and good, and her love was the flame that warmed the family's life. When the children, icy-cold and hungry, brought home strings of trout, she greeted them with "Lawsie sakes! Y'all must be the best fishermen in the whole world!" and "in less than ten minutes we were devouring hotcakes smothered in fresh butter and honey, washed down with gulps of hot cocoa that was made from fresh milk. The kitchen was warm and we were very, very happy."[2] The children continued to arrive (Margaret, Pearl, Edie, Ollie, Albert, Lloyd) but the last, Dorothy, almost killed her and the doctor said another birth would do just that. When Oland refused to give permission for an operation to prevent further pregnancies, Lona sent Joe and Tom to East Vancouver with $35 to buy a lot and build a house. Three weeks later, she moved in, bringing a trunk, an old stove, a couple of beds, a dresser or two, some blankets and a few dishes. She carried three-month-old Dorothy and was trailed by little Lloyd, Albert and Edie. Margaret came when her summer job ended. Ollie and Pearl were left with their father, who had given Lona $225 as a total settlement, even though he had recently banked over $40,000 from logging sales. Lona was just 42.

Much has been written of the loggers in their sweaty Stanfields and braces, whose skills and hard labour enriched British Columbians, and not much is said of the women like Lona. It was Lona who held the family together with good food and love, who was a model of courage, laughter and independence, who taught them to work for what they wanted. She might even have enjoyed taking her turn dancing on the whales.

KUPER ISLAND SCHOOL

In 1962 we stopped at the dock near Donckele Point on the west shore of Kuper Island. We had just come to live on a Gulf Island and were exploring our new world. In the lazy heat of a summer afternoon, we visited the impressive residential school and enjoyed its cool garden with a pool. I photographed our small daughter standing on a bridge that led to an islet in the pool. She gazed up, mesmerized. On the islet, on a pedestal, a tall, white-draped, marble male figure looked down at her. The Christ held a child in his arms.

Thirty years older, docking again at Kuper Island, we walked toward the row of five poplars standing motionless where we should have seen the school. Overgrown cement steps led into a tangle of trees and shrubs, but where was the school? Confused, we

Garden at Kuper Island School, 1962.

wondered if memory betrayed us. No, the school was gone. A passing truck raised a haze of dust which slowly sifted down onto the smashed cars at the side of the road. We struggled through the thorny arms of abandoned rose bushes, up the cement steps into the place where an alien garden had once been tenderly created. A large monkey-puzzle tree was blackened and dead almost to the top, but the tip was green. There were more steps, leading nowhere. White thistledown drifted like snow and rock music thudded softly in the hot afternoon, like drumming.

Thirty years ago, we walked here without knowing how some of the teachers had betrayed those they pretended to serve. Now, adults are talking about it; at the root of many social problems for native people (as for many in the non-Indian world) lies sexual abuse. Some say their aborted babies were buried in that garden. Three children (two sisters and a brother) fled in a canoe in the 1950s; only one body was ever found. All Catholic dioceses have agreed to set up, in collaboration with the native people, a process for the disclosure of mistreatment and the talking-out which may begin a healing. As we trudged back to the dock, the weight of the heat was heavy upon us. Blame? How unaware we were! The rape of the weak is a control policy in a patriarchal culture, but we, like the native people, were taught not to speak of it. The marble Christ is gone, the beauty of his compassion frozen in a society that nurtures unchristian violence, competitiveness and individualism.

When we returned to the dock, a young Indian girl was sitting on the rail. She tossed her shining black hair restlessly and twisted a bit of grass in her hand. When we asked about life on Kuper Island, she shrugged.

KULLEET BAY. VANCOUVER ISLAND. THE RAIN GOD

After the drought summer of 1993, the creeks were dry. Returning salmon could not spawn. During cloudless September days, they threw themselves out of the water at the mouths of the streams. Overhead the ravens squawked, or flapped at the eagles huddled despondently on the branches of drooping cedars. Back and forth across the tidal flats of eel grass and glasswort paced the bears, searching the dried-up pools. The fishermen prayed for rain.

Probably it was a shaman who grooved the dragon into a boulder on the beach south of Kulleet Bay, about a mile north of Nares Rock off Coffin Point. The native people called it the Rain God. We anchored off this shore on a hot summer afternoon, and rowed to a strand which shelved so gradually that we had to wade to the beach. The water was deliciously warm over a sand bottom thick with sand dollars. With the binoculars we had picked out a large rock which proved not to be the petroglyph boulder, but where we came ashore a tiny stream meandered across the beach. I looked at the stream and did a startled double-take: in the stream bed a boulder was shaped like the head of the mythical sea monsters at Petroglyph Park. I went closer and saw that a neat, round, five-centimetre eye had been pecked in the appropriate spot. This mythical creature waited in vain, for there were no longer salmon or fishtraps in what was once a salmon-spawning stream. As if that discovery were not thrilling enough, when we hiked north along the shore, looking for the Rain God, my grandson stepped upon a flat boulder and discovered he was standing on a petroglyph face!

Farther north we found the Rain God. The petroglyph channels are about an inch deep and wide, and within the channels are ridges cut so delicately that the sharp edges came out as fine lines on the rubbings we made for the museum some years ago. Peering out from the seaward end of the boulder, a non-outlined face was made by utilizing the eroded strata of the boulder. When we first examined this sea creature we noted that a line running from the

Rain God's ear to the top of the boulder connected the glyph to two circles, but it was only later that we realized that the circles were the eyes of a face. Perhaps this is the shaman and his "dragon" power.

I came here once with my psychic friend whom I will call Tom. His small daughter skipped and jumped ahead of us as we hiked along the beach. Then, as we three sat on a log near the petroglyph to eat our sandwiches, Tom remarked he saw the petroglyph boulder out in the shallow water. It stood, in fact, behind us against the bank. Although I knew that it had once rested where Tom saw it, I said nothing. The beach was empty in both directions, but Tom saw what he called "tent frames". I could not see them but knew that long ago, salmon-drying racks may have stood where he looked. I did not say so.

Then he got to his feet and announced that people were coming down to the shore and waiting for a boat that was approaching. I saw only the waves lapping on the stones. He watched for a while. "What are they doing, Tom?" I prodded. He told me that the people on the shore seemed to be forming themselves into two lines, and two children with brownish streaks on their faces were being brought down this corridor. The boat arrived and was pulled ashore, the crowd preventing Tom from seeing whatever was happening. Finally the children were escorted back up the bank. "The children are carrying something between them," Tom related, "and they are walking as if it might break." They disappeared up the path and Tom sat down to finish his lunch. I had seen nothing at all.

He had described a First Salmon ceremony. The salmon were regarded as humans who lived in the sea, who voluntarily sacrificed themselves to be food for people. They were treated as honoured guests. Hilary Stewart has explained how a ritualist would catch the first sockeye with a reef net and people formed an avenue from the water's edge to the cooking fires.

> Children, with red ochre painted faces and white eagle down in their shining black hair, each carried up a salmon by holding the dorsal fin in their teeth. They stroked and soothed the fish as they went in procession up the avenue, with the Ritualist singing songs and shaking his rattle.[1]

The first salmon were placed on a table and were sprinkled with eagle down or red ochre while chants and songs spoke of the salmon as a visiting chief. When the fish had been cooked, each person received a sacramental piece. All the bones were returned to the sea so that the fish might be reconstituted and return the following year.

In its original location the petroglyph boulder had snagged the log booms stored along this shore, so the loggers used a bulldozer at an extreme low tide to move it to its present location. Not until this was done, and the marine growth had fallen away, was the Rain God discovered.

Many years ago a Haida native told anthropologist E.L. Keithahn that some petroglyphs were made to cause rain, and in Puget Sound the Reverend Eels was told that if the petroglyph boulder at Eneti was shaken, rain would fall. The salmon, returning to spawn, may school up in deeper water offshore and wait for a heavy rain to raise the water level in a stream before they will enter it. Dependent on the salmon for their survival, the people watched the flicker of shining fins. The stone with the petroglyph eye, the spirit face on the flat boulder, and the Rain God may have been made to invoke spirit power to bring the downpour for which both fish and fishermen thirsted.

KULLEET BAY SHAMANS' POOL

We anchored off the north shore of Kulleet Bay, rowed ashore and walked along the top of the beach until we found in the bank two culverts (one metal, one cement) and a path ascending to the road above. On the other side of the road the path led us to the pool, a natural formation, an oval, sandstone basin about five feet wide and 15 feet long, part of a stream bed. What surprised me on this recent visit was the discovery that the petroglyph figures around the rim of the pool had almost disappeared under the moss. When the petroglyphs were discovered around 1930, C.F. Newcombe wrote that "the old Chief of the Kulleet Bay Band had no knowledge of their existence but thought they had probably been executed by ancient Shamans during their initiation, part of which consisted of prolonged fasting; the carved figures represented those seen in dreams."[1] Now, when the winter dance drums beat in the Big House at Kulleet Bay, the initiates come through the rain and darkness to bathe in the numbing water, to draw power from the ordeal, and from the spirits that inhabit this place.

The spring rains fill the pool to overflowing, but it is empty and dry in summer. Once, on a bleak winter day, when the wind rattled the leafless branches above us, Tom (my psychic friend) and I stood there with an archaeologist. The archaeologist and I were discussing the fact that the water was at the level of a dark line which, like a dirty ring in a bathtub, marked the winter water level. As the petroglyph faces were all above that ring, it appeared that they were made by someone squatting in ice-cold water (unless the artist drew upside down).

Suddenly Tom interrupted. "We must leave," he ordered abruptly, with an edge on his words that sent the three of us running to the car. When we were well out of the village I broke the silence by asking Tom if he could tell us what he had heard. "I heard nothing," he said, "but we were in great danger."

> Dark-brow'd sophist, come not anear:
> All the place is holy ground.[2]

MIAMI ROCK. THETIS ISLAND

North of Thetis Island, Miami Rock rose like a surfacing blonde whale; before the *Miami* struck, it was named White Rock. On the calmest sea (and one should visit it under no other conditions), approaching the *Miami* wreck has always made me nervous. We arrived at the red buoy at an extreme low tide. The prow of the *Miami* jutted from the sea like the tip of a knife waiting to rip the unwary hull. Leaving Ray aboard the boat, some of us put off in the dinghy to examine the wreck. The black-encrusted thing seemed to rise and fall as the slow swells lifted and lowered. I reached out and touched that sharp barnacled iron protruding from the green depths. Below us the skeleton of the *Miami* fell away into the deep darkness. Fascinated, horrified and silent, we looked down at pale ribs festooned with streamers of seaweed.

The *Miami* was a 3,020-ton steam collier. In the early evening of January 25, 1900, she left Mr. Dunsmuir's dock at Oyster Harbour, loaded with coal for San Francisco. The pilot was Mr. Butler. She hit the reef at full speed, and she hit at high tide. The rock tore a gaping hole in the hull. She hung there, this great wounded thing, with a black depth of water under both bow and stern; "She came very near going over the reef," Captain Wallace Langley later remarked.[1] They thought the fall of the tide would break her back, the ship being heavily loaded. Tugs hurried to the rescue but there was no use pulling her off and the men could only watch her die. "As the tide fell, the forward and after sections tore apart, the steel deck and sides ripping like so much paper," wrote the *Colonist* reporter.[2] Did Mr. Butler stand at the rail of one of the tugs, watching the death agonies? Captain Langley told the reporter that White Rock was not shown correctly on the chart. The reef, he said, extended farther out than indicated. "A very few feet would have cleared her."[3]

A very few feet...that fact must have rung in Mr. Butler's head. There was to be an inquiry, of course. In the following day's report, it was noted that Mr. Butler "did not return yesterday as expected."[4] However, both the ship (worth $150,000) and the cargo were insured.

BOAT HARBOUR. KEN KENDALL

No cannon boomed to welcome us to Boat Harbour in 1992 for Pirate Kendall had been dead for almost 20 years. We met him two years before he died. At that time we knew nothing of his eccentricities but were only searching for a rumoured petroglyph and were told that he would know about it. We talked on his terrace above the entrance to Boat Harbour. The sun glinted on his gold earring, and I remember the ring of his laughter. He knew where the petroglyph had been and when it was destroyed.

He was a lean man with the energy of a tiger. As we did not know about it, we did not ask to see his six-toed foot, which he considered the mark of the true pirate. Once when some tourists challenged him, he kicked off a shoe to display it. Kendall came to Boat Harbour in 1945 aboard the *Andante*, with wine-red sails; when the ship was old, he set fire to her, rather than see her rot away. His first wife asked to be buried at sea, so after her death he placed her body on a raft, soaked all in gasoline, towed the raft out into the channel and set it alight.

On his 50 acres at Boat Harbour, he devoted himself to living well on little money, his fuel from the beach, his food and medicines from the land and sea. His second wife Mary's recipes included the cooking of rattlesnake, cuttlefish, octopus, wolf-eel, beaver, coon, owl, crow, squid and ferret. She considered coon a delicacy and said that a fair-sized one would feed four.

During his years at Boat Harbour Kendall made more than a hundred cannons for his friends, turning them out in his foundry for $70, the recipients supplying the 16 pounds of brass required. He and Mary welcomed visitors, and one of their regulars was John Wayne, who always fired a Kendall cannon from the deck of his yacht to announce his imminent arrival. In the year 1962 Kendall's visitors' book had 600 names. There was a day when three of the guests signed the book before they showed their Royal Canadian Mounted Police badges and took possession of his still.

He died in 1974 at the age of 70. The cove seemed empty, when we came there in 1992. A large, four-foot iron pulley and hook leaned against a low rock cliff near the dock and behind them there was a crude fish cut into the cliff face, probably made with a screwdriver — one of Pirate Kendall's jokes perhaps.

CHAPTER THREE

Gabriola Island and Nanaimo

As this area has many petroglyphs, this chapter describes several sites. How old are the glyphs? Obviously there is no way to directly date a channel or a hole in rock. Carbon dating can measure the age of matter which once was alive; guesses about dates can be based on the similarity of a petroglyph design to a carved object found in an excavation, where that object has been dated by radioactive carbon at the same level. It is generally concluded that some petroglyphs may be as old as the first art objects, possibly 2,500 years old. But others, like the sailing ships cut into the rocks at Clo-oose, must have been made at the time of the arrival of Europeans. The petroglyph face at Fort Rupert was actually made while Hudson's Bay Company employees watched.

Giedion, the great art historian, wrote that art gives form to the inner life of humans: "Symbolism arose from the need to give perceptible form to the imperceptible", such as the fearful difference between life and death.[1] The making of prehistoric figures was a function of the religion called shamanism, but not all rock art was necessarily made by shamans.

Shamanism may be an intensification of the world view of the early hunting cultures. Yet it is also a psychological technique for bringing to life the mythological images of the group and thus giving potency to the collective psyche. To this end the images must be conceived, formed, displayed and transmitted.[2]

When we made rubbings of the glyphs (cloth stretched tightly across them and rubbed gently with a ball of black wax), our knees pressed the stone where the shaman once knelt to pound the figures into the rock. Petroglyph sites are protected by law, but their preservation depends on our respect for sacred places. The rock figures, many carved into soft sandstone, are gradually being eroded by wind and sea. For most of us the images cannot have more than a glimmering of the meaning they held for their makers, but few people discover petroglyph sites without experiencing some slight quivering of the nerve ends. Unconsciously, we feel the connection with awesome unknown dimensions and our own deepest anxieties: life itself is still the one and only ineffable mystery.

DEGNEN BAY. GABRIOLA ISLAND

In the northeast corner of the bay, a short distance east of the dock, we found the petroglyph killer whale cut into sloping sandstone, between the tide lines. This glyph may represent the "power" of a sea hunter, for, according to Wayne Suttles, "John Peter, one of the last of the Penelekut harpooners, had a blackfish guardian spirit."[1]

In the heel of the bay, the northwest corner, also between high and low tide lines, there once lay a large boulder with six bowls ground into it, arranged in pairs. Unable to find it in 1992, we questioned the people in cottages above the beach, then phoned enquiries to archaeology buffs on Gabriola Island. That night an islander came to visit us where we were docked at Silva Bay to tell us that the boulder was still there but had been buried by sea waves washing sand and silt over it. We also were told that there was a second boulder with two bowls which had been covered before the time when we recorded the six-bowl boulder. Moreover, our new friend had found a Seated Human Figure Bowl which he allowed us to photograph.

Mrs. Gray, who lived on the farm above this corner of Degnen Bay, first showed us the six-bowl boulder. In 1981 my article about Bedrock and Boulder Bowls was published. After observing one at Browning Harbour, I had accumulated a list of 26 manufactured (not natural) bowls, to which the years have added another 13. Most are single bowls in basalt boulders (27 in boulders, 12 in bedrock), slightly oval or round, the bowl diameters ranging from eight to 35 centimetres (with one exception, a very large bowl at Dogfish Bay on Quadra Island) and most are between the tide lines or found in middens at the edge of the sea. All but the large one are too small for cooking pots, and many show signs of having been used for grinding. No evidence survives to establish what substance was ground in these stone bowls, but it may have been ochre or clamshell.

The use of red ochre, an iron oxide, began in the Palaeolithic era and, as a symbol of blood and life, was an important component of shamanism. Ochre was painted on the faces of children in the First Salmon ceremony. Anthropologist Homer Barnett was told that when the annual run of salmon was late arriving in the Nanaimo River, red ochre was rubbed on the petroglyph at Jack Point. Possibly some of the bowls were used for powdering the ochre. If the bowls between the tide lines held ochre, the rising sea would devour it, and out of the sea came the salmon whose self-sacrifice sustained human life on the shore.

We modern folk casually and constantly examine our mirrored faces, but for people before the invention of the mirror, the image reflected in water was thought to be their soul, their very life. Mirrors were magic. The Elizabethan astrologer Dr. John Dee used them extensively in his predictions. Some of the shallow bowls may have served as mirrors, a basic article of shamanic apparatus throughout Siberia and North America. Marius Barbeau has described a Gitksan shaman using a slate mirror to predict the future.

Many years ago when Mrs. Gray's son, Bob, was digging in the family garden just above the six-bowl boulder, his shovel turned up a headless Seated Human Figure Bowl. A year or so later Mr. Gray, going through the gate on his way down to the beach, paused to pull up a large weed, and with the roots, the missing head of the Seated Human Figure Bowl was yanked from the midden soil. The Degnen Bay Seated Human Figure Bowl has disappeared into a private collection, and the sea has hidden the bowls; only the petroglyph remained to tease us with unanswered questions as we rowed back to the boat. Perhaps one day the boulders will be dug out of the sand and placed just out of reach of the waves, so that those who walk the beach at Degnen Bay can feel with their own hands the smooth bowls so hard won from the granite, and, touching the stone, can also bridge the gap of centuries and feel a connection with those who made them. We may never know how they were used, but we can share the deeper meaning: stone, which thwarts time, is about life.

WELDWOOD PETROGLYPH SITE. GABRIOLA ISLAND

A mile west from the government dock road at Degnen Bay, we found the United Church. Behind it, a footpath followed a barbed-wire fence and then turned into an open glade among the trees. At our feet lay the petroglyphs found, under their turf covering, in the 1970s by Mary and Ted Bentley and described in their book *Gabriola: Petroglyph Island.* Following their example, others have been peering hopefully under the moss blanket. Usually they find nothing, and the meadow moss will take a hundred years or more to repair itself. Once exposed, the rock pictures will slowly erode, and there is little to protect them from the vandalism of careless feet and motorbikes. It's a dilemma. Perhaps all that can be done has been done: rubbings of the petroglyphs have been made and are stored in the Royal British Columbia Museum, together with site diagrams and many photographs.

The main figure on the Weldwood site is a creature with a tall dorsal fin (or ear?), an open mouth with tongue and teeth, a large eye and foot-like appendages. Nearby is a delightful combination of bird and snake, with long beak, large crest and huge eye at the end of its writhing body.

The transition from child to adult has proven particularly difficult in Western culture — the "terrible teens" can be destructive and wretched for those without a sense of the sacredness of life, without a feeling of connection to the cosmos. The Indian cultures of the past understood that young people needed a spirit helper at this crisis. When a boy from the Nanaimo village felt ready for the ordeal, he would slip away to one of these clearings on Gabriola Island, as a Christian might fast and pray in a church. In these glades were images of the divine helpers who had appeared there, and might return. The seeker took no food, kindled no fire. He washed himself in the cold sea, scraped his body to cleanse it, induced vomiting so that he was ritually clean inside, felt the cramps of hunger, tried not to sleep, danced and sang and prayed, day after night after day, until — suddenly — the vision came. When he returned to the village, he said nothing about this transformational experience and no one asked, for it was considered dangerous to discuss it, lest the power vanish, or cause illness. But the other villagers recognized that the young person "had something", just from the new confidence with which he walked, for now he knew he had the power to play his role in the adult world.

Anthropologist Robin Ridington wrote:

> I cannot tell you what "really happens" to children in the bush, just as they cannot tell other people their experience directly. I was told that if a child has the right thoughts, if his head is in the right place, a medicine animal will come to him. There is a moment of meeting and transformation when he is "just like a drunk" or in vocabulary more familiar to us, "stoned." In these moments the Indian can understand the animal's speech.[1]

Nowadays the quest process may not be as stringent as in ancient times, but the initiation of new dancers at one of the Band Houses, those barn-like structures which dwarf the village houses, may still induce a trance state. Through the night the drums beat their insistent and hypnotic rhythm and the feet of dancers pound the earth around the fires. Perhaps this could be compared to the "possession" of a religious experience, when the converts experience ecstasy. To be a spirit dancer is also to recognize oneself as unequivocally Indian, to feel a sure sense of identity. This sense of one's own clan and land is more difficult for footloose young non-native Canadians.

We wandered about the meadow with the Bentleys' book in hand, trying to find all the glyphs they have recorded there. Our voices grew softer until we fell silent or whispered as one does in a church. People here had moments when they touched a great, unknowable power, and something of their experience lingered.

STOKES ROAD PETROGLYPHS. GABRIOLA ISLAND

We anchored off the southern shore of Gabriola Island on a windless day. At the place where Stokes Road turned east, we followed a trail across a treeless field; where the climb became steep and there were trees, we found the tall sandstone boulder with the petroglyph figure.

It has been called the Bear. The pose was oddly feminine, one hand loosely on the hip and the other behind an ear, like a modern mannequin. Her mouth was open and she had a conspicuous vulva. On the central coast, the Kwakiutl Tsonoqua, the wild woman of the forest, was Mistress of Wealth, her black skin and grizzly-bear eyebrows identifying her as a Bear divinity. This petroglyph figure

The Bear petroglyph, Gabriola Island.

may represent an ancient version of Tsonoqua. The young man to whom this divinity appeared would be a great hunter. The Masters and Mistresses of Animals could take human form. They were propitiated with gifts, and there are myths of them requiring sexual favours in exchange for wealth. There are many versions of the story of the Bear Chief who took a human woman to his lair. But Tsonoqua was like the wicked witch in the folktale of Hansel and Gretel, and one wonders whether the myth may not be an echo of the time when children were sacrificed to gain divine favour or protection. If the band's winter food had been consumed, and hunters and fishermen could find nothing, shamans might resort to the exchange of human souls for food, to save their people from starvation. In Nootka stories, shamans kidnapped infants from neighbouring villages to trade with the Master of Whales for success in the whale hunt.

Beside an uphill path slightly east of the Bear, stood the boulder channelled with a ferocious dragon creature and a beaked bird. There was much more bird when we first examined this petroglyph but the rock has spalled badly and only beak, crest and eye remained. The shaman/artist used a natural crevice in the boulder for the devouring mouth. The two figures may represent the Underworld/Upperworld division of the cosmos, the two halves together forming the universe, as light and dark, life and death are only known in terms of their opposites. The sun each night sinks into the Underworld, where it enters the great open mouth of the Dragon or Serpent, and passes through the divinity to be reborn in the east.

Returning to the False Narrows shore of Gabriola, below Stokes Road, we walked on the beach where a Gabriola resident a few years ago overturned a flat stone on the beach and was much surprised to find a petroglyph on its surface. The stone itself had the shape of the fin of a killer whale and probably once stood vertically on the shore, submerged by the rising tide so that it spoke to those who lived undersea. It had a round face with a large mouth and tall, fin-shaped hat. A Tlingit myth recorded in 1909 by J.R. Swanton, tells how Raven, the most important Tlingit divinity,

> ...came to an abandoned camp where lay a piece of jade half buried in the ground, on which some design had been pecked. This he dug up. Far out in the bay he saw a large spring salmon jumping about and wanted to get it but did not know how. Then he stuck his stone into the ground and put eagle down upon the head designed thereon. The next time the salmon jumped, he said, "See here, spring salmon jumping out there, do you know what this green stone is saying to you? It is saying You Thing with dirty, filthy back, You Thing with dirty, filthy gills, come ashore here."[1]

The face on this False Narrows stone may be the Master of the Seas in his whale form. Franz Boas wrote in 1890 that

> if the fish do not come in due season, and the Indians are hungry, a Nootka wizard will make an image of a swimming fish and put it into the water in the direction from which the fish generally appear. This ceremony, accompanied by a prayer to the fish to come, will cause them to arrive at once.[2]

The fin-shaped petroglyph stone is now stored in the Band Office in Nanaimo.

Although we were tempted to begin turning over beach stones in search of undiscovered petroglyphs, the tide was tugging the boat towards the boulder-strewn chaos of False Narrows and the wind was rising. Besides, there were salmon steaks for dinner.

BOLTON PETROGLYPH SITE. GABRIOLA ISLAND

Of all the Gabriola petroglyph sites, this one seemed the most remote, secret and silent, a haunted place. We came to it when rain had stopped falling but the trees were still dripping and a musty fragrance rose from the damp earth. A thin veil of mist was slowly dissolving. Then the sun sprang forth and the eye of the dragon figure glittered and winked. A powerful eye.

We had hiked almost three miles to the site. From the Degnen Bay dock, we had walked north on Peterson Road, then west on Dorby Way, to a gravel pit. From there, a logging road twisted through the woods to an open glade. The trail led us to the first glyph, a large female figure with heart-shaped head, and farther along the path we found the dragon with the eye that held a splinter of the sun. The Sechelt people pictured Tchain'ko, the God of the Sea, in dragon form, sometimes with sight, sometimes blind.

We had hoped to make a rubbing of the dragon figure, but we had just whisked off the pine needles when a gentle rain began; we

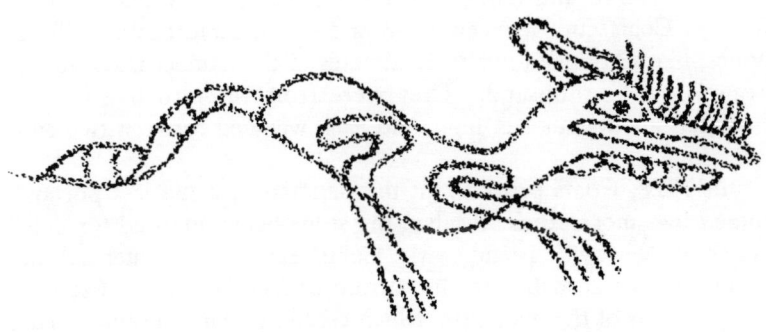

Dragon petroglyph, Gabriola Island.

could not rub wax on wet cloth. The dragons of ancient days were believed to control rain. Their voices thundered and their eyes shot lightning bolts. One of the oldest dragon figures, which had the same shape as the one at our feet, was made of mussel shells and was found in a 6,000-year-old tomb in Henan province in China. The place where it was found was once a marshland said to be inhabited by the God of Thunder; here a girl stepped on the dragon god's footprint, became pregnant and gave birth to Fuxi, the Chinese Adam, a tale that begs the question of who gave birth to Fuxi's mother.

What better symbol could be found to signify that force we call "life" than the serpent or dragon? Female in the laying of eggs, endlessly reborn in the shedding of its skin, it hibernates (dies) and is restored to life in the spring. At our feet a shaman had knelt to give form to an image in his head, to picture the most profound mystery, to make this glade a sacred place. The rain began to thicken. We bowed to the dragon and departed, hoping that we had not displeased this powerful divinity.

DESCANSO BAY. GABRIOLA ISLAND. MILLSTONES

We anchored in the bay behind the floating baulks at Descanso Bay and took a line to the shore to hold the boat securely. We climbed the road for about half a mile, until we could see, through an opening in the trees on the right-hand side of South Road, an open space in the forest. In this clearing we found a strange garden where waterplants grew in a series of perfectly round pools, five feet in diameter, with their rims touching. Dragonflies, like tiny blue bottles, hovered and flashed in the sun. This is the place where William Coats cut, between 1932 and 1936, hundreds of milling stones, like sections of pillars. Estimates of the number taken range from 500 to a thousand. They were from three to five feet in diameter, about four feet high, and each weighed between two and three tons.

In 1928, Coats proved that this sandstone, being less porous, pulped logs more efficiently than the stone being quarried for millstones on Newcastle Island. Mr. Coats' experiment sentenced the people of Descanso Bay to the torture of listening to the excruciating screams of the operation, which could be heard for miles. The torture instrument which left these exquisite holes was a machine like an open-ended boiler tank, the round bottom rim of the tank being the cutting edge. At this edge a ridge held "shot" (ball

Millstone pools, Gabriola Island.

bearings) which did the actual cutting when the tank was rotated. At the same time, a similar circular cut was made for the central core. Forty-five-degree slots in the side of the tank conducted the stone dust upwards. To break the column loose, a hole was drilled under the cut stone and a dynamite cap inserted and fired by a cable connected to an electric battery.

The millstones were lifted by a 50-ton derrick, trimmed on a giant lathe, loaded on James Rollo's one-ton, single-axle truck and taken carefully down the road we had just climbed, where another 50-ton derrick transferred them to a barge. For this ear-splitting work, men were paid three dollars a day. Each millstone was worth about $500. The business didn't last long. Cheaper, better stone was quarried in Tacoma and then carborundum made sandstone obsolete. We have been left with an evocative place, which should be preserved as a heritage site...fragments of Greek pillars in a Japanese water garden.

PETROGLYPH PARK, NANAIMO. VANCOUVER ISLAND

We came into Nanaimo Harbour past Jack Point, that long finger pointing towards Fairway Channel. The large petroglyph boulder, which once stood on the tip of Jack Point, is now beside the doors of the Nanaimo Museum, on the high rock outcrop above the bastion and the yacht basin. In ancient days, when the salmon were overdue and the people were anxious, these fish petroglyphs were rubbed with red ochre; ochre was put on pieces of four different substances (goat wool and a grass are the two that Homer Barnett identified) which were burned at the base of the boulder.

A legend about the Jack Point petroglyph tells how a dog salmon man came out of the sea and took away the shaman's daughter. The shaman grieved and made a long journey to find her. Although she would not return to Nanaimo, she promised to come every year to visit, and though the Indians caught many fish they did not touch the two who came first, leaping from the water side by side, the salmon man and his human wife. It was thought that the girl's father had carved the fish on the boulder.

A hike of about a mile and a half brought us to Petroglyph Park on the top of the hill south of the city centre. That slope sometimes ran with blood, the Nanaimo people told the first anthropologists. As we know that the Jack Point fish were rubbed with red ochre to empower them, possibly the petroglyphs at the top of the hill were also covered with ochre; heavy rains washing the paint down the sloping rock face could be responsible for the tale of trickling blood.

Once, a few years ago, my psychic friend Tom accompanied me up the path to the petroglyphs. Suddenly he darted ahead, climbed over the rail which separated the main panel of figures from the path, ran across the sloping sandstone, scrambled over the ridge where a shaman glyph was hidden under fallen leaves and branches, and hurried around to a spot where a ten-foot wall of bare rock descends from the peak of the hill. Teenagers often have parties in this out-of-the-way place, leaving the charred evidence of their campfires. But Tom jumped over the ashes and put his hands on the flat cliff.

"Here is the power centre," he announced firmly. "Right here."

We climbed up the cliff, examined the "altar" stone and another boulder which lay at the very highest point. It was a place of high anxiety, he said, for boys at puberty. I do not intend to relate all that Tom told me, but what I wish to record is a sequel: a month later, when I was coming down Vancouver Island with Hilary Stewart, she suggested that we stop at Petroglyph Park.

Capriciously, I pretended to be Tom and led her up and over the carved pictures and around to the back and — ! to my shock and surprise, someone, probably one of the teenagers, had pulled down a large flat rock from that cliff face, a rock that precisely closed off a horizontal, tomb-shaped chamber large enough to accommodate one human body. The rock had been so recently dislodged that the inside surface of it was clean and without lichen growth. The floor of the chamber had a mattress of white clay. Hilary immediately fitted herself into the cavity and in doing so knocked her head on a fine stone hammer which had been left where one end of the chamber was hidden behind the rock wall. I took my turn on the clay mattress and noted how small rocks had been used to chink the crack which opened upwards. Perhaps a speaking tube of kelp had once been inserted through that crack. How terrifying to the initiates above, when a voice seemed to come from the earth beneath their feet! Tom had put his hands on the very rock that closed off this secret chamber. A sample of the clay mattress (now dispersed) was taken to the museum, but its place of origin could not be identified. Such shamanic "tricks" do not negate the reality of a shaman's power any more than a doctor's placebo invalidates healing.

Ray and I leaned long on the wooden railing, examining the mythical creatures of the main panel — dream animals, reptilian and strange, like the composite animals of children's playbooks, head of wolf on snake body, rabbit ears on crocodile. Although we can never "explain" each figure, it is possible to say something of the world view from which they emerged. Generally, there was a thunderbird/serpent antithesis, upperworld/underworld, life/death, but these opposites were two sides of a coin, a unity. The sea, the underworld, the place of death into which the sun made its daily descent, was also the place of birth from which the sun emerged. This world was ruled by a sea serpent, or dragon, sometimes a two-headed snake. The power of this divinity could work for good or evil, could give or take life. This power could also be represented by the whale, the halibut, the sea lion, the frog, or the fantastic creatures from the shaman's vision.

The native people told anthropologists that the petroglyphs were made by a shaman named Thockwan, who lived "at the beginning of time".[1] The petroglyph figure of a shaman, on the path leading over the ridge, has power rays springing from his head. He has six-fingered hands, very long earrings almost to his shoulders, and his ribs and spine were drawn as if he were a skeleton. His strangely inturned feet may indicate the ghostly nature of this shaman. In a Salish ceremony which is a journey to the land of the dead to recover souls, the shamans may encounter a ghost; the dead walk crookedly, crossing one leg in front of the other. A ghost may weave back and forth "as his right foot stepped far to the left and his left foot far to the right."[2] Our pigeon-toed petroglyph shaman was accompanied by his spirit power, a wolf-like animal also shown as a skeleton, with "power" loops extending from his back and an extremely long tongue.

The shaman's earrings became particularly interesting when a gigantic stone earplug was discovered in the dig at the Pender Island Canal. This artifact was a flattened doughnut of smooth black stone, with a channel to hold the flesh of the ear around it, when the earlobe hole had been stretched to accommodate the heavy ornament. The stone earplug was dated to the Locarno cultural phase, about 4,500 years ago. Only one such earplug has been found in British Columbia, but they have been discovered in Japan and Mexico. We swept away the leaves and twigs that covered the pigeon-toed feet and heavy, six-fingered, dangling hands of this shaman figure who may be Thockwan. As we went away down the path I listened for the sound coming from the round opening of his mouth, but there was only the roar of traffic on the Island Highway.

PROTECTION ISLAND

Carried across Nanaimo Harbour to Protection Island in the small passenger ferry, we had come to look at a petroglyph discovered in the 1960s by young Harry Wilson. He noticed what looked like a toothed mouth chiselled into the surface of a flat rock jutting from the top of a bank overlooking a beach, on the narrows facing Newcastle Island. He scratched away the overburden of weeds and topsoil and uncovered an eye. At this point archaeologists took over the excavation, revealed a whale, determined that the midden covering was from the last century and then backfilled. What we found looked much as it did when Harry Wilson completed his preliminary work.

It was a 15-minute walk along Pirates Lane and down Pirates Spit to the beach. A yappy black dog seemed overjoyed to have someone to bark at. Our feet sank inches deep into smooth brown sand as he escorted us to the site, in front of the third house. Just below my eye level, the flat sandstone seemed to be held in place by a thick root. The blackfish face was partly covered, the great teeth chewing sand and grit, and bits of shell lying like teardrops on its cheeks. When I pushed back the leaves, the eye glared up at me, like an old man wanting attention but unable to ask for it.

Across the swift run of tide, the geese honked laconically from the sloping shore of Newcastle Island. Did the native people set here their exquisitely constructed traps made with split sticks? Sometimes wooden figures were attached to fishtraps, portraying the spirit power of the owner of the trap. Then I looked again at the petroglyph blackfish and recognized that the lozenge-shaped hole just inside his jaws was meant to represent a fish, and the black-fish teeth were like the split-cedar teeth of a basket trap. The petro-glyph teeth were even slightly in-curved. The prehistoric artist saw the natural hole as a fish and drew the voracious blackfish engulfing it. The killer whale, a powerful guardian spirit for success in fishing, was here a metaphor for a fishtrap.

Blackfish petroglyph, Protection Island.

CHAPTER FOUR

Northward, Nanaimo to Quadra Island

SCOTTIE BAY. LASQUETI ISLAND. SHARKS

When we anchored in Scottie Bay in 1968, we hiked up the road to look at the teapot house with brick spout and handle, which is said to have belonged, inappropriately, to a bootlegger. By the time we had returned to Scottie Bay, the evening had dimmed into that eerie time between daylight and darkness. We climbed into the dinghy to row to our boat. We were singing "Row-row-row your boat" to spur our daughter's oars, when suddenly she screamed. It was like a scene from *Jaws*. Sharks surrounded us. We could easily have touched the black fins slicing the darkening water and circling our tiny boat. The whole cove was filled with sinuous, glistening, black shapes. She could not stroke without touching one of them. It was a nightmare, terrifying. "Row!" we shrieked. "Row!" And when we reached our cruiser and were all safely on board, we shone flashlights on the black, roiling water. The elongated rubbery bodies (about five feet long), the two dorsal fins and the high lobe of the tail fin identified them: dogfish. Hundreds of glistening eyes looked up at us.

Michael Poole has written of drifting in The Tangles (between Fife and Blackfish sounds):

Beneath me was an undulating mass of thousands upon thousands of sharks, densely packed from the surface for as far down as I could see into the depths. Swimming with sinuous, hypnotic grace, they glided over and under. and around one another, never touching and never stopping.[1]

In 1939, Francis Barrow, rowing near Jedidiah Island, not far from Scottie Bay,

> turned the flashlight on the water and saw countless thousands of dogfish swimming about the boat. As far as one flashed the light one could see shining eyes. I have never seen so many dogfish in my life.[2]

We returned to Scottie Bay recently, seeking someone to tell us whether the dogfish always moved into this area in packs. And so it was that we met a charming Australian living in a hand-hewn house on a small barge draped with nets and white fishing floats and flying the flag of Gaia, (a banner blue as the sky with a picture of the Planet Earth floating in space). He was indeed a citizen of Earth, living in harmony with her winds and seas, consuming little, sensuously enjoying being alive. The barge was tied to a sandstone ledge with a cliff rising behind, and on the ledge stood his sloop, ashore for work on the hull. Tethered to the barge were his trimaran and dinghy. For a while, time slowed to a stop, as we sat with him. Through a square hole in the deck of the barge, we watched a thousand tiny fish doing synchronized water arabesques.

Once, when our Australian friend was fishing off the western shore of Texada, he suddenly found his dinghy in the middle of a school of fish. He had gaffed three of them with a hook and hauled them into his boat before he realized with horror that these were dogfish, not salmon. With disgust he hooked them back into the sea. He told us about two inexperienced fishermen, a Laurel and Hardy pair, who set off in a gillnetter to make their fortune with dogfish. Fishing in the deep water off the southern end of Texada, their turning drum pulled in a shark 12 feet long which came flopping onto their deck, its lashing jaws quite capable of slicing through an arm or leg. They leapt to the top of the cabin. We laughed at the thought of the mismatched pair waving wildly for help, clinging to the mast as their gillnetter rolled in the seas and the shark lusted for their blood.

There may be 350 different shark species. In British Columbia waters, the five-gill basking sharks, at 45 feet long the largest of our sharks, were almost wiped out in the 1940s; because they sometimes fouled commercial fishnets, the Department of Fisheries equipped boats to slice them in half by ramming them, destroying more than 4,000 of them. The white shark, the man-eater of *Jaws* fame, 40 feet long, has been sighted about ten times in British Columbia in 25 years, but the market value of their jaws ($5,000) may imperil them. The six-gill shark (26 feet) has the huge eyes of a creature from the dark depths, 3,000 to 6,000 feet below our keels; for some unknown reason, they drift lazily up for a few weeks each year to sunlit depths of 60 to 100 feet. They are dreamy leviathans, curious and friendly to scuba divers. The Flora Islet off Hornby Island is a good place to look for them. We also have blue sharks and sleeper sharks (25 feet), salmon sharks (ten feet), seven-gill sharks (eight feet), soupfin sharks (six feet), dogfish (five feet) and the little brown cat sharks (two feet). Laurel and Hardy probably had a salmon shark, the most voracious of the sharks and called "man-eater" by fishermen, although there are no reports of it attacking humans.

Many of us will have eaten dogfish in British fish and chips, and the Germans smoke dogfish belly and enjoy it as a bar snack. During World War II, dogfish were taken commercially for their livers, which provided a Vitamin A tonic equal to cod-liver oil. For a while the dogfish became quite scarce, but since modern children do not have their noses held while a spoonful of nauseating oil is forced between their teeth, the dogfish have once again flourished. They are a nuisance to fishermen, taking lures hungrily, then chopping the line with their sharp teeth and departing with bait, lure and all.

John Borgoni has written about the time he took out his friend Harry, a novice fisherman, to catch a salmon. The fishing was lousy, until, as a last resort, John put a six-inch 158 plug (a wooden imitation fish) on Harry's line. Then the line went screaming out with the rod doubling over so far and so violently that Harry could barely hold it. John thought perhaps they had inadvertently hooked a seal, or a giant ray, or a Russian submarine, or the biggest spring salmon in the world. Well, they finally netted the thing and what they had was a 35-pound spring with seven rather large dogfish still chomping away on it; around the stern of the boat swam about two dozen more dogfish. "After a lot of high stepping and shouting we managed to get rid of the unwanted guests that by now covered the floor of the boat."[3]

Though few of us may ever see a basking shark, knowing they are there inspires the vigilance of the helmsman. As for the dogfish: how fortunate we were to have seen them that evening in Scottie Bay — now we can enjoy the remembered horror.

FALSE BAY. LASQUETI ISLAND. SHARIE AND ALLEN FARRELL

This was not a comfortable place. We rode the rollers into False Bay and tied the *Liza Jane* to the bounding float at the government dock. Ray stayed with the boat while I hurried off to make enquiries at the blue-roofed restaurant, to ask if anyone had seen the vessel *China Cloud*, home of Allen and Sharie Farrell. At the top of the ramp I met a man headed down to his boat.

"*China Cloud*? She's lying in Mud Bay, safe from the wind. Saw her there this morning," he told me.

Mud Bay, a cove off False Bay, dries at low tide. When we had taken *Liza Jane* across to a sheltered anchorage, we set off in the dinghy for Mud Bay. At first we thought *China Cloud* had blown away, but then, in a hidden nook, we found her, settled comfortably on the bottom, in two feet of water. What a lovely sight she was, with the sweep of her oriental lines and the slanted masts of a junk, and the dragon's two red-rimmed painted eyes watching us.

Allen Farrell built this most unusual and lovely vessel. When Jim Spilsbury came to examine the work in progress, he looked hard at it and remarked, "Farrell, you know you've got to think of the resale value." Allen laughed when he told us this story, for of course the *China Cloud* has been his home for many years, "and how could we afford to live on land, anyway?" he added.

"Permission to board *China Cloud*?" I shouted as we came alongside, and Allen, once a champion gymnast, leapt from the hatch to take our line. Then Sharie emerged to welcome us. Allen was like a barefooted, nautical Santa Claus, but it was 86-year-old Sharie who amazed us. She was lithe like a dancer still, in a cotton skirt with a knotted cord around her small waist, her graying hair free and shoulder-length, the skin taut over a fine-boned face with dark eyes and a warm mouth. Down the hatch into the cosy cocoon of the main cabin we went, and eased ourselves into the cushioned bunks to talk. The interiors of most boats are spartan and impersonal, but this cabin felt soft and enveloping, like a seraglio. My eye fell on one of Allen's paintings, a Turner-esque shore scene in which two horses and a group of dark figures stood huddled in a swirl of mist, sand, sea and sky, evanescent, mysterious.

We had come to visit and we had come in search of an unpublished manuscript written by that amazing sailor George Dibbern, whose first book, *Quest*, was published in 1942 and is now a rare book indeed, rare and fascinating. We had heard that he had

CHINA CLOUD.

written a second book and that Sharie had the manuscript. In fact, Sharie was part of the George Dibbern story. In 1938 she was working as a secretary in a Vancouver office building when she heard about George Dibbern and the *Te Rapunga* from her cousin Roy Murdock. Roy and a very young New Zealander, Eileen Morris, had crewed across the Pacific aboard the *Te Rapunga*. It is our dreams that lead us, blind-folded, into our futures. Sharie (at that time named Gladys Nightingale) in her routine office life was perhaps unaware of the power of her sea dream. Taking her mother with her, she went down to the dock to visit the *Te Rapunga*. Later, she sent her mother home and went dancing with George. They danced all night, every dance, two people who loved life and were perfectly matched in the dance. When she came down the ladder into the ship the next day "light as a bird goes from twig to twig" [1] they recognized what had happened: "To think that only yesterday I felt completely useless and at a loss," she confessed. "And now that I have found what I want, it's out — you."[2]

It was Gladys (Sharie) who enabled George to begin work on *Quest*. He rented a room in Vancouver and each evening after work she typed from his dictation. When Eileen came, the two women worked together, revising and re-structuring. They were a happy trio, for Eileen's platonic friendship with George was not threatened when Gladys' dancing legs came down the hatchway. The three of them sailed north in *Te Rapunga*, falling in love with this coast. They experienced that astounding cruising moment when, coming around Sarah Point to enter Desolation Sound, the spectacular panorama of the Coast Range is suddenly revealed. They found the place of their dreams in the eastern corner of Galley Bay. Bubbling with plans for their future, they bought it. But it was 1939, and George, holding a German passport, was not allowed to stay in Canada. He and Eileen were forced to sail away.

Although Gladys, her heart wrenched with the decision, chose to remain in Vancouver, her dream did not die when George left British Columbia. Visiting Pender Harbour in 1945, she met Allen Farrell. He had come to Squitty Bay, Lasqueti Island, in 1934, in the Depression years, and had made his living as a hand-liner, trolling from a rowboat, until he got a job in a sawmill. By 1937 he had moved to North Vancouver where he built himself a 35-foot troller, and with a one-dollar salmon licence, he became a fisherman. He moved to Pender Harbour; like George Dibbern, he liked the seafaring life, but his wife preferred the city and they had become estranged. When Gladys and Allen met, two dreams collided and matched.

"I was cod-fishing and this guy introduced me to the two girls he had in his boat, so I went over and visited that evening, and all she and I did was sit in a corner and talk about boats. She told me all about George's *Te Rapunga*," Allen told us, with a grin. It was a huge step for Gladys to abandon her city job, adopt the name Sharie which Allen gave her, and live with him, helping to care for his youngest child, while he fished and in his spare moments built the sailboat called *Windsong*.

"Everything was much easier in the old days. If you wanted to build a boat you just sat down at the table and wrote out: a thousand feet of lumber, so many bolts, a 10-14 Easthope engine, a case of milk, six cabbages and so on," Allen explained. "My 10-14 engine for *Windsong* — they brought it up and lowered it right onto the engine bed." When they sailed *Windsong* to Fiji, Sharie's dream had come true. They sold *Windsong* in Fiji and the new owners lost the vessel on a Pacific reef after Allen and Sharie had returned to this coast to begin building another boat.

In 1953 Allen, Sharie and Allen's son Keray moved to Blind Bay, Nelson Island, where, in the 1960s, Ray and I came upon Allen building the *Ocean Girl*. Above the boat-shed on the sloping rock edge of the channel, the Farrells lived in a cabin enclosed on three sides by an amazingly high and long split-cedar deer fence. The house and parts of the fence were still there when we called at Colonel Pond's in 1992, but the boat-shed, weathered gray, was beginning to collapse. Someone once asked Allen how many boats he had built, all sizes; after much thought, he said the count went well over 40, but only ten of them were over 20 feet. Perhaps best known are *Windsong, Ocean Girl, Ocean Bird, Native Girl, August Moon,* and *China Cloud.*

It was time for our visit with the Farrells to end. From the shelf behind my head, Allen had pulled out a ragged brown envelope, the manuscript for George Dibbern's unpublished second book, "Ship Without Port". Dibbern had written the further adventures of the *Te Rapunga,* including an account of those few years when Sharie Farrell's life began the sea-change that led her to the *China Cloud.*

HERON ROCKS. HORNBY ISLAND. HILARY BROWN

Ford Cove, hardly a nick in the southwest corner of Hornby Island, has been improved by the building of a substantial break-water. Behind it, the tide came in over the beach as if determined to float the strange vessel propped up somewhat precariously on the shore, a fat-bellied sailing ship with the rakish look of a pirate vessel. At the top of the dock a small grocery store had benches and a table in the corner window where two islanders were drinking coffee and talking fish. Hilary Brown was only 28 when she and H.B. stepped ashore at Ford Cove beach in 1937. They thought the island was deserted until the sound of wood-chopping led them to an old man. "Is there anyone on this island?" they asked, and he sent them up the road to Parnell's place, a morning's walk that cast a spell upon them from which they never escaped.

From the Ford Cove store a path led us down to the strange shore of Lambert Channel, where the sandstone was swollen into huge mushrooms or shaped into solid waves edged with stone foam. Many times we have lingered along that mile of sandstone shore from Ford Cove eastward. We have photographed stone like solid froth, in which a million bubbles have been frozen, stone cracked in geometric shapes like the surface of cooled caramel pudding, caves I could curl up in, huge stone flower pots.

Then we came to the Heron Rocks co-operatively owned campsite, where trespassers are not welcome, and we would have returned to Ford Cove except that we were on our way to visit Hilary Brown. There are some special people, blessed by the circumstances of their birth and by their choice of parents perhaps, compassionate, intelligent and strong-willed people, who move through life doing good things for the rest of us. Hilary Brown, residing for 55 years in a small and cluttered house above the shore, amid the orchards and garden she and "H.B." (Harrison Brown) created, is one of those people.

Born in England, she was completing a master's degree in economics in Frankfurt when she and H.B. met. They were there when the Nazis came to power in 1933. H.B., a journalist and world traveller, had survived four years in the British Army in World War I and was the European Representative for the American Committee hoping to outlaw war. Sickened by the rise of fascism and aware that a second war was about to engulf the world, H.B. had just completed a lecture tour of the United States when Hilary came to Spokane to meet him. He wanted to find a place where he could have a garden by the sea, where he could read and think and write. Driving up Vancouver Island and seeing Hornby Island lying far offshore, they hired a fishboat at Deep Bay and came to Ford Cove.

It was one of those magic spring days when the world is newborn, with lambs kicking up their heels in the sweet spring grass of Stu Parnell's farm on the shore, and the great oak trees unfolding soft new leaves. Enchanted, they walked up the road east from Ford Cove, that road that twists and climbs through the oaks, curving up the ridge until you can see all the blue Gulf of Georgia glittering, stretching away southwards to the horizon. In all the world H.B. had never seen a place as lovely at this, and on that day in 1937 they bought ten acres next to Parnell's.

For the first years Hilary cooked on a wood stove, hand-pumped water from a dug well, and used kerosene lamps. In 1955 electricity was brought to Hornby, ferry service began and the Browns bought the adjoining land along the beach, which had unlogged forest. In 1956 they opened Heron Rocks campsite. In 1967, when the Browns wanted to give up running a fairly unprofitable campsite business, they reached an agreement with their campers and Heron Rocks Co-operative Campsite was born. Meanwhile, Hilary was instrumental in launching the Hornby Island Co-op Store, and was treasurer of the credit union. In 1974 her energy and expertise were recognized when she was asked to become the first chairman of the newly formed Islands Trust, established to "preserve and protect" these unique and vulnerable islands in the gulf, a new concept of area conservation which upset both the developers who hoped to grow rich by subdividing land and some of the islanders who were more interested in the rising value of their property than in the rural beauty of the islands. The Islands Trust confronted a primary issue: individual property rights as opposed to collective rights. Were these fragile islands to be intensively "developed" for the profit of enterprising individuals or was there an alternative? On Salt Spring Island, Ray and I survived angry confrontations as the islanders struggled to establish controls on land subdivision.

In 1977, when H.B. died at the age of 84, Hilary was left the task of finding a way to preserve and protect Heron Rocks. Many discussions under the great maple that towers over Hilary's house led to the establishment of the Heron Rocks Friendship Centre, and Hilary has transferred ownership of her land to the new society. The magnitude of this gift is astonishing: the old Parnell farm next door was for sale for several millions. The centre will preserve Hilary's ten acres and will explore the ways in which a rural community can contribute to environmental and peace and justice issues. For the past few years Heron Rocks has held workshops, seminars, retreats and countless potluck suppers, pursuing these objectives.

We came slowly through the campsite, admiring the ingenuity of driftwood shelters and benches, then followed the path past apple trees where much of the fruit had been knocked down by crows, and through the long grape arbour, with its tempting bunches of purple fruit, until we came to Hilary's house. When she opened the door to us, wearing a long blue gown, I had the impression that I was greeting a mediaeval figure from a brass rubbing. Her white hair was cut straight across her forehead, in a Joan of Arc style. Her steel blue eyes examined us, eyes that seek honesty and nobility. Then she smiled, and her face softened and her eyes sparkled. She made coffee in her small, higgledy-piggledy kitchen and talked with us for an hour punctuated by phone calls. A member of the co-op group now managing the 50-year-old orchard wanted advice. A meeting of the credit union was arranged. A friend invited her to dine. At 83, Hilary talked "retirement" but had just acquired a better computer for her writing projects. She moved purposefully and spoke firmly, and I thought of Tennyson's line describing old Ulysses:

...strong in will
To strive, to seek, to find, and not to yield.[1]

The central core of her life, its "meaning", has been the conviction that we *can* build a world of peace and justice, and the first step is the acknowledgement that our happiness is embedded in a happy society. She has given, not taken. She has fostered co-operation, not competition.

She came with us to the arbour's rickety gate and waited for the return of her scissors, as Ray cut off heavy bunches of dark grapes. We walked back, sucking grapes, through the campsite and along the shore. "Tell me," I had asked Hilary, "about that first spring morning in 1937 when you and H.B. climbed the road and looked south." She only smiled. Some moments are too wonderful to capture in words.

TRIBUNE BAY. HORNBY ISLAND. THE THOUSAND OAKS

To think that scientists are now considering the possibility of working from genetic material to remake the dinosaurs! A living Jurassic Park! And when we've killed the last elephant will they devote themselves to recreating that mountainous marvel of living flesh? But if we allow the last fragments of the Garry Oak meadows to be chopped into housing lots, will it ever be possible to reconstruct their amazing and delicate alliance of soil, air and more than a thousand very specific creatures and plants? Few people are aware that there exists, mainly on the western shores of the Gulf of Georgia, an ecosystem unique in Canada, in which there are plants that simply don't flourish elsewhere. Probably only about one per cent of the original Garry Oak habitat has survived the invasion of white-skinned people. Of the surviving pieces, the 45 acres above Tribune Bay is one of the largest, and may be the only one in pristine condition, undiscovered by that relentless intruder, the yellow broom bush.

We walked there on a soft morning with a gauze of cloud thinning the sunlight, on a toe-tingling path that almost falls off the edge of a sheer cliff. Old arbutus trees stretched their twisting, rust-red arms over Tribune Bay far below. An eagle flew by at eye level, ignoring us. Then the fir forest began to thin and the first oaks appeared. Suddenly we walked through waist-high grass, where the angular oaks stood in open, sunlit meadows. Dragonflies flitted by. We heard eagles screeching. A split-rail fence ran beside the path, reminding us not to trespass. We were in the Thousand Oaks woods, five hectares of pristine oak meadows, with the sea of grass bending to the sea wind. *Quercus garryana*: the dark-green leaves glittered on branches which twisted and bent in unexpected contortions; yet each tree achieved an almost perfect, convex outline.

Farther on, the path led us into the treeless slope on the sea-edge of Helliwell Park and we settled to eat our sandwiches in the long grass. The cliff here is not sheer but is composed of conglomerate rock, which bulges and swells and sags in uncorseted corpulence. We looked across Hornby Island's Downes Point to the blue ridge of Vancouver Island, topped with a scroll of cloud. To the south, Vancouver Island narrowed and faded to a vanishing point where sea and sky blurred together. Five eagles circled above us, squeaking and chirping to each other.

We are members of GOMPS (Garry Oak Meadow Preservation Society), a new organization attempting to warn coast people that a rare and lovely thing is at risk of being destroyed. The Garry Oak meadows will have to be parks, if they are to survive. The suggestion that houses could be built amid the oaks is not acceptable, because such land use would damage the wide-spreading root systems and introduce alien plants. The most vulnerable part of the mature tree is its network of shallow roots — but oaks die slowly and it might take years to kill the tree after trenching or digging around its roots. Hornby's Thousand Oaks have not been attacked

Garry Oak meadows, Hornby Island.

by broom, a legume, which fixes nitrogen in the soil; this process favours plants that compete with the Garry Oak meadow plants and ultimately displace them. The Garry Oaks are also threatened by a gall wasp and an aphid; the trees become vulnerable to these enemies when their whole ecosystem is out of whack. Some people in Victoria have ceased mowing and fertilizing their lawns; they pull up broom and ivy and allow the ancient meadow to be re-established.

We shall return to the Thousand Oaks in the springtime. In March, blue-eyed Mary, yellow monkeyflower, pink shooting stars and purple satin flowers bloom, followed by the glorious purple-blue camas, with Easter lilies, pink sea-blush and yellow buttercups. Even later the blue larkspur, white alumroot and brown chocolate lilies open. But we came in summer, in time for the blue brodiaea and yellow stonecrop, and the grass already bleaching in the sun.

TRALEE POINT. HORNBY ISLAND. OLIVIA FLETCHER

In the beginning of creation, when God made heaven and earth, the earth was without form and void, with darkness over the face of the abyss. Then, according to a Salish myth, Old-One formed Earth as a woman. "You will be the mother of all people," he said. "Earth is alive yet: the soil is her flesh, the rocks her bones, the wind her breath, and trees and grass are her hair. She lives spread out, and we live on her. When she moves, we have an earthquake."

After making Earth, Old-One took some of her flesh and rolled it into balls, as people do with mud or clay. Old-One transformed the balls into the first beings, the ancients, who were people and yet at the same time were the other animals. "Thus when we look around, we see everywhere parts of our mother."[1]

The native people also tell how the islands of the west coast of North America were formed. Once upon a time, when the king of the eagles was flying over the Nass River, small boys snatched up their bows and began shooting arrows at him. Instead of being frightened away, the king of the eagles circled low. Soon the warriors sprang from the houses, their bow strings twanging as the arrows flew into the sky. Even though it was apparent that the eagle had great power, for the arrows glanced off his feathered body, all the chieftains and nobles tried to kill him.

Suddenly the giant bird swooped down and seized one of the men by the hair. A second warrior clutched the legs of the first, trying to save him, but the eagle continued to rise. A third man grabbed the second, and then another and another until all the men and boys of the village were lifted into the sky. Straight toward the sun flew the king of the eagles with the human chain attached, until he had reached a height where the whole coastline could be seen. The eagle began to swing the chain in a great loop in the sky. Then he released his grip. The Indians fell through the air, one by one plummeting into the waves below, and where each splashed into the sea an island arose, the size of the island matching the rank of the Indian.

When Olivia Fletcher stood on the summit one of these Indians, the one now called Hornby Island, the mist thickened and she imagined the process of island formation in reverse. As the British Columbian coast moved back into the past, like a movie film run backward, she watched the ice grow deep, 10,000 years ago. By 40,000 years she had experienced four glacial advances and retreats. Then the mountains collapsed themselves and the land slid south until, 65,000,000 years ago, she stood on flattened rock in the vicinity of present-day California, in a forest of flowering trees, with ferns springing beneath her feet and elasmosaurs swimming in the warm sea. Then she travelled underwater while a billion billion organisms (brachiopods, gastropods and their like) fell on her like snow, softly piling up to one day become limestone. Then, 300,000,000 years ago, she was there when Hornby Island was born in the South Pacific, a piece of Wrangellia, in a violence of steam and dust, rumblings and hissings, bubbling basalt and mountainous tidal waves. The black basalt would one day lie in strange patterns on British Columbia's sea-washed shores, when the moving continental plates were carried north.

We walked with Olivia along the Hornby Island shore, where the sea was relentlessly erasing the petroglyphs. The mist turned to fine drops on our faces. She is a small person, with grey-streaked hair tied back from a round, soft face on which dark-rimmed glasses frame two far-seeing eyes. Her motto, from the *Talmud*, is: If you want to see the invisible, carefully observe the visible. She and John came to Hornby Island in the 1960s, but not until the 1980s did she begin the studies that led to the publication of *Hammerstone* in 1989, the year we met her at a party at Ford Cove. Underlying her life and work is the awareness that "time-structured linear thinking has been taking us 'western' people further and further from our roots, from our awareness of being part of the dance of the planet."[2] Conscious of Earth's vast and continuing upheavals of geological time, Olivia Fletcher has her feet firmly planted on Hornby Island, in the here and now of fresh-baked bread and the struggle to prevent the flood of new islanders from destroying the birds, beaches, plants, trees and rocks.

As she imagined time zooming backwards in *Hammerstone*, Olivia still had far to go before she reached the Big Bang and the Black Holes. And what happened before that? Ah...we are back in myth. Some people just prefer to believe that an old man with a white beard took seven days to make our island world.

COURTENAY. SEA SERPENTS

There were (and probably are) strange, long-necked sea creatures which we call "sea serpents" and we visited the Courtenay Museum to look at one of the oldest of them. Comox Harbour dries to mud flats at low tide, but the channel up the river to Courtenay was marked with pilings and range lights; we anchored and went up in the dinghy. From the marina it was a short walk to the museum. We had come to see the fossilized bones of the Elasmosaur, discovered near Courtenay in January 1988 by amateur paleontologist Michael Trask.

The Elasmosaur was a 45-foot sea animal which lived in our waters from about 98,000,000 to 66,000,000 years ago. That is a very long time as we humans measure time — we have only been human for something under three million years — so it is utterly ridiculous to speak of Elasmosaur in the same breath as we discuss Caddy or Ogopogo. And yet...other species have survived relatively unchanged for many millions of years. And if you were going to last out the ups and downs of eruptions, climate changes, glaciers and continents sliding around, where better to do so than in the depths of the sea? In an article about the six-gill sharks, Craig Piprell wrote "According to fossil records, they haven't changed much over the last 150 million years,"[1] which is more than 50 million years older than the Elasmosaur.

Is it possible that an Elasmosaur descendant may still be around? Yes, it is. In the archives one can spend eye-boggling hours reading the sea-serpent newspaper reports on microfilm. Howard White published an account of the day in 1932 when British Columbia poet Hubert Evans, Dick Reeves and Bob Stephens watched a sea serpent off the Sechelt Peninsula. Silhouetted against the calm, golden, evening sea they saw a series of black bumps looping up out of the water, and a shaft of neck which rose six or eight feet, measured against a spar buoy on the nearby reef. "Right there as we stood watching," Hubert told Howie White, "none of us breathing a word, the top end of this shaft began to elongate horizontally, until we were presented with the profile of a head, very much like a horse's in general shape, with eye bumps, nostrils and something in the way of a horn."[2]

It was Victoria *Times* news editor Archie Wills who made up the name "Cadborosaurus" in 1933, after he published Major W.H. Langley's story. Major Langley, a thoroughly reputable person, a barrister, and clerk to the B.C. legislature, was out in his boat with his wife, just off Chatham Island near Victoria, when they heard a loud sort of grunt-snort and there, on the edge of a kelp bed, was a dark, olive-green sea creature. Wills was swamped by calls and letters from people claiming to have seen the sea serpent. He weeded the list down to the hundred most credible witnesses, among them F.W. Kemp of the Provincial Archives who, in 1932, was with his wife and son when they saw the animal. "The creature swam to some rocks, shot its head out of the water and looked around, and then fold after fold of its body came to the surface." Then it slipped into deep water and was gone. "I did not report my strange adventure except to one or two trusted friends, for fear of ridicule and unbelief," he added.[3]

An October 7, 1936, *Daily Colonist* item described a snake-like thing 13 feet long, composed of a sinewy substance, with two fins, tentacles close to the head, which was found dead on the beach at Halkat Bay on Gambier Island. The caretakers at the United Church summer camp notified the Biological Station at Nanaimo.[4] In July 1937, the Naden Harbour Whaling Station announced that "there was taken from the stomach of a large sulfur-bottom whale a young monster named Cadborosaurus, attention to which will be given as fully as possible here."[5]

In 1968 William Hagelund, a former whaler, accidentally caught near the De Courcy Islands a three-metre-long creature "having a head similar to a large dog, animal-like vertebrae and having a tail resembling a single blade of gill bone as found in a whale's jaws." It thrashed during the night in the cockpit of his sloop: "I felt a strong compassion for that little face staring up at me," he said. "If he perished in my hands, he would only be a forgotten curiosity. I lowered the bucket over the side and watched him swim quickly away."[6]

There are stories of sea-serpent sightings in many other places around the world, but rarely are there pictures. A Mr. Gibson made

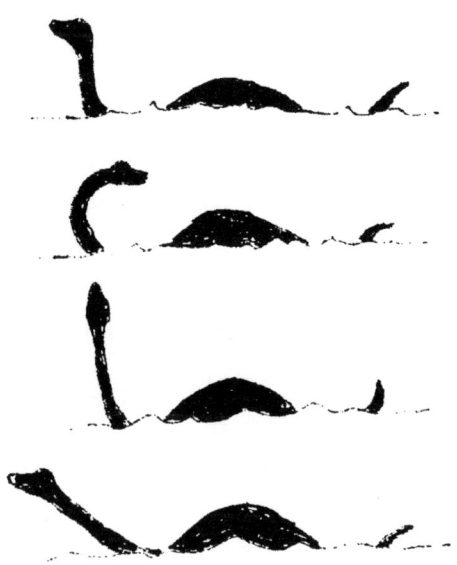

Four views of a sea creature seen at Mill Bay,
as sketched by Wilfred Gibson.

drawings of a serpent lunging at ducks and seagulls in Mill Bay, and in 1961 Mrs. A.R. Stacey sketched a long-necked creature who apparently ate a seagull stupid enough to mistake the serpent for a log and land on it. The only photo is the one of the half-digested "infant" sea serpent found in 1937 in the whale's stomach.

Could our sea serpents be descendants of ancient creatures like Courtenay's Elasmosaur? We examined the petrified pieces of the Elasmosaur in a row on a bed of sand in the Courtenay Museum. To bring them to life for the museum visitors, a small sign explained: "With a powerful thrust from its snake-like neck, the Elasmosaur would wrap its cage of teeth around terrified prey. Even in the age of dinosaurs, he was a giant. About fourteen metres long, the Elasmosaur was the largest of the marine reptiles. The fossils displayed here form only a portion of the neck."[7] It takes a bit of imagination to move the mind from those stony bones to a lively Elasmosaur wrapping its teeth around a terrified prey. Thinking about it could make diving from the swim grid more exciting.

According to Drs. E. Bousfield and Paul LeBlond, there were five separate encounters with a sea monster in 1992. In May, Professor John Celona was sailing on Cadboro Bay when he saw a serpent-like creature. He called to his companions to look at a thing "25 feet long and the way it was cutting through the water revealed several humps."[8] Reported in the *Times-Colonist* of August 16 of the same year, in the same place, a young sailor "heard a rushing of water and looked over and saw the coils rushing by the boat."[9] Are the creatures still swimming down below us? Watching for them will keep me alert when my turn at the wheel grows tedious.

COMOX. MUNGO MARTIN

We anchored in Comox Harbour and rowed the dinghy to the Indian Reserve, to visit the totem pole Mungo Martin carved to honour his son David. From the floats behind Portuguese Joe's fish store, we crossed the road to the Comox Reserve Ceremonial House; across the house front, a painted Thunderbird grasped a huge whale. Nearby stood David Martin's memorial pole. Its wooden faces stared into eternity, hiding the terrible grief accompanying their birth, when every blow of the adze chipped off a fragment of a father's heart.

Mungo Martin, who died soon after making this totem pole, was simply the best-known native person on this coast and the one most highly honoured in Canada. Of his work Hilary Stewart has written that "the slender thread of continuity, held by the last of the master carvers, was largely responsible for pulling Northwest Coast Indian art back from the brink of extinction."[1] He made his first totem pole in 1902, and from 1951 until his death in 1962, worked in Victoria at Thunderbird Park next to the Provincial Museum, repairing old poles, making new ones, and recording the songs and stories of his Kwakwaka'wakw people. He and his native helpers built Wa-wad-it-la in Thunderbird Park, a replica of the Fort Rupert house in which he was born. It is Mungo Martin's voice which is heard singing in the Indian exhibit longhouse inside the museum.

Around 1880, when he was still an infant in Fort Rupert on the north shore of Vancouver Island, his mother Nagayki, determined that her son would become an artist, took him to the famous carver Yakutglasomi. The old man, in ceremonial robes, performed a ritual in which he plucked four eyelashes from the baby's eyelids. He mixed these with porcupine bristles to make one of his paint brushes. So that Mungo would also be a singer, his mother put him inside a square, cedar-box drum; during a ceremony his father lightly drummed and sang to him. After her husband's death,

Mungo's mother married Charlie James, a master carver, who taught his skills to the boy. Mungo had little formal "schooling", for he spent only three weeks in the Indian Residential School in Alert Bay before he escaped and found a fisherman to take him home to Fort Rupert.

He was about four years old when the potlatch was declared illegal in 1884 but it continued to flourish in secret until the famous Dan Cranmer Potlatch in 1921. After the feast paraphernalia was confiscated (now restored to the Cape Mudge and Alert Bay museums), the making of masks and feast dishes came to a standstill for many years. Mungo turned to commercial fishing. He married Sarah Constance Abayah Hunt, a skilled weaver of Chilkat blankets and a widow with three children. Soon Abayah gave birth to Mungo's only son, David. Later they adopted a daughter, Helen Hunt. When Helen's son Tony was born, Abayah dried the umbilical cord and sewed it into a cloth bracelet which Mungo wore while carving, so that Tony would become an artist. It was Helen who accompanied Mungo when he took a totem pole to London to present it to Queen Elizabeth, and she was delighted to find one of Abayah's woven blankets in the Queen's Palace Museum.

When he was old and heavy with names and honours, fate dealt Mungo a terrible blow. In early September 1959 he learned that David had been washed off the deck of a fishboat in stormy seas off Comox. His body was never found. Two months later Mungo held a ceremony in Wa-wad-it-la at which he gave to the people of British Columbia all the things David would have inherited from him: the masks, the priceless Killer Whale Copper, the other ceremonial items. "Today I am in darkness," he said.[2]

The deep grief of this great man is enshrined in the carved pole on the Comox Reserve. At the top, the long beak of Hokw-hokw juts toward the sea where David died. Hokw-hokw, one of the three servants of the most powerful Nakbakwalanuksiwe, used that long beak to crack open skulls so that he might devour brains; in the winter dances the dancer wearing the Hokw-hokw mask opened and shut the beak with a clacking sound. Beneath the folded wings of this mythical bird, Mungo carved the sun mask, with the beaked nose of a sky spirit, and at the bottom he made a human figure, the high-ranking man with head and neck rings who represented the chiefly lineage to which David belonged.

Mungo himself died peacefully in 1962. His body lay in state in Wa-wad-it-la for a day while people filed past. After a private family ceremony, the casket was carried to Alert Bay on *H.M.C.S. Ottawa*, placed on the quarterdeck and guarded at four sides by soldiers with fixed bayonets. As the *Ottawa* moved slowly out of Esquimalt Harbour, flags on shore were dipped in salute. It was the first time in Canadian naval history that a native person was so honoured. In Alert Bay, as his casket was lowered into the ground, hundreds of seagulls took flight above him.

I wanted to reach out and touch the totem, partly to pay my own tribute to this remarkable man and to acknowledge that his bottomless grief had touched my heart, but also to take strength for my own old age. The cars thundered past on the Comox highway. I snapped a picture and turned away.

CHAPTER FIVE

Northward, Quadra Island to Sonora Island

At Manson's Landing, where Mike Manson, Cortes Island's first white settler, chose to build his trading post and establish his family in 1886, nondescript local boats rafted against the small government float. Resident boat owners were patching and painting, making jokes about woodrot. The store, located approximately where Michael and Jane Manson lived, carried local organic produce. The trail along the southwest shore of the lagoon, which brought us to a freshwater swim at Hague Lake, was probably old when the Mansons arrived, for he built on the midden of a former Indian village.

A mile south along the shore, not far from the Paukeanus Reserve, we found the nine-foot-long petroglyph of a marine animal, pounded into the flat side of a boulder, facing the sea. The Sliammon people say that it was made by Tl'umnachm ("only room for himself") whose father whipped him with a beaver tail for being lazy. (Was the beaver a symbol of hard work for the Sliammon too?) Humiliated, the boy went to Hague Lake, Anvil Lake and Gunflint Lake, training at each lake to acquire power; the guardian spirit power which finally came to him may perhaps be represented by this petroglyph creature. When he returned to his people, he was given the name Tl'umnachm because there were so many fish in his canoe that there was hardly room for Tl'umnachm in it.

In the days when the beaches were "black with Indians"[1] (as an old chief told John Manson), before the terrible smallpox epidemic of 1862, the men of Paukeanus village were whalers. Chief Billy Mitchell's father told his son that whalers in their canoes would line up straight out from the shore at Smelt Bay; when the whales

Petroglyph, Cortes Island.

came through between Cortes and Mary islands the waiting men would drop clam shells into the water, forming a visual wall of large white snow flakes falling through the sea. Avoiding this strange phenomenon, the whales were gradually driven onto the beach where they were stranded by the ebb tide, and butchered. The great petroglyph may have been made to call the whales to their deaths on the beach.

Enterprising Mike Manson, who became justice of the peace and a "big chief" in this area, came from the Shetlands and got a job in Nanaimo. When he eloped with lovely Jane Renwick, the daughter of his employer, he borrowed a dugout canoe from an Indian friend and paddled her all the way to Victoria to marry her. When the log trading post at Manson's Landing was ready, he went to Victoria to bring north a first schooner-load of supplies, including six cows, a pair of oxen, 24 hens and one rooster. As he approached Cortes, his centreboard struck a boulder in Sutil Reef, which runs out southwest from Sutil Point and is now marked with a flashing red light. It was a catastrophic moment, but the schooner did not sink and the wind and rough seas carried it to the landing place. The animals survived the incident, but that night a mink discovered the 24 hens and one rooster and sucked the blood from every one of them.

As we left Manson's Landing, the long reef off Sutil Point looked like a row of floating boulders. Perhaps it is this dangerous reef and the south wind's long reach which keeps Manson's Landing much the way the Mansons knew it. The bell in the buoy bonged dolefully, a bored bell.

CHANNEL ROCK. CORTES ISLAND. GILEAN DOUGLAS

When I phoned Gilean Douglas and she said we might visit her the following day, I asked if we could come at 9:30 (knowing that she usually rose at dawn). There was a gasp and she answered emphatically "NOT in the morning! That is for writing." In a column published in 1992, she wrote: "Writing is all I have ever wanted to do. It is all I have dreamed of, thought about, cared for. It embraces everything: solitude, silence, the satisfaction of constructing something."[1] And now, as death sidled in the distant shadows, she worked against time to finish her writing. We happened to visit just after the sale of Channel Rock had been settled, giving her life tenancy and the money to buy a computer.

The sea was smooth on a "brazen day of summer"[2] as we zoomed into Uganda Passage in the outboard dinghy, riding the swift flow of tide past the great, round, polished boulders that swelled out of the slick running sea. We saw the white weather-recording box on Channel Rock. Behind the white box crouched the low-eaved, silver-shaked brown house built by John Pool and long owned and beloved by Gilean Douglas. Her friend David waited on the beach to tell us that she was not ready to receive us. So we sat on a log in front of Mr. Pool's small boathouse.

A motherless child and without her father by the age of 16, Gilean, who always knew she would be a writer, took a first job with a Toronto newspaper. Now the author of several books and uncountable articles in more than 200 periodicals, she has received many awards for her work. She spent exquisite years in a remote corner of the Cascades, which she remembered in *Silence Is My Homeland*. She wrote of those mountain nights when she had "green dusk for dreams, moss for a pillow."[3] In her philosophy, as the colouring of flowers and leaves testifies to light, so the search for simplicity and solitude indicates a state of spiritual awareness. When her mountain home burned she also lost two book-length manuscripts on mountain flora and fauna — carbons, notes, photographs and negatives, everything. Distraught, cast out of paradise, she bought Channel Rock, sight unseen.

Arriving to claim her new home, she came to Whaletown on the Union Steamship *Cardena* and though it was after midnight, a small motor boat waited to bring her to the beach, the place where we now sat by Mr. Pool's boathouse. In the dark, the channel light blinked and blinked, welcoming her, and whales escorted the little boat. "I was feeling so intensely that my nerve ends were like fingers, groping for, touching, exploring this strange country where I was to live."[4] She found the path that climbed to the house, entered and lit a candle to look about her.

Now a phone rang in the boathouse, announcing that she was ready for us, and we ascended the path, ducking under the fishnet deer fence, approaching as John Pool's ghost had once come towards her door, disappearing as she opened it. Although Gilean and I had exchanged letters, we had never met. Now she stood in the open door and we looked for a long minute into each other's eyes. Such clear-seeing, wide-spaced, slightly oriental eyes, in that small, frail face. She made a movement as if to hug me, but I must have seemed a grotesquely large creature, and she stepped back to wave us in. David quickly stopped us, and showed us where we would wash in disinfectant to reduce the risk of bringing germs into the house.

We entered the kitchen, hardly more than a passage, walled with Elizabeth Pool's old cupboards and counter. The one large room had bookshelves on three sides, with Gilean's writing place below the sea-facing window. Chairs seemed randomly scattered in the room, with an oil stove standing amongst them. When we were seated, I asked about that first bright June morning when she woke on the canvas cot she had brought with her, and looked out for the first time on the shining sea and distant blue mountains. Her eyes misted and she made a gesture with her long, blue-veined hands, with their thin, bony fingers, but she found no words to recapture the glory of that morning.

In an article written in the spring of 1992, she stated, "I look out to sea and to the islands beyond and wish for the impossible: that this lovely land might be again as I first knew it."[5] She spoke of her nine years serving on the Regional Board of Comox-Strathcona and work with the Women's Institute and the Anglican Church, but the subject uppermost in her mind was her recent decision to sell Channel Rock, under conditions that will preserve it, supervised by an American conservation organization. So this small brown house will not be crushed and replaced by a monstrous place, nor will it be allowed to rot and collapse, and those of us who move through Uganda Passage may always look eastward and see it there, a monument to a life lived with wondrous awareness, a life we can experience vicariously in her writing. She described, for example, the night when she heard the wolves singing near her house, a night with Jupiter and Saturn hanging in the clear sky. The song of the wolves was

> like silver chiming on the chill, still air....I was lifted out of myself and out of this warring world. Back, back I went into the silence and serenity of the wildernesses I had known. The wolf song was a silver light in the universe....With Venus fading and dawn, there was one last glorious song — and then silence. "Thank you!" I called to the singers. "Safe journey, brothers!"[6]

In one of her Christmas letters, Gilean quoted Kafka: "A book should serve as the axe for the frozen sea within us."[7] Her work is more like a door flung open, so that those of us frozen in faraway places can share a life lived exquisitely on Channel Rock.

In her 1992 book of poems she wrote:

Salt on the wind and a full tide flowing,
dusk on the wind and a heart swung free —
What does it matter where I'm going
as long as this is part of me?[8]

Gilean died on October 31, 1993.

BURDWOOD BAY. READ ISLAND

This murder left no mark, no sudden shivering of chilled air, no ghost, and when we found the remains of the hotel, there was only a heavy, hot, summer silence. Burdwood Bay is a two-mile-long, irregular bite out of the southeastern shore of Read Island, full of islets, coves, fish pens, oyster leases, charted and uncharted rocks, some of which dry at low tide and others that don't, and no really safe anchorage. Here in 1893 the first post office was opened, with Edgar Wylie as postmaster. The Wylies had come from New York to build a hotel. They were joined at Burdwood Bay by their Yankee friends John and Laura Smith with their four children, and Chris Benson. Mrs. Benson and two daughters chose not to accompany Chris, perhaps for a good reason. One morning he was found dead in the bottom of a skiff adrift in Sutil Channel, with his face battered and bloody.

Up from Manson's Landing came Justice of the Peace Manson. He examined the body and asked a lot of questions before fitting the corpse into a rough coffin for a journey to the coroner in Vancouver. The autopsy led Manson to look for a motive for the killing: money, liquor or women? Manson sent in a local fisherman, Bill Belding, as undercover spy. Belding became chummy with chatty Laura Smith and it wasn't long before she whispered about hanging washing on the clothes-line as a signal for Chris Benson that the coast was clear. Unfortunately, one day Mr. Smith returned unexpectedly and found Benson in her bed. She had to help carry the dead man to the skiff, which they set adrift.

At the trial in Vancouver, the Crown produced blood-stained floorboards from the Smith bedroom, but Ed Wylie insisted the blood was from a butchered deer. Despite the testimony of the Smith children who admitted hearing blows and groans from the bedroom, and despite the fact that butchering is not ordinarily done in the bedroom, the jury found Mr. Smith not guilty. The long arm of the law had a kink in it. Mr. Smith returned to his Read Island duties, which probably included new planks for the bedroom floor.

Seeking the scene of this lurid crime, we explored Burdwood Bay on a calm morning. There was a deserted farm halfway along the shore and there we anchored, discouraged. We had encountered no one. "Unless there is someone to tell us where Wylie's Hotel was, we won't find it," I remarked. At that moment, a peapod dory materialized alongside our boat, with a charming, white-bearded man at the oars. At first I thought I had conjured him up.

"Can you tell me where Mr. Wylie built his hotel?" I asked immediately.

"Yes, of course I can," he replied, and climbed aboard to put a dot on the chart to mark the site. He also knew every hidden boulder in the bay and gave us the name of the farm: Stubley's Farm.

Wylie's Hotel was on the small peninsula which juts into twin bays at the northern end of Burdwood Bay. About 100 feet back from the shore and not visible from the sea, we found the cement foundations and graying fragments of boards and shingles which were once Wylie's Hotel. Fir trees 30 feet high, small pines and wild roses grew amid the debris; soon the concrete wall will be buried in forest and the site even more difficult to find.

I lay down in the tall, golden grass and listened to it whispering, but its lisping was as mysterious as this story. Surely the jury had been bribed, but why did the Wylies lie at the trial? Childless Mrs. Wylie taught three of the Smith children in a room behind the store and perhaps she feared to lose them? We know nothing of the later history of the Smiths, but Ed Wylie remained at his notorious hotel until he died in 1903. He was buried in a crack in a huge boulder at Healey's Point (Lot 340, Bird Cove) with cement poured into the crevice to conceal him, and small stones set into the concrete to spell his name. Time has crumbled both cement and bones.

HYACINTH BAY. QUADRA ISLAND. TOM LEASK

British Columbia's Paul Bunyan lived at Hyacinth Bay. Tom Leask's thick black moustache and beard hid an interesting feature: he had two sets of teeth. He occasionally amused the other loggers in a bar by biting chunks from the heavy beer glasses (called schooners). Leask ran away to sea from the Orkneys when he was 14 and stayed on the sailing ships for five years before coming ashore at Quebec and working his way to British Columbia by helping to build the Canadian Pacific Railway. He then joined the ranks of hard-drinking, hard-working, rough-living British Columbian loggers, but he was a gentle man, never quarrelsome. His stocky body and medium weight disguised his enormous strength. Misjudging Tom, a bully named Mickey-the-Brute challenged him to a fight outside the Heriot Bay pub. Mickey bragged that he got his name from a wager he had won by fighting, with one hand tied behind his back, a savage bulldog.

Encircled by a shouting audience of loggers, the fight between Mickey and Tom began about noon. For the first hour they punched and circled until blood ran down their faces. Then sometimes they clinched and wrestled, coming down hard on the ground, first one on top then the other, striking, clawing, biting. Tom's formidable teeth tore into Mickey-the-Brute. Their shirts were in shreds and dirt was mixed with the blood on their strong bodies. The sun went down but the fight went on. Now they were slow, swaying, blows sometimes missing, and when they clinched they took longer to break apart. The moment came when they rolled apart and were too exhausted to rise. But Mickey crawled painfully away, growling that he'd be back in the morning. Someone brought a blanket and covered Tom where he lay. Dawn came and Tom stirred, but Mickey had left the island, never to return. Some say that this was the most memorable fight in British Columbia's history, and those who witnessed it never forgot and those who missed it rued the day. But modest Tom Leask decided to give up logging and find some land to farm.

In a 12-foot rowboat, with groceries, ammunition, fishing tackle, a gun, an axe, blankets and cooking pots, he rowed away from Heriot Bay. Like the legs of a beetle on a stream, his little oars moved him northward, and each night he camped where he could find a niche ashore. Compared with the stony Orkneys, this was a land of abundance, huge and magnificent beyond his imagination. He rowed 400 miles, all the way to the Charlottes, and when he got there he had worn away the seat of his pants. He came ashore where some Indians were having difficulty clearing an enormous boulder from a beach in order to launch a cedar canoe. Tom motioned them aside, positioned himself with care and began to heave the great block of stone, which slowly yielded to him. Needless to say, he won the heart of a Haida lass. What is more surprising is that he rowed back to Hyacinth Bay with his bride and took up land there. The Leasks had five children when Mrs. Leask died. Down from the Charlottes came a Haida canoe, her family arriving to take back their grandchildren. But Tom, determined to raise the children himself, refused to part with them.

Many years later, Tom made a 120-mile round trip in a dugout canoe to buy an elegant rowboat, which he proudly displayed to his neighbour, Francis Dickie, on his return. But when he went off to cut firewood for a summer camper, he loaded his tools into his flat-bottomed skiff. When Mr. Dickie asked him why he wasn't using his new boat, Tom looked at him with shock. "And get it scratched?" he replied.[1] But his old skiff was overloaded, with the sea almost to the gunwales. The next day Tom was found, drowned, in two fathoms of water in front of his own beach, for he could not swim.

But where was this beach? With local guidance, we found our way to the lovely farm at the extreme north end of Hyacinth Bay, a bay that dries at low tide. There, on a garden fence, we photographed rusting tools from Tom Leask's time. The stream which runs into the bay has a salmon run, and the shore has the black earth and clam shells left by those who lived here before Tom Leask. There is an orchard of Leask apple trees, still producing Transparents and Gravensteins.

If we were Americans we would sing songs about Tom Leask and tell stories about him, and embroider the tales until he stood as tall as Paul Bunyan! But in fact, when I asked most Quadra Islanders about Tom Leask, they squinted at me and inquired, "Tom who?"

HYACINTH BAY. QUADRA ISLAND. FRANCIS DICKIE

Perhaps it is the writers who create the immortals, and Tom Leask was fortunate to have a writer as his neighbour. Doris Andersen has written that Francis Dickie was famous on Quadra Island for his vast library of books, his large stock of homemade wine and his 12 cats, but when I asked about him, Quadra Islanders immediately spoke of his sophisticated French wife. His best-known book bore the title *The Master Breed*, which led some islanders to refer to him as "Master Breed".

Born in Carberry, Manitoba, in 1890, and a protegé of Ernest Thompson Seton, at the age of 16 Francis Dickie gave up school to join a Canadian Pacific Railway survey party. At 19 he wandered through British Columbia and California, recording his experiences in *Strange Soul's Journeyings*. He returned to Canada to become a *Calgary Herald* reporter, then an editor in Edmonton. After he and a Parisienne, Suzanne Garnier, were married, they lived briefly in Toronto before buying the Hyacinth Bay house on the edge of the sea at the bottom of a steep lane now named Dickie Road.

A smooth sea rose and fell, licking the great rounded humps of bedrock that shelter the little beach where Francis Dickie's rowboat once lay. The house nestled on a green lawn shaded by tall trees. No evidence remained of the terrible forest fire of 1925. Dickie was awakened by a booming roar:

> May I never hear its like again! I ran up the nearest moss-covered ridge and looked toward the fast approaching sound. I saw miles of heavily timbered rocky slopes aflame. Along a five-mile front swept a wall of flame and rust-coloured smoke. It moved fast, mingling weirdly with the green ranks of the fir. The awful suction of fire created a hurricane of its own. Even with all my possessions in its path, I was held there, awed by this vision of an earthly hell,

destroying in a minute what had required a thousand years to grow. From the tops of the flaming timber vast clouds rolled to the sky. Ahead of the fire deer bounded at speeds varying according to how far they had run. Hundreds of grouse and smaller birds flew low over me, making for a tiny rock island a hundred yards out to sea. Here and there squirrels scolded defiant, until they were shrivelled.[1]

The Dickies fled down to their rowboat and there discovered that they had salvaged "the cats, an Airedale dog, bookshelves, a dictionary stand and several washtubs filled with books."[2] But at that moment the Columbia Coast Mission boat came into Hyacinth Bay, towing a Department of Forestry raft equipped with pressure pumps and hose. A heavy rain of saltwater drenched the Dickie house and the trees surrounding it, and turned back the leaping fire.

In the year after the fire, 1926, the Vancouver *Daily Province* sent Francis Dickie to Paris where he and Suzanne met Somerset Maugham, Ernest Hemingway and other Left Bank writers. The Dickies returned to Quadra Island in 1932 when seven years growth hid some of the scars of the fire. Among Dickie's 150 published short stories and countless articles was the one about Tom Leask, which appeared in *The Province* in 1936. Spilsbury laughed at Dickie's pretensions: "He'd been in Paris at the same time as Hemingway and never got over it." It was true that Dickie corresponded with Somerset Maugham — "the odd letter", in Spilsbury's comments. "He came to Quadra Island determined to write great things and spent a lot of time strolling around his garden with no clothes on, like William Blake."[3] Spilsbury described the tin-can bell at Dickie's gate which visitors rang so that Dickie could put on his pants to receive them.

Francis Dickie, who died in 1976, aged 86, whose books are forgotten, will survive in the articles he wrote about coastal people. Swells from Sutil Channel broke gently on his white-shell beach as we left his place.

SURGE NARROWS. READ ISLAND

It was like that scene in Nevil Shute's *On the Beach*, when survivors of the nuclear holocaust came from Australia seeking human life in San Francisco. The Surge Narrows dock, once a lively place, was deserted and silent, except for a tin shingle rattling occasionally on Mr. Tipton's abandoned yellow building. We explored carefully, avoiding the rotten planks in the dock, and holes which could break a leg. The buildings were empty. Where the doors stood ajar we ventured in, examining the furniture and pictures which someone had not troubled to take with them. Dead flies lay on the windowsills.

Feeling like the last inhabitants of Earth, we climbed the steep gravelled road, past a hoodless car in the ditch, to look at the million-dollar school (with a splendid gymnasium) which was constructed a few years ago when the school population appeared to be rising, but now serves only several dozen students. When it was built, there were fish-farm children, loggers' children, and welfare children, but disease forced the closure of the fish farms and loggers moved to other shows or were displaced by technology.

On the new school's bulletin board we studied a notice suggesting both the reason for Read Island's abandonment and a possible step towards recovery. Read Islanders had raised $70,000 (of a sale price of $140,000) to purchase 160 acres from Raven Forest Products to "return 90 acres of clearcut to a productive forest base for a community selective forestry woodlot," and at the same time to restore two salmon-spawning streams destroyed by bad logging practices. Community control of the forests to provide permanent jobs may be a first step to stabilizing these island communities, but acquiring ownership from the local or transnational corporations has not been easy.

The *Liza Jane* rocked, tugged by the tide. As we cast off the lines, the shingle clattered a tinny farewell.

OWEN BAY. SONORA ISLAND

No ghosts disturbed us at Owen Bay's government dock. I was awakened twice in the starless night, but heard only the sea chuckling as it sucked under the float. When Liv Kennedy lived here many years ago she overheard her parents discussing two men whose bodies had been sunk with boom chains wrapped around them. That was only one of several strange stories: "Whiskey Harry" disappeared, his body never found; Liv's friends Alex and Margaret Cameron, Owen Bay caretakers, vanished from their yacht moored here, never to be seen again; yachtsmen at this dock abruptly yanked from sleep by great clanging noises on their own decks; the builder of Owen Bay's Ghost Bay Lodge deciding to sell out and giving no reason. Even Bill Wolferstan found that "an ominous feeling pervades the bay!"[1]

It was cheerful enough when we tied here in 1968, but deserted except for one man selling gas at a dilapidated Esso station (no longer there). We explored the Schiblers' house at the dock. In that year, a path along the lagoon to the south led us to a boarded-up schoolhouse above the sea meadows. The classroom was illuminated by shafts of sunlight piercing the boarded windows. Amid the school desks stood an organ, so Ray promptly made the dust-motes dance with a fast-paced and wheezy rendition of "Sweet Lorraine". Our 1952 atlas announced that Owen Bay had "a school where dances are held occasionally on Saturday nights," but it had been a few years since that schoolhouse had rocked to the stomp of loggers' boots.[2] Farther up the lagoon the path ended at an abandoned floathouse whose owners had left personal possessions strewn about. We waded through toys, dishes and clothes, and studied family snapshots...now I wish I had kept them. There was a letter from Dad in hospital in Vancouver with a heart condition. Even the dresser drawers were full of clothes.

"Whiskey Harry" Pedersen, an aging logger, was one of the first to live at this corner of Owen Bay. When Logan and Gunnhilde Schibler came in 1925, he offered them his place in exchange for their care of him in his declining years. The large house was floated in and for many years the energetic, sociable Schiblers made it the centre of a lively community. Logan built and ran the mill on Mill Point, and in the 1940s cut the lumber and organized the construction of the schoolhouse. Gunnhilde's garden, now reverted to wilderness, grew abundant vegetables; according to Doris Andersen she wasted nothing, putting up over 500 quarts of vegetables, fruit, fish, grouse and venison each year. In those halcyon years, every little indent around the bay had a shack or two, and near Hyacinth Lake farmers raised vegetables, and cut the hay on swamp meadows for their cows.

When Logan Schibler died in 1957, Owen Bay's busy years were almost over. People preferred more populated islands where living was easier. By the time we arrived in 1968, Owen Bay was almost deserted. In 1992 most of the shore property had been bought by a real estate company, and we found that the path to the schoolhouse (transformed into a neat, white summer home) was Sonora Road.

This government "highway", running more than a mile from the dock to Hole-in-the-Wall, had been brushed out to make a delightful

Owen Bay, Sonora Island.

walking trail. Near the end of it, in a narrow, sun-trapping valley, we came upon a garden fragrant with sweet peas, with dark red-purple hollyhocks standing at attention. The gardeners, Joanne and her children Camil, Opal and small tousled, freckled Jody, offered us green peppers and tomatoes. When I invited nine-year-old Opal to return to the boat with us to get a book I wanted to give them, her mother demurred, explaining that there were too many cougars on the island for a child to be alone on the trail. This was Cougar Summer, when a cougar even found its way into the Empress Hotel in Victoria.

Joanne's children might have been safer in the 1920s, when August Schnarr lived here, for he was one of the greatest of British Columbia's cougar hunters. Born in Centralia, Washington, in 1886, Schnarr brought his family to Sonora in the early 1930s. He fished, trapped and hunted cougar for the bounty. Once Schnarr shot a cougar with four kittens, scarcely more than a day old. Tan-coloured, with darker leopard spots, the tiny creatures hissed and spat at him, but he bundled them into a sack and brought them home to his three daughters, Marion, Daisy and Pansy. Two of the kittens died but Leo and Girlie survived. A cougar can reach a weight of 200 pounds and a length of eight feet; with tremendous strength and speed they can break the neck of a deer with one blow of a powerful paw.

When Leo and Girlie matured, they had to be kept on chains if the girls were not with them, but "they would sometimes break loose from their chains and take off down a trail the girls used going to school. When they heard the girls coming, the cougars hid in the bush, then, as the girls approached, they would leap out at them, scaring them half to death before they recognized them."[3] Once Leo broke his chain and was about to spring upon the Schnarr dog when Pearl hit him with a stout stick. She then grasped the short length of dangling chain and dragged the dazed Leo to his den. Another afternoon, Marion, aged 13, saw Leo trotting free towards the pig pen and raced to intercept him. She coolly cuffed him across the nose with her open palm, and Leo, docile and purring, allowed her to lead him back to his chain. Leo got free a third time and chased the Schnarr goat through the brush, but his dragging chain snagged and stopped him a few feet from the goat, which was trapped by fallen trees. This time it was Pansy who seized a broken branch and whipped the snarling animal, then freed the chain and took him home. Leo lived to the age of seven and Girlie survived him by another two years. There was no obvious reason for their deaths. They seemed to pine away, when their beloved mistresses grew up.

As we walked back to *Liza Jane* on that path to the school, now Sonora Road, Camil, Opal and Jody accompanied us, first ahead and then behind us as they pedalled their bicycles at breakneck speed. I looked at the overhanging trees and almost expected to see a cougar watching us.

Later, in the gloaming, we sat on the dock and talked to Frank Istas, crippled with muscular dystrophy, who used to fish out of Alaska and now spends summers in his double-ended, Columbia river boat *Hoko*. He was waiting for the northwesterlies to blow themselves out, before he ventured into Johnstone Strait. Frank had visited Owen Bay in 1967, a year ahead of us, and like us, he examined the contents of the abandoned floathouse at the head of the lagoon. There he picked up a child's drawing, signed Sharon Godtin, a picture of an Indian woman cooking outside a teepee. Frank liked the picture and kept it aboard the *Hoko*. Twenty years later, when Frank was anchored in Cameleon Bay on the north side of Sonora Island, he talked to a man who arrived in a boat looking as if it had been built with a chain-saw. When the man said his name was Godtin, Frank showed him the picture made by his daughter Sharon before the breakup of the family.

Clouds, blown by the northwest wind, played peek-a-boo with the dying moon. The tossing trees hissed. Rocked against the dock, the boats groaned a little. But there were no clanking chains and we slept soundly.

OWEN BAY. ALDERS

Hiking an overgrown logging road, we entered an avenue of young alders, the slim, graceful trees springing up on both sides and forming an arch of flickering green light. I had been reading Mary Catherine Bateson's explanation of cybernetics, a science which allows us to recognize that the system which is a tree is the same as the system which is a human. "If you look beyond a tree's rigidity to see it as alive, then you see it as more like a woman than like a telephone pole, perhaps indeed, in a slowness of growth that only seems static, living the impassioned life of a dryad."[1]

Norse myths say the first woman was made from an alder tree. The red alder is woman-like in its role of nurturer. Those who do not understand it call it a "weed tree", good only for firewood, and it does, indeed, make an excellent fuel because it contains no pitch to spit and is easily split. Native people carved it into bowls and spoons, and used its sap to make a red dye; from its bark they brewed a stomach medicine. But the main work of the alders is the restoration of the land. Its roots form nodules with nitrogen-fixing bacteria which convert nitrogen from the soil into a form available to the trees. Alders heal mine tailings, garbage dumps, burned forests and logging scars. The alders are the first trees in natural reforestation, their roots converting nitrogen, their fallen leaves enriching the soil and their canopy sheltering the sensitive conifer seedlings. A monoculture forest policy, which reseeds logged areas with another conifer crop, overleaps the essential alder stage and tries to grow endless crops in ever more depleted soils. In Homer's sagas, the alder was revered as the tree of resurrection, a notion that has echoes in modern Ireland where people avoid falling it.

Peter Trower loves these slender dryads...

the forestfixers
bandaging brown wounds
with applegreen sashes —
filling in for the fallen
firs —

77

jostling up by the stumps
of grandfather cedars —
leaning slim to the wind
by logjammed
loggerleft streams.[2]

That summer morning on Sonora Island, the alder trail was a passage through a throng of whispering, curious maidens, who crowded to examine us.

CHAPTER SIX

Northward, Thurlow Islands to Minstrel Island

We left Owen Bay early, while the resident kingfisher could still dive into his own image, and went west out Okisollo Channel, intending to be out of Johnstone Strait and into Nodales Channel before the afternoon wind began to blow. We were throbbing north towards Chatham Point when a school of dolphins surfaced around us, under us, back and forth, rolling, banking, sideslipping, making rooster-tails of spray when they surfaced. I was on the deck in an instant, lying flat, hanging over the prow. They took turns riding the bow wave, almost under the keel, a braiding dance with each dolphin gliding beneath the prow for a few minutes then sliding off to right or left to give a companion a keel roll. They smiled their silly grin and I laughed with them.

Herman Melville gave the dolphin the nickname of "Huzza Porpoise":

They are the lads that always live before the wind. They are accounted a lucky omen. If you yourself can withstand three cheers at beholding these vivacious fish, then heaven help you; the spirit of godly gamesomeness is not in ye.[1]

They seem to live to play. There is, of course, the fact of their insatiable, ardent concupiscence: they love to make love. This is Aphrodite's animal, her sea horse — those old Greeks knew a thing or two about dolphins. In all seasons, all weathers, they eagerly copulate, nuzzling and necking, touching flippers, chasing each other, simultaneously surfacing in courtship foreplay. How odd if the function of their large brains, equal in size and complexity to ours, is simply love of life. Did we humans get side-tracked several thousand years ago into devoting much of our intelligence to cars and killing?

Play is supposed to be the hallmark of intelligence. Richard Ellis has described two captive dolphins playing with an eel, which escaped into a rock crevice. One of the dolphins swam away to capture a spiny scorpion fish which he shoved into the crevice to drive out the eel so the dolphins could continue their game. In captivity they invent games — throwing things out of their tanks the way an infant will push a toy off the high-chair tray so that someone will play the game of retrieving it. A wild dolphin nicknamed Donald had the disconcerting habit of clamping his teeth on the anchor chains of moored boats and towing them around a bay. Michael Modzelewski wrote that Cousteau, in a small boat over an Indian Ocean reef, looked down into the clear water and saw 15 dolphins poised on their tails, sitting on the bottom in a group, clicking and whistling to each other. Stories of dolphins rescuing people continue to appear in newspapers around the world. They turn a wet cheek and befriend us, their murderers.

Every year a million or more dolphins are killed, sometimes just for fertilizer or chicken food or because their sexual organs are thought to be an aphrodisiac or because they get entangled in nets. On many coastal docks we saw notices asking mariners to report to the University of Victoria any sightings of the harbour porpoise, a shy dolphin that hides in the shallow inshore waters. It can be distinguished by its small size (1.8 metres/six feet), its beakless profile and its small dorsal fin. Also, it makes a loud puff-noise when it exhales at the surface. Harbour porpoises (sometimes called "herring hogs") have been observed hunting herring by using the same technique which the orcas use on Common Dolphins — herding them into tight balls, then dashing in and gulping them down. Harbour porpoises do not ride bow waves, tend to avoid boats and humans and are likely to go into terminal nervous shock and die if captured. The Council of Europe has declared the harbour porpoise an endangered species. We may be killing off this species with pesticide runoff and industrial pollution in its shallow coastal habitat, with overkill (for fertilizer, etc.) and by the over-fishing of its major food, the herring.

In 1972 a law was passed prohibiting the sale in the United States of tuna caught with the driftnets which kill about 20,000 dolphins each year, but in 1991 this law was successfully challenged in international court by Mexico (a leading offender) under G.A.T.T. regulations. Dolphins are again being drowned in large numbers.

Our dolphin escort left us long before we entered Nodales Channel to take the "inside passage" north of the Thurlow Islands and Hardwicke Island. The strait seemed empty when they had gone. The Huzza Porpoises took some of the sparkle of the bright day with them.

SHOAL BAY AND BICKLEY BAY. EAST THURLOW ISLAND

Blown by northwest winds fetching out of Phillips Arm, we came bounding into Shoal Bay at noon, looking for the hotel where, in the 1920s, the loggers got tanked up before they buried Brown. There it was, on mouldering, encrusted pilings, at the head of the wharf, boarded up and left to rot. A new establishment spread itself over several of the Thurlow townsite lots. In the high days of the 1920s, the Thurlow Hotel was the centre of activity in this area and served loggers coming up on the steamships looking for work. We peered through the dirty panes of cobwebbed windows and imagined the loggers who buried Brown warming themselves at the bar.

When Brown drowned in Phillips Arm, his body drifted down with that northwest wind and washed ashore in Bickley Bay. Having examined him, the police asked some of his logger friends to build a coffin and bury him where he had emerged from the sea. They dug the hole before going to Shoal Bay to make the box and load it into Ed Dolby's boat; then they all adjourned to the hotel to fortify themselves for the burial. Dolby left first, and when he got to Bickley Bay, he got Brown into the box and nailed the lid down. When the others arrived, they found Ed asleep in the grave (the warmest place), with a bottle clasped to his chest. When they got Dolby out and were ready to lower Brown into the hole, the question arose: at which end of the coffin was Brown's head? They were convinced that he must be buried with feet pointing toward dawn if he himself were ever to rise again. Dolby solved the problem: "He's wearing his cork boots; whichever end makes the loudest thump, that's his feet."[1] By the light of an old Cold Blast lantern, they tilted the coffin first one way, then the other. The thump of boots was unmistakable, and Brown was lowered into his grave, oriented to rise on Judgment Day. Perhaps they threw a mound of stones on top, or planted a crude cross to mark the place.

In the 1920s, when the government was granting homestead land in 160-acre parcels, there were settlers along the shore of Bickley Bay, with vegetable plots, small orchards, chickens, cows and goats. When we arrived, looking for Brown's grave, the forest had devoured the little farms and there was no one there to remember whether Brown's grave had ever been marked.

BLIND CHANNEL. WEST THURLOW ISLAND. THE RICHTERS

When we stopped at the Blind Channel store in 1968, we lingered to listen to the elderly woman behind the counter, who was eager to find a buyer for the business. We talked late that night, weighing the pros and cons of purchasing this place and establishing a marina business. We didn't buy it, but I left the next day with her recipe for cooking rock crab: make a cream sauce with sauteed green pepper and green onions, pour this over fresh crab meat in a covered casserole and bake for a moment or two; but just before serving open the lid and add wine and a sprinkle of fresh thyme, then reseal and bake a few minutes more. "Serve with the lid closed," she said, "so that when you lift it at the table, you swoon with the beauty of the fragrance."

In the year following our 1968 visit, Edgar and Annemarie Richter, with sons Philip, Alfred and Robert, were cruising out of Vancouver. They stopped for a loaf of bread at Blind Channel, noted the FOR SALE sign and, unlike us, promptly bought the place. In a booklet written in 1984, Phil Richter explained that in the year 1969 "something was afoot, a different mood was definitely in the air. Besides complaining about 9 to 5 humdrum, the shackles of the rat race, a larger minority than ever before were actually taking the plunge and trying out alternatives."[1] With energy and imagination, the Richters began building up the marina business, and in spare moments Edgar built a 31-foot Carius hull, which we admired in 1972. The Richter children worked during the summers, and Annemarie's parents came to live at Blind Channel, occupying an old schoolhouse converted to a residence and lending a hand wherever they could. In 1992, when we tied at the modern floats, decorated with pots of daisies and murals made of stones, shards and shells, we found the next generation waiting to welcome us.

That evening we followed the trail through an 80 year-old, second-growth forest of mostly hemlock and balsam fir to visit the Thurlow Cedar. When the first growth was logged about the turn of the century, the loggers left one tree. "Educated guesses place it at about 2,500 years, give or take half a millenium."[2] The trail twisted upwards through a stately forest floored with sword ferns, the occasional huckleberry bush, thick mosses and salal. It was cathedral-like, yet when we reached the Thurlow Cedar the other trees seemed mere saplings. Will humans ever see again on Thurlow Island a forest like the one in which the Thurlow Cedar stood? Not in a "well-managed" forest of ever-weaker trees.

It was those first-growth trees which brought the first settlers to Blind Channel. The 1910 *British Columbia Directory* listed nine lumbermen, six woodsmen, a blacksmith and the mill manager, who took out the great logs by using teams of workhorses or oxen. In 1918 there were 120 people at Blind Channel but in that year the sawmill was dismantled and W.E. Anderson established a fish-packing plant on pilings just south of today's wharf. There was, in those days, a good-sized salmon run into the creek near the floats. A shingle mill was built next to the cannery. The Richters' diesel generator now stands inside the boiler room of the old mill, which is built of foot-thick concrete and double-lined with firebrick. Blind Channel's life reached a peak in the 1940s and began to dwindle when the old trees were gone and the local fishing declined. Small canneries closed as faster boats and refrigeration centralized the industry. When we came in 1968, Blind Bay seemed near the end of its community existence, but the Richters have given it a new lease on life. Perhaps their restaurant could serve crab in a sauce of green onions and peppers, with a dash of wine and a sprinkle of thyme?

FORWARD HARBOUR

Those persistent summer winds that roil the east-west inlets were prodding Chancellor Channel into a jarring chop and we were grateful to escape into Wellbore Channel. When we had sashayed through the Whirlpool Rapids, we turned west into Forward Harbour's sheltered corner, just inside the entrance. Suddenly, the sea was flat.

A small black bear emerged on the rock bluff next to the white beach, stretching a curious nose towards the smell of onions frying for a sauce. When we had enjoyed the spaghetti, we hiked the leg-bender over the ridge separating this anchorage from Bessborough Bay, singing marching songs to scare off the bear. John Chappell stated that the trail led to "a tiny abandoned farm"[1] but all we could find was the rusted remains of an iron stove among the beach stones, pounded by the driven waves. When the Barrows were here in 1933 they

> johnsoned out of Forward Harbour and into Bessborough Bay to the north and went ashore at Mr. McCulloch's place. He is a trapper. McCulloch came on board about 7 p.m. after we had looked at his garden close by our anchorage.[2]

Returning to Forward Harbour five years later, the Barrows anchored at the head of the harbour and went ashore near the old Indian house site beside Wortley Stream to examine the flat boulder covered with petroglyphs. "The wind died down at dusk, for which God be praised," Barrow wrote in his journal.[3] We too went to look at the petroglyph, after a delicious dinner at the resort which has been established in logging company buildings.

On the flat, sloping surface of the boulder, the central figure is a human with a heart-shaped face, but the emphasized feature is a

Creek Woman petroglyph, Forward Harbour.

deep pit on her belly, enclosed in a circle. It is women who give birth and this, surely, is a symbol of pregnancy and fertility and ongoing life. Above her a fish with x-ray skeleton suggests that this composition is about the fertility of fish. The petroglyph fish is headed up the creek, as if to spawn. The central figure is surrounded by pairs of eyes, one in a heart-shaped frame. On this coast, the spirits could be represented by eyes alone. In the oldest symbolism of Eurasia (and the natives of North America came originally from Asia), the eye itself was a symbol of fertility, for tears and semen were thought to have the same power.

The sun had slipped behind the mountains and the wind had stiffened; we were bumped and sprayed as we "johnsoned" slowly back to the one calm corner of the harbour. For us that northwest wind did not even die at dusk.

After I had written all of the above, I received a letter from an artist friend who visited the Forward Harbour petroglyph in August, at a time when salmon were heading up Wortley Creek to spawn. When she poured a libation over the stone, the water filled the deep eye sockets and the belly hole. In the Creek Woman's eyes she saw

an infinite world — sparkling, cellular, cohesive, locked and shaped like the cells of a hive but SPARKLING and glittering, as beautiful as the scales of a salmon fracturing the light. It was the beauty of the structures of nature, the beauty of the bloodstream, a butterfly's wing, a moon snail, the lenticular light on the water.[4]

She examined the toothy-faced creature at the knees of the Creek Woman and asked if this was the bear that devoured the spawned-out fish, their life incorporated into his. As the tide covered the boulder, the salmon splashed by on their way up the creek to spawn and die. The seawater in the eyes of the Creek Woman and the salmon and the bear glittered and winked. She understood that this is surely great art — not a dead image to be looked at, but a living, interactive symbol that may have been placed between the tide lines so that when the sea covers the Creek Woman, a cycle is completed and renewed, and there will be food so that life can spiral on. A true artist, my friend knows that art cut off from its deep roots in mysticism becomes merely a thing to sell, a commercial item. For those people for whom the petroglyph was made, the image explained, reassured and healed, connecting the individual with the universe. As my friend meditated there, the Creek Woman seemed to speak to her, saying,

The world is a web
there is no beginning nor end
there are no distinctions
there is continuity
everything is connected.[5]

PORT NEVILLE

Escaping the two-foot chop of Johnstone Strait, we slipped into Port Neville. Fishboats were rafted three deep at the government dock below the Hansens' log house on the eastern side of the entrance, so we anchored amid a dozen others in the kelp bed on the opposite side, where the high cone of Nelson Ridge provided a wind break. It may have been the full of the moon, or perhaps I was awakened by the fishermen who went out to fish in the dark strait when the night winds softened, but three times, I came out on deck to look about me in the moonlight. Three times, I saw huge glittering liners, like giant diamond brooches, sliding slowly past Port Neville's narrow mouth. Were there a thousand people dancing and drinking there, in saloons that could just as well be in Acapulco?

In the morning, the wind was buffeting the firs on the shore and the fishboats had all returned. When we crossed to the dock to visit the Hansens, a fisherman was patiently mending a sea-green net, which a liner had ripped during the night. The British Columbia ferry captains, he told us, were considerate. They saw the lights marking the end of a net, and avoided them, but the liners never altered course. Perhaps a 70,000-ton cruise ship travelling 20 knots in a narrow passage can't dodge nets.

Nor can the cruise people know much of Port Neville, as they swiftly pass this crevice in the wall of the continent. But in the spring of 1891, when one-handed Hans Hansen sailed his little boat in past Milly Island, he recognized the place of his dreams. Here would he live and die. He cleared and fenced the land above the curve of white-shell beach where proud Indian longhouses had once stood, built a home, married and was widowed, found his second wife Katrinka in Norway and raised a family.

Rare are the places on this coast where the old families survive, and rare are the buildings which the first settlers built. But at Port

Neville, the government dock (sadly in need of a new coat of red paint) led us straight to the front door of the old Hansen house, a two-storey log building. Once the coastal steamers tied here to disgorge passengers and freight, and Hans Hansen rented cabins to travellers for 25¢ a night, or for a bit of tobacco if that was all the visitor could afford. When we first came here, years ago, the great log house was still the post office and store. Now it stood empty, and if those responsible for British Columbia's heritage buildings do not immediately repair the leaking roof, this landmark will slowly collapse. When the first post office was opened in 1895 under postmaster Hans Hansen, it served coast people from Knight to Loughborough Inlet.

West of the log house, across a wide lawn with fruit trees, stood Olaf and Lilly Hansen's house, where they received us with gentle courtesy, the Hansen tradition. Olaf, born in 1909, one of Hans and Katrinka's sons, told us that the Hansens moved into the almost-finished log house in 1921. When young Olaf married Lilly Bendickson of Hardwicke Island in 1937, they built this, their one and only home, and their daughter is the present postmistress of Port Neville. Granddaughter Erica, with her straight blonde hair and bright eyes, wearing a turquoise and pink jacket, looked as Norwegian as her great-grandmother. In the field where Hansen cows used to graze, a deer lifted its head to watch us as we passed.

There are petroglyphs at the east end of the inlet and midden deposits at many points around Port Neville. An Indian reserve may mark the location of the main village at the mouth of the Fulmer River, which was once a major salmon-spawning stream. Nothing is known of this band, for they were gone before white settlers arrived, slaughtered, it is said, by Haida raiders. Port Neville has not always been a refuge for those escaping from Johnstone Strait's winds.

PORT HARVEY. CRACROFT ISLAND

Our 32-foot *Liza Jane* seemed to shrink as we emerged from Port Neville into Johnstone Strait's glittering magnificence. The one-foot chop was a great sheet of crinkled silverfoil, with the blue Vancouver Island mountains rising like a wall, each more distant slope a lighter shade of blue until the unseen end of the wall blended into sky. The waves came at us like endless rows of soldiers, flinging spray at our windows. We were plunging through two-foot waves by the time we reached the light at the Broken Islands and turned east into

Havannah Channel. We surfed into Port Harvey on the crest of a rolling swell which smoothed as we went to the north end of the bay. We passed Elizabeth Strondal's weathered cabin nestled into a golden meadow on Mist Island, and could see that the Mist Island pictograph was still clearly visible. Flowers bloomed on the deck of an apple-green floathouse moored to new pilings south of Tidepole Islet. The government dock at the end of the inlet was gone, so we dropped the anchor behind Tidepole Islet; with the click of the ignition switch, sweet silence and stillness engulfed us. I produced sherry and biscuits and we sagged to the cushions on the back deck. A heron flapped by. Out in the strait the wave armies marched relentlessly, but we rested in the glassy calm of Port Harvey.

We were awakened early when the rising sun smote us through the cabin window. A kingfisher was complaining in a ratchety voice. The reflected cedars were undulating seductively. We went in the dinghy to Mist Island, where bright green seaweed lay like wet lettuce on the barnacled beach. "This is the perfect place, the unbeatable place," I wrote in my sea journal in 1968, when we came ashore here to explore an abandoned house...or was it abandoned? Curtains fluttered at an open window. We had approached nervously, on that long-ago morning, through an overgrown garden of laburnum, lilac and roses. We knocked at the open door. No one answered, but I thought I heard whispering. We shouted a greeting and listened...and I realized that the blowing curtain was hissing to the teasing breeze. We walked in. There was almost no furniture, but a calendar with a bright green Irish scene hung on the wall. In the tiny bedroom, I opened a closet door — there hung a paddy-green silk evening dress! I closed the door as if I had seen a ghost. Who had worn this dress? Who had left it hanging there, the only garment in the closet? Searching about, we found envelopes with the names Elizabeth Strondal and W.A. Laird.

Later that day we called at the logging camp at the north end of the harbour to talk to two loggers, one a Swede who told us that Elizabeth Strondal had died of a heart attack in that house. Laird, who lived in the nearby cabin by the workshop, had found her. Laird himself was killed a year later, in a bulldozer accident. They had owned a logging operation. The following day, while buying gas at Minstrel Island, we asked again about Strondal and Laird.

"Betty Strondal was a fine woman, a fine woman," said the man at the gas pump, speaking with emphasis.

"And what sort of man was Mr. Laird?" I enquired.

He frowned thoughtfully. "Well, a bit unpredictable maybe. Got noisy when he drank."

But when we returned on that bright morning in 1992, scrunching the barnacles as we dragged the boat over the green lettuce, we almost wished we had not come back. Two large clumps of Elizabeth Strondal's white daisies bloomed bravely, but the lilac and rose bushes had grown grotesquely, enclosing her house as the thorns hid Sleeping Beauty's castle. Inside the house, squatters had left a ruin. The bushes were growing in at the windows and all was desolation. The closet was empty where the green silk gown had hung. Later we were told that Mist Island is owned by wealthy people from Liechtenstein who never come here but keep the island so that they can enter Canada without difficulty, if they should need to escape from Europe.

On a flat rock outcrop on the western shore of Port Harvey there once was a hotel. Its floor was pock-marked from the spikes in caulk boots and one wall was splintered because the loggers ran up it to see how high they could get and still land on their boots, each trying to leave an imprint higher than anyone else's. There was a story about the owner, Charlie Cavanaugh, deciding to save the wall by closing the pub, but the loggers returned with a dozen screw jacks; they began shifting the pub into the sea, so Cavanaugh re-opened it. In 1992, when we enquired about the Cracroft hotel, we were told that it had been towed around to Minstrel Island to serve as a store.

Ninety-odd years ago, when Martin Allerdale Grainger sat in that hotel, listening to a fiddler accompanied by another man who tapped on the violin strings with chopsticks, the room was crowded with loggers. "I'll tell you, feller," Ed Anderson held forth to Grainger, "there's a rough class of people in this country here — a rough class of people. And there's not a one of 'em 'ud fail in respect to a lady...you can't say the same of many classes of men."[1]

We "johnsoned" across the harbour to the site of the hotel, now reclaimed by the raincoast jungle. In this rugged world of loggers and liquor, a lady once lived serenely in her lovely garden, an Irish calendar on her wall and a green evening dress in her closet.

MATILPI. HAVANNAH CHANNEL

Under a ceiling of grey cloud, the surface of Havannah Channel was like mottled, shiny grey linoleum as we chugged east to the site of the abandoned Indian village of Matilpi. When we slid into the anchorage behind the Indian Islands, the tide was dropping down the steep slope of the white-shell beach. A path led from the beach through the wild rose and thimbleberry bushes into a ghostly dark place where trees dripped moss. Shiny black slugs lay motionless and a cloud of mosquitoes rose to attack us. Nothing of the great houses remained.

The path led us to two gigantic trees, a cedar and a maple, each about eight feet in diameter (measured well above their spreading roots). These giants stood close together, almost touching, clasping each other with their thousand arms. They had stood here, side by side, when people lived in the great houses beneath them. They had looked down on Francis Barrow when he hacked a path through the underbrush in 1934,

> to the only remaining standing door frame, with a huge house beam, round and carved, lying by it on the ground. The machete I brought along is the clear thing for chopping away underbrush, as it cuts very small stuff as well as fairly big. I took a photo of the house beam for Bill Newcombe, to compare with his photo of 1900. The house beam I photographed today was 53 feet long and 30 inches in diameter.[1]

The entwined cedar and maple giants watched us as we stumbled through the undergrowth, avoiding nettles and fighting off mosquitoes until we could escape from the clutching forest to the white purity of the beach.

On the shore of the smaller Indian Island to the west, a black, bent root stood vertical and I was startled, thinking for an instant that I saw an Indian stepping into his canoe. It was time to leave.

SODERMAN COVE. CRACROFT ISLAND

Leaving *Liza Jane* anchored at Matilpi, we zoomed by dinghy across Havannah Channel to Soderman Cove, trailing a cloud of mosquitoes. The wind had blown the last of them out of my hair by the time we arrived at the site of the Soderman logging operation, well known from Jim Spilsbury's account of a visit to this cove in the 1930s. In 1905 Oscar Soderman was living in a shack on Minstrel Island, hand-logging for six months, selling the logs, getting roaring drunk until the money was gone and then starting over again. This was the pattern of his years until Sidney snagged him. When the red-light girls were run out of Ocean Falls, Madam Sidney established them across the inlet (outside city limits) in a house on pilings, which was given the name Pecker Point. Exactly how it happened no one knows, but one morning Oscar, waking from an Ocean Falls spree, found himself married to Sidney. She invested her considerable money in his logging company, applied her expert management to their affairs, ended Oscar's binges, paid cash and had no debts. She selected their loggers with an eye that was a keen judge of capability.

According to Jim Spilsbury, Sidney was "of medium height, about fifty, with wisps of greying brown hair straggling out from under a red cotton bandana pinned around her head like a turban."[1] When she invited him and Glenys for dinner, she wore a flowered silk blouse and men's trousers tucked into knee-high laced boots, expensive jewellery but no make-up. Oscar died not long afterward, but Sidney long outlived him, and when her life ended she left a large bequest to the University of British Columbia. There is something elusive in this brief account of two lives lived extravagantly, excessively, intemperately, matching the challenge of the fierce landscape and frontier ethics. In Sidney's gracious deportment at the Spilsbury dinner, in the silk blouse, in the gift to the university there are hints of another Sidney who, in other circumstances, might have ruled other kingdoms.

We walked on the shore where an old log-dump crumbled and pilings rotted. Above us, up the logged-off slopes of Cracroft Island, the light, bright green alders were beginning the work of regeneration.

MINSTREL ISLAND

Coming through Chatham Channel was duck soup. Ignoring the anxious beeping of the depth sounder, we lined up the range finders and kept them aligned even though we headed straight for the keel of an oncoming vessel and the kelp almost stroked both sides of our hull. We tied up at the Minstrel Island dock and went ashore for lunch at the resort, a conglomeration of prefab aluminum buildings on a platform of stupendous logs overhanging the beach. The shore had been bulldozed; not a bottle was left from the wicked old days. As we studied the photograph on a postcard for sale at the restaurant, we saw that not much had survived even from the Minstrel Island of the 1950s; the tall, two-storey turquoise store building was the hotel that had been floated off its site near Tidepole Islet in Port Harvey.

Young Halliday was running this store when the Barrows arrived in 1934. They stayed for a few days so that Clarence Cabeen could take off the *Toketie*'s propeller and straighten the blades. Cabeen's boat-repair place is gone and the new hotel owners have built a golf driving range across the slope of green grass where the old hotel once stood. A driving range!..old loggers must be rolling in their graves. The helicopter pad and huge TV dish were other modern additions, but near them a smokehouse which looked like an outhouse belched smoke through every crack, and an ancient tin bathtub now held a few struggling flowers. The old hotel was still open when we came in 1968, and we drank beer there. Some changes are hard to accept.

There are many Minstrel stories and Sylvia Douglas at the resort said that she was determined to collect them all. As we ate lunch, fishermen were bringing in their entries to be measured in a fishing derby, and fresh-caught fish were dripping on the foyer floor. There was a prize for the smallest entry; a child presented Sylvia with an inch-long fish. Later, she found time to tell us about a murder that was done beneath the crooked pine on the point below the pub, "the oldest unsolved-now-solved murder in British Columbia history," she said. A Mr. Puglas from Alert Bay, in an angry dispute over a bottle of beer, killed a man under that tree, and fled. He could have carried his secret to his grave, but his conscience gnawed at him, and 50 years later when he thought he was dying, he called for the Mounties and made a full confession. And then he didn't die. The R.C.M.P. sent up an officer to examine the murder setting and seek further evidence. Puglas was duly tried, found guilty of manslaughter and sentenced to 18 months in jail. We wandered down to the tree, now decorated with strings of Christmas-tree lights, and sat on a bench which may be older than the crime, for it is cut out of a large log. On a hot mid-afternoon in August, the murder setting lacked the authentic atmosphere: a Saturday night, pale moonlight, and the noise of brawls, shouts and loud laughter from the old hotel.

In the early years of the century, Martin Grainger came to Minstrel Island on just such a night. Disembarking from the steamer *Cassiar* onto a large raft (there was no dock), he got ashore in an over loaded rowboat propelled by a drunken rower. Entering the hotel, he was at first half-blinded by the brilliance of the acetylene lamps.

Noise was my first impression — noise of shuffling feet, stamp of dancing men, loud talk and shouted cuss words. Then I saw that the room was crowded. A red-hot stove stood in one corner, and round it men sat in chairs or stood warming themselves or drying their wet clothes. A card game was going on at a small table, and men stood around, three deep, to watch the play. There was an incessant coming and going of men between the barroom and the public room, and men loafed about the rooms and passages and talked, or argued, or scuffled playfully. Some danced to the tunes of a fiddle played by an old man who swayed with shut eyes, rapt in his discordant scraping....Those who had fallen lay splayed out upon the floor in drunken sleep. [1]

It is a very long step from Grainger's experience to a prize for an inch-long fish.

KNIGHT INLET. MARTIN ALLERDALE GRAINGER

A roof of grey wool hid the tops of Knight Inlet's mountain walls and trailed dirty white wisps and threads down its steep slopes. With that low cloud ceiling overhead, the invisible mountains seemed as high and precipitous as the peaks in fairy tales. The fog closed in behind us. We weren't worried about fog — we could always keep a hundred feet off the shore and there aren't any rocks — but I thought about wind. This canyon, almost 2,000 feet deep below water and 65 miles long from Minstrel Island east, twisting and turning between peaks 6,000 feet high, is famous for its unpredictable and violent winds. And equally well known is the absence of sheltered anchorages.

Martin Grainger has written of the time when he and Bill almost lost the rackety steamboat *Sonora* at a creek mouth. Where the creeks and rivers come tumbling headlong into the sea there are tiny deltas, whose seaward edges drop abruptly from shallow depths to 2,000 feet. Grainger and Bill thought they had anchored safely, but while they slept, exhausted, the wild night storm dragged *Sonora*'s prow over "the drop-off", as they called it. In the night the tide fell and Grainger, waking to check their anchorage, discovered with shock that his pole touched bottom at the stern but there was nothing under the prow. Would the boat lurch over, forward and sideways, and fill and sink? Propelled by panic and fear, in the pitch blackness and raging wind, with rain as hard as hail, he and Bill rowed ashore to cut post lengths eight feet long. Imagine them tripping and flopping and clambering, feeling with their hands in the dark, somehow finding poles that would do and chopping them to the right lengths with the axe, unable to see either the pole or the axe as they worked. Imagine them alongside the steamer in a rowboat, struggling desperately to get those posts driven into the bottom to prop up the *Sonora*.

Although the *Sonora* clung to the delta on that occasion and floated with the rising tide, she was later doomed to sink when she slid down the drop-off at the very head of Knight Inlet, at Carter's camp where Grainger worked. And without the old steamboat, how were they to get supplies from Minstrel Island? Martin Grainger found himself rowing a sodden, heavy, 18-foot boat down that tortuous 65 miles of misery.

Grainger merits extravagant adjectives: a brilliant, wise, individualistic, good man, a man who ought to be remembered and honoured but who is, in fact, almost unknown. H.R. MacMillan said Grainger was responsible for the Forest Act of 1912: "There probably would have been no Forest Act if it had not been for the flaming zeal of Grainger."[1] H.R. MacMillan is well known, but how many people have heard of Grainger?

After graduating from King's College at 23 (in 1897), he pack-packed for the Hudson's Bay Company in northern British Columbia. His feet, badly frozen on one occasion, gave him pain for the rest of his life. In spite of bad eyesight and damaged feet, he fought in the Boer War and dispatched articles about it to the *London Daily News*. Back in British Columbia in 1901, he went to Samuel Island (one of the Gulf Islands) to buy eggs and fell in love with Mabel Higgs, who had come out to join her brother Leonard. When Grainger came back from logging up Knight Inlet, Mabel had returned to England. He sent her a cable asking "Will you marry me? Martin Grainger." She replied "Yes. Higgs".[2] Arriving in London still wearing his logging clothes and boots, and needing money, he gathered up the letters he had written to her and from them wrote *Woodsmen of the West*, a biographical and detailed account of logging in Knight Inlet in the first years of this century.

His book takes the reader into the logging world. At half-past six, you stumble through the dark into the cookhouse where the lamps had been lit. You see Pong Sam in spotless white flapping hot-cakes and sniff the fried meat and coffee. Today the old cookhouses have slumped and crumbled and alders grow through the frames of rusting donkey engines. The old trees are gone except for the spindly few left along the edge of the inlets, hiding the little new trees monocultured behind. Grainger admired the loggers:

> And if whisky was their bane, better this, to my mind, than that dreary scheming to indulge in Comfort that meets one everywhere in city life.[3]

In 1916, Grainger succeeded H.R. MacMillan as Chief Forester in the new Forest Service. "He especially wanted to save the forests from ruthless exploitation."[4] Wearing moccasins on his always painful feet, he was received by King George V at Buckingham Palace. He left the Forest Service to work for a private forestry company "determined that the B.C. forest industry should get back the good name that had been sacrificed by the ruthless tactics of early promoters."[5] Fortunately, he died before grapple-loaders and clearcuts. When he died in 1941, aged 67, Cambridge University founded a Grainger Fellowship to honour him. But we British Columbians have forgotten him.

The grey wind strengthened and *Liza Jane* began to buck the waves. In weather far worse than this, Grainger came rowing down the inlet, watching for an anchorage in curve after curve of cliff, darkness coming on, knowing that if he failed to find a ledge on which he could camp he would have to anchor and sleep in the boat, in wet clothes across the thwarts of the leaky boat, waking to bail her every hour or so. Grainger wrote, "I like the spirit of the thing: the quiet feeling that it is natural and right that a man should never admit that he cannot do a thing." [6]

But Ray and I, depressed by the dreariness of the scene and having no particular reason to proceed, turned *Liza Jane* around and abandoned Knight Inlet.

CHAPTER SEVEN

Around Queen Charlotte Strait

POTTS LAGOON. TRADE BEADS

We slid into Potts Lagoon with the mist thickening to rain; when the anchor was down and the motor had died with a sigh, we were wrapped in the soft grey silence. Nearby, on rotting, encrusted posts, the remains of an ancient dock now supported seedling trees. Tied to a small, neat assemblage of float buildings was a tall sloop. I raised the binoculars to examine it and was shocked to read its name: *Toketie. Toketie!*

"Someone is using the name of the Barrows' yacht!" I announced, outraged. We dinghied across to the floathouse, grumbling.

The man who took the line introduced himself: John Walders, the grandson of May John, the surrogate daughter to the Barrows. It was May who had snatched from a refuse fire the sea journals from which *Upcoast Summers* was written. Who better than her grandson had the right to use the name? The third surprise was the presence, in John and Wendy Walders' floathouse living-room, of the boulder bowl which once stood on May John's lawn at Toketie Point, Tsehum Harbour, and which had been found on the midden beach below the Barrow house next door. The next shock was when John showed us that this boulder bowl is a double bowl; he rolled it over to display a bowl of equal size underneath, chiselled as laboriously as the top bowl. Why would someone make that second bowl?

But when we settled down to discuss artifacts, we talked about trade beads, as I sorted and studied some of the beads in John's collection. Many and varied were the items traded for pelts by the fur traders — guns, knives, kettles, spoons, pipes, flints, scissors, mirrors, combs, jews harps, needles, red lead, blankets, salt, sugar, tobacco, even their own clothes — but the common denominator of the trade was the lowly glass bead. And one of the most interesting facts about beads is that almost all of them were manufactured on the island of Murano, Italy, a mile from Venice. Turning the blue glass bead in my fingers to watch the light refracted from its flattened planes, I remembered the terrible heat of the glass furnaces of Murano which I visited half a lifetime ago.

Blue glass, drawn out into a long, tubular wire was chopped into bead-size pieces. When their sharp edges had been rounded in a revolving barrow over a hot fire, the beads were polished by being poured into bags which two men shook from side to side. Bead-making was a fairly simple business, but Venice's rulers guarded their monopoly ruthlessly. If a bead-maker appeared to be selling his skills to another country, the law decreed that "an emissary will be charged to kill him."[1]

The large, ultra-marine beads, known sometimes as "Russian beads", were as Venetian as all the rest. Concerning trade on the Columbia River, Meriwether Lewis wrote, "As we have had occasion to remark more than once, the object of foreign trade which is most desired are the common cheap, blue or white beads...of these blue beads which are called *Tia Commashuck*, or chief beads, hold the first rank in their ideas of relative value. The most inferior kind are esteemed beyond the finest wampum, and are temptations which can always seduce them to part with their most valuable effects."[2] (*Tia* or *tyee* meant "Chief".)

In John Walders' collection there were some of the red and white beads called "Hudson's Bay beads", made by the Venetians but repackaged in London. The opaque, light, sky-blue beads, round and smooth, of varying sizes, called "China beads" because of their resemblance to Chinese ceramic wares, were also from Venice. On John's table lay one fragment of the rare "Fancy beads" or "Flower beads", polychrome beads with a flower motif inlaid in coloured glass against a solid white background. He also had several beads called "Cornaline d'Aleppo", distinguished by a semi-translucent red exterior and a core of opaque white or pink, ovoid, round or tubular in shape.

There, in Potts Lagoon, I fingered a few of the incalculable millions of simple glass beads traded all over the world from the 16th to the 19th century, which brought immense wealth to Venice. The next day, walking on the beach at abandoned Karlukwees

village on Beware Passage, we paused to watch visitors unsuccess-
fully combing the beach for beads, almost as infatuated with the
bauble as those who killed the animals to obtain them.

NEW VANCOUVER. HARBLEDOWN ISLAND

From Karlukwees it was a short (but careful) run through the
reefs of Beware Passage. Turning west around Dead Point we came
to the rotting dock of Tsadzis'nukwame, most inappropriately
renamed New Vancouver, an abandoned Indian village on
Harbledown Island. Looking back northeast across Indian Channel,
through a thin curtain of mist, we could see the empty houses of
Mamalilaculla on Village Island. We had come to look for two large
boulder heads which I had photographed many years ago. When
Dick Pattinson of Alert Bay saw the stone heads in 1971, he was
told by Jack Peters that one was found in the water at low tide; he
had pulled it into the village using a hand winch. The other,
belonging to his father, had rested in front of his longhouse.

The origin myth which Jack Peters recorded in 1980 does not
mention stone heads, but it is possible that the boulders represent
Da'naxdaxw, the New Vancouver Noah, who was told that a Great

*New Vancouver, Harbledown Island, photographed in 1933 by
Francis Barrow. (*COURTESY CAMPBELL RIVER MUSEUM*)*

Feast bowl, New Vancouver. (COURTESY CAMPBELL RIVER MUSEUM)

Flood was coming. The other men of Da'naxdaxw's band tied four canoes together and heaped their goods aboard this ark, but Da'naxdaxw built a house of small poles, coated it thickly with clay and sealed himself and his family inside. When the flood rose, the rest drifted away and were lost, but Da'naxdaxw and his family were snug and dry in their undersea clay box. After many months, he sent out a small bird but it returned, empty-beaked. After a while the bird brought a bit of root. Then it brought tree leaves, and finally, grass. Da'naxdaxw came forth to be the ancestor of his tribe.

None of Da'naxdaxw's descendants were at home when the Barrows visited in the summer of 1933 but they fed a hungry dog, and admired two 50-foot canoes and the totems:

> very interesting, & possibly older than at Mimkumlees [Mamalilaculla]. Amy got a couple of brass bracelets & the usual collection of trade beads.[1]

On that occasion Barrow photographed not only the house post and canoe but also two large feast bowls. They returned two years later with Mr. Oien, having attached the *Toketie* to his 28-foot cannery skiff to help propel it, in order to bring the Oiens' bull back to Village Island. On this second visit "we looked in the old lodge to see if the two old dishes we saw there some years ago were still there. They were not, and I am afraid we have lost the chance of getting them, which is too bad."[2] Unfortunately, when the people of the villages were away at summer fishing places, their possessions were easily stolen. Francis Barrow noted that two house totems lay in the nettles, the house having been cleared away. He remembered a photograph taken in 1900, with the chiefs in full regalia standing between the carved poles.

> Amy could find none of the old muskets she noticed last time, lying about, among the sand and clam shell on the beach.[3]

When we arrived in 1992, the beach was littered with rusted engine parts and broken glass, and a plaintive sandpiper followed us as we explored along the lonely shore. The mist thickened to rain, and we gave up our search for the stone heads.

MAMALILACULLA. VILLAGE ISLAND

We tied the dinghy to an encrusted post holding a few pieces of Mamalilaculla's rotting dock. A wide path led us first to the school, where branches of trees grew into the classrooms through broken windows. Once a small church stood nearby, with a metal plaque acknowledging the work of Kathleen O'Brien who, in 1900, left the confining life of a Victorian lady to build, in Mamalilaculla, with her own money, a small sanatorium called Lyuyatsi ("Resting Place") for tubercular Indian girls, and to establish a Church of England mission. Her friend Kate Dibben worked with her. On this visit we could not find the bronze plaque nor did the smiling young native guide who awaited us know anything of Kathleen O'Brien but she was most certainly there in 1935 when she showed the Barrows her little hospital.

> The totem with the sad face and tall hat that I took a photo of three years ago, the Indian boys rolled down the bank into the sea after uprooting it last Hallowe'en night. We saw a fluted house beam that was half sawn up for fire wood. I took some photos of totems and the ladies gave us afternoon tea.[1]

There were still fluted house beams and tall totems when we came in 1968, but in 1992 little remained from the high days of the culture. The village site had been extensively cleared with machete and axe, so that some of the Victorian houses stood clear of the rampant raincoast growth. The massive posts of a longhouse and the great beams were reminders of an earlier age. Carved on two rotting beam ends we saw the crumbling remains of wolves. Our guide led us to the sole remaining totem which lay flat, overhanging the beach. This was Henry Bean's pole, which he had left to his wife Mary, who declined $27,000 for it (according to our guide). The grizzly bear, supreme symbol of fearlessness, and the wolf survived, but a killer whale once rose above the wolf and an eagle topped them all. The eagle rotted away; when the pole fell over the bank, the whale floated off with the tide.

Behind us, as we examined Henry Bean's pole, a red roof sagged into the tangle of blackberry and thimbleberry bushes. It was the longhouse where that fateful last potlatch was held in 1921, an event which has epic importance for the Kwakwaka'wakw. I forced my way through clutching thorns and branches to get a closer look and was surprised at the small size of the collapsing building. During the first six days of the feast, Chief Daniel Cranmer of the Nimpkish tribe had distributed to 300 guests the equivalent of 30,000 blankets, hard-won wealth accumulated for many years. He gave away canoes, motor boats, pool tables, violins, guitars, sewing machines, gramophones, bedsteads and washtubs. He scattered cash

Mamalilaculla, 1992.

101

Mamalilaculla, 1992.

to scrambling children, and on the sixth day he handed out a thousand sacks of flour. Suddenly, into the dancing and the singing strode the Royal Canadian Mounted Police. We peered into the darkness inside that dank building and tried to imagine the moment...the drums falling silent...the startled faces. When Dan Cranmer was released from prison he was proud and unrepentent, and 30 years later he said, "I could call down anyone."[2] From the giving away of 320 blankets in 1849, potlatching had expanded to Dan Cranmer's 30,000 blankets in 1921. During those years the potlatch had become not merely a feast to announce status changes, with gifts to the witnesses, but a fight among chiefs for superiority, a substitute for warfare.

The Christian churches saw the strength of the old religion embedded in the ceremonies and sought to have them outlawed. The potlatch was prohibited in 1884 but not until the Cranmer potlatch was the law effectively enforced, mainly because of the efforts of Indian Agent William Halliday. In Mamalilaculla, on that calamitous December day, 45 people were charged. Of these, 20 men and women suffered the terrible humiliation of being sent to Oakalla Prison for two or three months. The ceremonial gear was inventoried, crated and shipped to museums or sold. In 1951 the Indian Act was revised to permit potlatching and in 1979 and 1980 the new museums at Cape Mudge and Alert Bay were built to display the potlatch regalia returned to the Kwakwaka'wakw.

We descended the steep bank to Mamalilaculla's shell beach, past the cement platform where the Indian guides had cleared the bushes covering a rusting Tetteryeovil motor, installed to drive a generator. What a noise it must once have made, when electric light shone from the windows of the Victorian houses. It was late afternoon. The guide and the other visitors had gone, and an eerie silence crept in from the forest pressing close behind the empty houses. Even the wind was still. The blank windows of the houses were like the staring eyes of the dead. Two ravens flew down and told us it was time to leave.

NATIVE ANCHORAGE. VILLAGE ISLAND

The following morning we went from Mamalilaculla around the southwest point of Village Island into Native Anchorage, off Canoe Passage. Muriel Blanchet called the bay "Indian Anchorage." One summer evening she anchored there in three and a half fathoms and woke to find the *Caprice* trapped in a little pool and lucky not to be aground, with the dinghy balancing on a barnacled reef. An old Norwegian, Mr. Oien, appeared on top of one of the reefs and invited the Blanchets for strawberries and cream. As they walked up to the Oien house they passed a pleasant cottage with windows, doors, verandah and chimney occupied by 150 White Leghorn chickens, which crowded to the windows to cluck at the visitors.

The Oiens sold milk, butter, cream, eggs, loganberries, strawberries and vegetables of all kinds to the many logging camps in the vicinity. On the 1936 visit, Barrow helped Oien turn the hay and get it into the barn and was rewarded with "one of Mrs. Oien's famed sausage pies with custard filling...a meal that should be recorded."[1] In his 1939 journal he made a note of lunch with the Oiens "the piece de resistance being coffee cream."[2]

Using Barrow's notes we identified a small shell beach where the Oiens' float must have been anchored, but the island shore looked as if the Oiens were a figment of Francis Barrow's imagination. A prefab building had been dragged up the bank, so we went ashore to enquire whether this was once Oiens' place. The young native men, the guides who were clearing at Mamalilaculla, assured us that we had found the Oiens' farm, but said the trail leading to Mamalilaculla was completely overgrown. Gone were the splendid garden, the clover field, the barn, the remarkable henhouse, the Oien house, and the acres of strawberries. They seem to have had as brief an existence as the sausage pie and coffee cream.

BERRY ISLAND PICTOGRAPH

Although it was a large face, the red ochre was so faded that most people, slipping through Village Channel in fast boats, would fail to notice it. It was on the Berry Island shore, a few feet west of the narrowest point of the channel, where a smooth, water-streaked cliff rose sheer above a ledge at the high-tide line.

Even less noticeable, because it is above eye level, was the large basin which hung in the cliff beside the pictograph face. The previous day, at Mamalilaculla, we were told by a native youth that this was the Chief's Bathtub, that slaves brought hot rocks from the village to heat the water. Perhaps we heard a faded remembrance of a time when the pool and the pictograph were powerful, possibly associated with puberty ceremonies.

As we came through Village Channel in 1993, my left eye felt bruised and my vision was slightly blurred; in the night a stab of pain had momentarily blinded me. As the eye had been more than thoroughly examined before we departed, I intended to ignore the discomfort, but I was feeling oddly fragile as we came to the pictograph. Would I lose the sight in one eye? When we came to the pictograph site the tide was high; Ray suggested that this was the time to examine the pool, since I could get into it fairly easily. I looked at the tide racing past the cliff and hesitated. Yes, I found myself saying, this is the moment.

I stood on the prow. Ray held the *Liza Jane* against the barnacled cliff, revving the motor to match the pull of the tide. I stepped onto a narrow edge of rock. Removing shoes and socks, I climbed into the pool, which was almost round, six feet in diameter, slightly pinched to a point at the outer edge. The water was about six inches deep, and below the water a pink algae covered the stone. I was surprised to discover that a large square block of granite had been placed at the back of the pool as a seat. I sat down, looking first at my feet in the pink bowl, firmly planted on a sand bottom, with a few stones scattered about. A small crab came to nibble the gigantic, white-lobed creatures which had invaded its world, and a tadpole darted about nervously. Then I became aware of the way the curving cliff wall enclosed me, as if I were inside a shell. Suddenly, all anxiety vanished and a wonderful feeling of deep calm enfolded me. The universe was as it was — perfect. I seemed to dissolve into it. For how many years — thousands, perhaps — have people come here to pray, to be silent and open, to wait for wisdom?

I wanted to stay there forever, but after a while, the *Liza Jane* came past and Ray shouted to ask if I was ready to leave. Reluctantly I climbed to the ledge, my shoes hanging around my neck on knotted laces, and when the moment came, I jumped back into my life on the *Liza Jane*.

SHOAL HARBOUR. CRAMER PASSAGE

It seemed never to stop raining, that summer of 1972, but the downpour had eased to a Scotch mist when we came into Shoal Harbour in search of the caves Alfred Williams of Sointula had described. I remember that the clouds were stuck to the trees like the angel-hair used to decorate Christmas trees. We couldn't find Alfred's trail, so we struggled straight up a hundred feet through dripping salal and worked our way along ledges of the steeply rising slope and just when we were ready to give up...there was the black hole in the cliff. Although our culture is only beginning to grasp the Gaia concept (the Earth as a feminine being), no one enters the womb-like darkness of a cave without some sense of the sacred. With the beam of a small flashlight probing ahead, we entered a water-sculpted series of four small rounded chambers, connected by passages; there was a narrow exit close to the wider opening we had entered. We did not know, at that time, that we had stepped into "the place where all the animals originated."[1]

This cave is called Nawalagwatsi, which means "receptacle of supernatural power." There is a dance, owned and performed by Mungo Martin at a potlatch in 1953, which was first danced in myth time in this very cave. When Mungo organized the Dance of the Animals, he had to make or borrow the masks and pay the dancers; he said that "formerly the performance involved more animals...he cut it in half because he didn't have enough money to pay dancers for all the animals."[2] The 1953 event was filmed. Visitors to the Royal British Columbia Museum can walk into a small, dark, inaccurate replica of the cave where a spotlight casts light upon some of the masks worn in 1953.

At that potlatch, many years ago, a central fire illuminated Mungo's house, flickering on the audience tiered around three walls and a screen across one end. Mungo reminded people that in "very old time" the animals held their own winter potlatch in the cave on Gilford Island. Four times animals could be heard stamping, crying and whistling behind the screen, then the drums grew loud and Wolf appeared, calling out the animals one by one: Raccoon, Mouse, Kingfisher, Owl, Marten, Wren, Land Otter, Squirrel, Deer, and Bukwis the wild man. During the dancing, Mouse was sent out four times because "We are not dancing very well, there must be a man around."[3] In the final scene, the animal masks were removed so the audience could recognize the human dancers.

In 1993 we found the beginning of the trail to the cave marked with a bit of red tape tied to a tree branch. The route up seemed even steeper than I remembered it, a matter of pulling oneself up from tree to tree, but the cave, when we reached it, was exactly as it had been in 1972. As we slid down the slippery trail through the wet forest, it was as if the rains of long ago had never stopped.

ECHO BAY. ALEXANDRA MORTON

As we were tying at Alex's float the dogs came racing down, the little terrier in the lead, barking hard, and the big golden retriever loping behind. Her son Jarret was at the top of the ramp, calling "Mocha! Kelsy!" The terrier retreated, unwillingly, the blonde dog following. We had arrived at Alex Morton's house not just because we loved *Siwiti*, her little whale story, but because all that summer we had listened to grumblings about the fish farms and we were told that Alex could answer questions. She came out to greet us, smiling, her long dark hair blowing in the breeze.

She has written her own story in her book, *In the Company of Whales*. At the Marineland of the Pacific in San Diego, it was her hydrophone that recorded the "raspy little cry" of Corky's baby orca, who died because Corky was captured too young to know about infant care.[1] When Alex had learned Corky's orca dialect, she piled pots, pans, tent, engine, food, tape recorder, camera, warm clothes and her new inflatable boat into her truck and drove to Alert Bay. On that first day, on the dock at Alert Bay, Corky's family came to welcome her: "It was sunset...the ocean was golden and their blows looked silver. It felt like the beginning of my life," she has written.[2] While studying the orcas, she met Robin Morton (a filmmaker), married him, gave birth to Jarret, and then, one terrible afternoon, Robin was drowned. Jarret kept her going, kept her moving, kept her from collapse. Now, when he isn't in school, Jarret sometimes steers while she observes and records.

Once, when she was alone in her boat, in the Blackfish Sound shipping lane, she was so absorbed in the activities of Corky's family that she failed to flee from the approaching fog. Suddenly she was engulfed in the white blindness. Then her hydrophone picked up the throb of an approaching vessel. Panic rose through her like fire. At any moment a towering metal prow could cut her in half. In this moment of blind fear...WHOOOOSH!...the orcas surfaced around her. She knew she was safe with them for they would avoid the ship, but if they dove she wouldn't be able to follow them. However, they stayed with her, so close she was afraid her propeller would hurt them. She followed them and when they had led her out of the fog, they disappeared. Although they had been travelling north, they had reversed direction in taking her to safety.

The Broughton Archipelago at the eastern end of Queen Charlotte Strait is Alex's place on the planet. She lived first in a floathouse, then bought land at Echo Bay and had the floathouse pulled out of the sea. Her boat is tied at her doorstep. Her camera and notebook are always beside the door, to be snatched up as she dashes out when the whales come into her area. Because she has spent so much time (since 1984) in her small boat watching the marine activity, she has witnessed the arrival and spread of fish farms. Far from being a benign industry, fish farming, which in British Columbia provides about 2,000 direct and indirect jobs, is having a devastating effect on the wild stocks which have supported 33,000 or more workers (commercial and sports fishermen and the businesses associated). In 1992 at Nelson Island, Colonel Pond shouted, "If you have no fish, you'll have no tourist industry!" Is it a coincidence that after Wells Pass (the entrance to the Broughton Archipelago) was sealed with fish farms, the oolichan, salmon and prawn stocks plummeted?

In 1993 there was almost no oolichan run at Kingcome Inlet; when the oolichan larvae come out of the inlet, the local fish farmers don't have to feed their fish, for the penned fish eat the oolichan. Prawn fishermen, complaining to Alex about "dead zones" down current from the fish farms, showed her the grey slime of decayed food and excrement which had smothered the prawn habitat. Recently, fishermen have been pulling in horribly diseased fish and there is "growing evidence that caged fish can stimulate disease epidemics and exponential population explosions of parasites."[3] Heavy fish-farm use of antibiotics has led to the emergence of new strains of disease for which no cures are known. There is also the uncertain genetic effect of the "Atlantics", escaped species from the fish farms.

After only three years of salmon farms in Ireland there was a "catastrophic collapse across all year-classes of sea trout" which had to migrate past the farms.[4] The accompanying sports-fishing industry also crashed. From Scotland, Norway, France and Chile have come similar reports. When northern European countries began to organize against them, the multinational corporations moved the farms to British Columbia's comparatively empty coast and lax protective legislation. In 1985 a staff of five people approved hundreds of fish-farm applications at the rate of one per day and some farms were given financial assistance; at the same time funding for Salmonid Enhancement was frozen. In British Columbia there are "guidelines" for salmon farms but all of them are being violated. "All the plants and animals in an area fit together like a puzzle," Alex has written. "If you have only one piece, like a whale in a tank, you really can't see how it fits into the whole picture. This kind of puzzle is called an ecosystem."[5] The fact that we humans are a part of this coastal ecosystem does not seem to enter bottom-line business thinking.

They escorted us down the narrow ramp to the float, Alexandra and Jarret in the lead and Mocha and Kelsy tumbling over each other and tripping us as they fought their way through the human legs. Not so long ago a fish-farm owner climbed this ramp to Alexandra's door and opened the conversation by asking, "How would you feel if I shot your dog?"

TRIVETT ROCK. PENPHRASE PASSAGE

North from Shoal Harbour the silvery morning mist dissolved and thinned and a soft light shimmered on a smooth grey sea. As we approached the opening to Simoom Sound, we watched for Trivett Rock, for the tide was low. A black lump poked through the pewter surface. Trivett Rock? Or the end of a deadhead? As we came up to it, it opened startled seal eyes and was gone, a magical act, leaving little circles on the silken sheen. It is the fact that we cannot see into that world below that makes it so fascinating, so threatening. Down there monsters linger amid the valleys and hills and the fields of waving plants; mountains rise up to rip our hulls.

Our depth sounder traced that invisible landscape but failed to find Trivett Rock, on which the *Cassiar* foundered in 1917.

It was the famous Captain Bob Wilson who was taking the *Cassiar* north from Simoom Sound on a dark night in August, "proceeding as usual when suddenly she was brought up with a crash."[1] She struck Trivett Rock at 2:30 A.M. and immediately began to sink. There were 58 people on board, including a Mrs. Johnson. Boats were quickly lowered. The *Cassiar* was going down fast, but no one abandoned the ship until Mrs. Johnson was safely seated in a lifeboat. Then the crew piled into the boats. The Vancouver reporter wrote:

> We rowed away, reaching shore in a few minutes. How long it took for the vessel to find bottom I don't know. We couldn't see very well in the darkness. When daylight came, nothing of the *Cassiar* could be seen.[2]

The story ended well. J.W. Dunseith, the postmaster at Simoom Sound, "looked after everyone in fine style, there being plenty of food and the ship's cook helping."[3] Four days later the *Cowichan* picked up the passengers. The *Cassiar* was patched, refloated and towed back to Vancouver. When she was repaired she gave several more years of upcoast service.

Best-loved of all the coastal steamships, the *Cassiar* was a lucky ship. Her stout, 120-foot wooden hull had been converted from a freighter in 1901. She had 42 berths, a "loggers' saloon" with open berths, a smoking room and a lounge. The crew of 29 included two bouncers, nicknamed Black and Red, who coped with the drunken rowdiness of the loggers. When she was "retired" in 1923, she had logged nearly a million sea miles along this inadequately charted coast without losing a single passenger. Anyone who seeks a glimpse of the *Cassiar* during her retirement years can rent a video of Charlie Chaplin's "The Gold Rush", in which she served as a movie set. Her only major accident was the smash at Trivett Rock.

J.W. Dunseith returned to his duties at Simoom Sound. Some years later he moved the floating post office (complete with the name) to an inlet just north of Echo Bay, thus putting two Simoom Sounds on the charts. In the new location, his community had a floating badminton court. Dunseith might have grown old in service if he had not swallowed drink provided by Sam Wong, who had added lye to his brew to give it more kick. Burning up inside, big

John Dunseith drank quantities of ginger ale as he waited for the steamer. When it came, he was winched on board but died on the way to the Alert Bay hospital.

No kelp marked Trivett Rock and nothing marred the shimmering grey surface except the prow of *Liza Jane* slicing into Penphrase Passage.

KINGCOME INLET. GWA'YI

As we rounded Petley Point I was so stunned by the splendour of the skyscraping peaks and the sheer verticality of the point that I almost missed the pictographs, tiny red figures just above the grey-green sea at the base of the cliff. Francis Barrow sketched them in 1933, finding them "quite amusing" but "from an archaeological point of view they are of little interest."[1] From his point of view they had been made yesterday, since they recorded a potlatch held in 1927. Above a black copper and a red copper (with two pieces removed), five cows (one white-faced) were marching towards a large copper and five smaller coppers beyond. This is, however, a pictograph of great interest: we are shown the power and wealth of the Tsawataineuk chief who gave the potlatch and some of Mr. Halliday's beasts which were consumed at the gigantic feast, and we

Pictographs, Petley Point, Kingcome Inlet.

110

know the date and event it records. Two holes have been drilled into a pictograph face. A logging cable hung from a tree far above. Farther along the cliffs, past the public float, there were more pictograph coppers and a sailing ship.

Coming up Kingcome Inlet we had neither passed nor met any boat and none were tied to the public float at Petley Point. In that colossal amphitheatre of towering peaks we felt very small. We read the guidebook's warnings about the changeable river channels and worried about the grizzlies and wild cattle that roam the delta meadows, and we seemed as lonely as the clouds that touched the snow fields above. Should we attempt to go upriver?

At that moment a fast outboard came out of the river. I waved. It slowed, turned and approached, and its occupants climbed out to talk. A few hours later Ray was given a quick lesson in how to find the main channel to the logging camp and how to avoid being hung up on shifting mud banks. The following day, after several excursions up the wrong channels, we found the camp; our new friends were there waiting to walk with us, carrying a gun, to explore the old Halliday house. Later, they went ahead of us upriver to Gwa'yi village.

At Gwa'yi we stepped ashore where the river curved east and children were splashing and shouting. We walked between the band's office and the store, then across the wide, close-cropped green grass of the soccer field, to visit Flora and Dave Dawson. They settled here 50 years ago after the village had been deserted. Dave, who was born here, has devoted himself to restoring the life of his village, and the soccer field is one result of his energy. Their turquoise house had four windows facing us, three of them shuttered with blinds; behind the open fourth window Flora was baking banana muffins and keeping one eye on her beloved village.

With her permission we visited the old dance house. Pushing open the door, we stepped from the sunlight into the dank, shadowy interior. Light slipped in under the elevated rain cover over the smoke hole. It was a small longhouse, about 50 by 35 feet. At the far end, on a dance screen stretched between two carved totem figures, a Sisiutl and two bears were painted. Below the screen, the log drum had a serpent's head and tail. On either side of the two figures, large coppers were painted on the wall. I sat on a bench of split-cedar boards and let the place absorb me. There was a musty smell of earth. Birds walking and dancing on the roof sounded like dry leaves crackling underfoot. Here, in 1974, the people had performed the Grouse Dance for Chief Sam Webber's potlatch.

Many years ago at 'Ksan (near Hazelton) I had watched a boy dance the Grouse Dance. Seated in the shadows at Kingcome, as the bird steps rasped and scratched over my head, I began to imagine the dancer entering from the curtained back door, cautiously, crouched, bird-like head jerking from side to side, winged hands fluttering.

When Mrs. Edward Joyce was a child in this village, more than a century ago, her family occupied an open compartment in a building like the one in which I sat. The women cooked at the central fire. The food was kept in wooden cedar boxes — mostly dried fish and dried berries.

> Eulachon oil was always mixed with what we ate, you know, and myself, I think that was really nice. I even long for it yet, but my husband doesn't. Deer was smoked and kept for the winter, and clams and everything, seaweed, wild crab apples, wild rice and porcupine, beaver — that's a delicacy if you know how to cook it.[2]

In interviews recorded in the British Columbia Provincial Archives, Mrs. Joyce explained that

> as far as crests go, well, we have so much of it...my dad was from Fort Rupert as well as from Gilford Island, as well as Kingcome, and he had so many in the family. I guess around the time when the white people first came there, he was in that tribe that was so respected or so high class that his great-great-grandfather went from village to village and he could choose any woman he wanted, chiefs' daughters. And he could say, "Well, I want her," and you couldn't refuse him. Didn't matter whether he had twenty wives...that was the custom. So that's why we've got so many relatives all up and down the coast.[3]

As we returned to the soccer field, we saw the gleaming white Episcopal Church of St. George and the brightly painted totem pole beside it, both like toy things against the background of Noisy Mountain, towering a mile high over them.

What is life like in Gwa'yi nowadays? We read the notices concerning sexual abuse and alcohol workshops, and heard about accidental deaths and suicides. The native people place blame for these on us, whom they call the "Europeans". Many people, aware

Gwa'yi, Kingcome Inlet.

that we are destroying the planet that sustains us, look to the native cultures for wisdom, but how can the native people escape being corrupted by television values? Welfare can satisfy the need for food, shelter, clothing and medical care but, more than these, all of us need meaning in life, love, respect, solidarity with others. We all bear the responsibility for transforming our world.

Is that what Flora Dawson meant when she told a *Province* reporter that "She would like to open the doors of the longhouse, and let the sunlight in"?[4]

KINGCOME INLET. THE HALLIDAYS

I kept thinking how angry Lilly would have been. Her gigantic kitchen stove was grimy and rusty and the dining-room was littered with old magazines, bottles, junk. I felt a surge of energy, as if her ghost had taken possession of me; I longed to clean and scrub and hang bright curtains at the naked windows. That cupboard against the wall — that, surely, was the one Ernest tied across the thwarts of his rowboat, the surprise that he brought to her after four days of rowing from Alert Bay. In the big living-room someone had scratched over the fireplace the words "The big house will always be" but I think this house began to die when Lilly left it.

Did young Lilly Elizabeth have any idea, when she married Ernest Halliday, that she would raise her children and grow old in this distant fiord? In 1894, the delta at the head of Kingcome Inlet seemed like Shangri-la to Ernest — hundreds of acres of natural meadowland at the base of towering mountains, with a river falling down from a glacier, and friendly native people welcoming them. The following spring, Ernest engaged the captain of a small steamboat to bring in Lilly, their two small children, household effects, four oxen, two cows and a bull. A small log cabin became Lilly's home for the next 35 years. When she decided to have her third child in Comox, she and Ernest, the two children and a dog travelled for 14 days in a tiny boat, in the bitter cold of December. Her next two children were born at Kingcome and her last two at Comox (when easier transport was available). Of her seven children, two died of tuberculosis. Although most of the descendants of the other five live in British Columbia, there are none at Kingcome Inlet.

For the first 17 years, Ernest Halliday made a monthly trip by rowboat to Alert Bay, 60 miles away, a four-day journey, to sell his beef at ten cents a pound. When the day came that he had a profit of $28 to splurge, he bought Lilly that kitchen cabinet. Lilly would never forget the day she saw her husband wearily rowing towards her with this large piece of furniture lying across the rowboat.

By 1927, when B.A. McKelvie arrived to write the Halliday story for *The Province*, there were other settlers at Kingcome. The Hallidays had constructed dykes to protect the fields from the high spring and autumn tides. In that year they had sold more than two tons of butter to the logging camps and to the boats that came up the inlet. By the time the Barrows came to visit in 1933, the Hallidays had moved into the big wooden house beneath the mountain on the south-facing side of the valley, looking across to the hanging valley in the Kingcome Range, with Smyth Cone rising more than a mile into the blue air. From Lilly's dining-room I watched white puffs of cloud tumbling into that sky valley. Did she ever grow accustomed to this magnificence of mountains? The evening the Hallidays moved into the ten-room house, Ernest and Lilly walked to the edge of the river and threw the key into the water, so that the door would never be locked against visitors. When we arrived in 1993 the front entrance was blocked by a rampant growth of roses and blackberries, the sky-blue flowers of a huge hydrangea

114

determinedly bobbing above the tangle, but the back door stood open and the grizzlies which had been eating Lilly's raspberries could have curled up in her living-room.

In the early 1950s, Gilean Douglas came on the Columbia Coast Mission ship *Columbia*, with a camera crew filming the work of the mission. The *Columbia* was left at the river mouth. As their overladen dinghy struggled upriver against the current, they swatted "bulldogs" (huge horseflies) and bailed out the icy grey glacial water. Mrs. Dick came sweeping down from the Indian village in a 30-foot dugout with a powerful outboard motor attached, to give them a tow upstream through the uncertain channels. Along the edge of the river, lines of washing flapped in the summer wind. Later, Gilean and the crew returned from the Indian village to a good supper that awaited them in that dining-room with the great black stove and the old cupboard. Lilly, then 84 years old, told Gilean that in the old days it was nothing out of the way for the table to be spread for 30 or 40. She showed her the guest book in which the Reverend John Antle had written, on the day Ernest and Lilly celebrated their 34th wedding anniversary, "The rains descend and the floods come, but the House of Halliday stands because it is founded upon a rock. May it ever stand and may there be many happy returns of this New Year's Day." There was another entry in his name in 1946: "Here we are again after 21 years and the house still stands and may it stand."

"I'd like to start all over again," Ernest Halliday remarked to Gilean as they stood together on his float, with the river whispering past and the rose-tinted peaks watching the light fade far below. "Sometimes I sleep in the old log cabin and the years go by like this river. Good and bad years, births and deaths — I never want to forget any of them."[1]

On our visit to the abandoned house, we noted that the roof had started to leak and the foundations needed work. Where will the money come from to restore it, and who would live here? Ernest and Lilly worked hard to make their dream a reality, but they also had a market for their beef and dairy products and vegetables. Now the loggers fly in and out, and only the people of Gwa'yi have homes in the inlet. The wild cattle have to defend themselves from the grizzlies who share the meadows. A logger once watched the cows bunch together in a circle, horns facing out; when a great bull lunged at the bear, it slouched away. Nowadays both the comfortable logging camp near the old Halliday house and the Indian village upriver are well supplied with fresh food flown in to them; no one grows food at Kingcome any more.

I searched in Lilly's cupboard and found an empty jar which I wiped clean with a handkerchief. At the back door, from the tangle of bear-trampled bushes we picked Lilly's raspberries for our supper.

FORT RUPERT. VANCOUVER ISLAND

Soft morning sea melts
Into air, an oyster shell day.
Fishermen troll in the sky.

On glassy Queen Charlotte Strait at dawn, when the wind was still asleep, seven knots of speed seemed almost motionless. We moved towards Fort Rupert like a tiny bug crossing a very wide wet pieplate with an indented rim of blue mountains. Fishboats were painted on the distant azure sea. The sky was brush-stroked with a few white clouds except in the south, where a small company of soft little puffy-bellies advanced over the Vancouver Island mountains. We came into Beaver Harbour and anchored.

Soft coal was mined here in the 1830s. The natives examined the coal brought from Wales to Dr. William Tolmie at the Hudson's Bay Company's Fort McLoughlin in Milbanke Sound (about 100 miles to the north of Beaver Harbour), then showed the Hudson's Bay factor that similar black rock was to be found on Vancouver Island. When the company's mining operations and settlement drew the natives to Beaver Harbour to trade, a fort was built in 1849, a log stockade structure with gallery and bastions. Almost overnight, Ku-Kulz village was built. A handful of white men found themselves vastly outnumbered by up to a thousand natives. Missionary Richard Dowson wrote in April 1859 that the fort consisted of a wooden stockade about 28 feet high and 120 feet square, with a gallery around the inside, about four feet from the top.

> When I was there there was plenty of heads and other human remains to be seen on the beach, and one body of a woman was found fastened to a tree partly in the water, and the lower part all eaten away by fish.[1]

The old patterns of the culture were cracking and breaking as the arrival of the white-skinned people brought both unprecedented wealth and deadly diseases. From time immemorial the potlatch had been a most important institution of coast dwellers north of the Coast Salish area. Basically, the potlatch was a feast and ceremony given by a chief and his band to another band for the purpose of validating the adoption of new names and status, or to announce a marriage or birth, or to mourn the death of a chief. Like our state ceremonies, rigid protocol controlled the issuing of invitations, the order of seating, the speeches, songs and dances. Gifts were distributed to the guests, who were the witnesses of legal changes for a people without writing or lawyers or land registry offices. The potlatches were competitive; the chiefs who could afford to kill slaves had the highest prestige, but the value of gifts distributed was relatively small. Then the new wealth from the European fur trade encouraged the Kwakwaka'wakw bands to abandon their traditional villages and establish themselves at Fort Rupert, and the close proximity of jealous chiefs led to the spectacular rival potlatches, when vast quantities of goods were given away or destroyed. "European" diseases contributed to the breakdown of traditional customs and inheritance patterns. Fort Rupert was a lively place during the 19th century, as the Kwakwaka'wakw were thrust into the industrial age. The old songs will be sung again, but the Indians are modern people now, at a different level of consciousness, and the old gods cannot be revived. But the old divinities were god-images only. Both native and non-native people, in our time, struggle towards an understanding of life which will enable all to live in harmony with other forms of life.

We anchored off shore. The 19th century seemed only a dream as we rowed towards the village sleeping in the sun. At the east end of the beach, faces have been pecked into an outcropping of sandstone. Having recorded this site some 30 years ago, I was disconcerted on this recent visit to observe how rapidly the petroglyphs are being eroded by the sea. Most of the surviving figures were probably made in the 19th century, when the ceremony associated with the making of one petroglyph face was observed by men standing on the gallery of the fort. Boas wrote that

In olden times, when the hamatsa was in a state of ecstasy, slaves were killed for him, whom he devoured.[2]

In about 1849, two men, Mr. Hunt and Mr. Moffat, watching part of the winter dance ceremonial from the safety of the fort, saw a slave (from Nanaimo) named Xuntem running down to the beach, where he was shot. His body was surrounded by the native bear dancers who leapt and squatted around him, crying "hap! hap!". Chunks of flesh were cut off and the dancers, growling, ate (or pretended to eat) it.

> In memory of the event a face representing BaxbakualanuXsiwae was carved in the rock on the beach at the place where the slave had been eaten. The carving is done in sandstone, which was battered down with stone hammers. Near this rock carving there are a number of others and much older ones. The Indians have no recollection of the incidents which they are to commemorate. They say that they were made at the time before animals were transformed into men.[3]

The hamatsa ceremony, when a high-ranking person was initiated into the cannibal society, was a re-enactment of the transformation of human animals into "civilized" people.

Sitting on the beach, watching the rising tide licking the petroglyph faces, it was difficult to imagine Xuntem's body lying here while chanting dancers pranced around him. A raven flew down to investigate us and squawked "hap, hap", but it wasn't convincing. The central theme of the winter ceremonials was overcoming death and I reminded myself that Christians ritually devour the body of Christ to obtain life after death. The aggressiveness, arrogance and extreme competitiveness of the Kwakwaka'wakw enabled the culture to survive. The giving away in potlatching is both generous and malevolent, as those who receive are also swallowed up, vanquished. Is western culture any less violent, less competitive? Christ advocated turning the other cheek but how many have died in "Christian" wars?

Man-Eater BaxbakualanuXsiwae, with mouths all over his body, devourer of lives, giver of life, source of weath, lived at the North End of the World, with Qominoqa (Rich Woman) and a woman rooted in the floor of his house. The rooted woman is the enemy within Man-Eater's house, teaching humans how to overcome devouring death. Ritual is the tamer of the raw power of nature. Man-Eater was the "power" of the hamatsa ceremony. The patterns of a culture evolve to sustain a people in the economic niche in which they live. I sat on the beach struggling with my thoughts. Violent competitiveness seemed to work for the Kwakwaka'wakw before Fort Rupert was built, and for western culture in earlier times, but I stubbornly held the opinion that our common future demands a different ethic.

When the tide had drowned Man-Eater's face, we climbed a path to the Hudson's Bay Company chimney, about 300 feet from the beach, a roughly built stone structure about 12 feet high. A cedar tree sprouted from a crevice near the top of the chimney and may soon split it. The village seemed asleep and no dogs ran out to challenge us as we went to look at the new Band House. Earlier that morning, entering Beaver Harbour, we had examined through binoculars the Sisiutl painted and carved across the front of the building, but now the size of the Band House astounded us: 90 by 72 feet and 32 feet high, the outside structure formed by steel beams and posts.

Plumbers were completing their work, but allowed us to enter. Inside the echoing space stood the longhouse framework; four carved houseposts held up 70-foot-long cedar beams. Only the boards of board-and-batten walls were in place, so the vast space was illuminated by thin vertical lines of daylight. Hot sunlight came down in a white shaft through the square smoke-hole in the roof and fell upon the smooth earth floor and a pile of half-burned wood inside a circle of stones. On both sides, bleachers stepped part-way up the walls. At the stage end of the house, the drummers' two long benches faced each other across a 20-foot log which served as drum, and was partly carved as a snake.

As I sat in the bleachers and listened to the wind whispers vibrating in the great enclosure, I thought about Mungo Martin, for he was born here in 1880. Mungo was only 26 years younger than George Hunt who recorded for Franz Boas, the anthropologist. George Hunt, the founder of the renowned Hunt family, was the son of a Scottish father and Tlingit mother, but was raised at Fort Rupert. When Mungo married Sarah Constance Abayah Hunt, they adopted Helen Hunt and when Helen's son Tony was born, Abayah made sure that he would become an artist also. Henry Hunt, Tony Hunt, Calvin Hunt, Patrick Hunt, Richard Hunt are all renowned carvers. At Fort Rupert, where the old culture began its painful decline, this gigantic building may signal a transformed culture emerging.

GOD'S POCKET. HURST ISLAND

According to our 1952 marine atlas, God's Pocket had a clean bottom. An accident taught us more than we wanted to know about this particular bottom. Because I liked the idea of sleeping in God's Pocket, in 1968 we had chugged west from Port Hardy and north through Christie Passage and entered this small indentation on the west shore of Hurst Island. We were well entertained that evening, watching the fishermen arrive and settle to the task of checking their gear for the dawn run across Queen Charlotte Sound. Aboard the seiner *North Wind*, roped against us, the crew stitched white and red floats to the edges of a new, pale green nylon net. God's Pocket was jammed full that night. After we were snug in sleeping bags we would wake to hear another boat arriving in the darkness. Ray got up once and reported that they were six deep around us. But they all slipped away in the half-darkness before dawn, and when we emerged on our deck there was just our boat and the *North Wind* at the almost deserted floats.

We slept again in God's Pocket in 1973, the summer we searched for petroglyphs up the coast to Prince Rupert and the Nass River. When we had stopped in Alert Bay on June 21 to have Dick Pattinson look at our radio, an old fisherman on the dock had surveyed the sky and warned us that wind was coming. I was painting the back deck and felt that fresh cool wind touch my cheek gently. Then it strengthened, blew back the grey overcast and revealed the shining, snowy peaks on the mainland, and scattered eagledown froth across peaked blue waves. Dick closed the cabin door to keep it out. We had planned to head to God's Pocket but instead we moved behind the breakwater for the night.

The next morning when the wind had gone elsewhere, we went west across calm water towards a grey-yellow fog bank. We entered the fog, running by compass and depth sounder. It thinned as we turned into Christie Passage and we came safely into God's Pocket in the mid-afternoon, with more fishboats behind us. I had baked corn muffins as we came along, but as I had no muffin tins, it was a corn cake. When I gave some of it to a fisherman tied alongside us, he said it wasn't bad with lots of plum jam. We planned to depart with the fishermen before dawn the next morning, unless the fog was too thick, but in the meantime we had an hour to explore around the shores of Hurst Island.

Ray hauled the outboard motor from the hold to fasten it to the dinghy, which I was holding firmly against the side of *Liza Jane*. As Ray leaned over the stern, lowering the outboard motor, a man on the float warned, "Don't drop that motor — there's 25 feet of water here." And Ray promptly did just that. The lid had come loose.

There was a splash and he was left with the lid in his hands. We were silent, in shock. Without an outboard we could not continue. We would have to go back to Alert Bay and find another motor, which was not in our summer's budget.

The fishermen gathered around and one produced a cod jig weighted with lead. Everyone had a turn trying to hook the motor. Then they put about 30 hooks and a lot of lead weights on a line and tried dragging the bottom. Next they collected everyone's pike pole and wired them into a pole more than 25 feet long. I emptied out several large-size cans of fruit juice and took off the bottoms and tops of the cans to enable us to look through them deep into the water, but even using the can, I could not see the motor. Everyone tried the composite pole, then one by one they returned to their boats to cook dinner. Ray and I were left, lying flat on the float, gazing down at God's Pocket's murky bottom through empty juice cans.

Then another fishboat arrived and a native fisherman strolled over to ask what we were doing. He looked through the can, then asked me to hold it as, with his face tight against the can, he moved the pole. "I've got it," he said quietly. Slowly, hand over hand, he raised it, and the fishermen came to watch, guiding the pole as it looped over the floats. The motor appeared. Ray got his arms around it. He began dismantling the motor and washing away the salt. Darkness came but Ray worked on. The lights in the fishboats went off, one by one. Then Ray had to run fresh water through the reassembled motor and the noise was excruciating in the night. Ray said the fishermen understood that he had to get it running immediately if it was to be saved.

We slept a few hours and then were up with the fishermen and departed with them, a great streaming line of us in the grey light, sliding over the smooth black swells of Queen Charlotte Sound, headed for Egg Island. The outboard motor never failed us during the rest of the summer and we left God's Pocket's bottom as clean as we found it.

We were again in God's Pocket at the end of that summer. John Chappell has written that a trail from God's Pocket to the south side of Hurst Island passes a small meadow and an abandoned cabin. "Strong evidence points to the existence of a Sasquatch family on the island, perhaps centred at Meeson Cone above Harlequin Bay."[1] The native people living on Balaklava Island, he said, refused to go ashore on Hurst Island. But we followed that path to the clearings with the remains of a settlement, and all we found were the delightful Silvey children from Nanaimo, bright and polite. We were all poking into a rotted cabin when the air was split with a boom. I thought one of the boats in God's Pocket had blown up, but it was only the signal for the Silvey kids to come to dinner.

Perhaps next year we'll sleep in God's Pocket once more. But the rest of this seven-knot summer will be homeward bound.

PORT MCNEILL. ELIZABETH COSGROVE

The forecast was for gales and the wind was rising when I first met Elizabeth Cosgrove. She was putting diesel into her little 26-foot sloop (a Haida) named *Quick Match* as the lively thing bounced against the Port McNeill gas dock. The dock was swaying. The breeze was flapping flags. Elizabeth's thin, straight white hair was streaming out from her head. We were hastening away to get four passengers and a lot of freight to Swanson Island. There was only time for quick introductions, but I knew we would meet again.

A year later, when we were storm-bound at Forward Harbour, the *Quick Match* came in. I watched with binoculars as she carefully placed her anchor. A solid, strong figure with that bright, blowing hair, she surveyed her location with satisfaction and disappeared inside the cabin. I gave her a few hours to rest and eat before I rowed across the anchorage and was invited aboard. I had immediately liked the square face and direct blue eyes. Not many people live aboard their craft and few women sail alone, but I now understand that Elizabeth Cosgrove is not truly alone.

Born in Australia, she went as a young woman to England, married, enlisted in the navy during the war and was trained in radar technology. After a divorce, she worked in Toronto as a television technician. But her dream was to own her own sailboat and when she saw the Haida sloop, it was a quick match indeed. Abandoning her job, she sailed the boat down the Hudson River and along the east coast to Florida, and back. To arrange a life in which she could live on *Quick Match*, she studied marine radio technology in Winnipeg; the *Quick Match* went with her, trailered behind a large car. She put it into the sea in Vancouver. At first she took a job on a tramp steamer and inadvertently became involved in the drug trade in the Caribbean, but then she found winter work on cruise ships. In summers the *Quick Match* might be found in any corner of the coast.

She has fitted her life neatly into a small cocoon indeed, and when I climbed down into the interior of *Quick Match* — the kitchen counter is the step — I felt like Alice in Wonderland after she had eaten the diminishing pill. But it was all there: kitchen, cupboards, comfortable bunks, a swivelling table, books crammed on shelves, a small TV screen, radios, a toilet compartment, clothes storage, forward bunks.

A year or so ago, Elizabeth thought she should have a small house for the winter months, so she purchased a lot overlooking Degnen Bay on Gabriola Island, and there she had a tiny, neat dwelling constructed. But when the house was ready, she began to have anxiety attacks. She poured out her misery to a stranger she happened to meet on the Degnen Bay dock, and he asked to see the new house. When she showed it to him, he bought it on the spot, and she sailed away, carefree again.

Although she sails singlehanded (and it is quite a feat sometimes to reef the sails, steer and read the charts all at once), she is not truly alone, for she is part of a network of ham radio operators. Each evening at six, she joins a conversation with friends dispersed from Northern California to Alaska; they keep an ear on her.

We were moored at Port McNeill in late July, again dodging in for shelter from a storm in the sound, when we saw the *Quick Match* coming in. This time she had trouble — the bleeder screw for her high-pressure diesel line had leaked oil because the thread had been stripped, the drips of fuel had heated, and smoke was rising from the motor well. When we left the following morning, she was competently taking out the faulty piece.

As we chugged away across the ruffled surface of Queen Charlotte Strait, with the clouds shuffling about, hiding the scraps of blue sky, I thought about the millions of words flying all about me. What magic! I imagined them zipping past, intersecting, zooming into space and bounding back, rounding the earth. Foreign voices. Music dancing in the sunbeams. Word spinners in the wind. With our VHF radio, we eavesdrop on the fibre-glass yacht conversationalists, bragging about fish, commercial fishermen who never say where or if they are catching anything, whale scientists identifying pods...but we can't listen in on Elizabeth Cosgrove's ham crowd for they use lower frequencies.

She has chosen to sail alone, and yet is as closely connected to others as if she were living in an overcrowded ghetto...and all she asked was a tall ship and a star to steer her by...and a VHF and an HF and the not-so-lonely sea and the sky.

SOINTULA. MALCOLM ISLAND

Some people go to Sointula just to sip the artesian well water, crystal clear and sparkling, but we went there to taste the flavour of a community that valued both socialism and self-sufficient independence. We happened to arrive on a sunny day without the usual morning fog and afternoon westerlies. When we were moored at the capacious government floats at the inside end of Rough Bay, safe behind a high breakwater wall of very large granite boulders, we phoned our Sointula friends, who bicycled down to the dock to cram a year's talk into one moonlit evening. After climbing from the float up to the dock to wave them off, we peered over our gargantuan wall. Across the Prussian blue-black Broughton Strait, glittering with moonlight, we could see the thousand sparkling lights of Port McNeill.

In the bright morning, the floats were noisy with big seine boats hoisting high their great nets to remove them from the drums for storage. The trollers and gillnet fishermen were permitted to continue fishing but the seiners were probably idle until next year. I wondered if the fishermen on seiners and gillnetters knew that the spool on their boats was invented in Sointula by Lauri Mattias Jarvis. He came to Sointula in 1901 at the age of nine to live with an aunt and uncle who were among the first Finnish people to establish the utopian settlement. What beautiful dreamers they were! Fleeing from Tsarist oppression in Finland, the Finns found themselves equally oppressed in the Nanaimo coal mines of Robert Dunsmuir. They sent for charismatic, handsome Matti Kurikka to help them found a colony on socialist principles. "If the whole universe, such as we see it and conceive it to be, is one great being whose spirit visibly or invisibly appears in us," Kurikka asked, "then is it difficult for us to know what that love is which must be uppermost in us? Nature in us, human beings, seeks harmony."[1] So they called the colony Sointula, which means "Place of Harmony".

Founded in 1901, the commune collapsed unharmoniously in 1905, partly because the founding folk were unprepared for the raincoast wilderness: instead of loggers and farmers, there were too many poets, writers, lawyers, teachers and doctors. And even these relatively enlightened people were unhappy with the utopian concept of the equality of men and women and rejected the idea that women should receive the same wages as men, should have the right to speak at meetings and should be able to vote. But the blow that crushed them was the fire which destroyed their three-storey communal house in 1903, with the death of eight children and three adults. The disaster seemed to take the heart out of the colony. When the commune broke up, half the colonists left and the land was parcelled out in half-sections to those who stayed, who lived by summer fishing and winter logging.

Lauri Mattias Jarvis' uncle and aunt had stayed. In those days the fishermen were towed to Rivers Inlet in small, flat-bottom rowing skiffs. Fishermen in as many as 1,500 skiffs at one time would be hauling in nets 200 fathoms long, weighted, wet and full of fish; young men's hands were too soon arthritic, doing this exhausting work. Jarvis, who had opened a boatyard in Sointula, noticed a logging spool cable abandoned on a beach. The concept sprang into his mind: he designed and built the first gillnet drum, using the rear-end system of a Model A Ford. It revolutionized the fishing industry around the world. The drum was adapted for seine boats by another Sointula gillnetter, Ted Davidson. Weathered boatyards line the edge of Sointula's long, curving, pebble beach; from each grey structure a pair of rusted tracks runs out under the clear water. Down one of those tracks, a fishboat with the first gillnet drum had skidded. Lauri Jarvis only died about 25 years ago, and ought not to be forgotten.

The Finnish fishermen of Sointula made the first attempts to unionize fishing, which suggests that the beautiful ideas of the first settlers did not die in 1905. We bought food in the co-operative store, established in 1909 and still the shopping centre for the islanders. Most Sointula people live in small houses strung along the beach on the eastern side of Rough Bay, but new homes dot the southern shore of Malcolm Island out to Mitchell Bay. During the 1960s war resisters and hippies arrived and have gradually earned the grudging respect of the old-timers. Probably only about half of the island people are of Finnish descent now. Gloria Williams (whose husband's name was anglicized from Honkala) complained that the old values were not as strong, and growth in numbers has tended to fragment the close-knit unity of the early years. Sointula's disadvantages (the long, wet, grey winters and a degree of isolation) balance the advantages, which are not as easy to assess: a feeling of community, of caring for each other, of making their own fun, of sharing. I listened to Sointula talk and caught echoes of the deep wisdom of its founders. I drank their clear, cold water and wondered about the strong underground river from which it flowed.

ALERT BAY. CORMORANT ISLAND

The government dock was crowded with fishboats, close rafted. There was a constant coming and going along the floats, with boxes and sacks of groceries and gear being carried aboard, for the fishing season was about to open and boats would be setting out the following day. In a soft drizzle we walked west along the water's edge road to the museum at the very end of the native half of Alert Bay. As it is an inconspicuously low, grey, modern building, what we saw as we approached was the old, three-storey residential school, whose white paint, scabrous, was peeling off the red brick. Worse, in front of it stood a hideous totem pole with a broken wing dangling and eyes glowering. As if to complete the symbolism, a mountain ash had strewn red drops of blood on the ground in front of the empty school. This is the place from which Mungo Martin escaped after only three days of captivity, hiding aboard a fishboat that carried him back to Fort Rupert. It is painful to think about frightened young children, torn from the security of their families and incarcerated here, whipped for speaking their own language. Maggots of anger and hatred gnaw that generation of native people.

Inside the modern museum, we examined the coppers, masks and costumes which were confiscated by William Halliday in 1921 and returned to Alert Bay in 1980. The power of masks is mysterious, universal. When the human animal puts on the mask of another animal, does he become that animal? By the light of leaping flames the animal/humans danced and were possessed, and the people were enchanted, bewitched. Such ecstasy can indeed pierce the unconscious, touching deep roots in our animal origins. This was a powerful culture and the loss of ecstasy a devastating blow to it.

Because the rain was heavy and the day grown dark, we took a taxi back to the boat. When we spoke of the opening of the fishing season, the native taxi driver immediately blamed the lack of fish on the Americans.

"They're takin' our salmon," he asserted. "They're greedy." He spoke of the American "Salmon for Washington" campaign. Having virtually destroyed the salmon-rearing potential of their own rivers with power dams, bad logging practices and industrial development, the American fishing industry is casting for the salmon bred in the Fraser River. Controls on American "interceptions" of Fraser-bound salmon were settled in 1985 by a treaty which limited the number of fish Americans could take. Canadian fishermen made sacrifices to allow more fish to escape up the Fraser to spawn, to enhance the numbers of fish. Now the Americans have arrogantly declared their intention to take some 500,000 more sockeye than the treaty limit by refusing to count the Fraser salmon caught in Alaskan waters. (As each salmon carries parasites unique to the creek where it originated, their origins can now be identified).

A recent book by Geoff Meggs, *Salmon: The Decline of the British Columbia Fishery*, is a tale of the short-sighted greed and government policies that are pushing the salmon towards extinction. "When resources are reaped for the gain of a few or the profits of a few seasons, they will be destroyed, along with those who harvest them," Meggs has written.[1] The economists who wrote the 1982 policy calling for the privatization of our fisheries have stated that "common property is repugnant to the principles of a market economy."[2] Maybe so, but those are my fish they are privatizing, mine as a world and Canadian citizen, and controlling their harvesting for the common good is not in the least repugnant to me. Meggs has written that "it is clear that a reorganized industry could support hundreds, even thousands, of new workers, particularly if all possible processing is done in this country."[3] As the taxi driver deposited us at the wharf, he declared, "We've got to stop that Free Trade. We've got to stand up to those Americans."

But we must also learn to work co-operatively, negotiating harmony with regard to aboriginal fishing rights, resource management and habitat protection, fighting the further concentration of resource wealth in fewer and fewer hands. The Kwakwaka'wakw lived harmoniously with the environment, it is true, not because they were less greedy but because their population was limited by the worst drought conditions that limited spawning; in the bad years, starvation curbed the rise in their numbers.

In darkness the following morning, when we heard footsteps on the float and the growl of motors, we only rolled over for another few hours of sleep. When we got up, we were almost alone at the dock.

BLACKFISH SOUND. FOG

As we entered Blackfish Sound from the west, Swanson Island lay ahead of us, a floating green pancake. Then, as we watched, it slowly vanished. A great grey fog bank, a shapeless beast, was swallowing the world. We checked the chart for a refuge, not wanting to be blind in this freighter and cruise-ship lane. By the time we had dodged into Spout Inlet, Hanson Island, and anchored, even the shores of our cove were filming over, melting into mist. Then the blinding, white wetness engulfed us. An unseen bird splashed into invisible water. In the distance, the soft, muffled chugachugachuga of a fishboat faded into the cottonwool and was gone. The world was Prospero's island and had "melted into air, into thin air", dissolved, "and, like this insubstantial pageant faded, leave not a rack behind." I shivered and reached for a jacket.

> We are such stuff
> As dreams are made of, and our little life
> Is rounded with a sleep.[1]

The white-out of the world was like a bright night. The world had disappeared, and we alone survived, cradled in a small boat floating in a milk-white silence.

SWANSON ISLAND. GEORGANNA MALLOFF

One midsummer day in the 1960s we dropped our anchor in Freshwater Bay, Swanson Island, and to this day I remember leaning over to watch it fall slowly down through water as invisible as air, and shrug itself gently into the sandy bottom 30 feet below. Puffs of sand lifted and then sifted down on the flukes. We were hoping to buy bread; our 1952 atlas stated that, at Freshwater Bay, "Mrs. Janet Proctor has a fish buying station, a general store, and Home Oil gas during the summer, although she lives here the year around."[1] But there was not a single structure or person to be seen, and we disturbed only a few gulls.

What a difference when we returned in 1973 to visit the Malloffs. As we approached, our binoculars showed us a sleek wooden sea lion rearing from an island in the bay, a random scattering of buildings above the beach, a tall triangular pole structure, some fruit trees, and a woman on the shore piling seaweed into a wheelbarrow. Our anchor splashed again into that clear water, and Georganna Malloff stopped her work to welcome us. A Rhodesian ridgeback bounded down to the beach, her barking quickly silenced. Georganna took us on a tour. The triangular structure (1960s "pyramid power"!) draped with fishnet, made a three-sectioned enclosure for clucking chickens, three angry honking geese and some shy partridge. A new bulldozer stood at the edge of a plowed field where a great pile of stumps awaited burning. A steep-roofed plastic-sided building was Will Malloff's blacksmith shop. A sculptured Pan figure danced among the trees at the edge of the field. A floathouse, pulled ashore to serve as their house, had stairs made of huge cedar rounds curving up to a front porch above the beach. On the porch stood a sort of totem pole, a life-tree writhing with plants and animals (which is now in the Coquitlam town centre).

We feasted well that night. Just as the day faded to dusk, Georganna stepped outside to the porch and began to squeal and screech. "I'm calling the blackfish," she explained. In the silence of the bay the high and eerie notes squeaked like a rasping piccolo, strange and otherworldly. She fell silent and waited. I heard the buzzing of a mosquito in the quiet night. And then we were transfixed — the orca were circling slowly in the bay below us, and very faintly we could hear their thin, high-pitched keening.

Arriving to visit the Malloffs only two years after they had begun their life on Swanson Island, we gazed with awe at the island dream come true. It did not last. During one of the years after Georganna and Will had separated, Michael Modzelewski lived in their house. In *Inside Passage* he wrote that it was like a tightly built boat:

> Plates, cutlery, spices, glass jars of bulk food all shelved and racked shipshape. In the 'bow' a round table six feet across, six inches thick, milled from a Mendocino redwood stump, then sanded and varnished until it glowed....Between table and front wall, a daybed covered with a red Navajo blanket.[2]

When Georganna came back to this place, which was legally hers, she found it stripped bare of everything not rooted in the ground. Not one building had been left, not even the outhouse. Gone was the carved seal she had placed on a rock at the edge of the bay which, according to Modzelewski, "stopped even the killer whales, as they repeatedly leaped up for a closer look."[3] During the summer of 1991, she began to construct a lodge from logs and beach stones. When the winter rains began, she moved into a winterized tent. It was fortunate that there was a visiting boat in the cove that night in December when, in the darkness, the island bear raided her outdoor kitchen. "I got him away the first time with much clashing of pots and pans and brandishing a shovel," she wrote to me. "Then at 5 am he came again but this time decided to hop into the cherry tree and not leave. I cried for help, but it took forever for Randy to get to me with flashlights and bear repellent!

Randy helped me get Stein away from the tree and let the bear run off. The next afternoon I was towing a log from West Beach and saw Stein jump into the water, three wolves following - lean and snarling! How I got Stein to walk the log, get into the kayak hole with me and not overturn the kayak, I'll never know."[4] Modzelewski also described how "a howling wolf pack had insisted on encircling the clearing, exhausting the dogs. But when the guns cut in, the wolves ran off and silence returned."[5] Georganna got a gun to fire over the heads of the wolves, if they should return.

When we arrived in 1992, she had the first floor ceiling in place on a hexagonal building. Stones and boulders had been dragged or wheelbarrowed from the beach to construct an eight-foot stone wall and pillars. She had even found time to begin the transformation of the centre post of her hexagonal room into a flowering, fruiting pole. When we had climbed to the first-floor level, we watched the kayakers on Flower Island (across Freshwater Bay) getting ready to embark. Fishermen trolled in glittering Blackfish Sound, leaving a thin skim of opaque polluted air on the surface of the sea. We could see the fog bank lingering between them and Hanson Island, and far away, the blue mountain ridge of Vancouver Island walling off the distance. Georganna and Ray went to work to put up the posts for the second storey and to set in place the first of five windows to frame the view. I walked in her vegetable garden, with its fishnet fence hung from sturdy posts eight feet high. Delighted with the vegetables crowding the raised beds, I also thought about the daily chore of carrying buckets of water from the stream.

The bear still shares the island with her, but they are getting used to each other. Sometimes she hears him bumbling down the creek, turning over stones to eat whatever tiny morsels of food he can find. Recently she came out of her winter-tent at five A.M. and found him standing in the dawn light with an apple in his paw which he had just taken from her basket, and the surprised look of someone caught raiding the refrigerator. He scampered off and Einstein hurried to check out his buried bones. Slowly, with sweat and joy, sometimes deeply happy, other times lonely, Georganna rebuilds a dream.

TELEGRAPH COVE. VANCOUVER ISLAND

We went into Telegraph Cove to see Jim Borrowman's bones. It was late afternoon; boats were jockeying for space at the floats and fishermen were lined up waiting for a turn at the fish-cleaning tables. Since this community is accessible to trailered boats, has trailer and RV accommodation, and is one of the most picturesque places on the coast, it was not surprising that it was crowded. We were allotted almost the last space. Exposed to the wash of passing freighters as well as the thoughtlessness of fishermen with powerful motors on small boats, *Liza Jane* was as skittish as an unbroken colt. No sooner were our lines secure than we saw Alex Morton bringing *Blackfish Sound* in through the narrow entrance. As soon as she had found a place, she came to tell us some amazing news.

That day a group from the TV program "Prime Time Live" had flown in to make a film to discuss with all of America the question of the release of the orca named Corky. Paul Spong had taken the TV crew by boat to Freshwater Bay on Swanson Island, where he hoped to pen Corky until her family reclaimed her. As Spong and the "Prime Time" interviewer stood talking, on camera, an unbelievable thing happened: Corky's mother Stripe surfaced beside the boat! Corky's mother came and her message was recorded! Of course, people will say that her arrival was coincidental...

Paul Spong, who has a dispersed network of underwater microphones to bring the orca songs into Orcalab, his whale research facility on Hanson Island, has been leading the campaign to free Corky. At 26 years of age, Corky is at the upper limit of life expectancy for a captive whale, but in the wild she might have 25 more years, or longer. Those who make money from the captive whales argue that their function is educational. It is true that the first captive orcas taught us to recognize their intelligence and their gentleness towards the humans who slaughter or kidnap them. But "a captive whale has only a year, maybe two, before his mental health starts going downhill. Some get bored, lethargic. Others turn neurotic and perhaps dangerous."[1] Some just die, but others have bitten their trainers, or held them underwater. Perhaps the first captures were justified, but there is growing public opposition to the imprisonment of these magnificent animals in cement tanks, making them into circus performers for the profit of their "owners".

In 1989, Sea World parks were sold to Anheuser-Busch, the world's largest brewer. It is not surprising that the investors are unwilling to free a star performer like Corky, but questions are now being asked about the morality of this business. Once, in a Los Angeles motel room, whale-researcher Erich Hoyt turned on the television "and saw an ex-Canadian killer whale wearing giant sunglasses and selling used cars for Ralph Williams, who cackled, 'Orky sez you'll get a whale of a deal'."[2]

It was the orca named Skana who, in 1969, taught Paul Spong to trust her. Spong, Skana's trainer, was dangling his bare feet in her pool when she suddenly dragged her mouth across his feet so that her teeth gently touched both the tops and soles. Shocked, he jerked his feet from the pool. Then, courageously, he put them back into the water. Skana repeated the slash. Spong pulled up his feet. They repeated this until he could sit unflinching as Skana's teeth gently raked his quivering feet. Then she stopped. Whether this was her intention or not, Skana had deconditioned Spong's fear of her. Perhaps killer whales, who have no enemies except humans, do not know what fear is. Possibly one of the barriers between them and us is that we are a species evolved through fear.

As the *Liza Jane* strained at the Telegraph Cove float, we watched the whale-watching ships return: the *Gikumi* (Fred Wastell's boat, once used for delivering lumber along the coast), the lovely old *Clavella,* and the big, 60-foot aluminum *Lukwa.* That evening Alex, Ray and I walked around the boardwalk to Jim Borrowman's house. Clinging to the curve of the shore, the houses had been tarted up with bright paint and historic information signs, but the place still retained the feeling of a coastal village of the past. A.M. Wastell's sawmill was operating until a few years ago and is, itself, a museum piece. The new tourist shops did not seem out-of-place. The freight shed had become the headquarters for Stubbs Island Whale Watching, the business in which Jim Borrowman, a diver, was now involved. After sharing some of the early orca observation work, Jim helped to organize the campaign (in the 1980s) to save Robson Bight as a whale sanctuary. As we sat with the whale researchers in his comfortable living-room that evening, he switched on the whale-monitoring channel and whale songs were woven into our talk. The orca were very close, just outside the entrance to the cove. Late that night, when all the salmon fishermen were asleep preparing for their dawn exits to fish, I stood looking out into the silent darkness of Johnstone Strait, where I knew the orca, who fish by night as easily as by day, were singing, so close to me, but beyond my sight or hearing.

Borrowman's bones? He showed us the collection the next morning, under the great timber beams of the freight-shed attic. The gracefully curving, white bones of a young 20-foot grey whale were aligned on a trestle table. The bones of an orca filled a carton. We saw a Steller's sea-lion skull, huge next to a Dall porpoise skull. Jim hoped to build a museum to display the bones, assembled as they were when clothed with strong muscles. As I reached out to run my fingers along the pure, smooth, silken whiteness of a grey whale rib, I put out of my mind the picture of Jim, in boots and mask, struggling to extricate these bones from stinking flesh.

ROBSON BIGHT. JOHNSTONE STRAIT

We were monitoring the whale-research channel as we approached Robson Bight, delighted to hear excited voices estimating that there were 30 to 40 whales in the area. It was a bright, serene morning in late July, with the gillnetters setting their nets in a glassy sea. We shut off the motor and drifted outside the Robson Bight Ecological Reserve, watching fragments of the blue mountain wall appear and disappear in the thinning mist.

Some 30-odd years ago I was coming south down Johnstone Strait aboard the ferry, on an autumn night so stormy that even that huge ship swayed and lurched. By happenstance, I fell into a long conversation with a tall, dark-haired young man, who told me about swimming with killer whales. On the night when Bruce Bott was born in Vancouver, Washington, a blackfish swam many miles up the Columbia River. Bruce thought of himself as a member of the whale clan. Bruce came to Vancouver Island, where two encounters furthered his life dream of swimming with his "kin". First, in Pedder Bay, when the rare white orca named Chimo was almost drowned, entangled in the mesh of nets holding the whales captured by Victoria Sealand entrepreneur Bob Wright, and the whales were thrashing about in a frenzy, Bott plunged to the rescue. In those days, divers were unwilling to risk being bitten by those great jaws. Bott's second encounter was with an old man in Sooke who gave him a sailboat, the *Four Winds*, a 32-foot yawl built in 1906. Having no engine, it was equipped with long sweeps.

In 1973 the *Four Winds* carried Bott, Michael O'Neill, Peter Vatcher and Erich Hoyt on an expedition to make a documentary about killer whales. Graeme Ellis and James Hunter joined them, in their inflatable Zodiac. Support for the project had come from the University of Victoria, the Koerner Foundation and the federal government, with hydrophones loaned by the navy, and tape recorders, amplifiers and generator from the University of Victoria.

A fascinating account of that amazing summer was written by Erich Hoyt. He described Skipper Bott at the helm in his

> long navy peacoat, white sailor pants and an old telescope (picked up in a secondhand store before we left) with which he scans the seas for orcas. Bott, the purist, is the only one of us with the patience to focus its ancient optics and to try to hold it steady in the swells.[1]

Off Robson Bight they encountered whales. Hoyt threw a hydrophone into the water, put on headphones and started recording. A bull's high, black dorsal fin knifed the water only 20 feet from the stern of the *Four Winds*; then he was gone, diving deep, leaving three rings of water on the surface. From under the boat Hoyt heard "Yeeeeeee-ooo-ee!", so loud the tape recorder's needles danced in the red band. The call was repeated, farther off. That night, he practised duplicating the whale's greeting on a synthesizer. A week later he had the opportunity to play it to whales as they circled the *Four Winds*, singing out the same phrase that he had recorded. With no notion of what to expect, he turned up the volume pots on the synthesizer, pressed the keys in the pattern he had devised, and monitored the imitation whale phrase as it was broadcast.

> I held my breath. Two seconds went by. And then it came: A chorus of whales — three, maybe four — sang out a clear, perfect imitation of what I had just played to them — in harmony. They did not repeat their own sound; rather, they duplicated my human accent. They were mimicking my mimic of their phrase — which was a slow, stilted version of their original — rather than repeating the original.[2]

There are moments in our human struggle to relate to other animals when all of creation seems to shout with joy. When Bruce Bott told me about that evening on the *Four Winds*, after the whales had departed and the crew members had played and replayed the tapes and sat in awed silence, hardly able to believe their ears, I felt tears of happiness under my eyelids.

In August of that wonderful summer of 1973, the researchers were ready to risk swimming with the killer whales. They called it D Day (Diving Day, Doomsday or Deadly Dentures Day). Graeme Ellis flopped from a Zodiac into the water and snorkelled into a circling group of bulls. Then it was Hunter's turn. He has described the moment when he hung just below the surface:

> then, silently, as if in a dream, a young whale glided into view, slowed almost to a halt less than fifteen feet away and looked right at me. I stared back at him — and I couldn't stop smiling. Then he swam off, leaving me vibrating.[3]

On August 31, when the underwater movie camera had arrived, the *Four Winds* rocked at anchor in Robson Bight, where it was rough weather above but calm darkness below. Bott went into the black water with the camera and within a few moments a cow and a calf swam into his view.

> Not ten feet away, the cow's winglike flipper turned slightly, banking, and the big whale pivoted, revealing her entire length. In the shadow of the cow's broad tail and pressing close to her white underside was the tiny calf. It was nursing. They swept past the camera and were gone. Bott had gotten the first in-the-wild underwater footage of orca.[4]

(Six months later I sat cross-legged on the crowded floor of a Salt Spring Island living-room and watched, mesmerized, as the whales glided silently in the 16-mm. film he had shot that August day. I could almost feel the cold water swirling around me as the blackfish came swimming toward me, sliding by so close that the screen went black as the camera photographed the wall of dark skin. Then a whale eye filled the screen, seeming to examine me as it passed.)

When I asked Bruce how I might see his whales, he told me to stand on the shore of Robson Bight on the evening of July 31st. In the summer of 1974 we were there on that appointed evening, with a group of friends. We had driven north on the Island Highway, slept on the shore at Telegraph Cove, and motored south in outboard boats on a bright midsummer morning. The Tsitika River at Robson Bight has washed down a fan of gravel on which the whales rub and scratch. The water at the edge of the fan drops off to a depth of a thousand feet of dark water, but on the shallow gravel shelf minnows flashed and a flounder darted away. We waited, expectant, uncertain, on the pebbled strand as the light began to fade. Then they came. High black knives slit the silken surface, and we could hear the puffs of air expelled from their great lungs. We danced and called greetings. And that night, when the tide swelled into the river, the whales came into the Tsitika river mouth where we lay in our sleeping bags. In the stillness of the moonless night, we listened to their deep breathing so near us, like the pulse of the universe, and we drifted into sleep, floating with them in the cosmic ocean.

The Tsitika watershed has, however, been the most unharmonious setting for angry confrontations between MacMillan Bloedel loggers and the people who want to save the whales' rubbing place. The small area of reserve land will not protect the estuary, for clearcutting leads to flash floods which plug the gravels with silt and sweep away the natural dams that regulate the river and make pools for fish. These logging companies have a sad record with regard to stream protection. In 1992 an environmental audit on Vancouver Island revealed "that B.C. logging companies' compliance with government guidelines for protecting fish-bearing streams and creeks had generally been 'poor',"[5] according to a Ministry of Forests press release. This report followed an earlier announcement of a joint federal-provincial initiative to protect killer whales in the Johnstone Strait area, working with the federal Department of Fisheries. Twenty-seven recommendations from the Johnstone Strait Killer Whale Committee are to be "assessed" and "appropriate recommendations implemented".

There are very few orca left. On this coast there are two known congregations: 64 pods (a total of about 380 whales) in the southern division from Washington state to the northern end of Georgia Strait, and 16 pods (about 190 whales) in the north. There are also about 100 transient whales roaming the coast.

As we drifted on the silken sea that morning, the clouds were shredding and we caught glimpses of the dark blue mountains behind the bight and flashes of bright sky. Snakes of reflected blue slithered and blended in the mottled grey surface, like grey and black, watered-silk paper come alive. Then we began to hear little puffs and my binoculars spotted the tiny exhalations against the dark green of the shore. Suddenly whales came Ka-whoof! to the surface a few feet behind us on the port side, and diving beneath us exploded out of the water off our starboard bow.

When killer whales appeared near the beaches of the Kwakwaka'wakw, sick people would go to the water's edge, take a mouthful of salt water and blow it toward the whale, saying "Carry away all that is bad in me, supernatural one, long life maker."[d] And that is the prayer I blew toward the blackfish as they went past us into Robson Bight.

CHAPTER EIGHT

Southward, Stuart Island to Desolation Sound

DENT AND YACULTA RAPIDS

In the maelstrom of rapids, my marrow bone mistrusts the pulsating diesel. To ease its anxiety, we came south down Cordero Channel just as the tide was turning to flood. The timing was precise. John Chappell confessed that he was caught here, with a dead motor, when the east side of the rapids was flowing south, the west half speeding north, with whirlpools and foam everywhere. "I mention this extreme case," he explained, "to inspire respect, not fear, of these rapids. Please watch the backeddies."[1] I am, unfortunately, unable to draw a line between respect and fear, so we always try to go through on the slack, which requires calculation.

Stupendous volumes of water crush through these convoluted passages. Down from Queen Charlotte Strait rushes the swelling surge of the tide, and it no sooner pours into the Gulf of Georgia than it turns about and roars north again. Much the same volume is pushing in through the Strait of Juan de Fuca and barging back out by the same route. In Desolation Sound where the floods meet, the sea stays relatively stationary, only rising and falling, and the sun warms it for swimming. One of the worst corners for turbulent tides is the Yaculta Rapids which turn to flood 25 minutes after Gillard Passage; the tables for Gillard Passage for that date stated that the northbound waters would turn abruptly southward at 11:30 A.M. That was standard time so we added an hour and then we added the 25 minutes and came plodding along at 12:45, bucking the last of the ebb.

We passed Little Dent Island, where in 1792 the current spun the *Sutil* like a top. Henry Maurin organized annual picnics there in

137

the 1930s, on the day when the full moon of June guaranteed the very largest flood of the summer. He was the King of the Yacultas, the only man who ran the rapids at any stage of the tide, night or day. He played with whirlpools: "They're not bad if you don't buck 'em...it's the boils that are dirty. They'll pick you up and set you on the beach, and there's nothing you can do about it."[2] For the June picnic he took all the Yaculta dwellers and their food baskets to the rocky point of Little Dent Island. Kathrene Pinkerton was there. She has described how the flood began with a low mutter. Then, as the mutter grew to a dull roar, masses of water surged up and broke in wide, swirling boils:

> Huge whirlpools formed, spinning dizzily. A great tree trunk came lunging down, and a whirlpool seized it, stood it on end, waltzed it around and sucked it from sight. A quarter of a mile beyond, the tree was spewed out and tossed into a fresh welter of turbulence...the tide snarled and surged and doubled its might in savage thrusts as it crowded through the narrow channel. And when the great tidal push increased in power, the roar intensified. The whole surface of the channel would lift suddenly. Then I understood why the Yacultas had been known to put a large steamship on its beam ends and hold it there, helpless in the rapid's grasp.[3]

Frank Lightbody has written about going through the Yacultas in the 28-foot gillnetter *Melissa* to fish in Rivers Inlet. They waited for the slack with some eight other fishboats.

> We entered in single-file some fifty yards apart....The wisdom of moving as a pack soon became apparent. Those with the less powerful motors seem to be at the mercy of the dark boiling swirling whirlpools. Several of the boats were unable to hold any kind of a straight course as the powerful currents swung them all over the place. Only one boat stalled! Immediately two others battled to close in on his sides, tossed lines and towed him slowly forward until safer waters were reached.[4]

In 1991, when we came through Gillard Pass between Jimmy Judd Island and the Gillard Islands, we found a tourist world. A sprawling hotel complex covered the point of Sonora Island jutting into the Yacultas, and all around the shore modern buildings stood, with sleek white yachts tied close in front. We gazed about like Henry Maurin awakened from the dead. Nor is there anything except the name of the rapids to remind us of the fierce Yaculta Indians whose villages were protected by a resident sea monster at Sea Lion Point. As we reached the monster's lair, the tide had turned to flood and we were running fast. A great shining boil of water tugged at *Liza Jane,* and struggled to drag it around, but the sea monster was not yet strong enough, and we escaped its grasp. Powerful yachts can ignore silly old sea monsters, but my marrow bone respects them.

FAWN BLUFF. BUTE INLET

When he went hunting with his older brother August, who lived farther up Bute Inlet, Johnny Schnarr, the rum runner, always anchored in the cove tucked into the mountain wall south of Fawn Bluff. When the fierce wind called "the Bute" comes raging, this bay is one of the few safe anchorages up this long, twisting stretch of water. After his anchor had been firmly set, Schnarr visited Henry Leask and his two brothers, "well educated men and very interesting to talk to."

According to Schnarr "the Leasks had quite a little place."[1] He described rock walls for a walkway from the beach to the southern point, a net shed on a rock foundation out in the bay, and a water wheel on the stream draining Leask Lake, three quarters of a mile and a couple of hundred feet above and behind them. The Leasks had built a wooden pipe back to the lake to spin the wheel and were planning to run a small sawmill. They had also constructed a stone kiln in which they had fired a large piece of glass that they were grinding into a lens for a telescope.

When we got there it was hard to believe the three Leasks had spent most of their lives in this place. The stream draining Leask Lake still cascaded out of the trees, and there was a narrow rim of sand, but dense forest overhung the beach. As we rowed ashore we could see a cross planted just above the beach. Had one of the Leasks been buried there? I climbed up to read the name cut into the cross piece: it read "Toilet" and an arrow pointed south. We found an opening through head-high salal and a small cleared campsite, but we couldn't locate a toilet and we searched in vain for a rock-walled path to the point. Creeks had cut through the dense undergrowth on that side of the bay. We climbed the trail to Leask Lake for a swim.

The lake lay silent, cupped in the mountains. Homalco people used to hear the singing of whales in this lake, and they thought an underwater passage connected the head of Ramsay Inlet with Leask Lake and with Bute Inlet.

When we came down to the beach again, some sports fishermen had arrived to picnic and to warn us that they had seen a large brown bear with two cubs and a smaller black bear nearby. When the fishing guide told us that the Leask cabin, which once stood in the corner of the bay sheltered by the south point, had been burned years ago, we were able to discover broken stone foundation walls. The midden soil above the beach spoke of the much longer native occupation of this bay — the trail to the lake must be as old as their arrival at Bute Inlet. Where the great mass of Fawn Bluff sheltered a tiny anchorage from the Bute winds, only a trail, a few sections of wooden pipe in the stream and boulders in a collapsing wall survived to remind us that people had made their homes here. So little, so briefly, did our anchor disturb the sandy floor of this snug anchorage. The great cedars closed ranks behind us. The whales no longer sing in Leask Lake.

VILLAGE OF THE FRIENDLY INDIANS. STUART ISLAND

It is only 200 years since the four ships, *Discovery* (Captain Vancouver), *Chatham* (Lieutenant Broughton), *Sutil* (Captain Galiano) and *Mexicana* (Captain Valdes) entered the Gulf of Georgia, each bearing smaller longboats. (When the vessels were being rowed, the natives thought they looked like floating islands with burnt trees thrusting skyward.) In July 1792 both the British and the Spaniards visited a village on the northeast shore of Stuart Island, and Thomas Heddington made a drawing of it. With a copy of his sketch and the accounts of the British and Spanish visits to the site in hand, we hoped to identify the Village of the Friendly Indians.

On June 30, 1792, Vancouver's men, in longboats commanded by Johnstone, came to an inhabited village near the northeast end of the Arran Rapids. Vancouver wrote that

many came off in the most civil and friendly manner, with a plentiful supply of fresh herrings and other fish, which they

Village of the Friendly Indians, from a sketch by T. Heddington in 1792.
(Courtesy BC Archives and Records Service)

bartered in a fair and honest way for nails....A very narrow
opening was seen stretching to the westward, and through it
flowed so strong a current, that the boats, unable to row
against it, were hauled by a rope along the rocky shores
forming the passage. In this fatiguing service the Indians
voluntarily lent their aid to the utmost of their power &
were rewarded for their cordial disinterested assistance,
much to their satisfaction. [1]

Ten days later, on July 10, some of the Spaniards came to the
same place in their longboats. When they reached the mouth of the
Arran Rapids they saw that

the water was running out with marvelous rapidity and they
at once took shelter at the southern point of the entrance,
mooring the boats with a cable on land. Many of the natives
surrounded our officers without showing the slightest
distrust. These men were of medium height, well made,
robust and of dark color. The number of natives in this

place would reach 140, and they seemed the happiest in the strait, for being settled on the slope of a hill, with flats close by, they dwell in a fertile and beautiful country.[2]

The little bay a mile south of Turnback Point on the northeast shore of Stuart Island appeared to match both the descriptions and the sketch. Having anchored in 50 feet of water off the beach, we went ashore, observing how the beach had been partially cleared so that canoes could be drawn up. The valley was logged many years ago. Vaguely resembling Heddington's sketch, there was a sloping hill on which small, temporary houses could have been built. He drew what appears to be a stream or trail falling down the slope; no stream could have existed on that hillside, but there was a slight gully which may have been the route of a path. To the south of the village hill, a creek burbled noisily through the valley and cut numerous streams across the beach. This site was probably a temporary village used during the herring run.

Soon after the departure of the first explorers these friendly natives were displaced by the Kwakwaka'wakw people pushing south. The fierce Euclataws who gave their name to the Yaculta Rapids at the south entrance to the Dent Rapids became the most feared tribe of the southern coast, and the Village of the Friendly Indians was abandoned.

HOLE IN THE WALL. SONORA ISLAND

Laughing at Raven, the Homalco people called the hole in the cliff his chamber pot. On the charts the name is attached to the narrow passage splitting Maurelle and Sonora islands, but it originally referred to the hole, about a metre deep and almost as wide, which we found at the high-tide line about half a kilometre north of Bassett Point on Sonora Island.

Raven's power is ancient. The Norse god Odin was accompanied by two ravens, Thought and Memory, but even earlier, about 10,000 years ago, a raven sat on a shaman's pole in the cave of Lascaux in France. Across Siberia and down the Northwest Coast, the eagle appeared supernaturally in the form of Thunderbird, the lord of the skies, but Raven was the trickster, transformer and clown. He was also a shaman bird, pitting his wit and insolence against the impersonal forces of the universe, a beloved culture hero. Selfish, greedy, lazy, gregarious, sometimes wise, other times stupid, ravens are very human birds. Their ability to imitate other creatures enables them to convey messages. They have bonded with wolves, leading them to game and expecting a share of the food. They will work co-operatively to steal an otter's fish, one raven pulling the otter's tail until the animal drops the fish to confront his tormenter while a second raven snatches bites of the fish. It was Raven who stole fire and light for the benefit of humans.

Ethnographer Charles Hill-Tout recorded the following Salish tale in 1907. Long ago, the world was always dark because Kwaitetek the Seagull kept daylight shut up in a box, until Raven tricked him into releasing it. To do this Raven made some torches and went down to the beach where he collected sea-urchins. When he had eaten the contents, he stealthily spread the empty shells, spines upright, on Kwaitetek's doorstep. In the dark Kwaitetek stepped on them and was in agony. Then Raven arrived — just on a friendly visit, you know — and offered to remove the spines. He dug into Kwaitetek's foot with his stone knife. Kwaitetek screamed with pain. "Am I hurting you?" asked Raven. "It's because I can't see properly. Open your Skwail-box and I shall be able to see better." Kwaitetek opened the box a little and some daylight shone through the crack. Raven went back to work and dug into Kwaitetek's foot again. When Kwaitetek cried out, Raven said that he needed more light. "Here, let ME have the box," he said, and he threw the lid wide open and all the daylight rushed out and shone all over the world. Kwaitetek the Seagull wept bitterly and has been complaining ever since.[1]

I stood on the cabin roof as Ray edged *Liza Jane* close to the cliff, so that I could look into Raven's chamber pot. Perhaps the Homalco people laughed because a pot on its side would challenge even so clever a bird.

WALSH COVE. WEST REDONDA ISLAND

From Pryce Channel, the narrow opening of Waddington Channel (which splits East Redonda from West Redonda Island) was invisible almost until the moment we entered it. A mile down the channel, we rounded the Gorge Islets and found Walsh Cove crammed with boats. With difficulty we joined them. All around the shore yachts were anchored with stern lines tied to trees, parked side by side like automobiles in a parking lot.

This was (is?) a sacred place. We rowed across to Butler Point, an impressively high, sheer granite cliff overhanging burial caves and rock shelters. We found the two pictograph panels about ten feet above high water. In one, a square-headed figure danced beside a copper, but whether this was meant to represent a chief buried in one of the nearby caves, or a spirit power, no one can say. In the second panel, leaping fish surrounded a symbol too blurred to identify. I crawled into a rock shelter close to the pictographs and felt the terrible mass of black granite rising 150 feet above me. Did a native boy once crouch here, learning to endure aloneness, hunger and fear in order to become adult? Did the rain sweep past and did the roar of wind in the trees sound like the voices of the ghosts of the dead lying close by? Above the rock shelter a large red hand was painted on the cliff. Perhaps a child-adult drew power from imprinting the bones of Earth, the source of life?

We picnicked on the smooth granite shelf below the pictographs and then I sketched while Ray pulled a small cod for our supper from the deep water where the cliff disappeared in the dark. We were part of the summer scene. Perhaps some day we will come in winter, alone, to feel the sacredness of this place.

TOBA INLET

We ate breakfast at dawn while the other boats slept, motionless and mirrored in their water beds. Perhaps some mariners heard the grinding of the anchor hoist and the growl of the motor as we slid out of Walsh Cove. We were going up Toba Inlet in search of the place where the Spaniards in 1792 saw the tabla (a painted sign) after which they named the inlet; although the British preferred to use naval and aristocratic names and usually ignored those on the Spanish charts, the name Tabla, corrupted to Toba, has stuck. Valdes made a drawing of the tabla, a unique sign indeed.

We had a few clues: According to Espinoza y Tello, Captain Valdes left to explore Toba Inlet on the morning of June 25, 1792, in the launch of the *Mexicana*, with provisions for eight days. Then, "at nightfall Valdes returned in the launch, having explored a considerable arm of the sea, which he called Tabla, because on the coast to the east he had seen on the shore a kind of wooden plank, on which were drawn various geographical figures, as was clear from the sketch which he made of it."[1] Erna Gunther's research led her to state that Valdes found the painting at a village site on a steep rocky island. There is only one tiny islet in the whole length of the inlet, and it does lie on the southeast side, a few feet from the shore, about two-thirds of the distance to the end. We set off to examine that islet.

As we entered the fiord, the rim of the sun burst over the mountains to the east — an orange ray shot across the water and we felt the warm, gentle stroke. The night mists still lay in the high valleys as we moved down a shining corridor of pale green water, between the shoulders of mountains, each one a fainter shade of blue in the distance. Our prow cut into the smooth surface like a knife slicing green silk stretched taut. About 12 miles into the inlet we approached the islet, which at first we could not see, so closely did it blend into the shore. Then, through binoculars we observed that it was inhabited by a family of seals; we moved towards them so slowly and quietly that they almost failed to notice us, and one female nursing a pup declined to budge at all. It was a small, low islet, with a few trees and a survey stake topped with a nail. It was neither steep nor high and did not appear to be associated with a village site.

The nearest possible village site was two miles away, south along the shore, where a collapsing cabin occupied some flat land near a stream. A mile farther, a spectacular waterfall came slithering down the smooth granite bones of the mountain from a great height, then dropped noisily into the sea. In the morning sun a hundred threads of silvery water glittered on the mountain slope.

The painted boards of the Indians have usually been associated with burial sites. The rainbow-crowned figure on this particular

The "tabla" seen by Valdes, 1792.

145

board with what looks to us like a pail between his legs has called forth some ludicrous comments. The five animals on the sign are probably goats. To qualify as a hunter, the young male had to kill a goat, which required great agility and skill. Among the neighbouring Sechelt, the blanket made of mountain-goat wool was the unit of wealth, and this sign may signify the wealth and power of a chief. To become a chief, a man had to accumulate wealth and give it away at feasts, and the strange circles may be a count of his wealth, or his feasts.

By noon the sheen was gone from the milky green water and it had crinkled into stretched seersucker as we descended the inlet. When we came out into Pryce Channel the westerlies had blown up a proper chop. Although the provenance and meaning of the tabla were still mysterious, we had been given a jade morning of rare loveliness.

REFUGE COVE. WEST REDONDA ISLAND. THE COUGAR

I had read about the Refuge Cove Cougar in the newspapers and all that summer upcoast people retold the tale. When we came ashore at Refuge Cove, serendipity led us straight to The Man Who Shot the Cougar. Reinhold Hoge was only talking us into purchasing the last of the sticky buns at his hamburger stand when he began to tell us city folks about city perils — his mother's house in Vancouver had been robbed while she was in the garden with her back to the unlocked door.

"Better a thief lifting a TV than a cougar in the kitchen, like the Refuge Cove Cougar," I remarked.

"But that was MY KITCHEN!" he replied, and the story tumbled out.

Reinhold explained that wolves, released from their isolated territories by clearcut logging, had moved south, exterminating the deer, and had even reached Redonda Island where they had wiped out not only the deer but also the resident beavers. Because there were no deer, the cougars were starving, and the young, inexperienced, hungry, teen-age cougars were the most desperate. One cougar had taken to eating cats and dogs.

Reinhold had city visitors. When his brother-in-law had come in with a salmon he had just caught, he was followed into the house by the dog Fritzchen, and very close behind Fritzchen came the cougar. In the middle of a living-room full of people, the cougar got

146

Fritzchen's head in its jaws. The dog screamed. Everyone shrieked. Reinhold leapt upon the cougar. The cougar released Fritzchen who bolted outside through his doggie door. Someone opened the front door to let the cougar out. "Shut the door!" shouted Reinhold, thinking the cougar would go outside and get Fritzchen again. Six people and a cougar sprang frantically about, furniture overturning, the cougar smashing its head against the unyielding glass of every window in the room. Reinhold's 82-year-old father attempted to tackle the beast, and took out a small table. In the midst of this bedlam Reinhold searched frantically in the closets for some bullets for his .22. By the time the gun was loaded, the dazed animal was standing motionless.

"While shooting a cougar normally requires a licence, in this case Hoge did the right thing," the regional conservation officer later conceded, as he pondered the question of issuing a permit. All the residents of the cove came to view the body.

"Well, I had to do it," Reinhold said sadly, "or this paranoia would have continued, and we would have still been looking for the cougar behind every tree." He went on to discuss the insanity of speaking about imbalances in nature when the human species is breeding out of control, and many people are being starved out of their own lands by the industrial world's greedy use of their resources. When I thought of the young, inexperienced, hungry, teen-age cougars being the most desperate of their kind, into my mind came the youth gangs in Los Angeles and Vancouver and elsewhere.

According to Reinhold, now that there are not enough killer whales to keep the seal population in balance, and it is illegal to shoot seals, the fishermen tell of seals taking the salmon from their hooks. Yet when three tourists in a large yacht recently found an abandoned baby seal and brought it into Refuge Cove, it was kept alive until the tourists found an agency for abandoned animals which would care for it. Then the seal was flown to its new life at considerable expense.

"Baby rats are also adorable little mammals, but Brigitte Bardot has unfortunately not cuddled one of them," commented Reinhold. Alexandra Morton has observed that mother seals sometimes leave their young on a beach while they go out to feed. Then people think the pup has been deserted and "rescue" it, and when the mother returns, her infant is gone.[1]

Fritzchen recovered. Reinhold's visitors went home with the best story of their lives. Life in the cove slowly settled back into relative placidity, and Reinhold could again contemplate the advantages of a peaceful rural life. But in the Real World, the pope and the Pentecostals insist that women bear and care for children they do not want and the world does not need. The cougar story is a cautionary tale.

REFUGE COVE. WEST REDONDA ISLAND. JUDITH WILLIAMS

The exhibit of her very large, darkly mysterious paintings, which I viewed in the Art Gallery of Victoria, was titled "Whose Story Is It?" She said the work came out of "rib-crushing encounters with the sublime"[1], and I understood this to involve her intense experience of past and present at Desolation Sound. I peered closely at the sinister, seething canvases, where layered artifacts and bones lay jumbled. She has looked past the brief white-skinned presence on our coast, past the Spanish and British explorers, past the arrival of the native people, into geological time; perhaps we humans are ephemeral actors in this story.

When she is not functioning as an assistant professor in the Department of Fine Arts at the University of British Columbia, she is part of the ongoing story of Refuge Cove. We rowed from the wharf on a black night when the wind thrashed the trees on the shore and heaved the dinghy about.

With a flashlight we located the beach below the log house she and Bobo built when the Refuge Cove co-operative was formed in 1972. From this home overhanging the tides, she has explored the region, digging through layers of history and archaeology (she calls herself a "poetic archaeologist") and in "Whose Story Is It?" she littered her canvases with a thousand artifacts and bones, mostly jumbled, disconnected, relying on the viewer to re-experience the whole by paying attention to the fragments. I suppose I do the same thing. In the struggle to find meaning in my own life, I too attempt to save scraps and bits of this coast's present and past, trying to tease some pattern from the tangle.

Like groping our way into the paintings, we struggled up the steep path from the beach, our flashlight illuminating fragments like those that emerge from the darkness of canvases. We came into the warm cave of her log house, where we sat around the candle-lit table to drink and talk. A solid, strong, fearless woman, with hair hanging free and a firm chin, she has explored in the wake of the first European explorers of 1792, Captains Galiano, Valdes and

Vancouver. Their problem, she has written, "was their duality. They saw, and most of us still see, nature, the landscape, and native people as the 'other'. We/they are encouraged to do so. The 'other' can be used, dominated. This I consider a fundamental error. I don't think the 'other' exists."[2]

Yes, Judith Williams, you have put your finger on it. Who knows when it happened? Did the Indians, by descending from folk who trekked off across Asia and into North America before that fatal split (between humans and the rest of nature) occurred, did they manage to remain embedded in nature? When did humans became conscious of themselves in landscape, separate from it? Prodded by post-glacial climate change, almost inadvertently, humans "domesticated" plants (or were domesticated by the plants?) and arrogantly we came to think we could conquer nature. We invented the plough and dug canals to grow food where it had not grown before. The world's human population began its exponential upward curve. Now, thousands of years later, we begin to see ourselves as monkeys expected to fine-tune a computer.

The captains were not aware that their civilization was painting itself into a corner. For Captain Vancouver the problem was only a dark night of driving rain when you could not see where you were in a region of unknown reefs, "and by the influence of the tides we were driven about as it were blindfolded in this labyrinth." How admirably Judith Williams' canvases express this mood! The heavy squalls drove the ships from their anchorage. To add to the desolation, Vancouver was ill. And "not a fish at the bottom could be tempted to take the hook."[3] Weary, storm-driven and the fish wouldn't bite — many a coastal story-teller can sympathize.

So whose story is it? It is a tale made up of many millions of stories told by stones and plants and beasts and all who have lived on this coast. We who write our stories today are struggling to un-learn dominance, to discover how to live in harmony with all the story-tellers. Judith smiled at us across the candle-lit table in the house on the edge of the darkness, and then Ray and I faltered down the path, holding hands as our feet fumbled over rocks and roots, to find the black waves licking the dinghy pulled up on the shore. All our stories are endlessly unfolding, but perhaps we are slightly less blindfolded in this labyrinth than Captain Vancouver.

LAURA COVE AND MELANIE COVE. DESOLATION SOUND

Bringing our old boat into Laura Cove was like crashing a Vanderbilt cocktail party in greasy blue jeans. One of the 50 or more expensive yachts anchored there was so large I wondered how it squeezed in, and there was another which looked as if it could take off to fight star wars. In the silence of an enchanted evening, I was almost embarrassed when our boat suddenly emptied its bilge. Ah, if Captain Vancouver, who named this place "Desolation", could see it now.

When we rowed around to the end of Melanie Cove to pay homage to Andrew Shutler, it was disconcerting to find a modern Parks Department outhouse where his cabin used to be. His famous apple trees, unpruned and dripping grey lichen beards, are hemmed in by new vigorous forest growth. The stepping stones he placed for a dock were there, and a path climbed past his hard-won terraces, but few of the people in the sleek yachts would know that a most remarkable man had once lived here. Stewart Edward White was his friend; the finest description ever written of the exquisite skill, strength and courage of the handlogger is in White's book *Skookum Chuck*, a portrayal of Andrew Shutler. I first knew Andrew Shutler in Muriel Blanchet's account of her annual visits with him (she called him "Mike") and loved him because his credo was the one I was taught as a child and still like to recite:

> Look well to this day....In its brief course lie all the varia-
> tions and realities of your life — the bliss of growth, the
> glory of action, the splendour of beauty. For yesterday is
> but a dream, and to-morrow only a vision...[1]

Melanie Cove ought to have a monument to remind us of this man. Shutler, who had almost died in a fight with another logger, had been in the cove for more than 30 years when Blanchet and crew arrived in the late 1920s. By carrying up earth and seaweed, he had built the terraces on which he planted his apple orchard. At the bottom of the garden a small, trellis-covered bridge dripped with grapes. Shutler sold fruit and vegetables to logging camps. He took the Blanchets up the mountain slope behind the cabin to explain how he had handlogged up there, as he had demonstrated to White years before. There were giant logs in those days, that came thundering, crashing, rumbling down into the sea. But it wasn't only

Shutler's gardening and logging they respected. Both White and Blanchet examined his books — Marcus Aurelius, Epictetus, Plato, Emerson — and acknowledged the profound wisdom and goodness of this solitary man. He was a seeker. He wanted to know what made life worth living.

Blanchet described him, as he rowed out to talk to them, standing up in the bow and pushing forward on the oars. Wearing logger's clothes (heavy grey woollen undershirt, heavy dark trousers tucked into leather boots), he reminded her of Don Quixote:

> High pointed forehead and mild blue eyes, a fine long nose that wandered down his face, and a regular Don Quixote moustache that dropped down at the ends. When he pulled alongside we could see the cruel scar that cut in a straight line from the bridge of his nose — down the nose inside the flare of the right nostril, and down to the lips.[2]

When the Blanchets came the year after the old man had been taken away to die, "the cove rang like an empty seashell" and a raven flew out from above the cabin croaking "Mike's dead! Mike's dead!"[3] In 1933 the Barrows picked the flowers in his abandoned garden. "The late occupant greeted people with a shotgun and he had to be removed," Barrow noted.[4] As we rowed away from Andrew Shutler's place, I wished for his honeysuckle to flavour the dusk.

The Blanchets found Shutler's cabin stripped, but discovered that his books had found a new home in Laura Cove nearby, in the cabin of Phil Lavigne who could neither read nor write. We examined the remains of Phil's cabin, a crumpled heap of rotting wood, perilous with rusty nails, at the head of Laura Cove. The Barrows have left us a photograph of Phil Lavigne in 1938, standing in front of his small cottage, with the water of the cove in the background, and not a tree in the picture. They bought lettuce, carrots, gooseberries, goat's milk and young roosters from him, when he was "over 70 but looks much younger & gets the old age pension, $20 a month."[5]

As the golden light faded in the west beyond Eveleigh and Scobell and all the other islands that shelter these quiet coves, and the stars began to appear, the fibreglass yachts became white ghosts of themselves and their riding lights joined Andrew Shutler's "celestial harmony of the stars".[6]

FLEA VILLAGE. DESOLATION SOUND

Such a morning that was — when Judith Williams, Liz Magor, Ray and I found Flea Village! It is odd that it was ever lost. The Barrows knew precisely where it was, for their friends Saulter and Frank lived there. Somehow, in the last 60 years, this much-discussed village of the fleas faded into the landscape.

The story is well known: in June 1792, a number of officers and sailors from Captain Vancouver's ships explored an Indian village of which Archibald Menzies, Vancouver's surgeon-naturalist, wrote a lively description. He recorded the "intollerable stench", the lanes between the houses full of filth, nastiness and fleas "which fixed themselves on our Shoes, Stockings and cloths in such incredible numbers that the whole party was obliged to quit the rock in great precipitation."[1] I have always enjoyed the thought of the sailors leaping down from the village, stripping naked and plunging into the sea! Frantic, they scrubbed themselves and their clothes but failed to reduce the liveliness of the fleas. Even after the clothes were towed astern of the ships, the fleas lived, only relinquishing life when the clothes were boiled. Tough fleas.

But where, exactly, did this flight from the fleas occur? I decided that it was not an island, as many assume, but probably Copplestone Point. I had based this view on Blanchet's account of that terrible night when Phil Lavigne fled from old Andrew Shutler, who had come from Melanie Cove to Laura Cove to sit in Phil's cabin with a gun across his knees, his finger on the trigger and madness in his eyes. When Shutler let Phil leave the house, on the excuse of feeding the chickens, Phil ran like blazes into the woods.

> He had a small mountain to climb before he could get help from anyone. It was only a rambling goat-trail, and it was dark when he finally stumbled into the Salter place....The three of them fell into the old fish-boat and didn't stop until they reached Bliss Landing four hours later, and got in touch with the police boat.[2]

If a trail led from the end of Laura Cove to Flea Village, the "village" was not on an island, and Copplestone Point was the logical site. So we four went carefully around the point in a small boat, watchful for the submerged islets that cluster in the corner behind Roffey Island...and there it was, plain as the proboscis it resembled on the chart! There was the small beach where Barrow's friends slowly built their troller. There was the stream to provide water for the village. The almost-island was high and steep sided, just as Menzies described it in 1792, but it had a flat top, where lay the remains of an old iron stove, perhaps Saulter's. The top of the peninsula was accessible from the saddle (which was covered by a deep midden deposit). There was ample room where the little peninsula joined the mainland for the large Indian house which once stood there, and later, for Saulter's big pea patch. Such joyful shouts as we recognized it, the long-lost village of the fleas!

When the Barrows first visited in 1933, Francis "watched Saulter & Frank putting a plank on their boat, a West Coast troller, Model C, Washington K.D. Boat Co."[3] In 1934 they had only six more planks to split from one of the Copplestone Point cedars, to complete the hull. By 1936 the troller was ready for caulking. Two years later there was no mention of the troller, and Phil Lavigne told the Barrows that Frank had had to take Saulter down to hospital for a second operation, but when the Barrows got to Princess Louisa Inlet some weeks later, they learned from Mr. Easthope (of Easthope Motor fame) that Saulter had returned from the hospital to Flea Village. I know nothing more. Two loggers dreamed of being fishermen and patiently, year after year, cut wood, shaped and nailed it to make a dream become reality. And then one of them was ill. Life, I reminded myself, is only lived in the present, but in Andrew Shutler's credo, to-day well lived makes every tomorrow a vision of hope. It was the dream of the sea that gave the tang of joy to the logging, the growing of peas, the wet cold winters, the annual visits of boat-inspector Barrow. One day someone may tell us the end of their story. In the meantime, I will remember Flea Village not only for the tenacity of its fleas, but also for those dreamers, Saulter and Frank.

The falling tide was retreating gently as we left Flea Village. No scratching, scrabbling, naked sailors splashed and dunked in the bay below the beach. Nor was there a troller on the beach, awaiting caulking. But it was easy to imagine these things, when we had discovered where to look.

HOMFRAY CHANNEL. ROBERT HOMFRAY

Coast scenery is so spectacular that it is impossible to choose a favourite viewpoint. But one August evening, returning from a run down to Lund from Refuge Cove, we rounded Sarah Point and looked east up Desolation Sound, and were stunned with the splendour of what we saw. The steep purple walls of the sound faded to distant mauve pinnacles, rose-tipped in the slant of sunset light. Perhaps the Sarah Point view is particularly breathtaking because most mariners labour up the long, western coastline of the continent from Pender Harbour without a glimpse of the Coast Range. Then, suddenly, at Sarah Point, they see the peaks holding up the sky. That August evening, I found myself thinking about Robert Homfray, who saw all this in October 1861.

What a foolhardy young man he was, that Homfray! Some Hudson's Bay Company officers, perhaps conscience-stricken because they were aware that the company was dispatching him to almost certain death, warned him against the task, but "having a great desire to see new and strange sights and being possessed of a fair amount of courage, I determined to go," he later wrote.[1] Well, during his 1861 experience, he found enough strange sights to last him the rest of his life in Victoria, where he lived (unmarried) at 3 Quebec Street, joined the First Volunteer Rifle Corps, sang in St. John's Church choir, collected seashells, and died in 1902 in his bed, aged 78.

Of course, in 1861 he had just arrived in British Columbia, from England by way of the California gold fields, so he could not know the perils he faced as the first white person to venture up the Homathko River at the head of Bute Inlet — and in the middle of a severe winter, when the likelihood of being frozen could be added to the other perils! Alfred Waddington, that wily, ambitious entrepreneur, was promoting the scheme to put a road through to the Cariboo gold by that route, and someone had to look at the pass. Probably Waddington had difficulty finding men willing to go. The HBC provided three French-Canadian voyageurs (Cote, Balthazaar and Bouchier), Harry McNeill, two Indians, two tents, two muskets, two blankets each, two axes, one hatchet, one spade, "a small supply of provisions," and the usual beads for gifts; all of this list, plus Homfray, travelled in one leaky canoe.

They left Victoria in October, were "buried in the waves" as they crossed the gulf from Nanaimo, and "almost lost in heavy seas" east of Texada. As he came north along the coast, he must have experienced that rounding of Sarah Point. Perhaps at that moment, he questioned the sanity of leading this small party into that towering wall of snowy peaks. His account of the expedition was not written until 33 years after he returned to Victoria, for Mr.

Waddington in 1861 was afraid that his story "would prevent parties joining him in making the road through to Cariboo." Its publication might have saved the lives of those who died in the Chilcotin War which the road-builders caused. To this day, the road has not been constructed.

Because it is named after him, we assume that Homfray's party paddled north up Homfray Channel. Somewhere in this region they

> saw a large canoe coming directly to us from a dark chasm in the mountains across the Inlet, paddling hard....One of the Indians who was sitting behind me was so frightened that he fired his musket in the air....They came swiftly alongside, seized our canoe, and one of them jumped into it, the others holding on to the sides, and we were completely overpowered.

They were taken to the chasm and expected to be killed, but just as they abandoned hope there was a loud war-whoop in the distance and their captors fled.

> On looking behind us we saw a tall powerful Indian in his canoe waving his paddles in the air and calling out loudly. He was coming quickly towards us; we got out of the canoe and stood shoulder to shoulder on the beach, determined to die together. We had only two empty muskets.

But the chief of the Cla-oosh explained, translated by Homfray's two natives, that their captors were marauders from a distant tribe which lived by killing travellers. Their new friend took them up a river to his encampment, fed them mountain sheep, beaver and bear meat, and finally was persuaded to accompany them up Bute Inlet to the Homathko River. No one can now identify the site of the chief's village. My guess, based on no evidence, is that the murderous Indians issued from the north end of Waddington Channel, and the rescuer's village was at Brem Bay, just inside Toba Inlet. The musket which one of Homfray's group fired accidentally may have alerted the Cla-oosh warriors, and so saved their lives.

The full story of Homfray's many narrow escapes from drowning, starving, freezing, exhaustion, avalanches, wolves, grizzlies and natives is too long for a telling here. The Cla-oosh chief rescued them a second time and even provided the two canoes with warriors that carried them back to Victoria.

Homfray concluded his account by noting that the Admiralty in London had named Homfray Channel in his honour, "not far from where the six Indians took us prisoners near Desolation Sound." The geographers also put Waddington's name on the narrow channel that opens off Homfray Channel, although one can be sure that the shrewd old man never risked rounding Sarah Point.

HOMFRAY CHANNEL. THE LINDBERGS

This is Bud Jarvis' story, and he will perform it for you any time you interrupt his gardening at his snug seafront home at Seaford, Cortes Island. Unfortunately, I didn't tape-record him, but my version is, I think, fairly close to Bud's. About 20 years ago, Homer Bergren from Bliss Landing wanted to send a repaired outboard motor to Ivor Danielson, who lived next to the Lindbergs at a cove about a mile north of Lloyd Point, Homfray Channel. Ivor kept an eye on Eric Lindberg and his sister Anna, ages 85 and 92 at the time of this story. Bud agreed to deliver the motor. He zoomed up Homfray Channel on a blistering hot summer day and went behind a breakwater of cedar-log cribbing filled with stones. Hobbling down to greet him came Ivor Danielson, a tough, six-foot-two, 75-year-old Swede, lean, with a hawk nose and a shock of iron-grey hair. Because of a broken hip, he walked with a cane. Bud had just out-performed himself getting the motor from his boat onto the log float, but Ivor lifted it easily, with one hand, and limped up the trail, pointing with his stick to the cabin where Eric and Anna lived. Bud looked as he usually did in the heat: old tennis shorts, no shirt, unshaven, sweaty.

He knocked. The door was opened by a skinny old guy in his winter Stanfield's.

"Who are ya? Whadda ya want?" he shouted at Bud. Hoping to gain acceptability, Bud explained that he was the nephew by marriage of Norm Hope of nearby Refuge Cove.

"Whadda ya want?" shouted Eric, even louder.

Peering from behind the old man's elbow, a bent little gnome of a woman queried, "Who is it, Eric?" in a high squeaky voice.

Eric bellowed again, "Whadda ya want? Did you bring me any money?"

Half irritated, half amused, Bud asked "What do you need money for?"

"I'd buy WHISKEY!" bawled Eric, his ho-ho-ho laughter bouncing back from the black cliff nearby.

Bud had brought a box of things for Anna, sent to Refuge Cove by Anna's and Eric's Chicago niece who had visited her aunt and uncle a few months before Bud's arrival. Concerned about their situation, the niece had loaded Eric and Anna into a float plane and then aboard a jet to Chicago, planning to keep them there, but Eric and Anna had managed to escape and get back to Homfray Channel. Now they asked Bud to help them, saying that the niece had stolen their bank-record books. When Bud confessed he was a lawyer and could get new bank books for them, Anna raised her withered old arms to the ceiling. "You were sent from heaven!" she shrieked.

Never before had anyone welcomed Bud as an angel. When he became their executor he found that they had $100,000 in cash in various savings accounts, their pension money accumulating because they spent almost nothing. He drew up wills, in which they left it all to each other and then to people in Sweden, relatives they had never seen. It did not occur to them to leave anything to old Ivor Danielson, who had watched over them for many years. Bud suggested they leave Ivor some money.

"What would he do with it?" demanded Eric. But they left him $5,000 which Ivor never spent. Ivor had a stack of uncashed pension cheques when he died.

Herman and Eric Lindberg had pre-empted the land on Homfray Channel some time after the turn of the century. Don Munday stopped there in 1932. Coming up Homfray Channel and facing the long line of unbroken granite cliffs ahead, Munday dodged into the Lindbergs' bay for a night's anchorage. He saw two men rounding up a big flock of goats, their only garments black bathing-suits, their bodies smeared with charcoal and sweat, from land-clearing fires. Don Munday described how one of them

> drove his axe into a big block of wood, heaved axe and block over his head, deftly twisting the axe so that its descent drove the other blade into another block. He heaved up the double load and rested the axe handle over his shoulder, this being his method of carrying wood to the house for splitting there.[1]

Capi Blanchet, who visited the Lindbergs in the 1930s, described one brother as quiet and domestic, the other as "a regular dynamo of a man."[2] Doris Hope thought that Herman was the dynamic one. Blanchet certainly had a kinder reception from Eric than Bud Jarvis received. Eric met the Blanchet family at the float and invited them to the large, neat cabin where half a dozen loaves of fresh-baked bread were cooling on the table beside jars of new-made cherry jam. What a tea party! — hot bread, cherry jam, honey from their own hives, butter from the goats. When brother Herman came bounding in, he was a sharp contrast to the quiet Eric. The two brothers showed the Blanchets the acres of overcrowded walnut trees (grown too big before they got around to transplanting them), trenches of Cascara saplings (never set out because the price dropped), the vegetable garden, the spring, the cherry orchard, and the storehouse with a double wall of logs. It was a dream achieved with hard work and determination...and yet Herman was always devising new projects, never satisfied.

We went up Homfray Channel in 1993 to visit the Lindberg farm. On the mainland side the peaks of the Unwin Range towered above us, Mount Pardoe rising 5,000 feet and Dudley Cone 4,130 feet above the shore. A conspicuous curving wall of smooth, blackened granite, beginning more than a thousand feet above, formed the sheer south wall of their cove. The little homestead seemed minuscule at the feet of such giants. We stepped ashore on the pier; millions of stones were transported from their land-clearing to make this hooked promontory to shelter their boats. Much else remained of the Lindbergs' work: their house, boathouse, storehouse, the house of their friend Ivor Danielson, the wildly overgrown orchard, the grapes hanging on the rotting trellises.

Herman was the first to die, and Eric buried him on the hillside behind the house. Sister Anna arrived to live with Eric. The last time Bud came here, Eric asked him for some "short-of-breath medicine" and not long after, Eric was dead of pneumonia. Did Ivor Danielson dig a grave and bury Eric beside Herman? Anna was forced to return to Chicago. The Lindberg farm is private property now, guarded by four lively dogs. But I wondered if two ghosts on the hillside behind the house grumble about the crumbling condition of this homestead? And when the winter winds rage down Homfray Channel, does Eric sometimes roar for whiskey?

GALLEY BAY. DESOLATION SOUND. GEORGE DIBBERN

The diesel throbbed as I sat on *Liza Jane*'s back deck, coffee at my elbow, reading an unpublished manuscript by George Dibbern.

Sailing his 32-foot ketch, a Norwegian double-ender named *Te Rapunga*, across the Pacific, George Dibbern liked to stand right out on the end of the bowsprit with his back against the outer jib stay: "From there I could see nothing but stars and waves, and the motion of the ship made me feel as if I had wings...the ship and I were one, outward bound."[1]

> Aha! she was a storm bird, spreading her wings, and I was a sea rover, riding my wild petrel. I sang. With fury and chaos and destruction around me I sang...I felt like jumping overboard, like flying high into the sun or down into the hollows of the waves, scooping up the millions of pearls and diamonds thrown by every breaker. I felt like diving into that creaming foam. I wanted to be one of those gannets that shoot from high, head first into the glass-clear sea. I wanted to dance over the waves, turn somersaults in them. Finally all I could do was jump out of the cockpit and climb to the crosstrees. I was living, living, and I knew it![2]

How mundane was the plodding progress of our *Liza Jane* as we ran toward Westview en route to Galley Bay. I went forward to sit on the anchor winch at the prow, to see if I could feel like a storm bird. The wind lashed me, blew my eyes closed, streaked through my hair.

We had just left Sharie Farrell, who is/was the Gladys on the typewritten pages I was reading. As *Liza Jane* (at 32 feet, the same size as Dibbern's *Te Rapunga*) yielded to the battering winds of the gulf, I imagined myself with George Dibbern, Eileen Morris and Gladys Nightingale in 1939, as this same Gulf of Georgia wind blew them toward the place of their dreams, at Galley Bay. Coming around Sarah Point at the end of the Malaspina Peninsula, entering Desolation Sound, I saw with their eyes that shockingly wonderful view of the wall of the Coast Range. The splash of the anchor into Galley Bay seemed to belong to that time, more than 50 years ago, which George recorded:

> Curving around a lovely sheltered bay, it was two hundred acres of forested land. At the highest part there was a lake with trout, high enough to give us electric power; there were good pockets of earth for gardening, and salmon, cod, flounder and shellfish in the waters around. We were so

enchanted that we could not tear ourselves away from the place, but lived there in a dream, building it up in our imaginations.[3]

They talked of trails and fruit trees, a long, low, log cabin and a community of friends, and they bought it for the unpaid taxes. But the year was 1939. The Galley Bay dream fled as Dibbern, holding a German passport, awoke to the reality of his expulsion from Canada.

How glibly we spout about freedom, we who are bound by invisible chains. I climbed to the high point of the tiny islet that sheltered his Galley Bay anchorage (and ours) and thought that it should be named Dibbern Rock. His book, *Quest*, published in 1942, is not only a fascinating account of the wind-blown track of little *Te Rapunga* from Germany to New Zealand, but is also the log of an inner voyage, a struggle to throw off the bonds of nationalism, sexism and racism, a search for true freedom.

Born in 1889, the son of a father who had sailed schooners in the China Sea, Dibbern at 15 went to sea on the square-riggers. Knowing that the days of sail were over and unwilling to work on steamers, he jumped ship. In New Zealand he found his spiritual home among the Maori. In 1913, aged 24, he went to Rarotonga. Oh, the enchantment! He chose a place, but before he could pay over the money for it, World War I began. His dream was shattered when he was interned in New Zealand. Shipped back to Germany after the war, he married a lovely woman (a Botticelli, he called her), had three daughters, and drove himself unmercifully trying to support them in the terrible years of the 1920s. In 1930 at age 41 he was on the dole like 6,000,000 others. Everything they owned had been sold except the *Te Rapunga*. He knew he must escape or rot. The agony of abandoning his wife never left him but in time she forgave him, knowing that he could not have endured Nazi Germany and that she would never leave the homeland.

"At first I thought only of breaking the fetters to be free, but now a little questioning voice asks, 'free for what?'"[4] Dibbern was a Taoist: he took up the path in order to become the path. He was not an escapist, for escapists adapt in order to ease their way through a world they do not fit. Dibbern sought to live his ideals. Sailing under a world flag he had designed, and carrying his own world-citizen passport, he was on a quest, his journey a means to an end: "I must sail into the unknown, and as crew I have law-breakers, criminals — my passions, lusts, lies, laziness, and many other handicaps; but one power I have also, a heart full of warm love, love for man, for the world, for beauty, purity, truth, which we call God."[5]

Dibbern's quest did not end, as his published book *Quest* ends, with his arrival in New Zealand in 1935, for the book was not written until he came to British Columbia in 1939. The story of the years of sailing with Eileen Morris and his friendship with Gladys Nightingale, and the account of the writing of *Quest*, are told in the unpublished manuscript which I had obtained from Sharie (Gladys) Farrell and which I was reading as we came to Galley Bay. It had been written during World War II while he was interned for the second time (in the same island prison) in New Zealand. When the war ended and he was released, George and Eileen had a daughter; George won a sweepstake and bought an island, but he and the dream had grown old. When George and Eileen parted, the island was sold. At 71 he was stevedoring at a New Zealand port. He intended to return at last to Germany to see his family, but he died of a heart attack.

I sat on Dibbern Rock and watched the burning sun dropping behind the purple ridge of Vancouver Island. I heard Dibbern's voice: "The worst is not death but being blind, blind to the fact that everything about life is in the nature of the miraculous."[6] I could almost hear him shout, "I was living, living, and I knew it!"

PENROSE BAY. OKEOVER ARM. NANCY CROWTHER

We came too late to meet this unusual woman, for she died several years ago, but we wandered through her house, haunted before she died and haunted still. We went into Malaspina Inlet and south down Okeover Arm and anchored in Penrose Bay, a mile and a half north of the government wharf. Through the trees we could see her log house, wide and low to the ground. The beach was guarded by two large dogs, one black, one blonde. A young woman, one of the new owners, came down to introduce us to the dogs and the dogs to us. The road from Lund ends at Nancy's house, and the peninsula between Trevenon and Penrose bays will certainly make an excellent campsite and launching place for kayaks or canoes or trailered boats, which is all part of the plan. The group also hopes to restore the log house.

When Mr. and Mrs. Crowther with their son Dick and four-year-old daughter Nancy arrived in Powell River from Hertfordshire in 1927, they had to blaze a trail across the Malaspina Peninsula to reach the 135 acres they had purchased for ten dollars. Nancy shot her first cougar at the age of 13, when her father's sight began to

161

fail. When she was a child, her dresses were made of flour sacks, and the children's feet were sometimes wrapped in cloth when the family couldn't afford shoes. In the Depression,

> I got to the point that I couldn't stand up for starving. It just so happened that a goat freshened that morning and that extra milk put me back on my feet. We were mighty glad when a logging camp moved into the area, because they would buy bread and eggs. The tourist was a goldmine...[1]

At first she shot her cougars with a .22: "the only place to shoot a cougar for a sure kill is right in the center of the neck. It snaps the spine and kills instantly,"[2] she explained to an interviewer, who came to talk to her in 1964, when she was a quiet, 41-year-old woman who had divorced a husband, reclaimed her maiden name and returned to live in the log cabin with her aging mother. At that time she had seven dogs: "I know I have too many dogs but if I don't the cougars will maul them or the bears will kill them."[3] Her mother had packed supplies in from Powell River when her father was away working: "she might have twenty pounds of rolled oats plus cans of milk plus other stuff."[4]

We tramped through leg-deep grass and went into Nancy's house. Our hostess described the chaos Nancy left behind, but no one should be judged by their last years of decline. She took care of her parents until they died, raised goats, chickens, dogs and cats, cut and split firewood, cultivated a garden which produced all their vegetables, milked the goats, got honey from her own bees, made goat cheese, preserved the orchard's fruit, harvested clams and shot the cougars and bears who threatened her livelihood. As we pushed through the grass, the scent of Nancy's lemon balm made my nose twitch with pleasure.

In her last years she often slept in a car outside the house, because of the lights that moved inside. "And you," I asked our young hostess, "have you seen strange things?" She looked uncomfortable but confessed that there had been unexplainable lights both in the old log house and in the cabin by the shore.

THEODOSIA ARM. VIRA MAY SALO

When she was old, Vira May Salo (*née* Palmer) lived alone on her brother's land at the edge of the mile-long tide flats of Theodosia Arm. One morning she slipped on wet grass while moving a timber to reinforce a fence threatened by an unusually high tide, and was knocked out. "When I came to," she told Bessie Banham, who interviewed her in the Powell River hospital, "I finished the job." Then she limped home, wet and cold, started a fire and crept into bed. "Shouldn't have done that, because my leg stiffened up. I'm sure, if I had kept walking it would have been all right. Shucks, when they x-rayed my leg they found two old breaks that had healed by themselves." She showed her hand where a lump of gristle had grown around a broken bone. "It's as good as new," she said.[1]

Vira May, the seventh of the 12 children born to Sarah Jane Palmer, took after her mother. "You can see where Mrs. Salo gets her grit," Banham remarked.[2] Sarah Jane never entered a hospital until her last illness at the age of 89. In 1877, when she was 26, Sarah Jane lost her fifth child, Hatti, who lived only 18 days. Then, in 1881, an epidemic killed nine-year-old Rufus, six-year-old Julia and the baby Zophar. Perhaps it was these tragic losses that moved James and Sarah Jane to leave Wisconsin and cross the continent to Oregon in 1883, with Vira May (aged two) piggy-backed on her brothers Al and Bami. On an Oregon homestead, William, Lionne, Irene, Nelly and Kit were born. Often, Sarah Jane and the children were left to manage the farm, while James went off to trap beaver. It was beaver that brought James to Theodosia Arm. In 1899 Sarah Jane sold their possessions in Oregon and moved the family to Lund. Vira May, 18 years old and very pretty, promptly married Fred Thulin and lived in comfort and a degree of splendour in the new hotel in Lund. She and Fred had three children before their divorce. Her sisters sometimes came to work in the hotel, sleeping in a room over the bar, "and when things got hot and heavy, they looked through a crack in the floor and watched the men fighting down there."[3]

It was late August when we went looking for the Palmer farm and the place where Vira May Salo broke her leg. We anchored the *Liza Jane* at the mouth of Theodosia Arm, in behind the Susan Islets. The inlet ends in a mile of mudflats, so we knew, when we took the dinghy in on the high tide of early morning, that we would not be able to leave until the tide returned in the evening. A few geese scattered, squawking, as we sped across the shallow inlet. We pulled the dinghy ashore where there were other boats on the mud. Suddenly, two very large black dogs came leaping at us. Zeus and Humphrey stayed with us all day, pleasant companions after we recovered from our initial fright.

We hiked up a trail, met the dogs' owners and got instructions about roads. Along the way to the farm we met Edie Bennett and

Theodosia Arm.

her son Bruce, who once owned the Palmer farm and told us its
history. Sarah Jane and James built a house on rising land on the
north side of the river, above the annual flooding of the pasture
land, "amidst a wild life paradise of geese and ducks in thousands,
huge runs of salmon, and plenty of game in the woods."[4] They
established a cattle ranch, with up to a hundred head of Aberdeen
Angus cows, which they butchered, and sold from their boat to
people in the inlet. Sarah Jane competently used her rifle to defend
the cattle from cougars and bears whenever James was away. The
Palmers also made money logging, and son Bill remembered
drawing $2,100 from the bank in gold. "It was mighty heavy in the
packsack and the banker looked at me as if he thought I was a mite
crazy. But we hadn't been used to paper money...I suppose we were
a bit leery about the lastability of paper."[5]

Meanwhile, Vira May, who lived in Seattle from 1907 to 1912,
had made a second marriage. Not until 1920, at age 39, did she
marry for the third time. She and Charles Salo moved to the
Theodosia farm to help her parents. A year later James Palmer died
and was buried at the top of the hill above the homestead. Now it
was Vira May's work to shoot the cougars and wolves which
attacked the cattle. On one occasion after shooting a wolf, she
encountered a second which she also shot. But the second wolf

howled before disappearing into the dense underbrush and to Vira May's horror, wolf howls came in reply from every direction. Having only one shell left, she ran for home.

In 1923 Merrill and Ring, a big logging company, built a railroad track for steam locomotives which ran eastward 25 miles or more, and life in Theodosia changed, as thousands of people moved in. In 1940, Sarah Jane Palmer died, almost 90 years old, rich with grandchildren and great-grandchildren. In 1941, Charles Salo was drowned. For 20 years, he had sold Theodosia beef from his boat, but in the spring of 1941 he took out a driver's licence and bought a Chevrolet truck. Then he accidentally stepped on the accelerator while the truck was in reverse gear and shot backwards off the Lund wharf to his death. Vira May had to sell the farm. Her brother had taken a pre-emption of 160 acres where Ray and I had come ashore, and it was there that Vira May lived in her old age. "Everyone is good to me," she told Bessie Banham. "My brother tows logs for my firewood. I cut them up with a crosscut saw, then roll the blocks to my shed." Banham described her bright eyes, ready smile and keen sense of humour. Vira May expected to return soon to Theodosia. "As long as my leg doesn't dangle, why shouldn't I go home? Still got two arms and a good leg."[6]

Ray and I hiked to the farm meadows, now neglected, fences broken, old equipment rusting. We crossed the river, seeking the original Palmer house and orchard, but found only a few old apple trees. Bruce Bennett showed us where James Palmer was buried; when his grave was dug, the site had a view over the farm below, but now it is hidden in the forest, marked by a gravestone. His name and death date were enclosed within a heart-shaped frame, but what was carved above? Our fingers traced the lumps and hollows. Flowers? No! Appropriately, it was a beaver with a branch in its mouth.

In the late afternoon we sat on the edge of the inlet, at the place where Vira May once lived. When she was old, and alone, did she sometimes rest here to watch the setting sun? A mile west across the mudflats, we could see the silver sparkle of water, and as we munched the tomatoes and cucumbers Edie Bennett had given us, we watched it creep slowly towards us. When it came close, we moved the dinghy into the dry stream bed and climbed into it, feeling like Mr. and Mrs. Noah. The fingers of water snaked toward us, touched the dinghy and curled around it. Nothing happened for about five minutes; then we felt a nudge and the dinghy shuddered, rose a few inches and floated. We waved goodbye to Zeus and Humphrey. As we zoomed down Theodosia Arm, cirrus clouds like brushed angel hair warned of a change in the weather. In the middle of the night as we slept in our snug anchorage, I woke to the tapping of rain.

TIBER BAY. CORTES ISLAND

We anchored in Tiber Bay, north of Mary Point on Cortes Island, to check out the location of another Bud Jarvis story. Some of the weathered buildings on shore looked as if they might have survived from the time of Henry Tiber, who named the little inlet. The original pre-emption was, however, in the name of Schofield.

Bud Jarvis, who told me this story, was living at Tiber Bay some years ago. One afternoon when he had kayaked up Homfray Channel to help old Eric Lindberg with the writing of his will, he happened to ask Eric if he had ever met Henry Tiber.

"No," Eric replied, "but I knew Schofield. Do you want to know something interesting about Schofield?"

"Don't tell him, Eric!" interrupted 95-year-old Anna, in her quavering voice. Now Bud was curious and he urged Eric to tell him, but "Don't tell him! Don't tell him!" cried Anna again.

"C'mon Eric," begged Bud, ignoring Anna. "What is the story about Schofield?"

Eric looked from one to the other. "He was a member of Jesse James' gang," he announced.

"You shouldn't have told him, Eric!" wailed Anna.

If Schofield was a member of the notorious gang, how did the Lindbergs know about it, I wondered.

Oddly enough, Schofield died in his rowboat when he was fishing off the Tiber Bay shore. He was hit in the head by a bullet fired from the shore. No one ever knew who fired the shot.

When I returned to Victoria I read some accounts of the Jesse James gang, although I knew I wouldn't find the name Schofield, for those thieves and murderers shifted aliases continually. I was impressed by the number of people who might have been hunting the members of the gang, in revenge for their cruel and callous crimes.

The strangest part of this tale is the way Schofield died. A constant pipe smoker, Schofield was sucking on his pipe when the bullet passed through his jaw. Bud was told that Schofield died slowly in his rowboat, but had time to write words in blood, on the floor of the boat. He wrote, "Don't know what happened. Pipe exploded."

CHAPTER NINE

Southward, Lund to Princess Louisa Inlet

DINNER ROCK

The surging swells rose and fell, leaving a wide, wet band around Dinner Rock. On a dark night in 1947 the *Gulf Stream* lay there, her after-cabins submerged, a pencil of light from the spotlight of the fish-packer *Betty L.* drawing white lines on the people clinging to the vessel or scrabbling over the rock. I found my hands tight on the wheel of *Liza Jane*. Who does not know that sudden switch from serenity to terror...that totally unexpected big foot of Fate descending? Dinner Rock is as big as a city block and never submerged, but it was wrapped in the black cloak of an October night, and there was a heavy sea and a strong southeast wind. Captain Craddock had checked the vessel on a familiar route and left the wheel in the hands of the second mate, a normal procedure. For a moment my hands on *Liza Jane*'s wheel were the mate's hands. I could hardly unlock their grip.

"It was all over in about ten seconds," Captain Craddock later remarked. In ten seconds three children and two women were drowned. The sea had burst in and snatched tiny Jeanie from the arms of her father, Henry Pavid. "Nothing could have been done that was not done," Captain Craddock insisted. "One of the passengers, Norman Hope of Refuge Cove, performed exceptionally heroic work," reported *The Powell River News*.[1] The *Betty L.*, which happened to be travelling north in the wake of the *Gulf Stream*, got on the lee side of Dinner Rock, and somehow the survivors, bruised, bleeding from shattered glass or the sharp teeth of the barnacles, were taken aboard the packer.

Henry Pavid was on my mind when we stopped at Westview to find the cup-marked boulders near Grief Point. Leaving *Liza Jane* at

The GULF STREAM on Dinner Rock, 1947.
(COURTESY *THE POWELL RIVER NEWS*)

the moorage, we sped south in the dinghy along the shore. The sea was calm that evening. The long beach below Westview seemed deserted, but what looked like a rounded beach boulder moved and became human.

"Let's go in and talk to that person," I suggested, hoping to find someone who had seen the pitted stones we were seeking. When I climbed from the dinghy and waded ashore, the man awaiting us was Henry Pavid.

Born in Geneva before World War I, Henry went with his family in 1922 to a ranch near Kamloops. In 1924 he was delivering groceries on his bike in Kerrisdale. Graduating from Lord Kitchener School, he worked in a sheet-metal shop, but the Depression forced his family to take up a vacated pre-emption near Powell River. They soon abandoned homesteading to try logging near Manson's Landing, and it was not long before Henry had a steam engineer's ticket to operate donkeys. He took to coast life, bought and sold a fishboat; then he had a tug, the *Natco*, built at Lund from Toba Inlet spruce, and the Pavid Towing Company was born. He had married in 1945 and it was less than two years later that his first child was snatched from him. According to Pavid, the second mate was very young and inexperienced. When the ship hit the rock, the bow climbed up the sharp slope. The stern went under and the seas flooded in. At the same time the vessel went over on her port side. In the pitch blackness, Pavid found himself floating under one of the plate-glass side windows.

"I managed to break it with the palm of my hand. I don't know how I did but I did — I crawled out of the broken window. Blood was running down my face — I crawled on the side of the hull up toward the bow, got a life belt and returned to where I had been."[2] His wife got out the same window, but Henry stayed back, looking for their baby.

Little Jeanie Pavid was never found. Dinner Rock is her gravestone. Diver George Unwin recovered the bodies of the others. Unwin, with 9,000 hours of deep-sea diving, was a 228-pound giant, a formidable sight when loaded with 125 pounds of gear. The men on the rock watched him smashing his way into the ship on its side. The reporter from *The Powell River News* was there, in the darkness. He wrote:

> It is an eerie sight, watching the flickering shadows and the green undersea glow of the diver's light as he slowly makes his way about the ship. At 30 feet nothing is visible in detail and the swirling waters around the Rock gave the effect of a nightmare.[3]

Henry Pavid lives now in a house built in front of the home he and his wife towed down from Refuge Cove. "Coming towards shore," he remarked, "all you could see from the tug was a mass of greenery in every direction. Now all you can see is houses."[4] He still swims regularly in Malaspina Strait. Or he walks down from his house in the evenings, to sit at Grief Point and watch the sunset. Perhaps Grief Point is aptly named. One cannot love the cruel and hungry sea — "the dragon-green, the luminous, the dark, the serpent-haunted sea."[5]

GRIEF POINT

When we filled our water tanks at the Westview dock, we were part of the problem. Those hundreds of Westview residents who built houses on the slope above Grief Point did not know that they were destroying a salmon run. As a boy, Roy Padgett crossed the stream draining West Lake on the backs of spawning salmon. In the 1930s little West Lake was tapped as the water supply for the new community of Westview. Until this happened, the creek had a run of sockeye, then a run of coho, and in December a run of dog salmon. Roy Padgett thought that 10,000 or more sockeye went up that stream to spawn, but "the dog salmon run was so thick that we kids at school used to see if we could run across the creek — over here, on the flat — on the backs of the salmon, because they couldn't even move; they were just wedged in."[1] When West Lake water began to run into the bathtubs and sinks and laundry tubs and swimming pools of Westview, and began to spray out through lawn sprinklers and shower heads and be flushed through all those toilets, the sockeye disappeared in two years and the other species dwindled away more slowly. If a reservoir had been built to store the heavy winter rains, would there have been enough water for both fish and humans?

Once, these runs of fish supported the people who have left deep midden deposits at Grief Point. When the tide falls very low along the Westview Beach, the remains of a mile or more of fishtraps are revealed. The mapping of the traps was done by Sid Riley in 1976. At that time a local resident, Charles Churchman, said that an old-timer, Dr. Marlett, had told him that the fishtrap walls were about four feet high in the early 1920s and the cleared canoe skids were visible.

We came to the beach in 1993, not to look at fishtraps (which can only be seen in spring and fall) but to make rubbings of the boulders in which small pits or cup-marks (about the size of an egg cup) had been made. Scraps of evidence allow us to speculate about these cup-marks, which are very common on the coast and are generally located (like the Westview boulders) just below the high-tide line. In the British Columbia archaeological literature, Teit in 1900 reported that a Thompson River youth

> made round holes in rocks or boulders with a jadeite adze which was held in the hand. Every night he worked at these until the holes were two or three inches deep. When making them he prayed, "May I have strength of arm, may my arm never get tired — from thee, O stone."[2]

A report from northern California states that holes in stones were connected with weather control, and shamans were credited with the power to cause or to stop rain or snow. Sometimes these

Boulder with cup-marks, Grief Point.

shamans prayed for rain while sprinkling the rock with water, or recited a formula while throwing pebbles at the boulder. Native informants stated that the conical pits on the Gottville rocks in northern California "were made to produce wind and rain."[3] In southern California, women hoping to become pregnant would sit on these holes. In Hawaii the umbilical cord of a newborn was spiralled tightly and placed in a small hole made in rock and covered with a stone lid. The Sechelt people had a similar custom: the umbilical cord was placed in a cherry-bark cup and hidden in a rock crevice as close as possible to the birth place.

We were also at Grief Point to look at an artifact collection. Henry Pavid had watched the machines biting into the midden at Grief Point when it was subdivided by his neighbour, Gus Court. Court placed some of the artifacts from his site in the Grief Point Elementary School, including one he called an earring because

> that's what one Indian told me. I know it's pretty heavy and it's hard to imagine any man having a big piece of stone like that clinging to the side of his head, but what else could it be?[4]

As only one large, oval earring has been found along this coast (at the excavation at the canal separating South and North Pender

171

islands), another earring would be interesting indeed. We went to the school but found no earring in the locked case. Then the principal said we might like to see the stone figures from the Court collection, and we were astounded when a large, white orca sculpture was dragged from underneath the shelves.

When we left Westview early the following morning the houses, row above row, were still in shadow, and their owners had not yet begun putting West Lake water into their coffee pots. The sleeping houses slid past. The waves licked the pitted boulders on the beach. It was difficult to imagine salmon so thick in the West Lake Creek that they made a bridge for the feet of small boys.

VANANDA. TEXADA ISLAND

Coming south from Westview to steep-walled Texada Island, we searched with the binoculars for the entrance to Vananda. We saw first the white horizontal lines of one of the limestone quarries and a pale road that curved down into it. North of this quarry, we slid into Vananda Bay's deserted government dock. Ours was the only boat tied to the float, and long grass sprouted from the end of the wharf where steamships once docked. A boy with peaked cap over unruly hair, sloppy t-shirt and jeans buttoned up the front was fishing from the float with a length of wire. He leaned off the float until his face was almost in the water, examining "a really big one this-s-s-s long." When I asked about life in Vananda, he said there wasn't much to do — "Only about six kids. None my age."

We walked up to the village to see what was left of Vananda's glory days, our footsteps noisy in the silence. It was hard to imagine the 1890s when there were more than a hundred mines being worked on Texada, as well as limestone quarries; Vananda had the first opera house north of San Francisco, and three hotels, including one called the Bucket of Blood.

Overlooking the grass-grown wharf where the lonely boy fished, a monument told the story of the stormy night in January 1913 when the Union Steamship *Cheslakee* sank at this very dock. Ninety people managed to get ashore, but nine were drowned. The sunken ship was later salvaged and stretched, and had a second life as the *Cheakamus,* in service until the late 1940s.

"Vananda, that ghost town, looked so dead that we went on," remarked Francis Barrow in 1935.[1] There was certainly an air of peace and tranquillity on the hot August day when we arrived. A clerk at the modern grocery store didn't know where the hotels once stood. Then Fate kindly led us into the Vananda Store.

It was a small building above the road crammed with objects old and new — toys, china, antiques, hardware. In one corner was an old desk sprouting papers from every pigeonhole, and beside it, a scale from Vananda's first store (more than a century ago) which still gave accurate weights. In one corner there was a glass-topped candy counter. Tiptoe on a stool so that he could hang over the wonders within, a small boy with tousled blonde hair was concentrating on his selection, while an old man waited to fill his order. It was quintessential Norman Rockwell.

"Ah, this young man has excellent judgment," the old man remarked. "Look at this—" (he held up a long cord of red licorice) "—you see, he really gets his money's worth with this." The boy's blue eyes looked up; with a satisfied smile, he returned to the business at hand. "Now you have 25¢ left," the old man reminded him. "Ah, yes, he knows what he wants...goes for quantity not quality." Not until the last penny had been carefully spent, and the small boy had been towed away by a slightly impatient mother, did Mr. Kempe turn his attention to us.

He had been tending this store for 52 years, and when asked about Vananda in its glory days, he told us that the biggest hotel was right across the road from his store. He produced a picture of it taken in 1911 and Violet Seaman's memories provided further details:

> Each evening from the shafts and tunnels that burrowed into the earth, streams of grimy, sweaty miners streamed forth, spilling into paths leading to homes, hotels or bunkhouses. But within an hour or so, the grime and sweat had vanished. Bathed and changed, the young men in particular, dressed for the evening stroll, appeared after dinner with their stiff white collars and coloured waistcoats a fine contrast to their tailored suits. In summer white flannels added to the smart appearance of the masculine set.[2]

Mr. Kempe's photograph showed the Vananda Hotel's great balconies, where, on Sunday afternoons, people met to sit and chat. According to Violet Seaman:

Very feminine was the costume of the ladies. Frills, bows and ribbons were copiously used to give finish to the full length dresses with their tight waists and high necklines. Great masses of ruffles, lace and flowers, to all appearances sat lightly on the upswept hairdo's (though really fancy hatpins secured them to the "rats" or "buns") and, of course, high-buttoned shoes, especially white ones, were the last word in fashion.[3]

We could hike up to some of the mines, Mr. Kempe said. A trail from Legion Road, a heritage trail kept clear by local people, followed an old tramway bed to the once-busy gold, silver and copper mines, but one must beware old deep shafts and open pits near Emily Lake.

As we walked back to the boat, the fisher boy came pedalling up the road, without the fish. "I'm getting my rod," he shouted. "I saw him. He's really BIG."

POCAHANTAS BAY. TEXADA ISLAND

On this beach a white horse led the police to the biggest whiskey still in British Columbia. South of Vananda, Pocahantas Bay is a notch in Texada's relentlessly steep coast, with the high peak of Mount Pocahantas rising above it. When the whiskey still was producing 500 gallons a week of 96%-pure grain alcohol in Prohibition days, a scow in Pocahantas Bay would have carried a couple of tons of barley and some sacks of rye, all labelled "Pig Feed"; when the white horse had carried the grain into hiding, the scow was swiftly removed to Raven Bay to avoid attention being drawn to Pocahantas Bay. We hoped to find loggers working there — surely they must have come upon the old mine shaft where the still was once hidden. But the loggers had finished their work and departed.

McKelvie, writing about "McDugald" (a pseudonym) in 1928, didn't believe the part about the white horse, but that is the version which has achieved the status of a myth and it may have described the operation after the mysterious McDugald had vanished. Some have written that the still was discovered by airplane but others claim that McDugald had tied trees together to hide it from aerial reconnaissance. McKelvie seemed to know who McDugald was but declined to disclose his true name since the gentleman later established a "respectable life".[1] Some time before World War I, according to McKelvie, McDugald, a Scottish engineer who had worked for a distillery, inherited $30,000 and came to British Columbia to invest it. But being young and inexperienced, he fell victim to shysters and lost it all in bad land deals. As there were no jobs for engineers, he did pick-and-shovel work, nursing his anger and determined to regain his fortune. Service in World War I as a commissioned officer gave him a new start; in 1919 he was seen in Vancouver and then he disappeared.

About that time a taciturn, bearded man, middle-aged, arrived in Vananda by steamer, with a dog of uncertain temper on a rope. He bought a pack-horse, grub and powder and headed down a trail. Some weeks later he returned and registered a mineral claim near Pocahantas Bay, but when people attempted to question him, he either faced them with a rifle or threatened to set his dog on them. He was considered mad and was shunned. One day when he came into Vananda for more blasting powder, an old friend from Vancouver happened to be there and recognized him as McDugald. When McDugald had sworn his friend to secrecy, he took him to his diggings six miles away. He explained that he had worked out a way of recovering his lost fortune, and when he had made $30,000, he would quit this place. He had built a still in a tunnel of the abandoned Raven Mine, the entrance concealed by bushes. He was producing excellent whiskey, which he put into gas cans. As he had arranged his contacts before building the still, small boats brought him the supplies he needed for the distillery, and picked up cans of whiskey. "Just sniffin' the bung on one of those tins set your eyes to crossin'."[2] The bootleggers were told where to find their orders cached near the beach. McDugald would set off an occasional charge of dynamite to maintain the fiction that he was mining. The Raven Mine's old pipes brought in water from the spring above, the pipes concealed under earth and brush.

The Mounties were well aware that there was a hidden still somewhere, but the bootleggers could not be forced to reveal the source of their excellent stock. The following year McDugald's Vancouver friend returned to Vananda, and when he was certain that he was not observed, he set off for Pocahantas Bay. But no dog barked as he appoached. The place was abandoned. When he made enquiries in Vananda, he learned that the "crazy prospector", shorn of his beard, had appeared in town, given away the horse and boarded the Union boat for Vancouver. Did he carry $30,000 in his baggage? What about the tale of the white horse on the beach? Some of the bootleggers, who knew of the existence of the still, moved into Pocahantas Bay, and it may have been those distillers who were caught.

We stood on the beach at Pocahantas Bay and gazed up disconsolately at the logged-off slope rising above us. McDugald's cabin will have rotted away and his molasses tins will have rusted into the earth, but the tunnels of the Raven Mine cannot disappear and one day I would like to find them.

NELSON ISLAND. PILCHARDS

Colonel Pond wanted to talk about pilchards, *Sardinops sagax*, the Pacific sardine. Colonel Pond, a man with the upright carriage and air of authority to which his rank entitled him, had spent summers on Nelson Island long enough, he thought, to be ranked as an old-timer. He had bought the place opposite Haven Island which had once belonged to boat-builder Allen Farrell, and he was carefully preserving Farrell's neat house, log cabin and his most remarkable fence of eight-foot-long cedar shakes, which Farrell had built to keep out the deer. When we had cruised this way in 1965 we had come upon Farrell building *Ocean Girl*.

Lorne Maynard, who had once been Colonel Pond's neighbour, told him that in the 1930s you could have walked from his dock to Colonel Pond's on solid-packed pilchards, and now there were none. Like the colonel himself, the pilchard once migrated between California and British Columbia, moving north in spring. It was a 16-inch fish, dark blue on top and silvery below, with round black spots along its sides. In 1929 the British Columbia catch totalled 86,300 tons, of which 81,250 tons were reduced to oil and meal, 4,900 tons went into sardine tins, and 150 tons were frozen for bait. Most of the pilchard harvest was fed to livestock. At this rate of harvest, the stock became so small that other predators caused them to become extinct. In 1939 the pilchard fishery disappeared from government statistics. The canneries closed and began to rot. Some people went on welfare. So much for pilchards.

Then the colonel turned to the subject of herring, which was not much of a turn as the pilchard is a member of the herring family. The herring, unlike the pilchard, once spawned in southern British Columbia coastal waters, and I well recall the early spring excitement when the herring fleet came into Ganges Harbour. The herring deposited pale amber, translucent, adhesive eggs in enormous numbers on eelgrass, seaweed, rocks, wharf pilings...everywhere. The gulls went crazy, shrieking and wheeling, and all the world shouted "Spring!" My friend Nonnie would row out to one of the herring boats; they would tip the net and fill her boat, so that she rowed home almost knee deep in herring. We ate rolled and pickled herring at island parties all year. The herring was the fundamental food for many marine animals, fish and fowl, sharks, seals, sea lions, jellyfish...the list goes on. In 1936 the total commercial catch was over 800,000 tons. We grumbled when the herring fleet began to use new technology to scrape the bottom of Ganges Harbour but we were not enlightened enough to do all the things people do now, fighting to save the earth for all creatures.

Colonel Pond said the herring used to leave Ballet Bay, a small notch off Blind Bay, every morning, returning in the evening, always accompanied by salmon which took the colonel's lure. Then the herring fleet grew more numerous and efficient, and the foolish government 15 years ago let the Japanese fleet come into Blind Bay; the Japanese placed high value on herring roe which is their caviar, but the little bodies were used for fertilizer. Now Blind Bay has neither herring, nor salmon. And, Colonel Pond warned, if there are no salmon, there won't be any American tourists. Will the colonel return in the spring if there are no salmon to catch?

BILLINGS BAY. NELSON ISLAND. THE MAYNARDS

That first time it was the seas fetching down Malaspina Strait that drove us to seek shelter in the hook behind Maynard Head, Nelson Island. We tied up at the Billings Bay float and enjoyed that delicious sensation of sudden ease when the floor stopped rocking and swaying. Exploring ashore, in an empty shed we read the names of the local people on the wooden mailbox compartments. A notice invited us to take a five-minute walk to the Maynards. Water jugs in hand, we followed a path into the forest and came to a cottage where we were warmly welcomed and fed tea and scones. We talked for two hours. "Exactly the sort of people I hoped to find and didn't really believe in," I wrote in my journal. "They've lived here for 27 years, knew Mrs. Blanchet, have such amusing stories to tell of local places and people, are warm and sympathetic and very fine indeed. The rain came down gently all afternoon, but we couldn't have been more entranced." That was in 1965.

In 1972 we returned. We came carefully towards Maynard Head through the narrow channel that separated Nelson Island from Haven Island, but even as I glimpsed their house (which faced the channel), I knew the Maynards were gone. We went around Maynard Head and managed to tie at the Billings Bay float but the wharf had a drunken angle and the float needed new logs. The little shed still had its named compartments but it seemed risky to mail a letter there and expect anyone to ever pick it up. In the hot afternoon the dry arbutus leaves on the path crackled crisply. Prickly blackberry vines clawed at us as we passed. The Maynards' house, when we came to it, looked much as we remembered it, but weeds had choked the flowers. We knocked. In the distance a raven croaked. Through the dusty window the kitchen looked as if the owners would soon return. Sitting on the porch where red roses bloomed, we decided to try to buy this cottage (but we had no money and nothing came of the dream).

On that same silent afternoon we climbed an almost vanished trail to the height of Maynard Head. We emerged on a high ledge, a hundred feet above Malaspina Strait with a view across to Texada Island and the blue ridge of Vancouver Island in the distance. Set into the cliff was a small bronze plaque: JOHN ANTHONY MAYNARD. IN LOVING MEMORY. He had died in 1957 at the age of 17. I sat there with a huge lump in my chest and wished I could cry and ease it. Was he their only son, I wondered? Once the steamer had docked at Billings Bay regularly; we had found a notice from Donald New of Coast Ferries, announcing rate changes with regret. Once there were all those neighbours greeting each other as they came for their mail, all those people who were now tattered, faded cardboard nameplates on empty boxes. Once a boy had climbed here....

In the soft, warm air of that summer evening, on an oyster-shell sea, we rowed into Cockburn Bay around the rock that guards its entrance, waiting until a mother duck had marshalled her frightened flock out of our way. The coastal mountains were like flat pieces of jagged paper, the distant peaks painted a pale violet and each nearer range a slightly darker shade of mauve, until the close mountains were washed with rich purple and cobalt. Small clouds, floating above the blue Vancouver Island range to the west, were edged with silver as the sky blended from blue to yellow and all the colours shimmered on the opalescent sea. It was hard to imagine that here, where we rested the oars and watched the colours fade, hijackers in 1926 had boarded the fishboat of William Gillis, who had a still in Hidden Bay. They murdered Gillis and his teen-age son, cut their bodies into chunks and dropped them overboard, abandoned the boat but took the rum.

That night in 1972, a fishboat came in late and tied next to us at the Billings Bay dock, and in the soft silence we heard them arguing about setting the alarm for breakfast; one of them operated on slow time, one on daylight time, but they finally agreed on a time halfway between. Also, one of them washed his feet before bed, which seemed to astonish the other.

Spilsbury described Lorne Maynard as a World War I vet with one leg who had a nice little boat named *Therma* and a regular contract to take the boiler inspector up and down the coast, year after year, to test all the hundreds of steam donkeys. Seeking to know more about the death of their son John, I learned that in 1979, when a man named Robert Harding had died suddenly of a brain aneurism, his ashes were taken to be scattered near those of John Maynard, his boyhood friend who had been killed in a road accident. The Maynards left Billings Bay in 1965, the year we met them.

Entering Billings Bay in 1992, we rolled and plunged in a very rough sea while reading the Loran bearings and selecting a course toward the waves breaking high and white on Maynard Head. The swells followed us into the crook of the bay. Rotting pilings marked the site of the old government dock and in its place there was a new float with a B.C. Hydro metal shed; we tied behind it to get maximum shelter from the gently heaving sea. FOR SALE, a sign announced. Ashore, we floundered through head-high salal but could not find the old path. To reach the Maynards' house we had to go out into the churning seas and into the channel between Nelson Island and Haven Island.

In that passage we found the Maynards' dock and the dockside path to the house. The cottage was still there, with the same white curtains with frilled edges at every window. We sat once more on the corner bench on the wooden deck at the front door, and looked down the path to the channel, where the gate post had fallen, taking the gate with it. The path to the memorial plaque had disappeared, but as we motored away we searched Maynard Head with binoculars and could see the dark stain running down the rock below the metal, like a track of tears down a cheek.

EGMONT. SKOOKUMCHUCK NARROWS

Egmont isn't where it was when we first went there. Before 1946 it was near Egmont Point, across the Skookumchuck Narrows from its present location. It seems that the postmaster moved and took the name of the place with him. We tied at the government wharf so we could meet the famous wharfinger, Vera Grafton, who is said to remember who you are from year to year. This is no mean achievement if there are, in fact, 17,000 boats going annually to Princess Louisa Inlet, most filling their gas tank and doing a last laundry at Egmont. The bright pink paint on Grafton's Store must be cheerful in the grey days of winter.

Judy Gill has related a story about Kwaht-ah-moass, which was the name of the place which became the first Egmont before it moved. It was told by Sophie Charlie about her grandfather. He and a grandson paddled from Kwaht-ah-moass to Tcka-a-Nayth-Chum, now called Egmont Point, to strip bark from a dead fir tree for fuel. As they stood beneath the tree, a massive sheet of bark broke free, came crashing down, and fell on the grandfather, crushing him. The boy paddled in desperate haste for help and many people returned to the rescue. They found the injured man lying on top of the slab of bark, injured, with a she-wolf standing over him. The man ordered them to leave him with the wolf, so they built a shelter over him and went away. When his wife returned with food, he would not eat it, for the wolf was bringing him the roots and plants to heal him. Soon the man walked into the village, limping but strong. Sophie Charlie remembered him picking bone chips out of his leg as they came to the surface. Afterwards, the wolf was his crest and it was said that the wolves herded deer into the hunting ground for him.

Wolf skins were never worn as robes or used in trade by the Sechelt people, and the wolf was not hunted. According to Lester Peterson, the young Sechelt man seeking guardian-spirit power always attained "Wolf Spirit Power", the power to do good deeds, whatever other powers came to him.[1] Legends often begin "Once upon a time when people were wolves..." and there are many stories of wolves helping people. A woman returning to where she had left an infant at the berry-picking camp might find a wolf guarding the child. A woman had to leave an ill husband, but neighbours saw a wolf bring a bucket of water to him.

Egmont wasn't where it was, and the world isn't as it once was; but Egmont Point still jutted into Jervis Inlet to remind us of wolf power, the power to do good deeds. And Vera's friendly welcome and helpful advice were proof that wolf power was still attainable.

PRINCESS LOUISA INLET

Up Jervis Inlet from Egmont, a snake of soft cloud lay like a white feather boa on the shoulders of 4,000-foot mountains. The tiny buildings associated with a few logging shows were dwarfed by the peaks. After hours of running up the corridor of water, almost at the end of the last reach, we saw Malibu Lodge nestled in a crevice in the mountain wall. This was the entrance to Princess Louisa Inlet.

Malibu Lodge was opened in 1941 (and closed four years later, when the reality of war made ostentatious luxury temporarily out of fashion) as a resort for Hollywood stars. In 1953 it was transformed into a holiday place for American Christian teenagers, mostly Caucasian, too young to care that William Holden, Bob Cummings and Alexis Smith once slept here. When we visited in 1965 we were given a tour by a charming girl from Tennessee, who gave us a brochure explaining that they "were committed to the aim of capturing the attention of the average teenager long enough for an intelligent look at the Christian faith."

Where we were shown luxurious buildings, a spectacular swimming pool, a golf course, tennis and volleyball courts, docks with equipment for kayaking, waterskiing and canoeing, and hundreds of brightly clad young people amusing themselves, there was once a Sechelt place: Sway-we-lat. But the Indian people no longer lived there when Judd Johnson arrived. Judd had married Dora Jeffries from Pender Harbour and for many years they and their children lived at the entrance to Princess Louisa Inlet, in a one-room shake cabin with benches around the walls for beds and an open fire in the centre of the room.

Then this place became the home of Casper and his cats. After young Herman Casper put his fist into the face of a German officer, he instantly deserted the army and fled to Princess Louisa Inlet, where he felt safe. In 1933 Francis Barrow wrote in his sea journal that "Casper now has 14 cats, one less than on our last visit" and that he had been reduced to smoking tea for two weeks until the Barrows brought him some tobacco.[1] Francis took an excellent photograph, by timer, of Casper giving him a haircut while Amy watched nearby, each of the Barrows clutching one of their dogs. They urged Casper to go out to get some teeth pulled, to stop his toothaches. Casper was a tool maker and a logger, a friendly man who welcomed visitors and entertained them by playing the zither or a guitar he had made. Thomas Hamilton, the founder of Malibu Lodge, paid him $500 for the property.

In 1992, on the glassy calm of the high slack we slid past Malibu's wide roofs and swimming pool, called greetings to the young people sunning on the smooth rocks a few feet from us, and entered Princess Louisa Inlet. After we were tied to a mooring buoy north of Macdonald Island, we lay on the front deck, drinking chocolate and looking up at the blue sky roof atop the mountain walls rising sheer up to more than 7,000 feet, or gazing down through the mirror to watch gulls flying past in the depths below our hull. I felt like a water spider. Looking up at these heights, Stuart Edward White once wrote:

> At the top of the precipice [the trees] had crowded to the edge. From this great distance they looked like little people venturing as close as they dared and peering over with the caught breath of wonder; while behind them the great summits, indulgent and benign, looked on with permitting tolerance.[2]

The British Columbia Ministry of Environment and Parks pamphlet told us that "The privilege of enjoying this bit of paradise comes through the generosity and foresightedness of James F. 'Mac' Macdonald." Mr. Macdonald, who in 1927 built a log house which burned in 1940, near Chatterbox Falls, was standing on the float when we first came to Princess Louisa and could hardly wait for us to tie up before inviting us to play chess. Years later he gave his land to a yachtsmen's society (the Princess Louisa International Society), which turned it over to British Columbia. The Parks folder quoted Erle Stanley Gardner: "There is no scenery in the world that can beat it. Not that I've seen the rest of the world. I don't need to, I've seen Princess Louisa Inlet," which seemed both illogical and arrogant. He viewed the scenery "with bared head and choking feeling of the throat" and Mr. Macdonald assured us in the pamphlet that here we "can find the peace that passeth understanding."

Most yachts carried a copy of Blanchet's *The Curve of Time* with them, as we did, and visitors sought to identify Trapper's Rock and the laundry pools. It was through Capi's eyes that we were able to "see" Mac's vanished house, built of peeled-cedar logs. One big room, about 40 by 20 feet, had a great granite fireplace. A stairway ascended to a balcony, off which there were bedrooms and bathroom. Bookcases, trestle table, and the chesterfield in front of the fireplace were all made of peeled and oiled cedar. Mac was 83 when he spent his last summer in the inlet, in 1972. We rose at dawn, when thin mists blurred the inlet, to leave on the change of the tide at Malibu. The teenagers were still asleep.

JERVIS INLET. PAINTED STONES AND PUBERTY

How does a boy know that he is no longer a boy? It is instructive to consider how the Sechelt people, who had no category of humans labelled "teenagers", dealt with the transition to adulthood. In the Queens Reach of Jervis Inlet, about three miles northwest of Malibu and on the same steep side of the fjord, we located the rock shelter with pictographs, a sacred place associated with puberty trials. It wasn't hard to spot the brilliant red of the figures, drawn on the curving surface of the cave-like hollow about 15 feet above high water. According to Lester Peterson, these pictographs were drawn with cinnabar (mercuric sulphide), not ochre. This panel of symbols, the work of shamans, included a large red circle, three blackfish guiding a serpent, and other designs. As we had no ladder, we were unable to climb onto the flat cave floor, where Francis Barrow found painted stones and the ashes of a fire. In 1935 Barrow's friend Casper made him a ladder,

> and at the right moment a hand logger came along to this spot to cruise for timber, and he helped me up to the ledge and took my camera up. I took some close-up photos and found some small stones all with pigment on them, which I took. I left quite a lot behind.[1]

When Lester Peterson came to this site in 1966 with Basil Joe, he too removed a few stones. To this place, Peterson was told, young Salish men came when they had sought and found the strength and confidence to abandon childhood dependency and accept adult responsibility. (For women, their first menstruation is a clear signal of awesome adult power, but for men the psychological transition is less distinct.) Peterson wrote:

> The late Chief Reg Paull told me that a novitiate who had completed his Guardian Spirit Quest was obliged to dance in a special cave, before a fire prepared by an elder, who

had waited there for him, and to sing to him his Ay-Yihm'uhss, his "spirit power" song.[2]

Their spirit power, "seen" as a raven or a fish or some other natural form, was sometimes painted on the rocks, even as we express divine power in symbols such as the cross, which we depict on objects to reinforce our own beliefs and confidence.

Here, in this rock shelter, the elder sat, tending a fire as he listened for the soft swish of an approaching canoe, and here he used the painted stones to protect the vulnerable initiate, even as priests waft incense to drive away evil spirits. From his anthropological research in the Nanaimo district, Homer Barnett wrote of "washing" an initiate in the puberty rites and specified that four stones were used. When Edith Cross in 1979 sold to the Provincial Museum a set of four painted stones (and the specially marked and split sticks with which they were moved), she had been told how the stones were used on Kuper Island. When those who had quested for their spirit power came to sing and dance in the big house before the assembled tribe, "the painted stones were heated around the fire, then picked up by the sticks and dropped in their washing water to cleanse and purify."[3] After the Kuper Island ceremony, the sticks were taken up the mountain and tied in young trees, perhaps with the hope that the young initiate would also grow in wisdom and in stature. In 1980 when I asked a Coast Salish person about painted stones, she replied that they had been used a few weeks previously in a dance ceremony at Musqueam, but she offered no further details, saying only that it was a private matter.

I have held in my hand a number of these stones, now in the Provincial Museum, and pondered the way we imbue objects with magic power — lucky coins, small figurines or, yes, small stones. Stones are Gaia's bones, and to feel the round, smooth pebble in the hand is to hold a piece of Her power. Some Salish stones have been painted with a fir-branch pattern, which may refer to the power to have children, a kind of miniature family tree. In James Teit's study of the Thompson Indians, he wrote that, as part of a woman's puberty training,

She made a record of her offerings and the ceremonies she had passed through, by painting pictures of them with red paint on boulders and on small stones....This was believed to ensure long life. The pictures were generally all of the same character and consisted of fir-branches, cross-trails, lodges, mats, men, etc. She painted pictures of men, symbolic of her future husband.⁴

Anthropologist Michael Kew wrote that the Salish recognized that people were in danger at times of change such as puberty, bereavement, etc.

At these times, one became supernaturally vulnerable. To guard against danger at such times...the Central Coast Salish had a variety of complex magical cleansing rites, which could be used to protect and strengthen vulnerable persons. These rites originated in ancient times.⁵

In the "western" world the evidence of vulnerability is in our medical statistics, which show that we risk illness at such crises. Perhaps at life's change points we need to strengthen our connection to the source of life, whatever name we give it. Our culture offers little support to our teenagers who long to be recognized as adults. They smoke cigarettes, drink, drive too fast, or think that by carrying weapons they prove they are no longer children. The Sechelt youth, in contrast, went alone to seek that transformational experience, and tested himself in trials sanctioned and supervised by the elders.

Coming down Jervis Inlet we paused in the Princess Royal Reach, about three miles south of Patrick Point, to examine the point called Kwah-oh'-tah, a high, narrow cliff rising about 60 feet from sea level with an overhanging lip at the top, marked with pictographs. During their puberty trials young men would throw themselves from this frightening height, recognizing their own courage in this leap into the deep inlet. A little farther down the same shore, we located the 75 feet of smooth, steeply sloping black rock which the young men ran across in another puberty test. A misstep meant a slide on back or stomach down 25 feet into the water, across the sharp teeth of the barnacles along the tide's edge. They must be swift and agile in preparation for the mountain-goat hunt, for the goat-wool blanket was the Sechelt unit of wealth, and to qualify as a hunter, the young man must shoot a goat with bow and arrow. Then, when he had passed these tests, he presented himself to the elders, danced his guardian-spirit dance and knew he was an adult.

CHAPTER TEN

Southward, Pender Harbour to Gibsons

MOUNT DANIEL. PENDER HARBOUR

Howard White, publisher and long-time resident of Pender Harbour, told us how to find the stone circles on Mount Daniel. We located the old gravel pit off Garden Bay Road, picked our way up the bank, and started a slow, steep, step-by-step ascent up a twisting path overgrown with alder. Gasping and sweating we emerged on a flat, open, mossy place, with a deep pool of dark water hidden in the trees. Howard wrote, "The site itself has the pulse-quickening thumb-pricking hair-raising impressiveness connected with most petroglyph and ceremonial sites".[1] We walked to the cliff edge, and felt like eagles, as we gazed down at Pender Harbour far below.

We found four circles of small stones along the open rock ledge facing southeast. Anthropologist Homer Barnett wrote in 1955 that a girl seeking a vision at puberty was secluded for ten days. If she belonged to a wealthy family she wore a bark apron and a fine cloak of marmot skins. On the eleventh day

> she went by herself to a flat place on a hill and laid out a circle of rocks which represented guests at a feast. In the center she put two rocks representing herself and her future husband.[2]

An 1857 account stated that a boy at puberty "retires alone among low hills near the sea-coast, and carries small stones up these hills, which stones he arranges in small circles."[3] Lester Peterson's informant, Basil Joe, said that the Mount Daniel circles of stones

186

View from Mount Daniel, Pender Harbour.

symbolized the moon whose cycles would affect the girls' lives, and that the boys built "serpent-shaped groins of stones" on Mount Cecil.[4]

We settled to the laborious task of measuring the site and mapping the circles, one with more than 50 stones. The mysterious and thumb-pricking feature of the site was the dark pool, the glittering eye of the mountain. The sparkling spring of water has been, for many prehistoric people, the eye of the dragon. If we had brought sleeping bags to stay the night on the top of Mount Daniel, would I have felt the presence of the young girls? I remembered my own ambivalence at age 12...did I really want to go through pregnancy and the pain of giving birth? Would I ever be able to give a dinner party the way my mother did? I remembered wishing that time would stop so that I need not grow up. I looked at the old woman reflected in the dark mirror of the pool and discovered she was laughing at me.

SECHELT

There was no longer a government pier at Sechelt, but the calm morning allowed us to safely anchor close to the beach. We had come to look at the totem raised, not to advertise the lineage of a chief but to celebrate REASONABLENESS, a wonderful notion. We also wished to examine the poles that were carved when this band achieved self-government, the first band in Canada to do so. With the binoculars we could see the totems standing in front of the Sechelt Band's hall, and noted that we must land where the two tall fir trees stood close together, the only tall trees left. Ray remembered when people came from Vancouver by steamship and picnicked under the trees, annual excursions like the Boilermakers Picnic and smaller family groups. One could easily get lost in the great forest of fir trees then.

The waves lifted the dinghy onto a strand of pebbles smooth as marbles. We climbed the bank and walked up Xenichen Avenue, less than a quarter mile to the cement-block building, on the far side of a playing field where a flock of geese was feeding. There were a number of poles and a circle of seven wooden figures (three natives and four faceless government officials, with the chief holding the talking stick). In the centre of the circle a large boulder had a plaque explaining their great desire for self-government. We stood there reading their words on the very day that in Ottawa, the government agreed that Indian self-government would be written into the Constitution of Canada.

Totem poles, Sechelt.

188

Behind the carved figures (one like the cigar-store Indian of my childhood) stood the Reasonableness pole, with Eagle on top of Wild Man of the Woods, above Bear embracing Salmon, and then Killer Whale standing on his head. Below his broad nose the plaque read: "In celebration of practicality, good will and reasonableness, showing what can be achieved when governments work together. This pole was unveiled during the inauguration ceremony for the Sechelt Indian Government District, a new form of government in Canada." Two other poles were raised to celebrate the achievement of self-government, one with a plaque: "Commemorative Pole Proclamation Day. October 9th, 1986. Enriched by our past, nourished by our vision of the future, this pole is dedicated to all those who laboured for so long in the great crusade to restore self government to the people of the Sechelt nation and thus to mark this new beginning."

"Our vision of the future"...aye, there was the rub. When people band together under some slogan such as "Freedom" or "Self-Government", individuals holding quite different visions can work together in temporary harmony. When we knocked at the door of their cement-block longhouse and the two Indians playing crib gave us permission to enter, we discovered a large room set up as a bingo hall: three cards for eight dollars, 18 cards for $48. It was empty: no drums beating, no celebration of another decision made by alien legislators. Harmony and compassion cannot be legislated. The native people have stressed the importance of their culture, but culture is a chameleon, growing and changing with economic circumstances. We are all shaped by culture; one of the greatest culture-shapers of today is television, which promotes competitiveness, violence and greed. *Kahtou*, a bi-monthly First Nations newspaper published in Sechelt, has advocated: "pow wows, drumming and war dancing, aboriginal feasts and festivals...we must utilize these sacred aspects of our heritage to the dominant society who have only an artificial (Coney Island) culture, driven by greed."[1] As we returned to the beach and rowed out to *Liza Jane*, we decided that reasonableness is in the eye of the beholder.

SELMA PARK

As Ray rowed away from the Sechelt shore, I wondered if long-lost stone figures lay beneath our keel. Diamond Jenness wrote in 1935 that many stone figures with bowls were made by a family at

189

Sechelt. When enemies carried off two figures, the family threw the remaining six or seven in their possession into the water, so they would not be taken too.

At the southern end of Sechelt Beach, a red beacon stood on the end of a massive stone breakwater. We could have sheltered behind the wall of rocks to go ashore where the Sechelt Image was found, but this area has been so changed by development that there would be no way to relate the Sechelt Image to the place where it was found. On the cover of Lester Peterson's *The Story of the Sechelt Nation*, the image is shown squatting on smooth, curving bedrock, presumably the Selma Park shore, but there is no evidence that it ever rested in such a place. It is now in the Vancouver Museum. An exact replica stands on a pillar in the Royal British Columbia Museum and is one of their most impressive exhibits.

A massively powerful human being grips an object which to me can only be a child. Some writers have reminded us that the Salish hoisted heavy oval boulders as feats of male strength, and others have thought that what is held here is a huge phallus. If so, it is a phallus with arms and two cheeks on its bum. Below the clasped child is a vulva; the image is the eternal mother and child.

When this sculpture was found, it was claimed by Dan Paull of Sechelt, who said an uncle had told him about the disappearance of an image during the smallpox epidemic. The uncle said it had been set up to the memory of the wife of a chief. The Sechelt Image may be that lost figure, for it is a powerful symbol of motherhood. The style of the image connects it to the Seated Human Figure Bowls.

Wilson Duff wrote that

> Images seem to speak to the eye, but they are really addressed to the mind. They are ways of thinking, in the guise of ways of seeing. The eye can sometimes be satisfied with form alone, but the mind can only be satisfied with meaning.[1]

He said that great art is about being human, ultimately about those aspects of being human which are most sacred. Duff saw the Sechelt Image as the eternal trio, mother, father and child, in contrast to the Christian image of Mary and infant Christ. The medium, stone — heavy, tough, everlasting — is part of the message. Wood may be carved to signify the wealth and power of a chief, but chiefs are mortal and totem poles rot. Perhaps the Sechelt

The Sechelt Image. (COURTESY VANCOUVER MUSEUM)

Image is about life endlessly renewed in the birth of the child, generation after generation. When I stand before this image in the museum, I feel as if I touch rock bottom. This is it. This is Life. This is the warmth and security we all need from parents. This is our basic duty: to nourish the young. This is not about power and prestige and wealth. This is about love.

Perhaps one day a replica of the Sechelt Image will be placed on the shore at Selma Park, for in my opinion this is one of the world's great sculptures, more meaningful than the Venus de Milo. Of course, it would have to be enclosed in unbreakable glass, for in our barbaric age vandals would paint their initials on her.

GIBSONS. LESTER PETERSON

We came to Gibsons a year too late to say goodbye to that remarkable man, Lester Peterson. I was glad that several times over the years I had told him how much I had learned from his writing and experiences.

191

Lester Peterson's father settled his family on a ten-acre stump ranch on Howe Sound; the Peterson boys worked with their parents from the time they could heft an axe. Lester grew up with the neighbouring native boys, and when he became a school teacher, athletics coach and youth leader, he came to know their children as well. His interest in their culture was deep, sincere, life-long and respectful. Acknowledging this, his native friends took time to show him their places, tell him their legends, and teach him their language. Because he was permitted to write this information, much has been preserved which would have been lost, for most natives during Peterson's lifetime were abandoning their culture.

Now I wanted to ask him about the "tabla" from Toba Inlet...but I had come too late. And I wanted to see the boulder bowl he mentioned in *The Gibson's Landing Story*:

A pestle was found on the Lowden property....What could be a corresponding mortar is a granite boulder embedded in the beach immediately below the property, into which a depression about the size of a soup-bowl has been made.[1]

The young man at the tourist-information office gave us the Lowdens' address on the waterfront along Marine Drive. We went down to the sand beach through the Municipal Park and spoke to a man at ease on his porch just above the beach. He remembered the boulder but said it had been moved to the lawn above. When we couldn't find it there, we went to the Lowdens' house and were told that the boulder had been placed in the museum. But when we had trudged a mile back to the excellent small museum, it was not there, and there was no Lester Peterson to tell us what had become of it.

Lester Peterson will be remembered in his writing: *The Gibson's Landing Story* and *The Story of the Sechelt Nation* should never be out of print.

DEPARTURE BAY. VANCOUVER ISLAND

We left the marina at Keats Island in the gray light before dawn, when the mountain tops were brushed with a delicate pink wash. Shoal Channel was smooth. On the boat's radio, the gravel-voiced weather forecaster was chatting about the pebbled surface of Departure Bay, our destination on the other side of the strait. But when we were too far across to return, a wind came rollicking out of the east, and an unexpected blast roared down out of Howe Sound. We lurched along, tossed from side to side on the sparkling waves, tipping, reeling, tilting, swaying. We went north off-course to ease the battering. Yet in all the roller-coastering, the horizon lay level and serene. There was something comforting in the sight of that ruler line between sea and sky. I became aware of watery Gaia swinging round the sun on an invisible string, held securely in eternity. We were only being buffeted on her wind-ruffled skirts because a weather forecaster failed to warn us of her mood.

When we came at last into Departure Bay, the surface was...yes...pebbled. We dodged half a dozen taxiing floatplanes which were lining up for fuel in the channel behind Newcastle Island, and headed for the marina below the Hudson's Bay Company Bastion. After a brief stop for a fill of diesel, we rode the tide through Sansum Narrows, the gateway to the region we have loved for so many years.

CHAPTER ELEVEN

Southward, Valdes Island to Salt Spring Island

SHINGLE POINT. VALDES ISLAND

A towering fig tree once stood there, a fig tree of enormous size. We first came upon it almost 40 years ago; sometimes we camped under it, during the years when the flat sandy point jutting into Trincomali Channel seemed abandoned by its native owners. Now it has been reclaimed: when we came past in 1993, houses stood above the beach and boats lay on the shore or were tied at the log dock. I was standing on the deck as we cruised past slowly, looking for the great fig tree. One of the men on the beach called, "Do you want to come ashore?" and I shouted back "Yes!", grateful for the invitation. We found the fig tree — but it was quite small! How could a tree shrink? When I climbed under the canopy of branches I found that the old tree had fallen and its top had been sawn off, but the old stump had sent out many shoots to cover its broken shape.

Forty years ago, near the fig tree, the cedar framework of a longhouse rose from the sun-bleached grass; it had no roof or walls. I remember seeing it silhouetted against the evening sea with the mauve mountains of Vancouver Island in the distance. At the back of the spit, close against the steeply rising ridge of the island, there was in those long-ago years an empty, ruinous, three-storey Victorian house, which (according to an article by columnist Mamey Moloney I once clipped from a newspaper) was built in 1860 by a family who also planted the plum trees we found there. She wrote that the native people, who owned the land, had displaced the family and moved into the house, using the chimney and fireplace brick to decorate their graves. Exploring nearby we found that those graves, edifices of brick and cement like outdoor brick ovens, had been vandalized.

Margaret (Shaw) Walter, who grew up on nearby Galiano Island, had another story, probably closer to the truth. She wrote that Chief Ce-Who-Latza of Shingle Point had served as a pilot for the British gunboats. He wore a naval cape and in greeting gave the naval salute with gravity and dignity. He and his sons were boat-builders and musicians, and they raised some cattle with fearsome spreading horns. "The family, in imitation of their new [white] neighbours, built themselves quite a big house, which outwardly was fairly true to type; but once indoors it was seen, not to be divided into rooms, but followed more the pattern of an Indian community lodge."[1] I cannot say what the interior of the building was like when we came upon it, for it was so near collapse that we did not venture in.

The chief inherited a tradition of courageous seamanship older than that of the gunboat captains he imitated. If we had been standing on Shingle Point on a spring evening a generation before Chief Ce-Who-Latza, we might have heard a strange call...ooo...ooo...ooo, in a falling and then a rising tone, coming faintly from Porlier Pass to the south. Hearing the call, the sea-lion hunters would have come running from the large shed houses that stood in a row facing the channel. Dropping their spears into the canoes, they would have pushed the boats splashing into the water, climbing aboard and snatching up the paddles. Then, digging the paddles into the sea with exquisite harmony, they would have raced to the pass. A lookout at Porlier had sighted the annual arrival of a herd of sea lions, following the spring herring run. The Steller's sea lion can weigh 1,500 pounds and is as dangerous as an angry bull. The call of the lookout could also be heard on Kuper Island and soon canoes would come darting from Penelekut Spit. The harpooners stood tall in the canoes as they hurled their weapons. Since a wounded animal would tow the canoe, the Indians tried to get a number of harpoons, from different boats, into the same beast, to tire it more quickly. It was a dangerous business and required spirit power; the hunter's wife must lie quietly at home, for her quiescence affected the behaviour of the quarry.

The connection between woman and quarry is an ancient notion. A Salish man from the Fraser River said that if a hunter's wife even scratched her head, the hunted deer's head would itch and the animal would be restless and harder to spear. But the sea-lion hunters needed more than a quiet wife before they paddled to the pass. According to Wayne Suttles, all harpooners had ritual knowledge and, awaiting the sea lions, would cleanse their bodies, avoid sexual intercourse and "train" for special power in the same way they sought spirit power as boys. One of the last of the Penelekut harpooners had a killer-whale guardian spirit.

No ghosts or spirits have ever disturbed our sleep on Shingle Point, but Jack Scott had a different story. This British Columbian writer and his wife spent a night in August 1961 on the point with their friends Gordon and Lou Graham. About midnight they all fell asleep, their campfire still blazing brightly. Some time later Scott was awakened by the sound of drums beating out a constant rhythm. At first he thought he was dreaming, but then he rolled over on his stomach, lifted the tent flap and looked out.

> Beyond the glowing embers I could see a great crowd of Indians dancing in the moonlight. There was no sound from them, only the steady, muffled rhythm of drums as they moved gracefully and sinuously in and out of the perimeter of the beach fire.[2]

Scott watched the spectacle until his friend Gordon crawled out to put more wood on the fire and the fantastic dancing images dissolved. In the morning he wrote the article titled: "The night I began to believe in ghosts."

SHAW'S LANDING. GALIANO ISLAND. THE SHAWS

From Retreat Cove, on a morning when the tide and wind were in disagreement along the Galiano shore, we bumped north in the dinghy to see where, exactly, the Shaws had landed in 1877, at the tiny cove locally known as "Shaw's Landing". The bays south of the North Galiano dock are not signposted from the sea but Spotlight Cove is named on the chart, and Shaw's Landing is the tiny indentation two miles to the south. The bay was almost tide-dry and the seas were breaking on the rocks at the entrance as we waded ashore.

When she was "fully four score years"[1], the old woman who was once young Margaret Shaw wrote her reminiscences. She had been named after her mother. John Shaw, a mason, had married Margaret Chivers in Glasgow in 1863, a year after she had travelled with her brother Jeremiah to Leith, the port of Edinburgh, to watch him depart for the glittering gold fields of the New World, his white terrier Foxy in his arms. In North America he was to be known as Jack or John Chivers. During the years when Margaret was bearing the children in Glasgow — Margaret in 1863, Robert in 1865, John in 1871 and Jeremiah Chivers Shaw in 1875 — her brother Jack was mining gold in the Cariboo. Little Margaret remembered her mother gathering the children around her to kneel and thank God for a letter from Uncle. By 1875 Jack Chivers was living at what was later Shaw's Landing, writing "such glowing accounts of the new country, its prospects and opportunities, advising us frequently to come out and perhaps take up land for ourselves." The Shaw family crossed the Atlantic in May 1877, aboard the *Ethiopia*. "In the very early hours of an exquisite June morning", Jack Chivers was awakened by the whistle of the *Emma* off his shore, and when he rowed out to the little vessel, he was greatly surprised and delighted to see his sister Margaret and her family waving from the deck. The letter John Shaw had written to him had reached Victoria but had not been picked up.

There were no staterooms on the steamer *Emma* so the Shaw family had spent the night crowded with other passengers in the saloon, singing to pass the time. In the filmy, grey, dawn light they went on deck to watch misty islands sliding past in the smooth sea. Then Captain Luckie shouted that they were approaching Chivers' place. The whistle shrieked. Uncle appeared on the shore and soon came rowing towards them. "This first little trip ashore in Uncle's rowboat remains a clear memory after between sixty and seventy years. We had never been in such a small craft before, so near the water, which was then like a mirror, showing quantities of medusa swimming gracefully almost on the surface." Probably several trips were needed to get the six Shaws and their luggage ashore. Included in this luggage was a wooden box, painted brown and plainly addressed in white letters.

They were dismayed to find that Uncle's house was a one-room cabin with a little verandah and a stone fireplace, and the only other accommodation a henhouse and shed. Of the 160 acres which Jack was pre-empting, only one was roughly cleared — no fencing, no crops or garden, only a few fruit trees. "To my Father with a family to provide for, the situation gave such grave discouragement that he thought the only thing to do was to go back to Scotland again. This distressed Uncle greatly, who pleaded with him to try conditions here for a year or so." Perhaps it was the beauty of the June morning that tipped the scales in favour of staying on Galiano, the "year or so" lengthening to become their lifetimes. What a lot they had to learn! None of them had ever handled an oar, or farmed. John Shaw went to Victoria, thinking they might do better in the settlement, but "found prospects not assured enough to justify moving his family there." Margaret remembered his return, when her mother met him "near the landing place, to lay her head on his shoulder, sobbing, while he tried to reassure her in his quiet, strong way." Some native people had come at dawn the previous morning. Their arrival had frightened her but she had slipped out to avoid waking the children and gone down to the beach and somehow made them understand they were to go away. "It was the first — and last — time that Indians gave her serious anxiety," Margaret commented, "and many of them proved kind and considerate neighbours."

The Shaw family settled at Uncle's place. John Shaw pre-empted adjacent Lot 84 in 1888 (the 160 acres behind Lot 83 which included the lake that was their water supply) but two years later he died. He had lived for only 13 years in the New World. Daughter Margaret was by that time married to Arthur Walter of Salt Spring Island, and son Robert had already applied for pre-emption on Lot 90. At Shaw's Landing, Margaret Shaw and her son John built the Victorian house in which, after they were both dead, the brown wooden box was found. We walked where this house and the Chivers cabin once stood, photographed the twisted old apple trees, and looked at artifacts dug up by the present owners: a small brass doorknob, a silver spoon, a rusted mattock. Until there is a museum in which to guard them, Alistair Ross keeps a few battered, discoloured books which were found in the Shaw house: a biography of Queen Victoria, John Buchan's *Greenmantle*. He also holds the notebooks in which young John and his brother practised their elegant, spidery penmanship under sister Margaret's critical eye.

About ten years after her husband's death, Margaret Shaw took in a boarder who became world famous. John Claus Voss lived at Shaw's Landing while he was outfitting the *Tilikum* at Vollmer's boatworks at nearby Spotlight Cove. In this 38-foot dugout canoe Voss went around the world in 1901. The canoe, purchased at Cowichan Bay, had probably been made on Vancouver Island's west coast and abandoned by natives who had died of smallpox. Adapting the dugout for the epic voyage, Voss was assisted by John Shaw Jr. They added a cabin, decking, a 300-pound keel, three masts and two watertight bulkheads, strengthened with an oak frame. They built the gunwales seven inches higher and installed floor boards. Boat-builder Harry Vollmers supervised the work and Mrs. Vollmers sewed the sails to catch the winds which blew the canoe around the globe.

During these years Uncle Jack Chivers was "engaged, with others, in trading ventures in northern waters, and spent enough time in Alaska to get a smattering of the Russian language." He never married. When he was over 50 he bought Narrow Island (later named Wallace Island) where he built a two-room cabin, with home-made furniture. His niece Margaret remembered his generosity, which she called a "pioneer trait". "When some one would ask for assistance or a small loan perhaps, then the hand would go into his pocket and he would give — even if never expecting to see it again — money he would not spend on himself." When he died at the age of 90, he was buried in the old cemetery on Salt Spring Island beside his sister Margaret (Chivers) Shaw, "the sister who had seen him sail from the Firth of Forth so many years before." The lines on his headstone were taken from Isaiah 41, the verse which begins, "Keep silence before me, all you coasts and islands."

In seeking the place where Margaret (Shaw) Walter first landed on Galiano Island, I heard about the brown box, and finally was fortunate to find the people who now own and preserve it. One autumn afternoon I examined the lid with them, turning it this way and that in the slope of the sunlight, to read the faded letters. We finally deciphered them:

NOT WANTED
JOHN SHAW
STEERAGE ETHIOPIA
VICTORIA BRITISH COLUMBIA
NORTH AMERICA

For a moment I could see the crew of the *Emma* handing down the box to the arms of Jack Chivers as he reached up from his rowboat. For a moment I was young Margaret Shaw, standing on this amazing coast, with all the adventures of my life ahead of me.

TRINCOMALI CHANNEL. MRS. G.B. YOUNG

It was here that the fishboat chased Mrs. Young.

When I first lived on Salt Spring Island, I volunteered for the Wednesday shift at the little Association Library in the back room of Mouat's Store; my partner on the shift was Mrs. G.B. Young, a spry and decorous old lady, brittle like a bird and just as sharp and perky. She always wore gloves, white in summer, black in winter, and she fastened her highnecked blouses with a gold pin. She had lived most of her life at Fernwood, on the Trincomali shore, walking the miles to church on Sundays to play the organ, and even longer miles on Wednesdays to join me in the library.

She told me about her grandmother taking her up the mountain slope behind her birthplace on the coast of Cornwall. Sitting in the ruins of the great hall of a castle, beneath the minstrels' gallery, her grandmother would listen, humming sometimes, and smiling. She would turn to her granddaughter and say, "Oh, my dear, can't you hear the music?" When the rumour about the music reached London, music historians arrived to record the grandmother singing for them the songs she had heard in the ruins. According to Mrs. Young, the historians knew many of them, but some were new. There are mediaeval songs known only because of Mrs. Young's grandmother.

When I knew her, Mrs. Young was growing old and her son worried about her living alone in a house heated only by firewood and no neighbours close by. He wanted her to move into Ganges. I agreed with her son.

"You ought to have help with the firewood," I said, thinking only of the task of carrying it from the woodshed to the stove. But she turned to me with one of her quick movements and answered, "If the tree is too big, I get someone else to fell it."

One snowy Wednesday she arrived late at the library. Apologizing as she shook the snow from her coat, peeled off her gloves, and unpinned her hat, she explained, "I'm late because that fisherman chased me." I knew that she was accustomed to swimming in Trincomali Channel but had no idea that she continued the daily routine right through the winter months. She had left her clothes neatly folded on the shore and was enjoying her swim when a fishboat came down the channel. The fisherman, spotting a white head and flailing arms, decided that she was drowning, or perhaps suicidal, and tried to get her out of the water. "I swam and I swam," she said, "but he kept right after me. I shouted at him, but he wouldn't go away. He chased me right to the beach."

MONTAGUE HARBOUR. GALIANO ISLAND

Lounging in one of Sutil Lodge's red canvas folding chairs, my feet resting on a thousand years of clam shells discarded by my predecessors, I looked westward across Montague Harbour through the narrow entrance towards the distant blue ridge of Vancouver Island, where the sharp point of Mount Benson, 57 kilometres away, had speared a passing cloud. I was thinking about Galiano historian Les Laronde's theory that this passage and peak served as markers for solar-lunar observations. At the same time I was watching a sailboat testing its hold on the bottom of this popular anchorage. The anchor flukes could not disturb the secret hidden there.

Under the sand and gravel the flukes might shove aside the live horse and butter clams, but beneath the layer of the living was a thick bed of fossil clam shell and, deeper yet, the archaeologists have found pebble and cobble layers, probably an ancient beach where the waves broke almost 2,000 years ago. But the exciting secret is that under that beach and above the basal clay, there is a thick organic level which contains evidence of "an occupation during an earlier period of lower sea levels on now-submerged shorelines."[1] The radiocarbon dates from wood found in the organic level were in the range of 6,700 years ago. People have looked towards Mount Benson for a very long time. "A fairly rapid transgression of the sea", the preliminary report states.[2] A flood? An earthquake? Earth's thin plates shifting on her molten core?

From one of the ancient maple trees shading the beach, a crumpled brown leaf made a wobbling crash landing onto my lap. How swiftly the days were flicking past, each a few minutes shorter than the one before. I needed no moon nor dead leaf to tell me that my summer was almost over, for my calendar was already marked with autumn events. If I had lived here those long years ago, someone would have made food quest decisions for my band, and that person would have had a firm knowledge of seasonal changes, moon and sun movements and tides — some kind of calendar.

When Les Laronde arrived that late summer morning, he led me up the steep slope behind the lodge, to show me the strange pile of boulders which he identifies as the place from which the shamans watched the sun touch Mount Benson. He explained how shamans could identify the summer solstice, the moment when the sun sets at its maximum distance north from the equator, the longest day of the year. From that tick of time the days will begin to dwindle...the maple tree will know it and signal slow death to its green leaves.

The June solstice was the time of the summer low tides when the native people gathered shellfish, camping where I had sprawled in the canvas chair, drying the clams for winter use. (We all now use the tide tables, circling in red the days for clams and crabs.) Winter low tides at the dark of the moon were for hunting waterfowl with flares. "To gain the greatest reward from nature, men had to be at the right place, at the right time, with the right equipment, and with the right complement of personnel."[3] The Coast Salish, knowing the relationship of tides and the moon, had to make their own tide tables. According to anthropologist Wayne Suttles they "observed the solstices and the changes in positions of certain constellations, especially the Pleiades."[4] From astronomical observations they would probably count the moon months. Anthropologist Homer Barnett was told by some informants that there were 12 moons to the year but others claimed 13: both were correct, for the moon is full 12 times a year but returns to the same place among the stars 13 times. So it was necessary, in matching the moon to the run of days, to fit together the solar and lunar years, to have a starting point to begin a new moon-month count. Barnett thought they counted from the winter solstice, but it is more likely (given our cloud-hidden winter skies) that they used the summer solstice. And if it was the summer solstice, then Les Laronde's idea may be correct, for in the early summer the people were at Montague Harbour, drying clams.

When I sank once more into that canvas chair, recovering from the climb, the earth seemed less stable under my feet. The sun was falling fast toward the darkening ridge of Vancouver Island. We cannot know the cataclysmic instant when our fragile Earth will twitch and cliffs fracture and tidal waves sweep over the land. How predictable, in contrast, are the circling seasons. Less easily forecast were the movements of the moon-drawn sea. Deep beneath the ruffled surface of Montague Harbour is the land which was once home to people whose lives depended on their mastery of the mystery of the vagrant moon.

They had more reason to watch the skies than I. I looked at my watch and scuffled off through the brown leaves to make dinner.

GANGES HARBOUR. SALT SPRING ISLAND. WILSON'S BOWL

In Ganges Harbour, along the north side of the Chain Islands, skirting the reef, we eased *Liza Jane* into the somewhat precarious bay behind the flashing light on Gunpowder Island. When the anchor was fixed we rowed to the beach, where a sloping path gave access to the end of Churchill Road. Above this white-shell beach an excellent spring of water has been enclosed in a cement tank. In the days when this fresh water came cascading down the bank, native people came here, perhaps for the herring run or to dig clams.

Near this beach, in 1973, an archaeological excavation went inch by inch down through eight feet of layered midden to expose 23 burials on the bedrock. There was one skeleton with a stone point embedded between its ribs. Another had been wearing leather leggings or moccasins on which thousands of tiny stone sequins had been sewn. Jars of the tiny beads, white, grey or almost black, were sifted from the midden soil around the burials. Late one afternoon, when the others had gone to scrub themselves and cook dinner for the crew, I was still brushing midden soil from the bones I was uncovering with meticulous care. When a white femur was fully exposed I lifted it, gently, delicately. Under it, a square inch of sequins was still arranged in zig-zag lines of white, grey and dark grey. I was stabbed with joy. For a moment I was the woman who held the thin bone needle which pierced the tiny hole in each bead to fasten it in the design. I replaced the femur and went off to dinner feeling high and other-worldly. For an instant, time had collapsed.

What was it like to be that person I was laboriously uncovering? Associated with the burials, there were a number of labrets — ornaments inserted through a cut made below the lower lip; the first puncture was small, like the hole pierced in an ear for an earring, then it was gradually enlarged until large stone, bone, shell or wooden ornaments could be inserted. The wearers of labrets can be identified by the abrasion on the lower teeth. Labrets, known from archaeological sites around the Pacific rim, have in this area usually been discovered in levels about 2,000 years old. But a 1990 dig at Tsawwassen found two 3,800-year-old human burials with tens of thousands of stone disk beads and the teeth of one burial showing abrasion from wearing a labret. Indicators of high status, the labrets signified that the buried people lived at a time when new trading contacts were bringing wealth; labrets marked an emerging "upper" class. This was a powerful person in a stratified society.

Was the rise of a ruling class inevitable? It may have been logical thousands of years ago, perhaps because rising numbers of people required a different kind of social organization in a warring competition over access to resources. Someone killed the people whose bones we excavated. But perhaps if we recognized that individual happiness is lodged in the community at large, and the welfare of that community is dependent on Gaia's state of health, we could limit populations and share equitably. On top of those Salt Spring Island skeletons, almost 2,000 years of garbage was layered. Invisible, but just as real, lay 2,000 years of human experience and learning that should enable us to change old ways.

At the other end of this beach there was an artifact which provided another glimpse of that dead person's world. On the rocky point which separated the beach from the main part of Ganges Harbour, carved into the bedrock, filled by the tide, a shallow round bowl was bright with reflected sunlight, a stone saucer with raised rim, more mirror than bowl. Here, perhaps, a shaman knelt to see the unseeable. I have stood by this bowl on nights of the full moon when the harbour glittered like a shattered diamond, and I have positioned myself so that a small brilliant moon-coin floated in the depths of this bowl, when the bowl was itself a dark moon on the rocks. Wilson Duff wrote:

> Stone images
> are
> always
> hard
> to see.
> The only thing they really, really mean
> is everything they only seem to mean.[1]

Wilson's Bowl, Salt Spring Island.

Provincial Archaeologist for many years before he became a
university professor, Wilson Duff was my mentor, a role he
played for many others as well. In a cottage near this bowl
there once lived a woman who understood Wilson Duff; they
never met but knew each other only in the letters they
exchanged. She named this stone saucer "Wilson's Bowl". He
called her his "twin". After his death by suicide, she walked
into this bay one winter's night when snow dusted the stones
along the shore. Her friend Phyllis Webb later wrote in her
book, *Wilson's Bowl*:

This is not a bowl you drink from
not a loving cup.
This is meditation's place
cold rapture's.
Moon floats here
belly, mouth, open-one-eye
any orifice
comes to nothing
dark as any mask
or light, more light/is
Holy *Cirque*.
Serene, it says silence
in small fish
cups a sun
holds its shape
upon the sea
howls, 'Spirit entered
black as any raven.'
Smiles -
and cracks your smile.
Is clean.[2]

BEAVER POINT. SALT SPRING ISLAND. THE RUCKLES

At Beaver Point, the 300 acres that Henry Ruckle (from Ireland,
by way of Ontario) purchased for $300 in the 1870s was, in 1973,
given to the people of British Columbia by his descendants. Lotus
and Gordon Ruckle and their daughter Gwen live in the handsome
Victorian house standing tall above the old trees that surround it,
with its back against the forested rise of the point.

Coming into the little bay on the north side of Beaver Point, we tied to the mooring buoy. In 1900 the steamer arrived three times each week; as the dock was taken down in 1960, we fastened the dinghy to a tree above the beach. At the top of the bank, marking the old dock and store site, we found a sign displaying two pictures of the docks: the one of the first wharf was painted about 1889 by Agnes Ruckle (whose father Henry built it); the other, by Gwen Ruckle, portrayed the later wharf that existed in the mid-1950s, with the general store, post office and home of the William Pattersons. When the post office was moved to Fulford Harbour, the Pattersons went with it. The road, at first a rutted trail bringing farm carts to meet the steamer, is now part of the park trail network. To the south we could see the stone steps which led up to the campsites along the shore, but we trudged through a parking area and then along the asphalt road to visit the Ruckles.

Sheep — great balls of dirty wool on spindly legs — browsed in the Ruckle fields. Gwen once said that when the ewes grew even fatter in lambing time she had to check them twice a day; if they got down on their backs they couldn't get up. "Everyone has to be the right way up,"[1] she remarked, with clipped humour. She also guarded them from dogs (those adored pets whose owners swear the dogs never leave home) which sometimes she has been forced to shoot. In 1990, dogs caused the deaths of 26 lambs. But dogs are not the only danger, for ravens will attack lambs, pecking at their eyes first. Eagles, Gwen said, would only attack dead or dying animals. She has solved the raven problem, for the moment, by shooting one of each of the pairs which nested on the ridge behind the campsites. In the bitter driving rains of January, when the first lambs are born, her mother, Lotus Ruckle, has always eased the difficult births; orphaned lambs had to be bottle-fed six times a day with a special formula. There is nothing quite as joyous as a spring walk through Ruckle fields, among the dancing lambs, when the great maples are putting out their bright new leaves and the ewes are bawling nervously.

I never unlatch the gate and walk up the wide garden path to the Victorian mansion without a wonderful feeling of time slowing down...not time to sit and stare, but time to be aware of being alive in a world of living things...time to paint pictures, play violins, hook rugs...time to laugh at the way the coons outwit every attempt to keep them out of the yellow plums. I found Lotus and Gordon in the kitchen. Lotus, who was twisting boiled corn cobs through a kernel-removing device, paused long enough to greet me, her bright eyes smiling. Gordon's long hair and beard gave him the appearance of a stern patriarch, but his smile betrayed his shy gentleness and goodness. When the Ruckle land was transferred to the province, Lotus said, "It's a dream come true for my husband. This is what he has always wanted to do, to turn this lovely land into a park for the people."[2] If they glimpse the old man walking in the fields, do any of the thousands of campers know what they owe to him? Gwen came in from feeding the chickens and put wood into the Monarch stove, which is itself a museum piece. The Ruckles have a lifetime lease on the 200 acres of the working farm and there are future plans to continue running it as a heritage farm, but when they are gone and strangers play the role of "pioneers", it will be artificial.

When the park deal was signed in 1973, and they were asked if it concerned them that this land, worth many millions to developers, was being sold for $100,000 cash and $50,000 per year (interest-free), Lotus answered that money was not everything. "What price do you put on a lifestyle that you want to preserve?" she asked.[3]

I watched her working the kernels off the cobs and wondered how I would ever put the Ruckles into words without sounding sentimental. If there are two ways of being human, either thinking of your own interests first or knowing that individual happiness is dependent on human relationships and community, the Ruckles are examples of the second alternative. The Ruckles give me hope that humanity will survive. I absorbed that hope as we sat in the living-room, Gwen's paintings on the ten-foot walls, Aunt Helen's bright rugs at our feet. When we had exchanged family news, we talked about ozone depletion and the ultra-violet radiation blinding of sheep in Australia and the American president's unwillingness to sacrifice American "interests" to environmental concerns.

As we walked away from the old house, some of the sheep lifted their heads to watch us pass. Tennyson's lines came to mind: "For what are men better than sheep or goats that nourish a blind life within the brain..?" and I remembered that the poem also contained the lines "More things are wrought by prayer than this world dreams of."[4] Visiting Ruckle Park was a glimpse of both the past and a possible future.

CHAPTER TWELVE

Southward, Mayne Island to Sidney

GEORGINA POINT. MAYNE ISLAND

As we came east through Active Pass, the Georgina Point light blinked. Near it, there once stood a palatial building, named Culzean (pronounced "Cu-lane"), and although we knew that nothing remained except the great Cedar of Lebanon which stood there, we decided to visit the site. Built in 1893 as the Point Comfort Hotel, its 35 rooms were much frequented by miners (after whom the bay was named), en route to the gold fields. From about 1875 until well into the new century, Miners Bay was the hub of life in the southern Gulf Islands, with post office, stores, St. Mary Magdalene and the only jail. At the wharf where we tied up, the Lady of Culzean and her friends sometimes grouped themselves around a small, wheezing organ to sing hymns as passengers disembarked from the steamer. Not a soul was there to greet us as we arrived to hike the Georgina Point Road.

About half a mile along the road, St. Mary Magdalene, almost a hundred years old, stood on the slope of the hill above us. Entering through the lich-gate, we climbed the path to the church. Mrs. Maude, who dwelt at the Point Comfort Hotel when it was no longer a hotel and was not yet Culzean, sometimes came here in the middle of the night, wearing a billowing white duster, her white hair ghostly, to play the organ in the darkness. Coming in from the sunlight to the shadowy interior of the church, we saw a shaft of light, rose-tinted by the round red window in the peak of the west gable, falling into the bowl of a natural stone baptismal font. The red light spilled out of the bowl and flowed across the floor. "Washed in the blood of the lamb," I said, my voice too loud in the silence. Soon after the church was built in 1897, this stone was found on the beach near the East Point lighthouse on Saturna Island and brought in a rowboat by Canon Paddon, Ralph Grey, Evan Hooson and Henry Georgeson — with what grunting, puffing and bruised knuckles did they heave that chunk of rock into a rowboat for the long pull into Bennett Bay?

We wandered down to the graveyard at the edge of the road and soon found the graves we sought: the Lady of Culzean, Lady Constance Fawkes, died in October 1946 at the age of 91. "And they shall be mine saith the Lord of Hosts in the day when..." — the rest of the words had been erased by the wind. I remembered reading that she was buried in her long black velvet gown. Next to her lay Colonel Lionel Grinston Fawkes, who had died 15 years before her, at age 82. Arbutus leaves were tangled in the dry yellow grass growing from their graves and a ferry hooted a long, mournful note as it entered the pass below us. I lifted my gaze and looked far west, down Active Pass, to the blue ridge of Vancouver Island in the distance. Lower down the slope of the graveyard lay Commander Eustace Downman Maude, 1849-1930, and his wife Grace, 1860-1946. It was a sad year, 1946, when these two friends, Constance and Grace, were laid here beside their husbands.

It was another mile to the Georgina Point lighthouse. Looking for the great cedar, we climbed down to the edge of Active Pass to walk along the smooth rocks where the wash from a passing ferry broke at our feet. A low-roofed private home occupied the place where Culzean once stood. Gigantic old arbutus trees were bright with red berries, but where was the Cedar of Lebanon? The historic tree had been cut down! It seemed wrong that nothing of the old hotel had survived.

According to historian Marie Elliott, from 1893 to 1900, "residents of Galiano would risk foul weather and strong tides to enjoy their liquid refreshments on the other side of the Pass."[1] In 1900 the hotel was purchased by Commander Eustace Maude, who had chased pirates in the China Sea, served on Queen Victoria's private yacht and lived at Hampton Court. His three pretty daughters flitted down the grand spiral staircase and the great house was filled with the laughter of young people. It became the social centre for the upper-middle-class British people of the islands. During the 25 years of the Maudes' ownership, little was done in the way of repair; when the foundation began to crumble, Commander Maude considered selling the place. At this crisis, in 1924, the Fawkes arrived as paying guests, seeking a new life in Canada after the deaths of their two daughters. Stepping down the gangplank at Miners Bay, the colonel, in black suit and straw hat, carried a canvas bag with sketching equipment and an easel, and Lady Fawkes followed in a full-length fur coat (the hem chewed ragged by her pet dog) over a long black gown. On her feet she wore high gumboots. They bought Point Comfort Hotel from their hosts and renamed it Culzean, after the castle in Scotland where Lady Constance had spent her girlhood.

In 1929 the English writer, Lukin Johnston, walked to the lighthouse with Colonel Fawkes at sunset. Johnston wrote that

> the whole horizon of splendid snow-capped peaks is like the teeth of a jagged saw. The glow of the setting sun tipped the peaks with delicate shades of pink and mauve, streaking the glassy water of the Gulf with faintest, ever-changing tones of blue, gold and red.[2]

The Fawkes restored and renovated Culzean. After ice-cold baths at seven, they had breakfast, Bible reading and prayers. Then the colonel sketched and Lady Constance cooked. After lunch and naps, Lady Constance might sew, for she continuously made undergarments for needy Vancouver children. In the winter evenings they sat before a roaring log fire while the colonel read aloud from the life of Disraeli or other such suitable book. Every summer Thursday at tennis parties, tea was served under the cherry tree on the north side of the house. On winter Thursdays there were afternoon games in the dining-room, the men playing chess and the ladies doing handwork or weaving.

Next door lived the Maudes. As Lady Constance was somewhat shy, Mrs. Maude was frequently pressed to assist with entertaining. Lukin Johnston also visited Commander Maude in 1929, describing him as a fine old sea-dog with silvery hair and beard, at age 81 bright of eye and keen of mind. In 1926 Mrs. Maude and her daughter Valerie made every effort to coax the commander to accompany them to England. He refused, and when they had departed he set off to sail his little 25-foot *Half Moon* to England, via the Panama. He was 77. He sailed more than 4,000 miles of the Pacific for 97 days, alone, and for the most part virtually blind. "While washing dishes after breakfast," he explained later, "a big roller swung the boom over, catching me on the base of the skull. I dropped unconscious into the cockpit and do not know how long I lay there."³ With a terrible headache and blinded by sunlight on the sea, he could not distinguish the points of the compass. He turned back. Sighted off Cape Flattery, with her red ensign upside down (the distress signal), the *Half Moon* and her commander were hoisted aboard the government vessel *Berens*. Shortly after Lukin Johnston visited him in 1929, the brave commander died peacefully at home.

Two years later, Colonel Fawkes was buried at St. Mary Magdalene. Fate had one more sad blow for Lady Constance. Her only grandchild, Lawrence Kirby, was drowned in the swift currents of Active Pass. A few days before she died in 1946, she asked that she might be buried in her black velvet gown, with her brooch of paste diamonds pinned to her dress. The brooch, bought at Woolworth's, was a gift from her grandson.

We sat at the site of Culzean and watched the tide swirling out of the pass, thinking about Lady Constance standing here to stare at the devouring sea. How swiftly they have all gone, leaving little except their names on gravestones. I wished the Cedar of Lebanon had survived.

WINTER COVE. SATURNA ISLAND

A strange thing happened one autumn night in Winter Cove: I saw the Christmas star! I was awakened by a dream voice announcing that Sagittarius stood above the eastern horizon, so I slipped out of the bunk to check. And there, in the east, a brilliant light hung motionless in the pre-dawn sky. The night was like obsidian, like black glass, the only movement the sparkle of the stars. They were flawlessly reflected in the dark mirror of the sea, but in the depths there were hundreds of tiny new stars exploding: the bioluminescence. The universe above was as dead as Jupiter but earth's watery universe was alive with tiny luminous creatures. As I climbed back into the warmth of the bunk, I wondered why we spend billions getting into space, as if Heaven were there, meanwhile trashing the planet where life exists?

Several weeks later, reading the October 1992 issue of *Omni*, I came upon an article by Fred Schaff in which he argued that the star the wise men followed when Christ was born was in fact a series of rare Venus-Jupiter conjunctions in the year 2 B.C. When the planets merged, then set together in the direction of Palestine, they led those adept skywatchers, the Magi in Babylon, to Jerusalem. From that city the wise men would have seen the bright conjunction moving from east to south as the earth rotated, thus "going before" them down the road to Bethlehem, five miles south of Jerusalem. Schaff informed his readers that they could see mid-October's Venus-Jupiter conjunction by rising before dawn and looking eastward.

On the bright Sunday morning after the star gazing, we walked around Winter Cove by road, hoping there would be a service at St. Christopher's, Parson Payne's chapel. In the rapidly "developing" island world, we were relieved to find that the tiny wooden church had been lovingly preserved, the white cross at the peak of the roof freshly painted. But the path into it was overgrown. This chapel, built by Japanese immigrants as a boathouse, was adapted for Sunday services by the Reverend Hubert Payne, who arrived from England in 1896 to visit his twin, Harold Payne. Harold's house is the lovely old home nearby, which faces the next bay. Harold and Hubert were not the first of their remarkable family to settle on Saturna Island.

Charles Payne came in 1884, with Warburton Pike. When Charles went "home" to visit England in 1886, he brought back his 16-year-old brother Gerald. Many young Englishmen and women came to the coast "partly in search of adventure and partly to escape the starchy routine of Victorian existence with its suffocating class distinction"[1]. In 1894 Harold stayed for a time at Warburton Pike's place at Saturna Beach before buying the land at Winter Cove. He went off to fight in the Boer War and then ran a trading post at Telegraph Creek during the Yukon Gold Rush, before he married Ruth Maude, eldest daughter of Captain Eustace Maude, and settled at Winter Cove. One summer day I sat on a beach log at the Indian reserve on Salt Spring Island with Dora Payne, one of Harold and Ruth's four children. She told me about the time the whale was towed ashore on the beach at Winter Cove, and she remembered her father's loud complaints when the stench of rotting whale drifted in at their open windows.

It is quite a tale, that whale story. In the days when the James Georgeson family kept the East Point light on Saturna Island, James would row and sail his small boat across the Gulf of Georgia to New Westminster, every six months, for supplies. Once, when he and Mrs. Georgeson and her brother were crossing a serene and smiling gulf, they came upon a dead whale. A whale, rendered down, produced a wealth of oil, but they needed a larger boat with a motor in order to tow it in. However, if they went off to borrow the boat, how would they find the whale again when they returned for it? Somehow it was decided that the brother would be put off on the floating whale, with a lantern, so that Georgeson could locate the great beast when he came back in a more powerful boat. I tried to imagine the man climbing from a bobbing boat onto the round, skin-covered islet. I imagined James looking back at him, a tiny bump on the swelling curve of whaleflesh, as he rowed hard for Boat Pass to borrow the motorboat. When Edna Slater lived on Saturna Island, she told the story in verse.

> Through forty years of joy and tears
> Oh, the sight has remained to me,
> Of Henry stride that horny hide,
> A speck in the empty sea!

Dora Payne could only tell me that the whale was towed in through Boat Pass and rendered down on the beach below the place where the park picnic tables are now set out, and the smell of it sickened them all for weeks.

> As the tide was high we warped her nigh
> The beach where the old church stands...
> Our whale's gone bad and old Parson's mad —
> He can't get a sinner to Church![2]

Dora grew up where there were no roads. All travel was by foot or by boat; Dora and her two brothers and a sister could row by the time they were four years old, and as soon as they could swim they were permitted to use the launch. They traded apples to the Indians for old, leaky canoes which they patched with tar and sailed with old sheets. When Dora was ten and her brother 12, they salvaged logs out in the gulf in January, when the storms broke the booms. Later, Ray and I watched the tide boiling through Boat Pass; the seagulls rode the surge as if it were a roller coaster. I imagined a wiry little girl towing logs through this dangerous gap. Their play-mates were the Grey children on Samuel Island (across the pass). According to Dora, "as soon as we got old enough, we used to swim across backwards and forwards. The Greys used to swim over to see us, or we'd swim over to see them."[3]

About 1900 Harold's sister Isabel Payne came to Winter Cove. She was a lovely young woman with auburn hair and blue eyes who never married and who lived an unusual and independent life in houses she acquired in Victoria, at Sproat Lake and at Kye Bay. Her niece thought she was in love with Warburton Pike, and it is strange that his ghost came to Winter Cove on the day when Pike died in England. Dora Payne told me about the knock on the door and her father recognizing his old friend...but this story belongs with Warburton Pike's place on the Plumper Sound side of Saturna Island.

No Payne descendants live on Saturna now. Harold's house at Winter Cove and Gerald's at Boot Cove are well cared for by their new owners, and Hubert's little chapel stands on the shore, but the ghosts can only survive as long as their stories are told. We peered through the chapel window and tried to imagine islanders crowding the six oak pews. Crows noticed us and cawed raucously. Then the dogs guarding Harold Payne's house were roused to bark and run back and forth behind the tennis-court fence. Our presence had shattered the opal calm of the Sunday morning.

EAST POINT. SATURNA ISLAND. MOBY DOLL

We went to East Point to find the petroglyphs carved in 1964 by Sam Burich, a member of the crew who harpooned Moby Doll. East Point hooks slightly to the north to enclose a small bay with a sand-and-shell beach, where the Ritchies always kept their boat when they were the light-keepers. Here in 1964 the *Corsair* was anchored, ready to chase a harpooned whale. This cove is not a safe anchorage when the nor'westers rage but good enough for a few hours on a calm day. When James Georgeson (the man who towed the dead whale to Winter Cove) was stationed here in the 1890s, he and his brother-in-law, Peter Garrick, built boats on this beach, for themselves and other islanders. "No Trespassing" signs prevented us from taking their path up to the lighthouse above. Negotiations to designate most of this point as park are now proceeding, but until they are completed, one has to ascend to the road along a path which follows the wire fence of the light-station property.

The path climbed to the end of East Point Road, crossed the road and started down again, still following the wire fence. We emerged on the sea-sculptured sandstone cliff, with the easterly breeze chasing the tide around the point and a view that almost surrounded us — a 300-degree arc of brushed cotton clouds in a blue dome and a horizon of blue mountains, and islands in a cobalt sea. Far to the south the Olympics were draped in clouds. As we turned our heads slowly, we saw the distant Cascades and followed the mountain chain until it peaked in the bright white cone of Mount Baker. Northwards, the Coast Range was lightly iced, white tips holding up the clouds. Below the mountains lay the coast lands and the San Juan Islands, and beneath our feet the tide swept into the Gulf of Georgia, with some seals fishing in the swirling current that washed the base of the cliff.

We found the first glyph easily, for we knew that it was near what we used to call the "Trappers' Bathtub". I remembered this bowl filled with sun-warmed water and our children splashing into it, but on this dry-summer visit the bowl was empty, with dead grass lying on the bottom. On the smooth curve of sandstone above the line left by rainwater, Burich had chiselled a mother cradling a child. Nearby he had carved a petroglyph whale and a salmon, and a low-relief fish whose gaping mouth was a natural bowl. Once the mouth was sharp-edged, the light-keeper Ian McNeil told us, but some idiot children smashed it.

A few feet from these rock carvings was the flat rock platform on which a harpoon gun was mounted and above the killing place was the most impressive sculpture of all. Leaping from a massive curve of sandstone was a huge killer whale with mouth open so wide

East Point, Saturna Island.

215

that Ray could put his head inside the jaws. This natural rock form had been touched up by human hand, the eye added and the fin perhaps shaped a little.

Dr. Murray Newman, curator of the Vancouver Aquarium, chose this spot. On May 21, 1964, he stood here with Burich, harpoonist and sculptor, Vince Penfold, assistant curator, and Joe Bauer, a fisherman. Waiting at their university laboratories to do research on the whale's brain and organs were Dr. Pat McGeer and Dr. Gordon Pike. It is amazing to consider how little was known about the killer whale in 1964, and how much almost 30 years of research have altered our understanding of this intelligent creature and of our own interdependence with all life on our tiny planet. Here on this cliff edge, Burich loaded the gun with powder and a four-foot harpoon.

They should not have had to wait long. From 1960 on, the light-keeper and his family had been keeping a log for the Department of Fisheries which showed that killer whale sightings were almost an everyday occurrence. They had seen pods of more than 50 whales stretching between East Point and Patos Island, three miles away across the international boundary. But two months elapsed before an orca came near. During the long wait a small Department of Fisheries vessel had recorded the conversations of whale pods passing beyond the harpoon's reach and had played the recording through a loud-speaker on the deck, as the tide carried the boat past the whale hunters. The men lounging at the harpoon gun listened to the strange squeals, squeaks, clicks and chirps; perhaps they began to recognize that they were listening to amazingly complex and intelligent animals.

Then, on July 16, 1964, at 11:30, a pod of whales swam swiftly below the point, breaching and hissing on a flooding, six-knot tide. Burich fired. Harpoon and 600 feet of line whistled through the air and disappeared. They saw that one had been hit and two of the other whales were trying to buoy up the wounded animal. Zurich and Bauer ran for the chase boat. Up that path we had just descended, and down to the beach they leapt. Out in the swift tide stream they picked up the line and chased the whale, trying to kill it with rifle shots. When it was clear that the harpoon had missed vital organs, they decided to tow it to Vancouver where Newman had quickly arranged to have Burrard Drydock flooded to contain the animal he named Moby Doll. Vancouver newspapers alerted the public with headlines like "Battle with Sea Monster!" In drydock the harpoon was removed and Vitamin B and penicillin pumped in. Many people became involved and when a pen was built into an old dock at Jericho Beach, thousands came to see Moby Doll. The whale was filmed by the National Film Board. Offers of more than $20,000 were received from aquariums; the capturing of orcas was seen to be a lucrative business.

For three weeks Moby Doll refused food, but when she began to eat she astounded everyone by taking fish gently from the keeper's hand. When a pod of orca came near the harbour, Moby Doll's whistles became louder and agitated and her pod responded. Animal-rights people began to campaign for her release, as the shine of her slick black-and-white skin slowly turned grey and dull. Eighty-five days after her capture, Moby Doll was dead. At this point it was discovered that Moby Doll should have been named Moby Dick.

Sitting beneath the East Point stone whale, we watched seals and wished for whales,

> Where the salt weed sways in the stream;
> Where the sea-beasts rang'd all round
> Feed in the ooze of their pasture-ground...
> Where great whales come sailing by,
> Sail and sail, with unshut eye,
> Round the world for ever and aye.[1]

TAYLOR POINT. SATURNA ISLAND

Off Taylor Point the kelp bed rose and fell in the slow swells from Haro Strait. We anchored behind the kelp and went ashore on the curving sand beach, aware that this was only a calm-day anchorage. The steep path where the beach ended led us to the ruins of what was once a magnificent, cut-stone mansion.

George Taylor was a young man when he came from England in 1892 and bought the Potato Point property (later named Taylor Point) from Warburton Pike. Here Taylor, a stone mason, quarried the stone for Craigdarroch Castle, for the old Carnegie Library on Victoria's Blanshard Street, and for buildings in Vancouver and on the prairies. He also built a handsome, two-storey house for his wife Annie and their children. When we first came upon the house, only the walls remained, rising from a sloping greensward close-cropped by sheep, in an orchard of crooked old trees. Trees also filled the interior of the building and sprang from it like green branches from a vase. When we returned in 1992 the trees had been cleared from the interior of the building but most of the walls had fallen or seemed about to fall. (Later, I learned from Lorraine Campbell, a present owner, that the walls were pushed over by Bible-camp teen-agers.) Little remains of the iron tracks on which stone was carried to the barges moored to the cliff.

Was life without neighbours lonely for George and Annie Taylor and their five children, Valey, Chrissy, Thomas, George Junior and Derwent? Did Annie sometimes long for the company of other women? Geraldine Payne remembered that they occasionally hiked over the high central ridge of the island to have tea with the Taylors. She described Mrs. Taylor as "a tall, dark, gypsyish-looking woman, but she was Scotch. I think she had a very hard life, but she was always pleased to see us and made wonderful cakes. We would run the last mile because we were so hungry and we knew what was at the end for us."[1]

The problem of the children's schooling was partly solved when the East Point Georgesons bought property on Mayne Island and built a six-room cottage there for their children to live in while they were attending school, the older girls in charge of the younger children. Valey, Chrissie and George joined this house of children, away from Taylor Point for months at a time. An island resident remembered that one of the Taylor boys "was brought to the island to come to school with us when he was 14. He had never seen a school before and was quiet and shy, but I remember how smart he was. He went through four grades in one year and got good marks too."[2] Was the great stone house lonely when the children were gone?

George Taylor lived on Saturna for nearly 50 years. Irene Ethelwyn said that the stone house was gutted by fire when Mr. Taylor was old, and "the last time we saw the old man he was living in a shack at the end of his orchard, all alone."[3] He showed his visitor the tobacco he grew and cured. When he died in the Royal Jubilee Hospital at the age of 74, he was survived by Annie and his five children, but neither Ethelwyn nor the death notice said much about Annie. Jim Campbell talked to her once, when she was living in a boathouse at Hope Bay. He remembered her saying, "I told the old fool to put on a slate roof, but he would use cedar shakes."

218

SATURNA BEACH. SATURNA ISLAND. WARBURTON PIKE

Above us, as we chugged eastward along Saturna Island's south shore, towered Mount Warburton Pike, named after the extraordinary man who once owned all this side of Saturna Island, including East Point. We rounded Croker Point and anchored off Saturna Beach where Pike once lived. For many years we came here for the annual Saturna barbeque, anchoring amid flag-bedecked boats, while the scent of roasting lamb drifted tantalizingly in the summer heat. Awaiting dinner time, we drank beer on Pike's tennis lawn, used as the barbeque beer garden. Nearby, the site of his house was marked by the rubble of his chimney. How different the mood in 1992, when we were greeted at the dock by a caretaker with a large yellow dog on a leash, who seemed eager to discourage us from walking on the smooth beach. There is a story of Pike and a friend drinking daiquiris until they were running races against each other, stark naked, on this beach, and it is also said that on that occasion, a careless match set the dry grass of the island aflame and burned Pike's house. As Pike's friend Harold Payne remarked, "Pikey was a most offhand sort of chap."[1]

In 1993 we wanted to examine the beach to find out if the boulder bowl was still there. It was found by Lorraine Campbell who, for no reason known to her, chose to overturn a boulder and so discovered the bowl. Close to it she picked up the grinding stone which exactly fitted the curve of the bowl. She has now moved the boulder to a safer place outside her kitchen door, a mile from the beach, for Jim and Lorraine Campbell farm the land once plowed by Warburton Pike.

Pike was often away, exploring. He wrote *The Barren Grounds of Northern Canada* (1892) and *Through the Subarctic Forest* (1896). One of the few memorials to Pike is to be found at the northern end of Dease Lake, near the Yukon border. There is also a plaque over the door of St. Mary Magdalene on Active Pass, for Pike gave the land on which it was built. The mountain above his farm is his most conspicuous memorial. He attained a world reputation as an explorer and hunter and if he had been American we might have seen a film about his exploits, with Kevin Costner playing Pike. Theodore Roosevelt entertained him at the White House. Tall, handsome, upper class and Oxford educated, he was also a loner, a wanderer, an explorer, a scientist. A friend in an obituary described him as "modest of achieve-

Warburton Pike. (COURTESY BC ARCHIVES AND RECORDS SERVICE)

ments, reserved in manner, indifferent to the opinions of those who held conventions in esteem."[2]

Pike was notorious for his habit of borrowing clothes which he never returned. Dora Payne told about an expedition to the Cassiar, when her father Harold and some others had left their luggage at 150 Mile House and gone on from there, travelling light. Pike, arriving after them at 150 Mile House and needing a jacket, opened Harold's trunk and put on the first garment to hand. He joined his friends to dig for Cassiar gold wearing "Dad's soup-and-fish, boiled shirt and all! Dad said that was a really wonderful sight — to see him arrive like that in the midst of the wilds. He wore it until it fell apart."[3]

Now Jim Campbell's boat seemed lonely in this place which was the earliest centre of Saturna social life and the site of the first post office (but before there was a post office, the mail bags were just up-ended on the wharf and people scrambled for their mail). Geraldine Payne wrote that "while waiting for the mail boat, games of grass hockey, football or cricket were organized, and the post-master usually provided tea — and sometimes food. If night fell," Geraldine added, "and still no mail boat in sight, a game of poker would pass the time. Then it was over the sea home, by moonlight."[4]

When Pike was about 40, he was watched from Prairie Hill by a lovely pair of blue eyes. Isabel Payne had come out to Saturna to keep house for her brother, the Reverend Hubert Payne, at Winter Cove. One of her nieces remembered that "Aunt Isabel was very beautiful when she was young. She had auburn hair and beautiful blue, English eyes."[5] She was an accomplished artist, played the piano well, had a private income and was a good shot with a rifle. Once when a cougar was scrabbling on the roof of one of her three houses, she snatched up her gun and shot it. She never married.

"But I think, looking back on it," remarked her niece Geraldine, "she had a romance with Mr. Pike." When she stayed with the Paynes, she frequently took her paints and disappeared, "and that's the last you'd see of her perhaps until midnight." According to Geraldine, this behaviour worried Mrs. Payne and "upset her terribly." Once her brothers got a search party together to look for her. "All night they climbed and shouted, and by morning found her, quite calm, resting in a shack at Murder Point."[6] Murder Point is not far from Pike's place.

When World War I started, Pike returned to England to fight, but he was 53 and not in good health. Given a position on a patrol boat on the English Channel, he became ill and was sent to a nursing home in Bournemouth, but he got no better. "The unutterable disappointment of finding himself unfit to serve his country, when at last an opportunity had been given him, seems to have been a death wound." Eluding the nurses one evening, he left the hospital. "He was found dead on the edge of the tide with a knife wound in his heart. The verdict of the coroner's jury was that it was self-inflicted."[7] And that same night, at Boot Cove on Saturna Island, he mounted the steps of the Payne house. Dora told me about seeing him there. I like to think that he came seeking Isabel Payne, who often stayed there. If a movie were made of his life, perhaps it would end with Merle Streep playing Isabel, sitting on Prairie Hill watching Plumper Pass turn blood red as the day and her dreams died.

Isabel continued to live in all of her houses, and to the terror of her nephews and nieces, she kept goats. They hated goats' milk, which she splashed lavishly on their porridge when they came to visit — in fact she poured goats' milk on everything and made the desserts with it.

The memorial plaque at St. Mary Magdalene quoted lines from Robert Louis Stevenson's poem, "Requiem":

Under the wide and starry sky
Dig the grave and let me lie.
Glad did I live and gladly die,
    And I laid me down with a will.
This be the verse you grave for me:
'Here he lies where he longed to be:
Home is the sailor, home from the sea
    And the hunter home from the hill.'

BREEZY BAY. SATURNA ISLAND

From the beach at Breezy Bay, a steep path climbed to the end of the lane which is the driveway of the Gerald Payne house (the Jim and Lou Money house during the years when we lived on Saturna). Nowhere on the islands can the flavour of pioneer island life be better caught than coming upon this old house (now a bed-and-breakfast hotel) in the warm light of an afternoon at the golden end of summer. I stood still, listening to the silence, when suddenly I heard a pitter-patter like raindrops — but it was only a shower of maple leaves sifting down. A rooster, idly pecking as he came, made a very loud scuffling.

Through the gate opening off the lane, a wide path of flat stones led to steps ascending to the porch of the blue-trimmed white house with the bright red roof. The present owners have a photograph of the Payne family standing just there, at the head of the steps, and it is easy to imagine them posed for the family picture. The house has been painted to match the colours in Dorothy Payne Richardson's oil painting, done in about 1929. There have been some changes in the house over the years, but the panelled dining-room was as I remembered it when the Moneys presided over island life, with the tall narrow French doors (one still jammed closed with a silver table knife, I noticed) and the stone fireplace. I particularly remembered the fireplace because a log often lay with one end burning brightly while the rest of it, running between the chairs, waited to be shoved forward.

Here until 1935, when they sold the property to the Moneys, lived Gerald and Elizabeth Payne and here their four children, Katherine, Dorothy, John and Geraldine, spent storybook years. Until they were about nine years old, they did not attend school. They just read. Dorothy could never remember a time when she

222

couldn't read. "We even climbed up in trees and read when we were supposed to be doing other things."[1] They rowed boats and fished. They had Irish water spaniels, St. Bernards, fox terriers, collies and once a Gordon setter. They had guns — "my youngest sister at the age of 8 was allowed to have an air rifle and she became quite a good shot,"[2] Dorothy remarked. They had pet rabbits, chickens, ducks and pigeons. On Sunday afternoons they climbed the island mountains, the children struggling to keep up with their father's long strides. In Dorothy's words: "He always wanted to go and see something new or something different and that was the thing he sort of taught us in a way; we always want to go and see what's around the next bend."[3]

Ultimately, they were sent to boarding schools. Dorothy "used to nearly die...you could never run out anywhere and hear the wind blow or hear the waves blowing on the beach."[4] As I stood in the panelled library upstairs, walled with books and furnished even now with deep chairs and reading lamps, it was not difficult to imagine a Payne youngster curled up with a book.

Their father, Gerald Payne, came to Warburton Pike's place on Saturna Beach with his brother Charles in 1886. He lived there until, in 1892, he pre-empted the 900 acres at Breezy Bay, which he cleared with the help of a formidable ox named Bismark. On one page of his diary he wrote:

Finished fence around cow pasture...logged with Bismark...Split rails, picked rocks, ate first cucumber, started to paint boat. Bought 140 pounds of beef from Trueworthy for six cents a pound. Started to salt it down...Cut those damn chickens' wings. Hoed thistles...Old fighting cock very sick, gave it coal oil. Planted cabbages. Made fence. Started to build smoke house...Hoed potatoes...Picked first strawberries...Logging in fine rain. Fruit trees came: six Gravensteins, six Bartlett pears, six Canada Kings, six late pears and two cherries. Paid Layritz Nursery one dollar for the lot.[5]

I wandered down towards Boot Cove through the meadow Gerald first cleared and fenced, following a path he had worn into the slope, to examine the surviving orchard trees and the large vegetable garden where seven tall sunflowers hung their heavy heads, and the mauve cosmos swayed delicately against a background of yellowed cornstalks. What a clear dream he held, working to make it a reality. Did he grieve to leave it all, after 43 years?

The sale of the estate to Jim and Lou Money marked the end of one era and the beginning of the next, for Jim Money in his time would earn the title "Patriarch of Saturna", which is cut into the granite stone that stands on his grave. Lou, who died a few years ago, was his equal, the matriarch of the island. The first time we came to visit, she had loaves of bread ready to bake and I remember her thrusting wood into the great stove, placing the high risen loaves carefully in the oven, closing the iron door gently and then knotting a rope around it to keep it shut.

There are more than half a century of stories to be told about Lou and Jim, but their preparations to survive an atomic war reveal as much about island life as about the Moneys. They were all sitting around that fireplace, with one end of a log burning, when 12-year-old John asked his dad, "What are we going to do when the big white clouds mushroom around us?" It was the Cuban nuclear crisis.

"I guess we would have to cope with the situation, all right," his father answered thoughtfully, and that began what they called "The Survival Game."[6] Jim, as magistrate, game-conservation officer, road-construction superintendent and police officer, felt responsible for the 120 islanders, and certainly Lou was not a woman to sit down and wait to die. What would they do if civilization disappeared in chaos but the people of Saturna survived?

They added up their resources: firewood, fish, deer and grouse, chickens, vegetable gardens, wild goats, a few cows, sheep. The island women knew how to spin wool and weave. "We could make candles from mutton tallow," said Jim. They had a resident doctor, and for medicines, "there's a woman on the island who knows quite a bit about herbs. We would have to preserve every bit of written matter and make sure that anyone with any knowledge gets it written down before paper is lost or destroyed, so we can pass knowledge on to our children. We would put the most intelligent person on Saturna Island in charge of this." If they ran out of paper they could write on cedar bark. When Jim was asked about law and order, he said everyone would have to get together and lay down a code of law, and if anyone didn't want to obey the law "we would have to turn them adrift. The democratic principle would have to be maintained, absolutely."

Island people like the idea that they are self-sufficient and that they have the skills and resources for such an emergency. When the last ferry has departed for the night, they cherish the wide moat of water that protects their safe refuge. And, as the stock markets of the world shiver and our civilization seems unable to stop its lemming-race towards collapse, The Survival Game may once again be played in that hundred-year-old room at Breezy Bay.

At the gate to Payne Road, tall poplars planted by Gerald Payne formed a high cathedral passage, like a guard of honour of old soldiers; down the slope, the slim young trees crowded close, fluttering their yellow-green leaves. Although the world has changed since Gerald Payne built this home for his family, the place still looks much as it did when he built it, sometime after 1892. Perhaps it will be there for another century.

PORT BROWNING AND BEDWELL HARBOUR. NORTH AND SOUTH PENDER ISLANDS

Homeward bound and loath to leave the sea, we loitered through a bronze and golden day of late summer, crossed Plumper Sound and went into Port Browning to look at a boulder bowl. We had no sooner tied up at the red-railed government dock on the north side of Port Browning than a crab fisherman arrived; two lively crabs gave us an unforgettable lunch. Walking on this strand at a low tide, many years ago, I ducked under the dock and went past the waist-high boulder of dense black stone which still rests almost beneath the dock. I paused to examine the bowl of water in the top of the boulder. Since it had not rained, this bowl must have been filled by the tide, I thought, as I glanced into the bowl. Then I did a double-take and looked more closely. The bowl was oval, and I could see that it had been abraded; the polished smoothness ran over the two ends of it. A natural bowl, worn round by the grinding action of a stone, would not be so shaped. I splashed the water out of the bowl, feeling with my hand how the smooth surface flowed over the ends and contrasted with the natural roughness. Suddenly my hand was not my hand...it seemed to belong to someone standing exactly where I stood, someone grinding something in this bowl.

Why was it so laboriously shaped here, between the tide lines and unusable when the sea covered it? A stream emptied into Browning Harbour a few feet to the east. Could this bowl have some association with the return of spawning salmon? Thus began my search for bowls through the archaeological literature and along

Port Browning Bowl

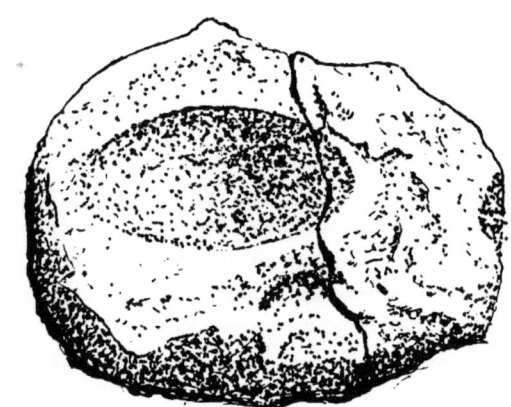

Pender Canal Bowl

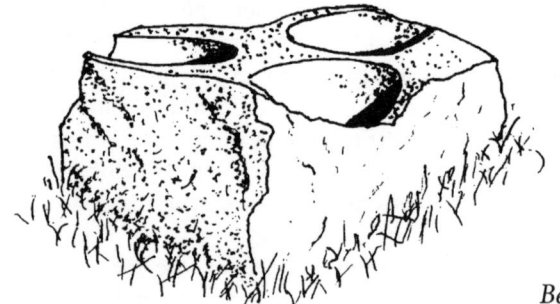

Bedwell Harbour Bowls

Bedrock and Boulder Bowls.

the island shores. And when I began looking for bowls I found them, and now have a list of almost 40.

Crossing Port Browning we entered the canal, dug in 1903, which separates North from South Pender Island. The current swept us past the place, about two metres before the bridge on the North Pender side, where Mr. and Mrs. Herbert Spalding in the 1950s took a boulder bowl out of the bank. It had been partially uncovered by tidal action; if the canal had not been cut, this boulder might have remained hidden. Before the canal existed, people hauled their canoes across the narrow isthmus. The deep midden on the North Pender side has been excavated, first by the Provincial Museum and later by Simon Fraser University, and it was here that the large, black, oval earspool was found.

We stopped at the Bedwell Harbour Marina to check out a small boulder with three bowls which lies beside the path to the pub. I have always feared that one day I would come ashore and discover geraniums growing in the bowls! This boulder was originally on the midden beach below the marina.

The great maple tree burned yellow on Hay Point, the flames turning red-bronze as the late sun touched it. A chill breeze ruffled the harbour. How swiftly the day had gone. So soon the summer was over. In the morning we would run to Tsehum Harbour, our home port.

SUMMER'S END

When we came ashore at the end of summer, we seemed to close the door on the universe. Instead of moon and stars, we had streetlights and neon signs. That last night at sea, we sat on the damp deck and felt the dew like a blessing as we watched the moon rise. Long ago, like all other living things, we were tuned to the rhythms of sun and moon, and a woman's fertility waxed and waned with it. Timothy Findley, who once slept in the kennel to observe the nocturnal habits of his dogs, described how they would wake and go outside to just sit and stare at the moon. They also greeted the sun, waking before dawn, lying quietly, waiting. Then,

simultaneously, they lift their heads and look at each other. Then she gets up and makes for the door. He rises and follows. I do likewise. Then — we bow. That's it. We bow...what we are bowing at is not just the new day and the

east and the sun. We are bowing at its precise and exact
moment of emergence over the horizon.... I've checked on
it often from the window of the house. They know — I
swear it — they know when the sun is going to appear — to
a second.[1]

Alexandra Morton spent many nights beside the Marineland of
the Pacific pool, studying Orky and Corky's night-time activities.
She was amazed to see that they always and precisely greeted the
sunrise "with their mouths open and tongues stuck out."[2]

I am transfixed with wonder when I happen to be awake to
watch the brilliant orange rim appear as my chariot of Earth turns.
At that marvellous moment the sun stretches out a warm hand and
touches me, gently, and I am Liedloff in that forest glade, and life is
unspeakably GOOD. But, for most of my days, tall buildings
prevent those first rays from touching my city windows.

As we entered Haro Strait on the bright morning of the last day
of our summer at sea, a fishboat, moving into a dancing pool of
spangled light, trailed its own crystal sparkling tail, and when the
boat passed us, the bursting stars on the surface of the rippling sea
exploded like miniature rockets, but more brilliant by far. We
foolish humans, having invented artificial light, ignore the maestro,
Sun, whose rhythm and power activate and control all life. In a
mink-farm experiment, the mink subjected to rosy light filtered
through pink glass turned aggressive; 90% of the males became
sterile, and four died unexplained deaths. Violent mink put under
blue-filtered light became gentle and affectionate, the males became
potent and the females got pregnant. Consider the egg producers
who illuminate the tiny prison coops in the dark days of winter:
when the light enters those little chicken eyes, it stimulates the pitu-
itary gland and out pop the eggs. We too are puppets dancing to
the sun's command. Yet we destroy the ozone layer that prevents
ultraviolet rays from damaging our immune systems.

There is no exile from this Eden,
we have made it all ours,
and nakedness reveals us
as tenderbodied fools
who must turn this time and face
the avenging angel, Sun,
with his sword, the wind.[3]

We have lived these summer months with wind and sun. There is much to be said for an old boat and a maximum speed of seven knots — roughly 13 kilometres per hour. We had to keep an eye on the tidebook, for in some of the passes the tide could run against us faster than our best forward speed. We pushed a button and the Loran flashed out our latitude and longitude so that I could quickly fix our location on the charts, our precise place on the great ball called Earth. At seven knots there was time to FEEL things — the grip of purple and red starfish on a rock, the air current carrying an eagle up into the ethereal blue, the crunch of the crackling bladder-wrack, the push and pull of currents. Like the long, streaming pennants of kelp, we knew ourselves to be held, shoved, buffeted by solar winds, tied by invisible threads to moon and stars. It was a comfortable feeling, most of the time.

Inebriate of air am I,
And debauchee of dew
Reeling, through endless summer days,
From inns of molten blue.[4]

Many of the coast people are interesting and distinctive, not aligned in square streets, never cutting their grass to conform with their neighbour's lawn. But they are constrained by different laws — bound to stand on their own feet, bound in times of trouble to help their neighbours or be helped by them, whether they like them or not, and bound to live with an awareness of tide and wind.

We throbbed in past Coal Island, and Curteis Point came into focus on our starboard side. "Hello Capi Blanchet!" I shouted. With the engine turning slowly, we slid into Tsehum Harbour and saluted the Barrows' house standing on the far shore. I wanted to tell the Blanchets and the Barrows about our summer and thank them for their good company up the coast.

On my first night at home in my city bed, I woke before dawn. The drapes were closed and in the dark the bed rocked gently. It was not until I stood up that I realized that I was not aboard *Liza Jane*. Sadness and loss washed over me and I longed to return to sleep and recapture the summer. It was already sliding away, dream like, or like the turbulence so swiftly smoothed in the wake of the boat; the places and people were like swirls of foam curling briefly before the sea swallowed them. It was not, I thought, just this particular summer whose departure I mourned. It was all the summers past, all the adventurous days, and before our turn to be the voyageurs, the summers when the Barrows and the Blanchets woke in rocking beds to sniff the salt wind blowing. That morning I bemoaned the thefts of time, and knew that there would not always be another summer.

> Yet meet we shall, and part, and meet again
> Where dead men meet, on lips of living men [and women].[5]

FOOTNOTES

INTRODUCTION: THE END AT
THE BEGINNING
1) Liedloff, J. 1977:5
2) *Ibid.*
3) Dickinson, E. 'There's a
Certain Slant of Light'
4) Tolkien, J. J. R.

CHAPTER ONE. NORTHWARD
OUT OF TSEHUM HARBOUR

TSEHUM HARBOUR. 'CAPI'
BLANCHET
1) W.A. Percy: 'March Magic'
2) Daly, E.I. n.d.:44
3) *Ibid.* 42
4) Blanchet, M.W. 1968:212
5) Daly, E.I. n.d.:40
6) *Ibid.* 42

TSEHUM HARBOUR. AMY
AND FRANCIS BARROW
1) S. Butler: 'Life after Death'

TSEHUM HARBOUR. SEATED
HUMAN FIGURE BOWLS
1) Duff, W. 1956:56
2) Woodcock, G. 1977:59
3) Duff, W. 1956:57
4) Barnett, H. 1955:150
5) *Ibid.* 58
6) Duff, W. 1975:18

D'ARCY ISLAND
1) Hilson, S.E. 1979:29
2) Hall, E. 1898
3) Corney, H. 1993:16

ISLE-DE-LIS
1) Bruce, M. 1970

PORTLAND ISLAND
1) *Colonist* October 17, 1932

CHAPTER TWO. NORTHWARD,
COWICHAN BAY TO DE
COURCY ISLAND

COWICHAN BAY. CHIEF
TZOUHALEM
1) Cryer, B.C. 1935
2) *Ibid.*
3) Davy, H. 1949
4) Turner, D. 1993 pers.comm.
5) Turner, D. 1992:54
6) *Ibid.*

MAPLE BAY. VANCOUVER
ISLAND
1) Lugrin, N. deB. 1932:21
2) Maud, R. 1978:161

VESUVIUS. SALT SPRING
ISLAND. THE GARNERS
1) Garner, J. 1982:50
2) *Ibid.* 74

KULLEET BAY. VANCOUVER
ISLAND. THE RAIN GOD
1) Stewart, H. 1977:167

KULLEET BAY. SHAMANS'
POOL
1) Newcombe, C.F. 1931:6
2) Tennyson, A. 'Politics'

THETIS ISLAND. MIAMI ROCK
1) Victoria *Daily Colonist* Jan.26,
1900
2) *Ibid.* Jan.27, 1900
3) *Ibid.* Jan.26, 1900
4) *Ibid.* Jan.27, 1900

CHAPTER THREE. GABRIOLA
ISLAND AND NANAIMO

GABRIOLA ISLAND AND
NANAIMO PETROGLYPHS
1) Giedion, S. 1962
2) Lommel, A. 1967:146

DEGNEN BAY. GABRIOLA
ISLAND
1) Suttles, W. 1987:237

WELDWOOD PETROGLYPH
SITE. GABRIOLA ISLAND
1) Ridington, R. 1971:190

STOKES ROAD
PETROGLYPHS. GABRIOLA
ISLAND
1) Swanton, J.R. 1909:3
2) Boas, F. 1890:108

PETROGLYPH PARK.
NANAIMO. VANCOUVER
ISLAND
1) Royal British Columbia
Museum files
2) Miller, J. 1988:15

CHAPTER FOUR. NORTHWARD,
NANAIMO TO QUADRA ISLAND

SCOTTIE BAY. LASQUETI
ISLAND. SHARKS
1) Poole, M. 1991:111
2) Hill, B. 1985:6
3) Borgoni, J. 1992

FALSE BAY. LASQUETI
ISLAND. THE FARRELLS
1) Dibbern, G. n.d.:113
2) *Ibid.* 115

HERON ROCKS. HORNBY
ISLAND. HILARY BROWN
1) Tennyson, A. 'Ulysses'

TRALEE POINT. HORNBY
ISLAND. OLIVIA FLETCHER
1) Teit, J. 1917
2) Fletcher, O. pers.comm.

COURTENAY. SEA SERPENTS
1) Piprell, C. 1992
2) White, H. n.d. (*Raincoast
Chronicles 10*):51
3) Tomlins, A. 1973
4) *Colonist,* October 7, 1936
5) Davis, M. 1993
6) Murphy, P. 1992
7) Courtenay Museum
8) Davis, M. 1993
9) Murphy, P.1992

COMOX. MUNGO MARTIN
1) Stewart, H. 1990:232) British
Columbia Indian Arts Society
1982:27

CHAPTER FIVE. NORTHWARD, QUADRA ISLAND TO SONORA ISLAND

MANSON'S LANDING AND SMELT BAY. CORTES ISLAND
1) Andersen, D. 1979:84

CHANNEL ROCK. CORTES ISLAND. GILEAN DOUGLAS
1) Douglas, G. 1992
2) Douglas, G. 1980 pers.comm.
3) Douglas, G. 1979a
4) Douglas, G. 1979:12
5) Douglas, G. 1992
6) Douglas, G. 1980 pers.comm.
7) Douglas, G. pers.comm.
8) Douglas, G. 1992a

HYACINTH BAY. QUADRA ISLAND. TOM LEASK
1) Dickie, F. 1967

HYACINTH BAY. QUADRA ISLAND. FRANCIS DICKIE
1) McVeigh, R. 1974
2) Andersen, D. 1979:58
3) Spilsbury, J. n.d.:85

OWEN BAY. SONORA ISLAND
1) Kennedy, L. 1991:73
2) Morris, F. 1952:33
3) Emery, M. 1960

OWEN BAY. ALDERS
1) Bateson, M.C. 1984:230
2) Trower, P. 1978

CHAPTER SIX. NORTHWARD, THURLOW ISLANDS TO MINSTREL ISLAND

JOHNSTONE STRAIT. DOLPHINS
1) Melville, H. 1942 Book 3, Chapter 1

SHOAL BAY, BICKLEY BAY. EAST THURLOW ISLAND
1) Andersen, D. 1979:163

BLIND CHANNEL. THE RICHTERS
1) Richter, P. 1984:25
2) *Ibid.* 25

FORWARD HARBOUR
1) Chappell, J. 1979:44
2) Hill, B. 1985:97
3) *Ibid.*
4) Pers.comm.1992
5) *Ibid.*

PORT HARVEY. CRACROFT ISLAND
1) Grainger, M.A. 1968:103

MATILPI. HAVANNAH CHANNEL
1) Hill, B. 1985:105

SODERMAN COVE. CRACROFT ISLAND
1) Spilsbury, J. n.d.:125

MINSTREL ISLAND
1) Grainger, M. 1968:23

KNIGHT INLET. M. ALLERDALE GRAINGER
1) Schieder, R. 1967:10
2) *Ibid.* 7
3) Grainger, M.A. 1968:30
4) Atkinson, C.M. 1973
5) Schieder, R. 1967
6) Grainger, M.A. 1968:84

CHAPTER SEVEN. AROUND
QUEEN CHARLOTTE STRAIT

POTTS LAGOON. TRADE BEADS
1) Woodward, A. 1989:6
2) *Ibid.* 16

NEW VANCOUVER.
HARBLEDOWN ISLAND
1) Hill, B. 1985:119
2) *Ibid.* 118
3) *Ibid.* 119

MAMALILACULLA. VILLAGE
ISLAND
1) Hill, B. 1985:118
2) Andersen, D. 1979:60

NATIVE ANCHORAGE.
VILLAGE ISLAND
1) Hill, B. 1985:116
2) *Ibid.* 118

SHOAL HARBOUR. CRAMER
PASSAGE
1) Royal British Columbia
Museum Files, P.Smith letter
1973
2) *Ibid.* Notes 1953, Mungo
Martin potlatch
3) *Ibid.*

ECHO BAY. ALEXANDRA
MORTON
1) Morton, A. 1993:8
2) *Ibid.* 11
3) Morton, A. 1993a
4) *Ibid.*
5) Morton, A. 1993:15

TRIVETT ROCK. PENPHRASE
PASSAGE
1) Rushton, G.A. 1974·78
2) *Ibid.*
3) *Ibid.*

KINGCOME INLET. GWA'YI
1) Hill, B. 1985:128
2) Usukawa, S. 1941:10
3) *Ibid.* 12
4) Strickland, N. 1974

KINGCOME INLET. THE
HALLIDAYS
1) Douglas, G. 1983:10 and
previous two quotes.

FORT RUPERT. VANCOUVER
ISLAND
1) *Colonist* October 26, 1975
2) Boas, F. 1895:439
3) *Ibid.*

GOD'S POCKET. HURST ISLAND
1) Chappell, J. 1979:76

SOINTULA. MALCOLM ISLAND
1) Lawrance, S. n.d.

ALERT BAY. CORMORANT
ISLAND
1) Meggs, G. 1991:253
2) *Ibid.* 251
3) *Ibid.* 252

BLACKFISH SOUND. FOG
1) Shakespeare, W. *The Tempest*
II,2.

SWANSON ISLAND.
GEORGANNA MALLOFF
1) Morris, F. 1952:38
2) Modzelewski, M. 1991:2
3) *Ibid.* 24
4) Malloff, G. pers.comm.
5) Modzelewski, M. 1991:40

TELEGRAPH COVE.
VANCOUVER ISLAND
1) Hoyt, E. 1990:125
2) *Ibid.* 19

ROBSON BIGHT. JOHNSTONE
STRAIT
1) Hoyt, E. 1990:29
2) *Ibid.* 54
3) *Ibid.* 91
4) *Ibid.* 108
5) 1992 Environmental Audit,
Vancouver Island
6) Boas, F. 1932:182

CHAPTER EIGHT.
SOUTHWARD, STUART ISLAND
TO DESOLATION SOUND

DENT AND YACULTA RAPIDS
1) Chappell, J. 1979:32
2) Pinkerton, K. 1991:82
3) *Ibid.* 83
4) Lightbody, F. 1991:3

FAWN BLUFF. BUTE INLET
1) Parker, M. 1988:155

VILLAGE OF THE FRIENDLY
INDIANS. STUART ISLAND
1) Hilson, S.E. 1979:76
2) *Ibid.*

HOLE IN THE WALL. SONORA
ISLAND
1) Hill-Tout, C. 1907:212

TOBA INLET
1) Kendrick, J. 1991:140

REFUGE COVE. WEST REDONDA
ISLAND. THE COUGAR
1) Morton, A. 1993:41

REFUGE COVE. WEST REDONDA
ISLAND. JUDITH WILLIAMS
1) Surrey Art Gallery brochure
2) *Ibid.*
3) *Ibid.*

LAURA COVE AND MELANIE
COVE. DESOLATION SOUND
1) Blanchet, M.W. 1968:62
2) *Ibid.* 58
3) *Ibid.* 64
4) Hill, B. 1985:49
5) *Ibid.* 49
6) *Ibid.* 63

FLEA VILLAGE. DESOLATION
SOUND
1) Marshall, J.S. 1955:41
2) Blanchet, M.W. 1968:149
3) Hill, B. 1985:48

HOMFRAY CHANNEL.
ROBERT HOMFRAY
1) All quotations: Homfray, R.
1894

HOMFRAY CHANNEL. THE
LINDBERGS
1) Munday, D. 1948:183
2) Blanchet, M.W. 1968:151

GALLEY BAY. DESOLATION
SOUND. GEORGE DIBBERN
1) Dibbern, G. n.d. 16
2) *Ibid.* 20
3) *Ibid.* 125
4) Dibbern, G. 1942:315
5) *Ibid.*
6) Dibbern G. n.d.:152

PENROSE BAY. OKEOVER
ARM. NANCY CROWTHER
1) Thompson, G.W. 1990:401
2) *Ibid.* 399
3) *Ibid.* 400
4) *Ibid.* 401

THEODOSIA ARM. VIRA MAY
SALO
1) Banham, B. 195?
2) *Ibid.*

3) Thompson, G.W. 1990:91
4) *Ibid.* 367
5) *Ibid.* 369
6) Banham, B. 195?

CHAPTER NINE. SOUTHWARD,
LUND TO PRINCESS LOUISA
INLET

DINNER ROCK
1) *Powell River News* October 12,
1947
2) Pavid, H. pers.comm.
3) *Powell River News* October 15,
1947
4) Pavid, H. pers.comm.
5) James E. Flecker 1913
Prologue to 'The Golden Journey
to Samarkand.'

GRIEF POINT
1) Thompson, G.W. 1990:149
2) Teit, J. 1900:32
3) Heizer, R.F. 1953
4) Thompson, G.W. 1990:176

VANANDA. TEXADA ISLAND
1) Hill, B. 1985:36
2) May, C. 1960:25
3) *Ibid.*

POCAHANTAS BAY. TEXADA
ISLAND
1) McKelvie, A.J. 1928
2) Thompson, G.W. 1990:300

EGMONT. SKOOKUMCHUCK
NARROWS
1) Peterson, L. 1990:55

PRINCESS LOUISA INLET
1) Hill, B. 1975:29
2) White. S.E. 1925:178

JERVIS INLET. PAINTED
STONES AND PUBERTY
1) Hill, B. 1985:31
2) Peterson, L. 1980 pers.comm.
3) Cross, E. 1979
4) Teit, J.A. 1900:317
5) Kew, M. 1980

CHAPTER TEN. SOUTHWARD,
PENDER HARBOUR TO
GIBSONS

PENDER HARBOUR. MOUNT
DANIEL
1) White, H. 1975. pers.comm.
2) Barnett, H. 1955:151
3) Grant, W.C. 1857:302
4) Peterson, L. 1976 pers.comm.

SECHELT
1) *Kahtou News* March 8, 1993:4

SELMA PARK
1) Duff, W. 1975:12

GIBSONS. LESTER PETERSON
1) Peterson, L. 1962:10

CHAPTER ELEVEN.
SOUTHWARD, VALDES ISLAND
TO SALT SPRING ISLAND

SHINGLE POINT, VALDES
ISLAND
1) Walter, M. n.d.:3
2) *Vancouver Sun*, August 28,
1971

SHAW'S LANDING. GALIANO
ISLAND. THE SHAWS
1) All quotations: Walter, M.S.
n.d.

MONTAGUE HARBOUR.
GALIANO ISLAND
1) Easton, N.A. 1992:12
2) *Ibid.*
3) Suttles, W. 1987:68
4) *Ibid.* 70

GANGES HARBOUR. SALT
SPRING ISLAND. WILSON'S
BOWL
1) Abbott, D. 1981:311
2) Webb, P. 1980:64

BEAVER POINT. SALT SPRING
ISLAND. THE RUCKLES
1) Clogg, G.C. 1991
2) Thomas, L. 1973
3) *Ibid.*
4) Tennyson, A. 'Morte d'Arthur'

CHAPTER TWELVE.
SOUTHWARD, MAYNE ISLAND
TO SIDNEY

GEORGINA POINT. MAYNE
ISLAND
1) Elliott, M. 1984:34
2) Johnston, L. 1929:7
3) Bulic, I. 1992:14

WINTER COVE. SATURNA
ISLAND
1) British Columbia Historical
Association 1961:52
2) *Ibid.* 147
3) Reimer, D. 1976:35

EAST POINT. SATURNA
ISLAND. MOBY DOLL
1) M. Arnold: 'The Grande
Chartreuse'

TAYLOR POINT. SATURNA
ISLAND
1) Reimer, D. 1976:26
2) Ethelwyn, I. 1957
3) *Ibid.*

SATURNA BEACH. SATURNA
ISLAND. WARBURTON PIKE
1) Clark, C. 1952
2) Gosnell, R.E. 1915
3) Reimer, D. 1976:23
4) British Columbia Historical
Association 1961:60
5) Reimer, D. 1976:24
6) British Columbia Historical
Association 1961:61
7) *Colonist* October 30, 1915

BREEZY BAY. SATURNA
ISLAND
1) Reimer, D. 1976:25
2) *Ibid.* 27
3) *Ibid.* 23
4) *Ibid.* 33
5) British Columbia Historical
Association 1961:54
6) Hesse, J. 1961

SUMMER'S END
1) Findley, T. 1990:102
2) Morton, A. 1993:9
3) Chambers, C. 'Logging the
Amazon'
4) E.Dickinson: First Series, 'Life'
5) S.Butler: 'Life after Death'

BIBLIOGRAPHY

BOOKS

Abbott, Donald. 1981. *The World is as Sharp as a Knife*. Victoria, British Columbia Provincial Museum.

Andersen, Doris. 1979. *Evergreen Islands*. Sidney, Gray's Publishing Ltd.

Barnett, Homer G. 1955. *The Coast Salish of British Columbia*. Eugene, Oregon, The University Press.

Bateson, Mary Catherine. 1984. *With a Daughter's Eye*. New York, Washington Square Press.

Bentley, Mary and Ted. 1981. *Gabriola, Petroglyph Island*. Victoria, Sono Nis Press.

Blanchet, Muriel Wylie. 1968. *The Curve of Time*. Sidney, Gray's Publishing Ltd.

Boas, Franz. 1890. *Second General Report on the Indians of British Columbia*. British Association for the Advancement of Science. Report on the North-western Tribes of Canada, v.1:10-163.

Boas, Franz. 1895. *The Social Organization and Secret Societies of the Kwakiutl Indians*. Washington, National Museum Annual Report.

Borradaile, John. 1971. *Lady of Culzean*. Victoria, Borradaile.

British Columbia Historical Association. 1961. *Gulf Islands Patchwork*. Sidney, Peninsula Printing Co.Ltd.

British Columbia Indian Arts Society. 1982. *Mungo Martin: Man of Two Cultures*. Sidney, Gray's Publishing.

Chambers, Carol. 1992. *From the Gulf*. Hornby Island, Moonsnail Press.

Chappell, John. 1979. *Cruising Beyond Desolation Sound*. Surrey, Naikoon Marine.

Cummings, Al and Jo Bailey-Cummings. 1986. *Gunkholing in the Gulf Islands*. Edmonds, WA, Nor'westing Inc.

Cummings, Al and Jo Bailey-Cummings. 1989. *Gunkholing in Desolation Sound and Princess Louisa*. Edmonds, WA, Nor'westing Inc.

Dibbern, George. 1942. *Quest*. New York, W.W. Norton.

Douglas, Gilean. 1979. *The Protected Place*. Sidney, Gray's Publishing.

Douglas, Gilean. 1992a. *Seascape with Figures*. Victoria, Sono Nis Press.

Duff, Wilson. 1956. *Prehistoric Stone Sculpture of the Fraser River and Gulf of Georgia*. Anthropology in British Columbia No.5. Victoria, British Columbia Provincial Museum.

Duff, Wilson. 1975. *Images Stone B.C.* Saanichton, Hancock House Publishers.

Elliott, Marie. 1984. *Mayne Island and the Outer Gulf Islands, a History*. Mayne Island, Gulf Islands Press.

Ellis, Richard. 1982. *Dolphins and Porpoises*. New York, Alfred A. Knopf.

Findley, Timothy. 1990. *Inside Memory*. Toronto, HarperCollins.

Fletcher, Olivia. 1989. *Hammerstone*. Hornby Island, Apple Press.

Garner, Joe. 1982. *Never Fly Over an Eagle's Nest*. Nanaimo, Cinnabar Press.

Giedion, S. 1962. *Eternal Present: The Beginnings of Art*. New York, Pantheon Books.

Goodson, Gar. 1988. *Fishes of the Pacific Coast*. Stanford, Stanford University Press.

Grainger, M. Allerdale. 1968. *Woodsmen of the West*. Toronto, McClelland & Stewart Ltd. (First published 1908).

Gunther, Erna. 1972. *Indian Life on the Northwest Coast of North America*. Chicago, University of Chicago Press.

Hill, Beth and Ray. 1974. *Indian Petroglyphs of the Pacific Northwest*. Saanichton, Hancock House.

Hill, Beth. 1985. *Upcoast Summers*. Ganges, B.C. Horsdal & Schubart.

Hill-Tout, Charles. 1907. *British North America. I. The Far West the Home of the Salish and Dene*. Toronto, Copp Clark Company Limited.

Hilson, S.E. 1979. *Exploring Puget Sound and British Columbia*. Holland MI, VanWinkle Publishing Co.

Hoyt, Erich. 1990. *Orca*. Camden East, Ont., Camden House.

Johnston, Lukin. 1929. *Beyond the Rockies*. London and Toronto, J.M. Dent & Sons Ltd.

Kendrick, John, trans. 1991. *The Voyage of Sutil and Mexicana 1792*. Spokane, Arthur H. Clark Co.

Kennedy, Dorothy and Randy Bouchard. 1983. *Sliammon Life, Sliammon Lands*. Vancouver, Talonbooks.

Kennedy, Liv. 1991. *Coastal Villages*. Madeira Park, Harbour Publishing.

Liedloff, Jean. 1977. *The Continuum Concept*. New York, Alfred A. Knopf.

Lommel, A. 1967. *Shamanism: The Beginnings of Art*. New York, McGraw Hill.

Marshall, James S. and Carrie Marshall. 1955. *Vancouver's Voyage*. Vancouver, Mitchell Press.

Maud, Ralph, ed. 1978. *The Salish People*. v.4 Vancouver, Talonbooks.

May, Cecil, 1960. *Texada*. Texada Centennial Committee.

Meggs, Geoff. 1991. *Salmon: the Decline of the British Columbia Fishery*. Vancouver, Douglas & McIntyre.

Melville, Herman. 1942. *Moby Dick*. New York, Dodd, Mead.

Miller, Jay. 1988. *Shamanic Odyssey*. Menlo Park, Ballena Press.

Modzelewski, Michael. 1991. *Inside Passage*. New York, HarperCollins Publishers.

Morris, Frank and Willis R. Heath. 1952. *Marine Atlas of the Northwest*. Seattle, P.B.I. Co.

Morton, Alexandra. 1993. *In the Company of Whales*. Victoria, Orca Book Publishers.

Munday, Don. 1975. *The Unknown Mountain*. Seattle, The Mountaineers.

Parker, Marion and Robert Tyrrell. 1988. *Rumrunner*. Victoria, Orca Book Publishers.

Peterson, Lester R. 1962. *The Gibson's Landing Story*. Toronto, Peter Martin Associates Ltd.

Peterson, Lester. 1990. *The Story of the Sechelt Nation*. Madeira Park, Harbour Publishing.

Pinkerton, Kathrene. 1991. *Three's a Crew*. Ganges, Horsdal & Schubart.

Poole, Michael. 1991. *Ragged Islands*. Vancouver, Douglas & McIntyre.

Reimer, Derek. 1976. *The Gulf Islanders*. Sound Heritage 5.4. Victoria, British Columbia Provincial Museum.

Rushton, Gerald A. 1974. *Whistle up the Inlet*. Vancouver, J.J. Douglas Ltd.

Spilsbury, Jim and Howard White. 1987. *Spilsbury's Coast*. Madeira Park, Harbour Publishing.

Stewart, Hilary. 1977. *Indian Fishing*. Vancouver, J.J. Douglas Ltd.

Stewart, Hilary. 1990. *Totem Poles*. Vancouver, Douglas & McIntyre.

Suncoast Writers' Forge. 1990. *Our Sunshine Coast*. Sechelt, Fleming Press.

Suttles, Wayne. 1987. *Coast Salish Essays*. Seattle, University of Washington Press.

Swanton, J.R. 1909. *Tlingit Myths and Texts*. Washington, Government Printing Office.

Teece, Philip. 1988. *A Dream of Islands*. Victoria, Orca Book Publishers.

Teit, James A. 1900. *The Lillooet Indians*. American Museum of Natural History, Jesup North Pacific Expedition, v. 5

Teit, James A. 1917. *Folk Tales of the Salishan Sahaptin*. Memoirs of the American Folklore Society, v.11.

Thompson, G.W. 1990. *Boats, Bucksaws and Blisters*. Powell River, Powell River Heritage Research Association.

Trower, P. 1978. *Bush Poems*. Madeira Park, Harbour Publishing.

Turner, Dolby. 1992. *When The Rains Came*. Victoria, Orca Book Publishers.

Usukawa, Sacko, ed. 1984. *Sound Heritage*. Vancouver, Douglas & McIntyre.

Vancouver, John, ed. 1798. *A Voyage of Discovery to the North Pacific Ocean...under the Command of Captain George Vancouver*. London, John Murray, 3 vols.

Walter, Margaret (Shaw). n.d. *Early Days among the Gulf Islands of British Columbia*. Hebden Printing Co. Ltd.

Webb, Phyllis. 1980. *Wilson's Bowl*. Toronto, The Coach House Press.

White, Howard, ed. 1976. *Raincoast Chronicles First Five*. Madeira Park, Harbour Publishing.

White, Howard, ed. n.d. *Raincoast Chronicles Six/Ten*. Madeira Park, Harbour Publishing.

White, Howard, ed. *Raincoast Chronicles 12*. Madeira Park, Harbour Publishing.

White, Stewart Edward. 1925. *Skookum Chuck*. New York, Garden City.

Woodcock, George. 1977. *Peoples of the Coast*. Edmonton, Hurtig Publishers.

Woodward, Arthur. 1989. *Indian Trade Goods*. Oregon Archaeological Society. Binford and Mort Publishing.

ARTICLES, LETTERS, BOOKLETS, NEWSPAPERS ETC.

Atkinson, Corday Mackay. 1973. 'Pioneer of B.C.'s Forest Industry'. *The Daily Colonist*, September 9.

Banham, Bessie. 195?. 'Came to Lund Before Turn of Century'. *Powell River News*, May.

Boas, Franz. 1932. 'Current Beliefs of the Kwakiutl Indians'. *Journal of American Folklore* 176,45:177- April/June.

Borgoni, John. 1992. 'Dogfish Harry'. *Island Fishfinder Magazine*, July:7.

Bruce, Marian. 1970. 'Owner wants gov't to buy her Gulf Island of dreams.' (Rum Island) *Vancouver Sun*, October 26:36.

Bulic, Ivan. 1992. 'The Ulysses of Mayne Island'. *Gulf Islands Guardian*, Spring:12-14.

Clark, Cecil. 1952. 'Warburton Pike - The Man Who Went North.' *Times*, February 23.

Cleaver, Basil C. 1949. The Story of Martin Allerdale Grainger. Typescript. British Columbia Provincial Archives.

Clogg, George C. 1991. 'Island shepherdess cares for a family of 227'. *Gulf Islander*.

Corney, Heather. 1993. 'D'Arcy Island Ghosts'. *Pacific Yachting*, May.

Cross, Edith. 1979. Report accompanying stones from Kuper Island. Victoria, Royal British Columbia Museum.

Cryer, B.M. 1935. 'Memories of Tzouhalem' *Daily Colonist*, January 20.

Da Gem. 1988. 'China's Oldest Dragon Figure'. *China Reconstructs*, 37,7:48. July.

Daly, Edith Iglauer. n.d. 'Capi Blanchet'. *Raincoast Chronicles*, 40-44.

Davis, Marc. 1993. 'The Search for the Monster'. *Monday Magazine*, 19,3:6 January 14.

Davison, Liane. 1990. 'Whose Story is It?' Monograph to accompany Judith Williams' exhibit Whose Story is It? at Surrey Art Gallery.

Davy, Humphry. 1944. 'Island quaked at name of Terrible Tzouhalem'. *Victoria Daily Times*, October 1.

Dibbern, George. Ship Without Port. Unpublished manuscript.

Dickie, Francis. 1936. 'Skookum Tom's feats led legends of the lusty'. *The Province*, August 4.

Dickie, Francis. 1967. 'Irony and Heroism'. *The Daily Colonist*, January 22. (Tom Leask).

Douglas, Gilean. 1970. 'John Pool Came Home'. *The Daily Colonist*, March 8.

Douglas, Gilean. 1979a. 'Land of Summer'. *The Daily Colonist*, June 10.

Douglas, Gilean. 1980. unpublished Christmas letter.

Douglas, Gilean. 1983. 'Bible Barge to Kingdom Come'. *Raincoast Chronicles*, 10:4-10.

Douglas, Gilean. 1992. 'All I ever wanted to do was write'. *Times-Colonist*, March 1.

Duff, Wilson. 1981. 'The World is as Sharp as a Knife'. In Abbott,

D.N. *The World is as Sharp as a Knife*: 209-217.

Easton, N. Alexander. 1992. 'More Findings from Down Under'. *The Midden*, 23,3:9-12 June.

Emery, Maud. 1960. 'Never Believe Them'. *The Daily Colonist*, October 2. (August Schnarr).

Ethelwyn, Irene. 1957. 'Stone-cutter of Saturna Island left Solid Record of his Residence Here'. *Saanich Peninsula & Gulf Islands Review*, January 2.

Fisher, C.B. 1958. 'Incredible Adventurer'. *The Daily Colonist*, December 11.

Fletcher, Pete. 1992. 'Hunt for a Sacrificial Killer Whale'. *Times-Colonist*, March 8.

Fletcher, Pete. 1992. 'Huge Knife Slices Basking Shark'. *Times-Colonist*, September 27.

Gill, Judy. 1990. 'A Quiet Miracle'. Sechelt, *Suncoast Writers' Forge*:1-6

Gosnell, R.E. 1915. Obituary, Warburton Pike. British Columbia Provincial Archives.

Grant, W.C. 1857. 'Vancouver Island'. London, *Journal of the Royal Geographic Society*, v.27.

Hall, Ernest M.D. and John Nelson. 1898. 'The Lepers of D'Arcy Island'. *Dominion Medical Monthly*, xi,6:3-11.

Hamilton, Bea. 1965. 'In a Corner of Beaver Point Lives Aunt Helen Ruckle.' *The Daily Colonist*, October 10.

Heizer, R.F. 1953. 'Sacred Rain Rocks of Northern California'. *Archaeological Survey #20*. Papers on California Archaeology. University of California, Berkeley.

Hesse, Jurgen. 1961. 'They'll survive on Saturna.' *The Daily Colonist*, December 10.

Hill, Beth. 1981. 'Bedrock and Boulder Bowls'. In Abbott, D.N. ed. *The World is as Sharp as a Knife*. British Columbia Provincial Museum, pp.127-143.

Homfray, Robert. 1894. 'A Winter Journey in 1861'. *The Province* 1,43:613-617 December 22.

'Huge skeleton discovered up-island may..or may not..be that of Caddy.' *Colonist*, December 6, 1947.

Keddie, Grant. 1983. 'Ritual Bowls of the Salish Indians: Some Theories.' *The Midden* 14,6:2-4. February.

Kew, Michael. 1980. Sculpture and engraving of the Central Coast Salish Indians. Museum Note No.9. Vancouver, University of British Columbia Museum of Anthropology.

Laronde, Les. 1987. 'A Solar-Lunar Observatory, Montague Harbour, Galiano Island'. *B.C. Historical News* 20,4:16-17.

Lawrance, Scott. n.d. 'Sointula: Saltfish and Spuds Utopia'. Madeira Park, *Raincoast Chronicles: First Five*: 164-170.

Letter re Voss. 1978, *Colonist*, November 26, p.5.

Lightbody, Frank. 1991. 'A Moon-lighting Adventure'. *British Columbia Historical* News 24,2:2-7. Spring.

Lugrin, N. deBertrand. 1932. 'Indian Saga'. *Maclean's Magazine*, December 15:21.

MacDonald, George F. 1981. 'Cosmic Equations in

Northwest Coast Indian Art'. In Abbott, D.N., ed. *The World is as Sharp as a Knife*: 225-236.

McKelvie, A.J. 1928. 'Texada Island Rum Runner Proud of His Product'. *Province*, December 23.

McKelvie, A.J. 1949. 'Chief Tzouhalem'. *Province*, March 12.

McKelvie, B.A. 1954. 'Chief Tzouhalem Attacks Fort Victoria'. *Vancouver Province*, February 22.

McVeigh, Ruth. 1974. 'Quadra resident writes and reflects'. *The Province*, May 10.

Malthouse, Rex. 1972. 'Kendall of Kenary Cove, 'Pirate' Extraordinary'. *Nanaimo Daily Free Press,* May 27.

Morton, Alexandra. 1993a. 'Risky state of affairs'. *The Fisherman*, June 21:5.

Murphy, Patrick. 1992. 'In search of Cadborosaurus'. *Times-Colonist*, June 14.

Nathan, Holly. 1992. 'It's time for healing for natives traumatized by life at Kuper Island 'concentration camp' '. *Times-Colonist*, May 15:A12.

Newcombe, C.F. 1931. Annual Report. British Columbia Provincial Museum.

Peet, Fred. 1978. 'Warburton M. Pike'. *The Daily Colonist*, June 18.

Piprell, Craig. 1992. 'Sharks'. *Monday Magazine*, 18,35: August 27.

Richter, Phil. 1984. *The Guide to Blind Channel and Surroundings*. Kask Graphics.

Ridington, Robin. 1971. 'Beaver Dreaming and Singing'. *Anthropologica* 13(1971):115-128.

Schaff, Fred. 1991. 'Heavenly Messenger'. *Omni*, October:25.

Schieder, Rupert. 1967. 'Martin Allerdale Grainger.' *Forest History* 11,3:7-13 October.

Scott, Andrew. 1991. 'Harmony Island'. (Sointula). *Equinox* 10,2:89-107 March/April.

Scott, Jack. 1971. 'The Night I Began to Believe in Ghosts'. *The Vancouver Sun*, August 28.

Smith, Edgar D. n.d. 'Mother's Courage saves her family'. BC Archives. (re Tzouhalem).

Strickland, Nicole. 1973. 'Echo of pioneers'. (Nancy Crowther). *The Province,* December 23:27.

Strickland, Nicole. 1974. 'The Winds of Change'. *The Province*, October 5:39.

Thomas, Lew. 1973. 'Saltspring park deal called a steal'. *The Vancouver Sun*, February 3.

Tomlins, Alice. 1973. 'Is Caddy Alive and Well?' *The Daily Colonist*, February 25.

Tomlinson, Alice. 1979. 'Islands of the Living Dead'. *The Daily Colonist*, September 2.

'Unidentified sea monster found dead.' *Colonist*, October 7, 1936.

White, Howard. n.d. 'The Cadborosaurus meets Hubert Evans'. *Raincoast Chronicles* 10:50-52.

Wild, Roland. 1962. 'The man who makes cannon'. *The Province,* October 22.

INDEX